OUT OF THE
COLD DARK SEA

Enjoy!

Jeffrey D. Briggs

May 2019

OUT OF THE
COLD DARK SEA

A Seattle Waterfront Mystery

Jeffrey D. Briggs

WATER'S END PRESS

Shoreline, Washington

Published 2019 by Water's End Press

First Edition

Cover design by Kari March. www.karimarch.com

Inquiries should be addressed to:
Water's End Press
2329 NW 198th Street
Shoreline, Washington 98177
206.619.9139
www.watersendpress.com

ISBN: 978-1-7337316-0-7

Printed in the United States of America

For Mary Jo

For love and support beyond compare

ONE

If he showed up now, everything would be all right. If he arrived in the next few minutes, his cane tapping steadily against the wooden planks, she could dismiss her worries as an overreaction to standing alone on the end of a pier in the dark. The wind tugged at her umbrella. She clutched it tighter and stamped her cold feet.

Still, if he showed up now, everything would be all right.

Knowing Hewitt had never been on time for anything in his life did little to ease her growing fears. At any second, she expected to see him hobbling down the pier, calling to her in that deep baritone voice, brushing aside his tardiness without a word, as if a predawn meeting on the end of a pier on Puget Sound was the most natural thing in the world. But she couldn't dislodge the growing suspicion that he wasn't coming, that this was no longer just the wait for an endearing but perpetually late old man.

What could have happened? Another heart attack? A car accident? Another stroke? In the silent gray dawn, one thing was clear—this meeting was too odd even for her eccentric old friend. Why would he choose this location and time? Something had spooked him. He was scared. But why hadn't he shown up?

Beyond the flashing red light at the end of the breakwater, the starless night sky had graduated to pewter, revealing a lid of low, thick clouds. Water continued to sluice down in sheets. The wooden planks of the pier shone black and slick—and empty. Five more minutes, then she would . . . what? The only thing she could think of was to drive to his houseboat. He refused to use a cell phone, and his home phone kept going straight to voicemail. She envisioned him sprawled on the floor of his houseboat, too weak to summon help. It had to be her next stop.

A text to Crystal, her admin assistant, said she'd be late to the office. Crystal texted back instantly saying she had cleared her calendar until ten a.m. Did she need anything? "No," she replied and dropped her phone in her pocket. Her fingers, restlessly plucking at an old fishing line tied to the wooden rail, felt the heft of its weight. Someone's illegal crab pot on the other end. Not wanting the distraction, she dropped it and thrust her hand into her coat. Five more minutes.

Once again, she replayed his cryptic phone message, letting it reel through her mind, searching for a hint of anxiety, a clue to hidden meanings. "My dear Martha, this is Hewitt. I'm afraid I've gotten into a spot of trouble with work and I need your help. I know you're busy protecting the corporate world from the insidious attacks of the little guy, but if you'd be so kind as to meet me at the same place where we took that photo for my seventy-fifth birthday party, I'd be forever in your debt. As I already am, of course. Let's say tomorrow at seven o'clock. That is, unfortunately, in the morning, by the way, an hour when no civilized person other than you would be up and about. I'm unavailable this evening so you won't be able to reach me. Till tomorrow at seven, then, my dear, ta ta."

Hewitt was being Hewitt—a little playful, a little sarcastic, anything but normal—and how he hated the notion that he might be normal. That's what she'd thought at first. And the jaunty tone of it—like he'd just bounced a check or offended some fellow rare book collector. But seven o'clock in the morning? Hewitt hated mornings. And why the secret meeting place, far from other ears and eyes? No, this was more than "a spot of trouble." She had assumed he needed her as a friend; now she wondered if he needed his attorney.

And why so vague about the meeting place, a reference only a handful of people would understand? Was he afraid of being overheard? Did he think his phone was tapped? Someone must have been with him, someone he was trying to keep in the dark. But who?

None of it made any sense.

She paced back and forth across the end of the pier, the same pier where she and a small group of friends had celebrated Hewitt Wilcox's birthday over a dozen years ago. She had flown back from Michigan for the party, the last of many classes she had taken with him just months behind her, her first law class just weeks away. It was a time of tension between them. He argued for a career in cultural anthropology, but she had already decided on law school. She loved how he had instilled in her an appreciation for the esoteric realm of rare primary source documents and how they shine a light on our history—if a person knew where to look. He was an expert on nineteenth-century American documents, devoted to uncovering the paper trail that illuminated a nation in flux as it fractured in the east while still doggedly pushing west until the whole country had been settled.

But she'd had enough of meager paychecks and constant travel while growing up, thank you. That was his life, his profession. The party on the pier had been after his heart attack and a battle with prostate cancer, and before his first stroke, any one of which could have killed him. None of which did. He kept bouncing back, his wit and humor and intellect as sharp as ever, even as his body grew frail and stooped. He'd begged her to follow in his footsteps. She'd refused and was glad of it. But it had damaged things.

It was only after Hewitt's stroke that they had reconciled. On countless trips up and down the halls of the rehab center she had held his arm, steadied him, commiserated with him over his latest lover who had packed his bags and moved out the night the ambulance raced Hewitt to the hospital. She had felt like a daughter comforting a grieving father whose physical state only emphasized his emotional pain. His already thin frame was little more than blotchy skin stretched over old bones; he swung his left leg in a stiff arc until, exhausted, he let it drag like a dead tree limb. She wanted to pick him up and carry him back to bed. She begged him to rest.

But no. His skinny chest swelled. Using the professorial voice honed over decades in the classroom, he said, "My dear Martha, rest will only hasten the inevitable, and I am yet unprepared to go to my grave. I have too much unfinished business here to bother with questions of eternity." Tears leaked out of his rheumy eyes. He started to say something but stopped, his words slurred. He struggled for control. "It was vanity to think George would stay with an old man. Still, I hoped. You, however, have shown your true character. I have loved you, Martha Whitaker, as Dante loved Beatrice, from the moment you appeared in my class, balm delivered by angels to a soulless man." Even then, he couldn't resist a poke. "You're wasting your time and talents with your continued defense of the indefensible."

"And making a hell of a lot more money in the process," she snapped. It had come out harsher than Martha intended, but she let the words linger, tired of the long-standing argument.

"Even the fallen may find redemption," he replied, shrugging free of her support.

She watched him struggle on without her. His hair, freed from the ever-present ponytail, fell in an avalanche of dirty snow down the back of his blue bathrobe. Following him, she said, "Making a decent living is not evil, Hewitt."

Both hands on the walker, he stopped. The gaunt face, mostly hidden behind a white beard, turned back. "No, my dear, it's not, unless it requires the sacrifice of your soul. Then it is the ultimate evil. That I shall fight to my dying breath." Then his voice softened, as if he too wasn't up to the battle. "Be a dear, and help an old man with his exercises."

And now the old man was late, even by the standards of one with a habitual disregard for time.

A flock of gulls huddled against the rain in the far corner of the empty parking lot. She turned back to the Sound, counting the seconds between flashes of the distant harbor light. Rain drummed against her umbrella. Suddenly, she heard footsteps behind her on the wooden pier. Too fast for Hewitt and without the accompanying *tap tap tap* of his cane. She whipped around and stepped back, shifting her weight to her back leg, bringing her body into balance. Her shoulders squared, her breathing slowed. She looked out from under the umbrella.

A jogger with a dark goatee and deep-set eyes came to an abrupt halt. He wore a yellow foul weather jacket over black leggings. He had her six-foot frame by an inch or two, and was lean and sinewy. Like a gladiator in the arena, Martha calculated how she might disable him and immediately dismissed him as a threat. She tilted the umbrella back, raised her head, and smiled the smile that men had died for.

Disarmed, he nodded, mumbled a quick apology, made a sharp turn, and in a couple of easy strides, was trotting back down the dock.

Nice calves, she noted absently. Maybe it was her nerves, maybe it was his dark, brooding eyes, but Martha wondered why Jogging Man had run out to the end of a pier only to stop short when she turned around. He reached the shore and veered away toward the boat ramp and Little Coney's. He hadn't found what he was looking for. Who were you expecting, Jogging Man?

Hard pounding rain was the only answer she received.

No other answers would be provided here, waiting for a rendezvous that wasn't going to happen. Martha started to follow the jogger down the pier. His yellow rain jacket disappeared on the far side of the empty parking lot. A mallard rested in the water of the boat ramp; then stood up to flap rain from its wings— stood up where it should have been swimming in five, six feet of water.

There, in the growing light of morning, Martha saw the faint outline of a submerged van roof. She dropped her umbrella, fumbled in her pocket for her cell phone, and sprinted down the slick pier as she dialed 911. The shock of the icy cold water brought her to an abrupt halt. The duck swam away. Knee-deep in Puget Sound, she informed the emergency dispatcher of her location, of the back windows and flat roof of a van—Hewitt's van, she was sure—barely visible but there, a splotch of blackness in a dark sea. It had been there the entire time.

Within minutes, sirens wailed in the distance. She retreated backwards up the incline, her eyes locked on the submerged vehicle, rain cascading down her face like tears.

The first police officer arrived in an unmarked car. Hatless, his thin gray hair was instantly plastered against his head. He fumbled for his wallet under a trench coat, finally producing a badge that identified him as Lieutenant Peter Lolich, Harbor

Patrol. He had a face like bread dough. Rain-speckled glasses magnified fade blue eyes.

"I'm sorry, I'm terribly sorry," he said. "Are you the one who called?"

"It's been there since at least seven o'clock," Martha responded in a rush. "That's when I . . . we were supposed to meet. It's why I didn't go in. It wouldn't've mattered."

"Of course, of course," the officer said. "Who were you supposed to meet?"

"Hewitt Wilcox," she said. "An old friend. But he didn't show up. Or I thought he didn't."

A squad car screeched to a stop on the loading ramp, lights flashing. The shrill *whoop whoop whoop* of its siren blasted away the dull silence of the morning. A police officer hurried out.

Martha felt pressure on her arm. Lolich had taken her by the elbow. "I need you to step aside," he said. "I'm sorry, but I'd like you to remain here until we find out what we have. Would you like to sit in my car? Get out of the rain?"

She shrugged herself free. "I'm fine."

Martha watched from the shore as more police appeared in a flurry of sirens and lights. Two squad cars blocked off the approach to the boat ramp. A boat from Harbor Patrol came around the breakwater and held a position off the end of the ramp. A tow truck was waved into the parking lot, its driver not bothering to get out of the cab. It became clear the unassuming Lolich was in charge. People moved with purpose after talking with him. He had an officer bring her coffee and sent a second out to retrieve her umbrella. She accepted coffee gratefully, holding the thermos lid in both hands before taking her first sip. A blue police van arrived. Two divers stepped out, already dressed in dry suits. They fastened on weight belts while talking with Lolich. One strapped a knife to his forearm. They donned masks, flicked on headlamps, and waded out toward the submerged vehicle. Their black bodies slipped silently under the water.

Martha paced the pier waiting for their return. It had to be Hewitt's van. The dread of waiting, the dread of what they might discover, matched her every step.

The sirens and lights had drawn a straggly line of bystanders who pressed against the rail that extended from Little Coney's out to a small boat-launching crane perched over the water. Martha caught sight of a yellow rain jacket. Jogging Man was back. He wasn't watching the police activity. He was staring straight at her. She stared back hard until finally he turned away.

The first diver surfaced. His fins slapped the pavement as he waddled up to Lolich. Martha tried to hear their conversation, but she couldn't make anything out until Lolich yelled at a uniformed officer to get on the horn and find out what the tides were doing early this morning.

They waved the second diver in, and the two men proceeded to gear up, adding tanks and regulators and additional weight. Each checked the other's gear, and this time when they descended under the water their trail was visible as a line of bubbles breaking the surface. The bubbles continued out past the submerged vehicle.

When Martha glanced back at the line of bystanders, Jogging Man had disappeared. Lolich stood beside a squad car, leaning into the window. He nodded and slowly made his way toward her. At some point he had donned a blue baseball cap with "Police" written across it. It was now as soaked as the rest of him, as if he had just come out of the water himself. He paused for a moment and wiped rain spots off his glasses with a handkerchief, and then said, "It's a red or burgundy van, with a handicap license plate. DOL just confirmed it's registered to a Hewitt

Wilcox. I believe that was the name you mentioned. Keys are still in the ignition. There's a cane wedged beside the passenger's seat. The front driver's door is open. There's no one inside."

The lieutenant kept his voice respectful, deliberately low. They sat in a booth at Little Coney's, sipping weak coffee. The restaurant was still closed, but the owner, seeing the storefront flash by on the morning's news, had hurried down to the waterfront and opened the doors for the police.

"Would he have done this deliberately?" Lolich finally asked. Large, soft hands engulfed the mug.

It was a logical, if misguided, question. There was no way Hewitt had driven his van down the ramp and into the water. At least not intentionally. Not the man who had struggled so hard to regain control over his life. Not the man who had pushed his body to the brink just so he could get medical clearance for a driver's license. The man who had hired a personal speech therapist so he could again stand in front of a class and deliver a lecture. The man who had driven his mind with word games and puzzles and memory tests. No. He wouldn't have given up now.

When Martha, lost in her memories of his unending efforts to come back, didn't answer, the lieutenant continued, "You say he's been in poor health. Maybe he just decided it was time. Old people reach that point sometimes. When it's no longer worth the struggle. Can't really blame him, of course, can't blame him at all."

Martha glanced at him and then out the window. A few hardy souls still lingered along the railing. Little remained to gawk at except the flashing lights of the patrol cars and an occasional police officer in a rain-slick poncho. She expected the Harbor Patrol divers to appear at any time with Hewitt's old and broken body in tow. Lolich let the silence linger between them like a gift.

"No, it wasn't deliberate," Martha said, finally. "It's not like him. He may've been old and frail, but he was a fighter. Besides, he's on enough drugs, he could've killed himself any time without driving into the water. If he was behind the wheel when his van went down that ramp, it's because he was in trouble. Another stroke. A heart attack. But then he wouldn't have had enough strength to open the window or the door underwater." Lolich nodded his head, before she added, "Besides, he was scared."

"You said that before," Lolich said. "What was he afraid of?"

"Lieutenant, if I knew that, I'd have already told you," Martha snapped. "It had something to do with his work. That's why he called yesterday and wanted to meet. I don't know if he needed an attorney or a friend."

"Seems like an odd time and place to meet. Middle of winter at the end of a pier. In the dark. Seems odd indeed."

"That's what I've been telling you: It *is* odd. Even for Hewitt, who is as odd and eccentric as they come. That's why I know he was scared and why I know he didn't drive his van down that ramp."

"But you don't know what it was?" When she didn't answer, he asked, "Do you know what he was working on?"

"Not really. We haven't talked much lately. I've been busy at work, Hewitt's been busy. He tends to disappear when he's in the middle of a big project."

"And he didn't give you any indication of what this project might be?"

Martha gave him a weak smile and a shrug. "Lieutenant, asking the same question in different ways won't change my answer. I still don't know what he was doing." She leaned forward. "If I did know, I'd tell you. This isn't him! He didn't go into that water willingly, I can assure you. Surely there must be more that you and the Seattle Police Department can do than just wait for a body to show up."

Fatigue lined the lieutenant's face; his shoulders seemed to slump with unexpected weight. He clasped his hands across his thick middle. His voice remained calm, hinting at a deep well of patience. "You have every right to be concerned about your friend, Miss Whitaker. While I appreciate your conviction that he didn't drive down that ramp himself, it is my professional responsibility to be open to all possibilities and skeptical about each. Until we learn more, we'll be doing everything we can to determine what happened. But right now, I have no evidence a crime's been committed, and I certainly have no evidence of foul play. My divers will continue to search the surrounding waters, but let me be frank: with the tide and currents and the cold water, it may be weeks or months before we find a body. An officer will be assigned the case. He'll be contacting the hospitals, Mr. Wilcox's family, his work colleagues to see if anyone might know of his whereabouts."

He rose with a grace that surprised her and handed her a card. "Please call me at any time if you remember something. And I'll be sure to let you know if we find anything here." He extended a hand. When she grasped it, he said, "Thank you, Miss Whitaker."

"What happens now?" Martha asked.

"We keep looking," Lolich replied. He glanced out the window. His voice became even more deliberate. "The tide was at full ebb between six and seven o'clock this morning. It would have created a two to two and a half knot current through here."

He didn't say more. He didn't need to. Deep and cold, the waters of Puget Sound could hide a body for a long time. How far would the tide carry a lifeless body? Martha wondered. Would the crabs pick it clean before it had a chance to surface? A pile of white bones on the murky bottom . . .

TWO

Mid-morning, the trip from the boat ramp to Lake Union proved easy. To the steady beat of the windshield wipers, Martha wove the Mini Cooper around the north end of the lake. At a red light, she closed her eyes. Rain beat on the hood. Blood pounded through her veins. A deep breath was followed by a second, a third. Her body began to respond to years of training, replacing fear with control.

A horn shattered the moment of meditation. As she sped away, Martha tried to regain a sense of calm. She needed to think. Needed her thoughts clear. Needed to master her fear. Don't deny it or ignore it; don't let it paralyze you. Accept it and let it become a part of you. From a place of stillness, she could formulate a plan.

People are taught to be afraid but seldom taught what to do about it. Hewitt had been afraid and had reached out to the one person he could trust. But afraid of what? Why call her and not the police? Had he disappeared or been kidnapped or had someone driven him into the water to let him drift off on the ebb tide? But who? Who would want him dead?

Tucked back off a gravel side road, the modest headquarters

of the Seattle Harbor Patrol appeared on her right. She flashed on the image of Lieutenant Lolich, his face steady and bland, like a bored uncle at a junior high commencement. She knew the police were only going to poke around the edges of Hewitt's disappearance, waiting for some irrefutable piece of evidence that might suggest something more sinister had happened than a decrepit old man driving himself into the water and opening the door. A favorite cliché of her father's came to her: "I ain't got a dog in this fight." It had always been his excuse for doing nothing. She suspected it now applied to Lolich.

Gas Works Park, despite the abandoned, rusting towers that gave it its name, appeared like a sodden green sanctuary amid the industrial landscape. Across the street, condominiums built in the past ten years crept up the hillside like rabbit warrens.

At the next light, she texted Crystal: "Cancel all appts today. Won't be in."

A text came back immediately: "Wise? Gksu lunch. Mtthws at 6."

Martha knew her billable hours had slipped since she had agreed to work pro bono for Zahit Göksu, the poor Turkish immigrant, and his comatose son. No doubt Matthews had slipped her into his schedule for an end-of-day chat to remind her of that. But neither her boss nor any of her colleagues at Carey, Harwell and Niehaus had experienced the grief of seeing a loved one lying unmoving and unresponsive day after month after year. She could not deliver revenge, but she could seek justice to help Göksu manage what could be a lifetime of medical bills. Having no faith in miracles, she could only hope that the boy's life would be mercifully short.

Another horn got her moving again. Quickly, she thumbed her response, "Tell srry. Family emrgncy."

"Need plane ticket?" Crystal knew her family lived in Michigan's Upper Peninsula.

"No but thxs."

Martha tossed her phone onto the passenger seat and zipped through the last curves before the merge onto the University Bridge. Where she came to an abrupt halt. The bridge was going up, the bells clanging. On the far side, just visible over the bridge deck, was the top of a mast. It began to inch toward the bridge, making a slow transit from Lake Washington to Lake Union. Behind her, stopped cars formed a line snaking back toward the U District. A bedraggled bicyclist, head down against the rain, hung on to the deck railing, spinning the pedals backwards to stay warm. Fucking rag baggers, she muttered, and always when you're in a hurry. She killed the engine and settled back to wait.

For the umpteenth time this morning, she called Hewitt's number, only to hear his message machine pick up after four rings. She disconnected without leaving her umpteenth message. In her Contacts, she found the phone number for University Rare Books and Manuscripts, a bookstore Hewitt owned in the U District. His former lover, Ralph Hargrove, ran the store, and had slowly transitioned it away from rare books and old manuscripts to used books popular with the university students.

On the second ring, a male voice answered, sounding as if he had just woken up to take the call. "Ralph, it's Martha Whitaker."

"Yes, Martha. How may I help you today?"

"Have you talked to Hewitt recently?"

"Not in a couple of weeks. We had lunch. It was a Wednesday, I believe. Yes, Wednesday, the day Haley comes in early to the store. I picked him up and we went to the new Italian bistro on 65th and 15th, La Cucina. Hewitt said he had—"

"How did Hewitt seem to you?" Martha interrupted.

"Fine. Actually, he seemed kind of groovy."

"Groovy?"

"Yes. I'd say he was borderline giddy, said he was wrapping up a big project. He even treated." Ralph didn't have to explain to Martha that such events were as rare as finding a first edition Shakespeare folio. After a pause, he asked, "Is everything okay?"

"No," she began and offered a condensed version of the morning's developments.

"That is disturbing," he said, when she finished. "And he's not home? Should I go check? I can close the store if you want me to run over to the boat."

"I'm on my way there now," Martha said. The sailboat had passed and the bridge spans slowly inched their way down.

Ralph knew nothing about the big project, had not heard from him since their lunch date. But that wasn't unusual. They hadn't talked business; Hewitt seldom did. Finally, Ralph said, "How may I help?"

The spans closed with a final shudder. Martha restarted the Mini Cooper. The bells sounded again, and the light turned green. She shifted into gear. "Just let me know if you hear from him."

Once across the bridge, she dropped back down to the waterfront and sped past marinas and houseboats until she pulled into a parking spot at Pete's Supermarket. A dark sky provided the backdrop to a row of houseboats that extended out along a dock into the dull, gray lake. She waited, scanning the empty road, the empty dock, the empty parking lot. Stop being paranoid, she chided herself, and pushed the door open.

Inside the grocery store, she chose a "Gold Label" 1996 Ruffino Chianti Riserva from their well-stocked wine selection, a favorite of hers and Hewitt's. She hefted the bottle, pleased with the weight and grip. Anything could be used as a weapon— an umbrella, an open hand, a closed fist, even a fine bottle of wine—one of the many lessons from Jonesy, the first of a series of teachers who had taught her how to protect herself. And if it turned out she didn't need the bottle for her arsenal, she would relish every drop. Its coffee and tobacco and deep loamy earth scents triggered one of the few pleasant memories, one of the only memories she had, of her mother, a woman who was never without a cup of coffee in hand, a woman who had abandoned her husband and her seven children on Martha's first day of kindergarten. Back home for lunch, full of excitement, with stories to tell, Martha had found the house empty except for the baby, Rachel, crying.

Loss. Her mother. Rachel. Now, maybe Hewitt. At the cash register, she swiped her credit card and feigned good cheer. She recognized the thin, bald man in a green apron. His nametag reminded her that he went by "Brownie."

"Have you seen Hewitt recently?" she asked. "I don't want to waste a good bottle of wine if he's not home."

Brownie glanced up. His eyes went wide and he stared at her for a brief instant. Martha was accustomed to the look and let him study her one hazel eye and one blue eye without comment. The one remaining gift from her mother.

Finally, he said, "Sure. Yesterday, day before I guess, he was in. Picked up a few groceries, and I helped him with a package. He should be around. Anything else I can help you with? Got some new postcards of the store you might be interested in."

"No thanks," Martha said. "Just the wine today."

Disappointed, he handed her a receipt and a pen. "Hewitt's a popular guy."

"Oh? Why's that?" Martha struggled to keep her voice light.

"Last night, a couple of guys came in looking for him. Said they were former students. They bought the 2008 Ruffino Chianti, so I believed them. That's a good wine. This is a great wine.

Hewitt will like it."

"Hewitt's the one who introduced me to it. He just can't afford to buy it. Did they find him?"

"I assume so. It's not like the old man is out dancing with the stars at night."

"Only because he can't anymore."

Martha hurried down the wide wooden planks of the dock—a boulevard that reached out into the lake with houseboats crowded on either side, one off-kilter as if it had lost half its flotation. At another, a fat, bearded man stood at an open door talking to a couple of young men, their heads bare under a black umbrella. Clean-cut faces, the white shirts and dark ties just visible under their rain jackets. Mormon missionaries spreading their gospel. She hurried past decks with empty planter boxes and upside-down canoes and kayaks, and stopped at the last houseboat.

Modest in comparison to its neighbors, it was a small wooden structure with a narrow deck—a tiny bungalow magically transported to its float on the lake. It had been Hewitt's home since he had finished his stint with the Navy after World War II and had come to Seattle as an unemployed, indigent sailor, relegated to the cheapest housing available. But it was on the water and within walking distance of the University of Washington, and he had the GI Bill and an insatiable thirst for knowledge. So Hewitt never left. Now, millionaires vied for a berth along the dock—the farther out the better—where they could marvel at the breathtaking vistas of the Space Needle and the city skyline lights reflecting off the dark waters of Lake Union.

An old ship's wheel, varnish peeling, served as a gate. It stood ajar. Martha stepped onto the deck and felt the slight sway as it rocked in the water. Two pots containing the desiccated rem-

nants of last summer's tomato plants framed the front door. She
knocked loudly, and then again. No one answered. She found
Hewitt's key on her key ring. There was no click or pressure of
the deadbolt releasing.

Martha eased the door open. The destruction nearly knocked
her back. She froze, alert to any sound, the slightest movement.
All was still. Was Hewitt's body somewhere in the debris?

She tightened her grip on the wine bottle and stepped inside. Winter jackets and parkas, their linings slit open, had been
tossed in the corner of the tiny foyer. Cabinet doors hung ajar,
boots and gloves and half a dozen berets were strewn about the
floor. The bookcases were empty, books splayed open on the
floor, magazines, newspapers, and clothes in a mad jumble. A
picture frame sat propped against the wall, its backing torn off.
It took her a moment to realize that the carpets had been pulled
up. The desk had been overturned, its drawers pulled out and
dumped. Martha's heart sank at the sight of Hewitt's first edition of Cotton Mather's *Magnalia Christi Americana* buried in
the pile, spine cracked. "A horrible man," Hewitt had said of
the early American puritan. "Without his influence, we probably
would never have had the Salem witch trials. Religion has been
the destruction of so much of civilization." But he cherished the
book and what it told him about early America. Now its yellow,
brittle pages lay tossed on the floor with last week's newspapers.

She took it in like snapshots as she moved from room to
room, careful not to touch anything. Former students? Hardly.
Then she remembered they had known what wine to buy.

The small kitchen looked like a bomb had gone off. Pickle
juice permeated the air and puddled in broken glass among cans
of tomato soup. The refrigerator had been pulled out from the
wall, its back unscrewed and the insulation ripped out. More of
the same greeted her in the bedroom and the bathroom. They

had torn the stuffing out of the mattress, dumped the dresser, and slit open the lining on the window curtains. The contents of the medicine cabinet—with enough pills to start a pharmacy—had been thrown into the old porcelain bathtub. The trap door in the floor to the plumbing under the deck had been removed. Even the cover to the toilet tank had been tossed aside.

But there was no body.

Was he really adrift in the tides of Puget Sound? Martha shut the image down as grief threatened to consume her.

She exhaled slowly and relaxed her grip on the wine bottle. What the hell were they looking for? From the extent of the search and the torn-off backing of the picture frame, it must have been something small and flat. Papers? A book? Several first editions, some quite valuable like Mather's, lay scattered in the debris. A special book? Documents from Hewitt's latest research project? They hadn't stopped looking until they had searched everything and everywhere.

The realization came to her suddenly—whatever it was, they hadn't found it.

Martha dug the cell phone out of her pocket and hit the Received Calls button. Hewitt had called her from the houseboat the night before at 5:58 p.m. Whoever did this had come after that.

She slid through the broken patio door onto the deck. The dull water of Lake Union was pounded flat by the nonstop rain. Under the eaves, she dialed Lolich's number. He picked up on the second ring, and she identified herself. "I'm at Hewitt's place right now, Lieutenant. It's a houseboat on the lake. It's been ransacked."

"I'm sorry, hang on a sec." His voice grew faint but was still audible. "Andy, you and Ronnie start sweeping grid six. Then you're done. You've already spent too much time underwater."

While he was talking, Martha looked around. Hewitt's smoking lounge, which is what he called the white plastic lawn chair tucked under the eave, was undisturbed. She sat down and looked across the lake. The flying saucer top of the Space Needle was just a faint outline in the clouds. At her feet, brown hand-rolled butts swam in the ashtray. She kicked it into the lake, which brought a curious duck over.

"Have at it, dude," she said. The police didn't need to be distracted by Hewitt's penchant for easing into the evening by with a little dope. As his body continued to fail, the once purely recreational habit had become medicinal, relieving the pain in both body and spirit. Martha had rolled plenty of joints for him, leaving them neatly lined up in an old silver case that even a one-armed stroke victim could manage.

"What do you mean, ransacked?" Lolich said, coming back on the line.

"Someone's turned his houseboat completely upside down and inside out."

Silence followed. Finally, Lolich said, "Okay, I'll get someone over there. Don't touch anything."

She gave him the address. The image of his shoulders slumping with the news came to her. Lolich's wish for a tidy little suicide wasn't going to happen. Maybe he would believe her now.

Just inside the patio door, Martha stopped at a double light-switch cover. The intruders hadn't disturbed it, which indicated either they weren't former students or they hadn't been particularly good students. Hewitt had little use for hiding anything—being gay, smoking dope, teaching his students about fine wines. If you were among his favored few, he shared everything—his stash, his knowledge, even his bed if you were the right gender. She popped off the false cover plate, revealing a little compartment and a surprise. His marijuana and the silver cigarette case were gone. She scanned the floor. Nothing in the debris indicated they had found and scattered his stash with the rest of his possessions. She sniffed. No aroma of marijuana lingered in the air.

Still puzzled, she searched the small compartment, feeling around the corners and edges. Then her fingertips brushed something tucked out of sight. She tried to loop a finger over the top and drag it out, but she could only get a fingernail on the front edge. She snatched up a hanger from the floor.

A rap on the door. She dropped the hanger and took a deep breath to center herself. She opened the door, expecting to find the blue uniform of the Seattle Police standing there. Instead, she found herself staring into the face of a young man whose razor had played havoc with his acne. A second man, with a phone to his ear, stood back on the dock staring at her.

"Hi, I'm Matthew," the first man started, "and this is Nathan. We're with the Church of Jesus Christ of Latter-day Saints, and we were wondering if we might talk with you about—"

"No." Martha slammed the door shut.

She grabbed the wire hanger on her way back to the hole in the wall. She bent the end and fished out a small bundle. It was something wrapped around one of Hewitt's pill containers, tied there with a piece of fishing line. Martha had only enough time to drop it into her pocket and toss the hanger before she heard a new rapping on the door, this one followed by the announcement, "Police."

THREE

Eyes closed, her breathing slow like someone in a deep sleep, Martha continued to wait. Hour after agonizing hour had dragged on with nothing to hold her attention except the *tick tick tick* of the clock on the blank gray wall of the interrogation room. She had no idea what was going on. Hewitt was missing, and she was trapped here like an animal in the zoo. Every hour she had pounded on the door; three times, she had been informed she would have to wait. The last time, no one responded.

Finally, she took off her wet boots and shook out her black hair, curling to damp ringlets on her shoulders. She tried to meditate herself into a trance. It didn't work. The clock kept ticking.

She was trapped. Helpless. "You're never helpless," Jonesy had told her long ago. And, in time, she believed him. Marcus Jones, retired Marine sergeant in Okinawa, had also taught her that you rarely had time to prepare. So you always had to be prepared. Others had taught her to respect her ability, to control and limit it. They carried her training to levels Jonesy never could. But Jonesy understood she wasn't in it to win a competition. She had her reasons, even back then. Watching her fight, he knew. He instinctively knew.

"I don't know who hurt you so bad, honey, but you know bad guys won't approach the *tatami* and bow before an assault," he told her. And taught her. From the moment she locked her bike until she began the ride home, he'd attack without warning. It didn't matter that she was only fourteen and he was six-four, lean and sinewy as a feral cat. Her youth and size just made her more vulnerable, he said, more attractive to the scumbags and lowlifes who preyed on the weak.

She wasn't about to be weak. Not ever again. When she thought she couldn't make another move, strike another blow, ward off another attack, he would increase the intensity. "Pain's just on the surface," he'd shout. "Breathe through it, in and out, like me now, follow me. In and out, in and out. You're stronger than pain. Falter and you lose to him again."

She would never lose to him or anyone again. She breathed through the pain and attacked. When they were done, he ignored her tears, as he had her pain. "It's the way life works, honey. Bad guys don't play by the rules. Neither should you."

It was a lesson she'd learned all too well before she ever met Jonesy.

But she wasn't under physical attack now. Still, caged in the interrogation room, the old demons rose up. Let them go. Breathe them out. Let them escape, she told herself. Far more difficult than fending off a physical attack. But just as critical to survival.

Eventually, a dark-haired man in a tailored suit entered the interrogation room. He set some files on the table and shuffled through them. She glanced up at the clock and smiled at him, a smile that carried neither warmth nor impatience. After he looked into her eyes, he glanced away and reshuffled his papers. He massaged his temples. All the while, she kept a solemn, unblinking stare focused on him. The styling gel he used on his hair glistened. Two little cowlicks like imp horns stood in defiance on his crown. Finally, he introduced himself as Detective Eric Metcalf.

"It's called heterochromia iridium," she said. "It's benign."

His lips parted in an attempt to speak, but when she arched a dark eyebrow, all he could say was, "I'm sorry?"

"It's a fancy medical term for having one blue eye and one hazel."

Metcalf nodded but otherwise didn't respond.

"Do you want to tell me what's going on," she said. "I probably know Hewitt better than anyone, and I've been stuck here for hours. I can help."

"I'm sure you can," Metcalf said. "But first, I just want to talk, clear up a few things you told my colleagues earlier." He leaned forward and spoke into the recorder, giving his name and the date and time. He looked straight at her. "State your name, please."

"Martha Whitaker."

"You are a Seattle resident?"

"Yes, I am."

"Where do you live?"

She gave her address in Ballard.

"Are you married?"

"Is this relevant?"

"I don't know what is or isn't relevant at this time. You tell me."

"No, I'm not married."

"Partner? Significant other?"

"No."

"Children?"

"No."

"So you're alone?"

"Not at all. I come from a big family. We're in touch frequently."

"Do they live here?"

"Could you tell me what these personal questions have to do with finding Hewitt Wilcox?" she snapped.

"Please just answer the question, Ms. Whitaker."

Martha rolled her eyes and glanced at the clock. Over four hours this cop had left her sitting here, and all he could think to ask was where she lived? But of course. It was the old trial technique taught to every first-year law student—establish authority by getting the witness to answer simple mundane questions. Get them talking. It was designed to put her at ease and him in charge. Fine, so she would talk. She caught a whiff of his hair gel. She put the detail in an imaginary balloon and let it float away.

"No, they're all in the Sault Ste. Marie area in Michigan."

"And you have lived in Seattle how long?"

"Just shy of sixteen years total."

"What does that mean?"

"I did four years of undergraduate work at the UDub and then I went back to Michigan for my JD. I moved back here after law school. That was a little over twelve years ago now. I'm thirty-six years old. I'm employed as a junior associate at Carey, Harwell and Niehaus. My boss is Ben Matthews, one of the senior partners. It's the second law firm I've worked for in Seattle."

"So who is Hewitt Wilcox, then?" he asked.

For a moment, she thought about answering, A vain, egotistical man who was also compassionate and fun and funny. A college professor who cared about his students and his friends, and who had no qualms about sleeping with any of them as long as they were gay and younger and better looking than him. She looked at the detective, the little horns sticking up from the back of his head, and knew this was a conversation she didn't want to start. Instead, she said, "A friend. A dear friend."

Metcalf shuffled some papers, scanning for something. At one, he paused. "It says here, Mr. Wilcox is eighty-seven years old. And you're thirty-six?"

"Both correct," she said. "Congratulations on—"

She cut herself off before she said something she regretted.

Metcalf studied her for a moment, his lips pursed. "How did you know Mr. Wilcox?"

"I took classes from him as an undergraduate. Cultural anthropology." When he glanced at her like she had just spoken Klingon, she added, "You know, a historian who studies culture. Hewitt focused mostly on American history, the books and letters and artifacts that make us who we are and define our differences. Civilization is not something absolute, but . . . is relative. It's why Hewitt believed the American West developed in a distinctly different way than the East Coast."

"That hardly explains—"

"We became close when I was in school—he was one of my advisors—but our friendship developed after I returned from law school. He liked to cook—and was really good at it. I like to eat good food. We both liked to fish—though neither of us were particularly good at that." There was so much more to it, but Martha knew Metcalf neither cared nor had the time to understand the nuances of their relationship. She leaned forward. "Now why don't you tell me something?"

"What do you think I should be telling you, Ms. Whitaker?"

"Whether you've found Hewitt's body or discovered what happened to him?"

"Maybe you should tell me."

"*What?*"

"Oh, I believe you heard me, Ms. Whitaker."

She would have laughed if the situation hadn't been so serious. She had been ushered out of Hewitt's ransacked houseboat within minutes of Metcalf arriving on the scene. Then she had been asked to come downtown to make a statement. What had they found since? Hewitt's body in the Sound? Her voice steady, she said, "Maybe I do need to call an attorney."

"No one's charged you with anything, Ms. Whitaker."

"Nor will they, because I'm guilty of nothing, Detective. Hewitt was a close, dear friend of mine. I was concerned about him. I did not murder him."

"That's an interesting choice of words. 'Was.' 'Murder.' Why do you think he was murdered?"

"Detective, please. Obviously, Hewitt is missing under suspicious circumstances and very possibly dead. Or did Lieutenant Lolich forget to bring you up to speed on the tides and currents out at Shilshole? Your implication that I know what happened to him, that maybe I'm responsible, is preposterous."

"So now you're a police detective, as well as an attorney."

Martha sighed. This idiot was in charge of finding Hewitt?

"Or could it be you're the one playing with me, Ms. Whitaker?" For the first time, there was a sharp, menacing tone to his question. Dark eyes flashed at her. "No one has charged you with anything, no one has read you your rights. So, as you well know, nothing we discuss is admissible in court. I've read the statement you made to Lieutenant Lolich. I've read what you told Officer Crawford at the houseboat, and you know what troubles me?"

Rhetorical questions were not meant to be answered, so Martha let this one hang in the air until he answered it himself. Silence unnerved most folks, even the best of cops.

"Here's what's troubling me, Ms. Whitaker. You keep showing up at all the wrong times. You just happen to be where the Harbor Patrol fishes a car out of the water. According to the lieutenant, you're soaking wet because, you say, you've been waiting in the rain for some ancient professor to show up on the end of the dock at o-dark thirty in the middle of the fracking winter. Hmm, I ask myself, what doesn't sound right about this? Then you show up at the houseboat of the man who owns the car in the water. The place is trashed. Hmm, I say."

"But we don't know whether anything's missing or not. It's clearly not the typical looting. They didn't take the television, no collectables, no jewelry, stuff that normally disappears in a robbery. It was old stuff for the most part and maybe the person doing the searching just didn't find it worth much. Maybe they snatched the better stuff and ran. But we also found a few hundred bucks and a jar full of coins. They weren't hidden, just out in the open. So, what gives, I keep asking myself? What happened here? They've gone through this place floorboard to attic but they leave the money, a diamond ring, some two-hundred-year-old books . . ."

His voice trailed off into silence. Again, Martha didn't try to fill it. She suddenly remembered the old barrel-chested Rottweiler with black eyes—Walt Boudreau's dog—chained to the shed even during the Michigan winters. When the dog went silent, you knew you were in trouble. Those same hard dark eyes surveyed her now. With contempt.

"We dig a little deeper," Metcalf continued. "We find a couple of marijuana butts outside, fallen down between the deck planks. We find a hidden compartment behind a fake light switch. Marijuana flakes are pushed back into the corners. And scratch marks inside. Like he's hiding his pot. Did Mr. Wilcox have a doctor's prescription for marijuana?"

"Not that I know of," Martha said. "But maybe he did."

"Well, it's not on record anywhere, but this was just a preliminary search, I admit. I've got someone looking into it more. Pot isn't legal yet, but looks like that'll change with the next election. So our missing person hides his pot. Now, it's gone. Is this a drug deal gone bad?"

"Hewitt didn't hide anything, and certainly not his pot smoking. If someone wanted Hewitt's pot, he would have given it to them."

"Not if he's unconscious. Not if he thinks it well hidden behind a false light switch in the wall. If he didn't want to hide it, why not just put it in a drawer? One of my forensic techs finds a bent coat hanger with drywall dust on the hook. Like someone used it to pull the stash out of the secret little compartment. None of this is making any sense. So, we poke around some more. Know what we find?"

Martha was no different from any other attorney—a slave to analyzing every comment, forming a rebuttal, searching for a precedent, trying to remember some arcane law that might apply. But what she wasn't doing was listening. She forced herself to stop jumping ahead, to slow down and just listen. To hear the searching in his voice. She noticed his damp forehead, the restless fingers, the probing, questioning eyes. He was rambling. The evidence he laid out offered nothing that any judge would find remotely credible. He was flailing at ghosts.

"Know what we find?"

Again, she didn't answer. She knew what they didn't find: A torn postcard of Pete's Supermarket and a key, tied up with fish line. She had no idea what it meant, but she sure wasn't about to tell Metcalf about something that would implicate her further.

"No? No idea what we located in the mess?"

"I'm sure you're about to tell me."

Metcalf opened one of the file folders on the table. He pulled out a few sheets of yellow legal paper. Chicken tracks ran at odd angles across the top page. He stabbed it a couple of times. "'The Last Will and Testament of Hewitt Wilcox.' It was probably in one of the desk drawers that got dumped." Metcalf began to read. "'I, Hewitt Wilcox, being of sound mind and failing body do hereby . . .' Okay, I won't bore you with all the details, but you probably already know them anyway."

"Sorry." She shook her head and clasped her hands in front of her. Hewitt had a will? He had always run away from that topic whenever she brought it up, like a nun fleeing a navy base. This wasn't going like she had expected. She stared at him. "I have no idea. I've never seen that document."

"Really?" He flipped through some papers. "But you told Officer Crawford that you were his attorney, as well as a friend."

"Both of which are true," she said.

"So you've never seen the will of your client, Hewitt Wilcox?"

"I have not. Sorry."

"How convenient." His sarcasm was amplified by a look of suspicion. "You can imagine *my* surprise when I notice that Mr. Wilcox's primary beneficiary is the same woman who keeps showing up at all the wrong places. One Martha Whitaker. That is you, isn't it?"

"Yes." She felt like a trap door had opened beneath her and she was teetering on the brink of falling through.

"Signed and notarized. Even have two witnesses. Legal will determine if it's a valid document, of course, but it does make me wonder. I don't know how much money is in the bank. But that houseboat out on the end of the dock must be worth a round at the bar—I heard the *Sleepless in Seattle* houseboat sold for a couple mil. Not a bad little inheritance in and of itself. But we're not done. The old guy also has some property in Utah and a bookstore over in the U District in a building he happens to own. All this doesn't come free, of course. Says you're to take care of his cat. Hell, you might even like kitty cats."

"And you receive all this bounty for what, I ask myself? You're not family, or so it would seem. I wonder if you're the mistress of a dying man. You get to change his Depends? Or maybe you're supplying his dope. I find it puzzling. See, we're talking about enough money here to get my attention. Which makes me wonder if it was also enough to get yours. So I did a quick profile on you, Ms. Whitaker. No priors, no convictions. But it seems you were acquitted a few years back of doing a number on a guy that put him in the hospital."

"He tried to rape me." At great cost, the words came out. She struggled to find a breath. How dare they try to use that against her? "Self-defense is not a crime."

Metcalf shrugged. "Like I say, you were acquitted. Now DOL shows three cars registered to your name. A single woman with three cars? And it appears you own a pretty piece of view property in Ballard. Up there in the high-rent district. How many thirtysomethings own three cars and a million-dollar estate? Maybe it's not worth a million bucks anymore after the recession. Maybe you're upside down in the mortgage or maybe the bank's making noises about repossessing it. You wouldn't be the first person to face foreclosure in recent years. So I ask myself, maybe you're in over your head. Maybe you've sold your soul to the devil, and now you're desperate to get your hands on some cash. You find a sugar daddy. Someone old. Only he doesn't produce enough money to get you out of trouble. How hard can it be to knock off an octogenarian who's got enough pills in the cupboard to start a pharmacy? So you make it look like someone busts into his place—only we can't really find anything missing, except his marijuana stash. Odd, don't you think? You don't smoke dope by any chance? We might need you to pee in a cup. Or how would you do on a blood test? It may be legal soon, but it's not yet. Then maybe you drive him into the water and open the car door, knowing full well that the tide will wash him and any clues out to sea. And Lieutenant Lolich tells me that with the water temperature this time of year it could be weeks, even months, before it bloats enough to rise to the surface. In the meantime, you create a cockamamie story about secret phone calls and how he doesn't appear for some hush-hush rendezvous. You walk out of the water, change your clothes, and call the cops. 'Oh my, what happened to my dear Hewitt?' Only, there are never any tears. Oh, did I happen to mention that DOL also has a yacht registered to your name? And that Shilshole Marina has you on the books as one of their tenants? You must know the area and the tides pretty well. And, gosh, we take a look at the old man's phone and his outgoing call register. Guess what, Ms. Whitaker? You're not there. But you say he phoned you about meeting him this morning."

Martha said nothing. There was nothing she could say that the detective would believe anyway. She didn't think it prudent to tell him that if she had wanted to kill the asshole that had tried to rape her, she could have. Now was not the time to quibble about her "yacht" being a twenty-three-foot fishing boat, bought used, nor to try to explain how Hewitt hoarded nickels like a miser his gold. The only thing the detective wanted to hear right now was something that would confirm his line of reasoning. She had no intention of giving him anything that might take him further into this idiotic fairy tale.

Metcalf nodded and leaned forward. "You're in a tight spot here, Ms. Whitaker. You see, you're no longer just some person of interest, you're not just the friend—the dear friend—who found Mr. Wilcox missing. You're now a person of suspicion, and if the lieutenant's men find a floater, you may be the prime suspect in a murder case. The best thing you can do is talk to me."

"I have nothing to say about your bullshit theory," Martha said. "I've made my statements, I've signed them, I stand by them." She paused. "Now, I'd like to call my attorney."

FOUR

By the time Martha walked out of police headquarters, the dark streets glared with the streaking headlights of evening commuters hurrying out of the city center. Sidewalks were packed with people scurrying by, heads dipped low against the continuing rain. The day had passed while she waited, dueled with Metcalf, waited some more, and then watched as her attorney berated the detective for hypotheticals that were bereft of evidence. Finally, her attorney, Kirk Eckersley, had leaned across the interrogation table and snarled, "Charge her or release her, but we're through playing charades."

A wasted day—with no news of Hewitt. She stood rooted to the pavement, sick with the memory of the van and the trashed houseboat.

Eckersley hurried toward her, his trench coat flapping against tailored wool trousers. His was a pretty, effeminate face with delicate features—thin nose, cheekbones, lips. A touch of gray highlighted his dark, wiry hair. "Sorry. Discharge papers always take longer than you think." He popped open an umbrella. "Here, we can share."

"I'm fine, thanks, Kirk." Eckersley had once been her boss, a good criminal attorney who was building a reputation as a great one. "I appreciate your coming on such short notice."

"Metcalf's bluffing," Eckersley said. "He has no evidence. With no body, no weapon, and no blood, there is no murder. He's investigating a disappearance, nothing more. Metcalf was just hoping you'd implicate yourself in some way. They'll find Hewitt's phone call to you if they subpoena the phone company for his records. Hell, he might have hightailed it out of town, rather than wait to meet you. Most likely the Harbor Patrol will find him once he washes ashore."

"I had no idea I had so much motive. That was a shock," Martha said.

"Motive and opportunity don't add up to murder. Who would've known? Can I buy you a drink—or maybe you should buy me one, come to think of it—or give you a ride somewhere?"

"Thanks, but no. My car's just around the corner."

It wasn't, but it was a handy excuse. Eckersley deserved his reputation as a good criminal attorney and as a womanizer as well. After getting an STD from him, his last wife had gathered his three mistresses in the same room and told him to pick one because she was gone.

"You look like a puppy that's just been whipped," Eckersley said. "Maybe you could use a friend."

Martha was too tired to play this game. "Kirk, that line might work on some overwhelmed housewife, but not me. What I need are answers, and I don't think you can help me get them over drinks. Being a good attorney doesn't change the fact that you're a scrub. And knowing you, you always will be."

"A scrub? Oh, that's brutal. Old-fashioned, but brutal." Perfect white teeth gleamed in the light. "Well, if you change your mind . . ." He handed her a card with his cell phone number scrawled on it.

"Trust me, if I hear from Metcalf again, you'll be hearing from me. In the meantime, have your assistant send me a bill."

"First consultation is always free. You'd be surprised how often they take place in an interrogation room at police headquarters."

"Okay, thanks." She hesitated, before adding, "Kirk, I'd really appreciate it if this didn't get back to anyone at CH&N, especially Matthews. I don't need that right now."

"No problem. It's our little secret."

"I'd rather think of it as an obligation. You know, attorney-client privilege."

He nodded, adding a smile that was really a smirk. "Of course. Being too trusting was never one of your faults. I'm surprised you called me."

"I called because you're good." She extended her hand. "Thanks, Kirk. I really do appreciate your coming down."

She strode off, hoping she looked more confident than she felt. After rounding the corner, she savored the moist air—noticeably warmer than it had been that morning—and the wind on her face. She let the rain fall steadily on her shoulders. The storm, a Pineapple Express blown across the Pacific from the tropical waters of Hawaii, would only bring more rain and wind.

The Lyft driver dropped her off at Pete's Supermarket. The parking lot was empty except for her Mini Cooper in the far corner. Lights from the store windows reflected off the water but fell short of the car. Trees swayed and branches whipped with the wind. Across the street, the dock leading to Hewitt's houseboat was empty.

At the car, she used her phone light to look up the tailpipe. Hewitt's mystery package still sat there, dry and out of sight. She fished it out and dropped it in her jacket pocket. What could it mean? A key in a pill bottle, wrapped with a torn postcard of Pete's Supermarket, all tied up with fishing line. She had barely had time to hide it before she had been bundled into a patrol car and taken downtown.

Maybe this little package had nothing to do with the houseboat search, but that was about as likely as Hewitt driving himself into Puget Sound. Whether the mystery key was important or not didn't change the fact that whoever ransacked the houseboat probably hadn't found what they wanted. And they would still be looking.

On edge, she glanced around. In the dark, water and wind and shining streetlights gave the scene a rippling, surreal quality without depth enough to see movement. It was time to go home and try to figure out what all of this meant. As she searched for the key slot, her phone light flashed across the inside of the car. Something caught her attention. She swung the light back, peering through the window. The glove box hung open, its contents scattered across the passenger-side floor. She tried the door. It opened, the dome light softly illuminating a mess of papers, power snacks, and spare tampons. The seat cushions had been popped up and not replaced. If they had taken anything, she couldn't immediately identify it.

She jerked upright, scanning the parking lot again, this time pausing at each shadow, peering into the dark corners of a dark night. She saw nothing new, and began to shiver. If they had searched her car, they knew where she lived. She touched the lump in her pocket. And now, she was certain. She had what they wanted.

The popped up seats and jumbled contents of the car brought the chaos in Hewitt's house—the coat liners slit, the mattress spewing forth their stuffing, the refrigerator dismantled—back

to mind. She looked around again. The realization came to her
slowly, like the creeping of the dawn. It was there in the un-
slashed, intact seat cushions; it was strengthened by the curious
fact that nothing was stolen; it crystallized in the unmistakable
scent of . . . Metcalf's hair gel.

Anger replaced panic. The police could have easily put the
car back together to hide their search. Instead, they chose to send
her a message. What was Metcalf telling her? We're watching
you? You can't hide? Don't screw with us? At least it partly explained why they had kept her waiting all afternoon in an interrogation cell. If they had found anything, they would have had
time to put the car back together, get a search warrant, and show
up at police headquarters with the charges in hand.

"Bastards," she shouted and kicked the car. A cat darted out
from under the car, disappearing into a row of shrubbery.

"Dante?" she whispered. In an instant, she realized it wasn't
Hewitt's cat. Dante, like his twin Beatrice, was black as the night.
This one was some kind of tabby.

"Oh, Christ," she groaned. She had forgotten about Hewitt's
cat.

The dock to Hewitt's houseboat was a ribbon out into the
lake. She was suddenly tired. All she wanted was to go
home, draw a hot bath with lavender, play some Mozart, and
wash away all thought. Wash away Metcalf and his stinking hair
gel. Something, anything to just let her brain shut down and let
her subconscious work on this puzzle. The last thing she wanted
to do was walk down that dock, enter that houseboat.

She slammed the car door and did just that—hurried past
the other houseboats, ignoring the flicker of television screens
and folks gathered around tables. Low lights lined the dock and
cast feeble halos to guide her back toward Hewitt's houseboat.

All this for a cat? Yes, for a cat. It was what friends did. It was what family did.

The houseboat at the end of the dock was dark against the dark lake. Police tape stretched across the gate and the door. She hesitated no more than a second, then ducked under the tape and stepped onto the deck. The houseboat rolled with the waves whipping across Lake Union. Her knees bent in time with the rise and sway of the big, water-soaked flotation logs below as the whitecaps pounded in. This time, when she turned the key in the door, she felt the pressure and heard the click of the lock.

In the foyer, she stood motionless. Too much had happened in the past twelve hours for her to assume anything or anyplace was safe. Least of all this place. She listened to the creak of the boat, the wail of the wind, the waves slamming the hull. Natural sounds. Sounds of a storm. Between gusts, she strained to hear anyone breathing, her eyes darting from shadow to shadow. Nothing.

Only then did she whisper, "Dante. Dante, kitty. Wanna come visit Beatrice?" She repeated it all again, only louder, adding a purr at the end. She punched on her phone light, saw an overturned chair, and turned the light off. Righting the chair, she sat down. The skittish Dante would need time to recognize her before he ventured too close. She sat there in the dark, occasionally calling his name, offering companionship, bribing him with the promise of canned tuna, which she knew drove him into a catatonic bliss. If Dante was still on the houseboat, he ignored her. Who could blame him?

Martha was about to call out again, when something made her pause. Had Dante come home? She waited to feel the brush of Dante's fur against her leg, as she had so many times in the past. Instinct told her it was something else. The houseboat heaved and groaned in the storm, a perfect camouflage for footsteps. She slipped into the darkest shadow in a house of shadows, her every sense on high alert.

The reflected glow of a neighbor's light winked out and came back. Someone had scurried past the window. The light winked again. Two of them on the deck. Fine. She was ready, and she wanted answers. They were heading around back. Had they come through the front door, they would have surprised her. Now, she had the advantage. They would either come through the tarp or head back to the front door like she had. The trick was to be patient, let both of them enter before announcing her presence. They would be harder to catch if they fled down the dock. Trapped in the houseboat, they were hers. The only question was weapons—a gun, a knife, a policeman's baton. She dismissed the last option. Cops would have used the front door. Up close, she could disarm someone with a gun. But she had to be close. And quick. A knife was more dangerous. She'd have to make sure she didn't give them a chance to use either.

"Survival. That's always your first goal," Jonesy had said, like the drill sergeant he had been. "Kick 'em in the balls. Disable them. Make them run. Whatever it takes. No rules. I'm not training you for competition. I want you to survive in the *real* world."

He had taught her well.

How she wished Rachel had met a Jonesy earlier in her life. But some people just weren't survivors.

Unwanted distractions. Let it go, she told herself. Breathe. Focus. Murmurs reached her, but not words, indistinct sounds moving back and forth in the wind. Whoever these guys were— for now she was sure they were guys—they were back for a second search to find what they hadn't found before. Or maybe to find her. They whispered back and forth like they were at a Sunday afternoon potluck. Amateurs. Obviously. But amateurs could be dangerous. Now they were at the tarped-off patio door. She forced herself to be patient.

"Never rush into a fight," Jonesy had warned her. "Slow time down. But when you're ready, strike fast, strike hard, and strike to end it then and there."

She flexed her fingers and her toes. She let her body relax, breathing deeply, silently.

She moved deftly into a shadow near the patio door. A blue spot shone through the tarp and glinted on a knife blade as it sliced the bottom edge of the tarp, then up one side. The light snapped off as suddenly as it had appeared. The bottom corner of the tarp lifted. A head poked through, followed quickly by a body. Was he the one with the knife? She let him enter and move past the opening. He stumbled on some of the debris on the floor and swore before righting himself.

The second head appeared. A flashlight snapped on. The light glinted off the steel of a knife in his hand. When it was dark, she had planned a more general, close-in assault. Now she had enough light for something more specific. He started to right himself. Martha stepped forward and delivered an open palm to his forehead. At the last instance, she pulled her blow. She wanted him alive and disabled, not dead of a broken neck. He dropped like a sack of wheat, the flashlight and knife clattering to the floor. In less than a heartbeat, she spun and drove a foot into the other man's thigh. He went down with an *umph*, the air escaping his body like deflating a balloon.

"Oh, God," he screamed. "My leg's fucking broken."

Martha picked up the flashlight, kicked the knife into the dark, and stood over him. "If I'd wanted your leg broken, I'd have gone for your knee. Do you have a knife, too?"

He reached in his pocket and removed a small pocketknife and handed it to her. "That was my grandfather's."

"And now it's mine. Evidence in a breaking and entering. Who are you? What do you want? And where the fuck is Hewitt?" The arc of the flashlight reflected off a pair of glasses on a bearded face. Longish blond hair, a receding hairline. She put him in his thirties.

"You're a girl?" His voice sounded incredulous.

"A girl? A *girl*? Shut up and don't move or I *will* break your knee cap." Martha turned to the other man. The upper half of his torso had fallen back through the tarp. She grabbed him by the legs and dragged him inside, a trail of water following him.

"Oh my god, you fucking killed Lance," the bearded man said.

"Shut up. I didn't kill him. But he'll have a headache in the morning."

"Lance!" the man cried out. "He's not moving."

"He's unconscious," she sighed. "He'll come around in a minute."

She didn't add that an open palm to the forehead could knock someone senseless without leaving a bruise. It made assault charges harder to prove if there was no evidence. Thank you, Jonesy.

She shone the light on the man's face to see if he was coming around. The darkness hid her surprise. The last time she had seen that goateed chin it had also been soaking wet. Jogging Man.

Finally. Maybe now she would learn something useful about Hewitt's disappearance.

"Start talking," she demanded, shining the light again at the first man. "What's your name? Why are you here?"

He moaned and grabbed his leg. She crouched over him. When he didn't respond, she said, "Okay, I can just find out from your wallet. Left side, I believe. Thin. Like there's not much money in it. Hint. If you're going ninja, don't leave your wallet in your pocket."

"Going ninja? That would be you, not us."

She pressed his thumb back along his wrist, and he started to roll over to escape the pain.

"MacAuliffe," he screamed. "James MacAuliffe. Jesus. Call an ambulance. We both need an ambulance."

"You'll be fine. Your buddy, too. What the hell are you doing here?"

"We're reporters."

"Reporters? Christ, they're worse than attorneys. So what are you doing here, Mr. MacAuliffe?"

"How do you know he's okay? I'm calling an ambulance."

"Because I hit him." Martha released him. "If I didn't want him to be okay, I would have hit him harder. You're a slow learner, aren't you? I'd hate to think I'm dealing with someone that stupid. Oh, that's right, you're a reporter. If you so much as touch your cell phone . . ."

MacAuliffe scrambled away from her, shaking his hand.

"So who's your partner in crime?"

"We're not criminals."

"Oh no? Breaking and entering? Through a police barricade? Give me a break. In fact, as it happens, you may be breaking into *my* houseboat, which, of course, gives me the right to kill you. Now, again, what's his name?"

"Lance Trammell."

"And what are you doing here?"

"I told you. We're reporters. Lance said this houseboat belonged to an old professor of his, some guy named Wilcox. Hewitt Wilcox. Said Wilcox had a big story for him, but then the old man disappeared."

"Now we're getting somewhere. So what was this big story about?"

"No idea. Wilcox was supposed to tell Lance in person. Lance seemed to think it had potential."

"'Potential.' Interesting. So, again, Mr. MacAuliffe, I ask, what are you doing here?"

"We thought the old man might be home."

"Right. That's why you sliced through a police tarp and let yourself in? Don't lie to me."

"I'm telling the truth! Lance said the old guy sounded scared last time they talked. We thought he might've come back. And if he wasn't home, we thought we might find something to tell us where he is."

"Like a note saying, I'm hiding at the Olympic Four Seasons for the night?"

"People leave unintentional clues all the time. A copy of a boarding pass, a hotel number, a trip planner."

"You know they pulled Hewitt's car out of the Sound this morning? Police divers were looking for his body."

MacAuliffe hesitated. "No, I didn't know that."

"That's interesting, because your friend here certainly knew. He was there. Nearly ran me over."

She pulled Trammell's wallet from his pocket. His driver's license confirmed what MacAuliffe said—at least about his identity. She glanced from his license to his face. He was maybe thirty-five; a thin, almost gaunt face made him appear older. She continued searching his wallet. A couple of credit cards, one in his name, one in the name of the *Ballard Gazette*, a couple of receipts, a little cash. On a business card, she noted that Trammell was "Publisher and Editor" of the *Gazette*, the free alternative weekly with a leftist social agenda and citywide distribution. People loved it or hated it. Once a regular reader, Martha now largely ignored it.

She dropped the card into her pocket, returned everything

else, and tucked the wallet back in Trammell's pants. In her peripheral vision, she saw MacAuliffe move. She swung toward him.

"Just trying to get comfortable with my leg." The words rushed out of him. His eyes darted around the houseboat. "Fuck, what happened here?"

"Good question. What do you think that police tape was for? It's a crime scene. Or, aren't you used to that kind of thing at the *Gazette*. Maybe you're the criminals."

"Fuck. I told you. How about you tell me why you're here?"

"Same reason as you. Plus I came back to get Hewitt's cat."

"Why should I believe you?" he said.

"I don't care if you do or not. And it looks like I'm in charge."

"Look, I'd feel a whole lot better if I saw him move. At what point *do* we call 911?"

As if on cue, Trammell moaned, his body twitched. Martha didn't expect him to rise up like Lazarus. She turned back to MacAuliffe. "What do you do at the *Gazette*?" When he hesitated, she added, "It was on his business card. Do you write that disgusting sex column?"

"No. We prefer to think of it as kinky. It's the most popular section in the paper. Why do you care?"

The tarp lifted in the wind. Why *did* she care? She wanted to be done, done with those nightmares, those memories. Why did the bad ones linger sharp and crisp, and the pleasant ones fade away? Finally, she said, "You're right, I don't."

MacAuliffe's head seemed too large for his body, but then she realized it was just an illusion created by the flashlight beam illuminating only his head. "If Hewitt was his professor, if Hewitt called him about the story, what are you doing here?"

"He thought it would be better if there were two of us."

"Sounds like he was covering his ass, or expecting trouble."

"Yeah, well, it looks like we fucking found it. I'd have stayed on the sidelines if he'd warned me there was a chance of meeting Bruce Lee. He thought the story might be big enough that it would take two of us to track it down, okay? So he wanted me in from the beginning."

"He wanted you in on it from the beginning but didn't tell you what the story was? And you've no idea what would make your boss risk getting caught breaking and entering? That's an interesting management style."

"He's my friend. I trusted him. And the answer is still the same—no, I don't know."

She took a chance. "What'd you do with the bottle of wine last night?"

"I'm sorry?"

"Your buddy bought a bottle of wine at Pete's last night before coming down the dock. The 2008 Ruffino Chianti."

"You seem to know a lot for someone just looking for his cat. When the old man wasn't home, we took it back to the office and drank it."

Martha waved the light across the debris. "This was done some time last night. I'm sure the police will want to talk with you two."

"I'd be glad to talk with them. I'm sure Lance would be, too—if he wasn't fucking unconscious. People with nothing to hide usually are. Maybe we should call the police now."

"And you saw nothing amiss?"

"I never left the dock. It wasn't late, but it was already dark. Lance knocked on the door, no one answered, we left and went back to the office. We drank his bottle of wine and a couple more. We're on deadline."

Martha didn't know if this was a justification or an excuse. Before she had a chance to respond, Trammell moaned again.

This time he also moved—first his legs, then an arm. Martha shined the light in his eyes. They blinked, even if they weren't focused yet. Finally, he tried to struggle up. He failed and fell back onto the wet carpet. She helped him into a sitting position. She found a glass that wasn't broken and filled it from the tap. Trammell sipped, then gulped the water. His eyes fell on Martha. "Who are you?"

"I'm Martha Whitaker, Mr. Trammell. Let me buy you a cup of coffee. I think we may be able to help each other."

D ante continued to prove elusive. By the time Martha gave up the search, Trammell was feeling better, a lingering headache the only reminder of being knocked unconscious. A private conversation with MacAuliffe seemed to satisfy him, and Trammell agreed to join her for a cup of coffee. Trammell handed his keys to MacAuliffe. Side by side, they were a study in contrast: Trammell, all sharp angles and well-defined muscles; MacAuliffe, short and square, moving toward pudgy.

"Hope to see you again," MacAuliffe said in parting at the car. "Maybe some time when you're not trying to kill me."

"I wasn't this time." She broke out in a smile, and handed him back his grandfather's pocketknife. "Alternate heat and ice on that leg and load up on ibuprofen for the first twelve hours. Three every four hours or so. You'll be out jogging with Trammell in a day or two."

She offered no apology. She didn't believe in apologizing for things she didn't regret. Survival.

FIVE

Most of the coffee drinkers were gone for the day. Only one young man sat at a table, laptop open, unblinking eyes staring at the screen, fingers tapping away. Flame from a gas fireplace flickered. Martha took the first sip of her latte standing inches from the fire, soaking up the warmth. She shuddered with fatigue and nervous energy. It was crazy to be here with Trammell. But she didn't believe coincidence had put him at the boat ramp this morning. And she needed to know what had.

She pulled a leather chair close to the fire. Trammell, latte in hand, pulled one up beside her. He shed his wet parka. Long, thin fingers curled around the coffee mug, warming his hands. He wore no rings or other jewelry. In a black fleece vest and black turtleneck beginning to fray at the neck, he looked like a cobra coiled in a basket. He wore his dark hair short. A few strands of silver were visible in his goatee.

She sipped her latte and studied his eyes, a deep brown with lighter flecks near the pupils. They were tight with concentration. She was in no mood to waste time. "So, what were you doing out on the pier this morning?"

It was a challenge as much as a question. If it angered him, she didn't care.

"I could ask you the same thing." His lips barely moved. His voice was harsh, a challenge of his own.

Good, he was pissed. She had been trained to watch for such moments—and to then pounce. Keep him off balance, press the advantage, don't let him get comfortable. The lessons from Witness Interrogation flicked through her mind, as automatic as sipping her latte—which she now did. Then she responded with a harsh whisper of her own. "I'm not the one facing a B&E rap for breaking into a missing man's home, Mr. Trammell. I'm not the one who showed up last night on his dock—when, by the way, someone ransacked his houseboat. No one has talked to Hewitt since, which means you may be the last person to have been in contact with him. Now he's missing and presumed drowned. You can talk to me, or you can talk to the police." She paused. The pause of being in command, the pause to let him consider how a conversation with the police might go. She waited, she watched. When his lips moved to form the first word, she interjected, "So, Mr. Trammell, what were *you* doing out on the pier this morning?"

"Who exactly are you?"

"I told you, my name is Martha Whitaker."

"That's like telling me the sky is blue."

"I'm a longtime friend of Hewitt Wilcox—and his attorney."

"I was jogging. Like I do nearly every morning."

"Very informative. Next you'll tell me it's a wet January."

"Why should I trust you?"

"That's the first good question you've asked."

His momentary surprise passed, and he held her gaze.

"The next good question is why should I trust you?" she said.

"That's easy. You want to know what I know. You want to know why Hewitt called me. You have to trust me to get it. But I still don't know why I should trust you."

Martha stood up abruptly. "Fine. Maybe the police were right. Maybe Hewitt was just a tired old man who decided to take one last drive into the Sound. God knows he had reasons enough."

"You can't believe that line of bullshit."

"No, I can't. The cops don't either, by the way. But I'm really not interested in this little cat-and-mouse game you're playing. I thought maybe we could help each other."

"Oh, I'm not playing. And neither should you."

"Thanks for the warning." She set the mug on the coffee table. Fatigue hit her like an open palm to the forehead. She took out a business card and scribbled her cell number on the back of it. She dropped it on the table beside the empty mug. "If you decide you want to talk, give me a call."

"Just sit down," Trammell said, motioning to the vacated chair. "Let's start over, shall we?"

"Okay. What were you doing on the pier this morning, Mr. Trammell?" She made no move to sit back down.

When he didn't answer, she started to walk away. That hot bath beckoned like a siren's lure. She needed time to think about a key, a torn postcard, and some fishing line. Mostly, she just needed sleep—deep and dreamless sleep.

"I was supposed to meet Hewitt on the pier this morning. Please call me Lance."

Martha paused, and turned around. "What time?"

"Seven thirty, on the end of the dock. I'm thinking you were too."

"Yes." She didn't bother to add that she and Hewitt had planned a seven o'clock rendezvous. Why the difference? "Why were you meeting him there?"

"He had a package to give me."

"What was it?"

"I've been working on a big story. Would you please sit back down?"

The notebook and pens in his pocket, the business cards, the corroboration from MacAuliffe—everything, right down to the frayed turtleneck, indicated he was speaking the truth . . . or an elaborately constructed lie. She chose to believe the simpler explanation. Occam's razor.

"What story?" Martha asked.

"Suppose you tell me why you were meeting Hewitt this morning?" Trammell countered.

"I don't know," she said. They were doling out honesty like chips in a poker game. Her turn to ante up. "He called me yesterday and left a message. He asked for the meeting, but didn't say why. I think he was scared."

"He should have been scared," Trammell replied.

Martha remained silent. She lowered herself into the leather chair and faced him.

"What do you know about the Mormons?" Trammell asked, leaning forward.

"Just the usual stereotypical stuff. Polygamy. A great choir. One of their own ran for president and lost. More to do with being a conservative asshole than a Mormon. Anything deeper is a remnant from Hewitt's classes. He loved to talk about them because they are obsessed with their own history and genealogy."

"Good, sounds like we took the same classes," Trammell said. "That's what I wanted to talk to you about. You know I run a newspaper."

"If that's what you want to call it." Martha arched an eyebrow.

"Whether you like it or not couldn't matter less to me. We're not for everyone, but we're not controlled by corporate media either. Yes, we're political. Yes, we have an agenda—be the social conscience, speak up for the person whose voice is lost amidst the money, speak up for the environment, freedom of the individual. And freedom of the press. We expose things the big boys won't cover and do it on a budget smaller than the sports department at the *Seattle Times*, okay?" He took a breath. "So a couple of weeks ago, Hewitt called me, claiming he had uncovered evidence of a longtime church scandal. Why me? Maybe because I had been a student of his and over the years we've stayed in touch. Maybe because I wasn't the *Times*."

He sat back. Martha nodded. She leaned in slightly, encouraging him.

When Trammell continued, his voice had softened a bit. "When Hewitt and I met, I was skeptical. Most so-called scandals are just people seeing boogey men that don't exist. Conspiracy theories started by people bent on discrediting something or someone. I've followed enough of them down the rabbit hole to be cautious. But Hewitt's story was different. He showed me this old letter. It was from a guy named Samson Avard and addressed to 'Brother Port.' Avard was the leader of a Mormon secret militia known as the Danites, a group willing to do the church's bidding, right or wrong. Ever heard of them?"

Martha shook her head.

"Few have. This was back when the church was still in Missouri and Joseph Smith was still alive. There was this huge tension between the Mormons and the state of Missouri. That tension led to what's called the 1838 Mormon War. And that ended with Smith a martyr at the hands of vigilantes."

"Okay, so there was a guy named Orrin Porter Rockwell who was known as 'Old Port,' aka 'The Destroying Angel of

Mormondom.' He was Smith's bodyguard and later Brigham Young's. Basically, he was a thug, an assassin, fast with a gun and not afraid to use it. He was arrested for an assassination attempt against the Missouri governor, a guy named Lilburn Boggs, but Rockwell was acquitted for lack of evidence. At the trial, he testified he couldn't be guilty because if he had shot at Boggs, Boggs would be dead."

"Sounds like a nice guy," Martha said.

"But exactly the kind of guy you'd want heading up your hit squad. For years, people have speculated that Mormon leaders had a secret vigilante group. They've been called a bunch of names—the Danites, the Army of Israel, and later, the Destroying Angels or the Avenging Angels. Mormon hit men."

"Those rumors have been around as long as the church. No one's ever proven any of them."

"And the church, of course, denies their existence. But a lot of people swear they exist. A Mormon named John D. Lee said Brigham Young gave the order for the Mountain Meadow Massacre. Do you know about that?"

Again, Martha shook her head.

"Over 120 settlers—men, women, and children—were killed, guilty of nothing more than being on a wagon train traveling through Utah."

"God," Martha said.

"I know. So, another Mormon, Wild Bill Hickman, not to be confused with Wild Bill Hickok, confessed to several murders and said he'd been working under the direct orders of Young. But there's never been any direct evidence linking Smith or Young or any of the church Elders to a church-sponsored death squad."

"How does this relate to the letter that Hewitt showed you?" Martha asked.

Trammell sat back and offered her a faint, almost shy smile.

"Sorry, I get carried away sometimes. But trust me, it's a complicated, violent history, a part of what made the Wild West wild. So, the letter from Samson Avard to 'Brother Port' basically said 'the Prophet,' which always means Joseph Smith, had a vision from God in which Orrin Porter Rockwell would be the 'Sword of Zion against the Gentiles,' and that he would be safe from all bullets as long as he never cut his hair."

"And apparently 'Old Port' never questioned the prophet about how this sounded suspiciously similar to the story of Samson and Delilah?"

"But it worked. Despite being in many gunfights, Rockwell died of natural causes. No one knows exactly how many people he killed, but it was a lot. There's an old Mormon proverb that goes 'God could use a thunderstorm. Or Porter Rockwell.' In his own defense, Porter said, "I never killed anybody that didn't need killing.""

"Oh, Christ, that's a false logic as old as the oldest religious war and as new as the latest terrorist attack."

"No kidding. So, Rockwell, as 'The Sword' of Joseph Smith, was supposed to bring the Lord's wrath down on those who sought to, quote, 'exterminate God's chosen people.' A direct reference to Governor Boggs. In 1838, Boggs issued 'Extermination Order 44,' calling for all Mormons to be exterminated or driven from the state of Missouri."

"How Christian of him," Martha said. "Ethnic cleansing right here at home."

Trammell nodded. "If you don't think like us, look like us, or worship like us . . ."

"But what made Hewitt, or you, for that matter, think the letter's authentic? Remember the Salamander Letter? And the Hofmann forgeries back in the '80s? Hewitt taught them in class. Wasn't he part of the FBI investigation that eventually caught up with Hofmann?"

"That's what I mean. Hewitt knew what he was about. That's why I think this is authentic. Why else would he bring it to me? Ever since the Hofmann forgery, the church has gone to outside experts to authenticate new discoveries. Hewitt was one. And there have been a ton of documents presented to the church in recent years. When people heard how much the church was willing to pay for them, everyone with an ounce of Mormon blood started tearing apart family Bibles and dusting off old trunks in the attic. Hewitt said most of it was authentic but insignificant. Settlers concerned about crops and weather. Mothers writing families back East with news. But . . ."

"But amongst the swine, a pearl."

"Exactly." He slapped the table.

For the first time, Martha had a glimpse of how Hewitt had augmented his meager pension. Metcalf had found his assets, but he wouldn't find much cash. Too many years as an adjunct instructor at the U had left his retirement small, while his moorage was high. *Sleepless in Seattle* had ensured that. She hesitated. She still hadn't given up hope that Hewitt might turn up. Maybe in an out-of-the-way motel frequented by hustlers and prostitutes, where no one would ask questions of an old man behind closed curtains. But if Hewitt was hiding, why hadn't he called again? Her heart sank at the thought Trammell might be right. Had the Avenging Angels caught up with Hewitt?

"Do you think the church is involved here? That they have some idea about the letter implicating Joseph Smith in the murder attempt on Governor—what'd you say his name was—Boggs?"

"Exactly," Trammell repeated.

"But Joseph Smith didn't even write the letter," Martha said. "How do we know this Samson guy was actually speaking for

Smith? It's circumstantial evidence. Remember Henry II saying
about Thomas Beckett, 'will someone rid me of this meddlesome
priest'? He said it in frustration, not as an order to go murder the
guy. Beckett ended up with his brains spilled across the cathedral
floor because some stupid knight misunderstood the king."

Trammell's voice dropped to a whisper. "Hewitt showed
me one letter, but he said there was more. He wanted to know
if I was interested. And how do you explain what happened?
Hewitt's houseboat ransacked, his car in the water? He goes
missing? I think we're getting a new kind of authenticating here.
From the Church. They have no trouble deflecting rumors and
innuendoes, so something more is happening."

Martha nodded slowly and stared into the fire. She had always figured Mormon death squads were lies and exaggerations
spread by the disenfranchised and the disillusioned. Then she
remembered the two Mormon missionaries on the dock that
morning. One had stood back away from the door, talking on
a cell phone. Had they been watching the house? What if they
weren't missionaries at all?

"Two guys stopped at the houseboat this morning," she
said. "Crew cuts, white shirts, black ties, black rain coats. The
whole bit. When one of them said they were from the LDS, I
just slammed the door in his face."

Trammell remained silent for a moment. Then he said,
"Who knows? Doubt they'd come knocking politely at the door
if they hadn't found what they were looking for the night before.
Unless you surprised them and they'd intended to enter on their
own and keep looking."

"But it doesn't make sense. Why would they go after the guy
they hired to authenticate the letter?"

"Not because he authenticated the letter—because he was
going *public* with it. Don't you get it? Smith is their founder. It's

like the Catholic hierarchy discovering that Jesus was in on a plot to kill Pontius Pilate. Can you imagine what they'd do to keep that out of the headlines?" He paused. "Do you have any idea how big it would be if I broke the story linking the LDS with the long-rumored death squad? The little *Ballard Gazette*? This is a journalist's dream." Trammell leaned forward, his long, lean frame perched on the edge of his chair.

Martha looked away in disgust. What about helping an old friend and professor? Trammell was just in it for himself. As if he knew—and didn't care—that Hewitt was already dead. Maybe he was, but until she knew for certain, all she could think of was that he was in trouble, not some journalistic coup. Maybe kidnapped, tortured. She fingered Hewitt's mystery bundle in her pocket. "Does anyone know Hewitt approached you with the letter?"

"No idea. I mean, other than Mac."

"How long have you known him?"

"Years. We started the paper together."

"He's not a lapsed Mormon or a secret Death Angel?"

"If he is, he's hidden it well through the years."

Martha and Trammell stared at each other. She said, "They're still looking for whatever documents Hewitt had. And if your theory is correct, they think we have them."

SIX

It was a day without end. Back in the cocoon of her Mini Cooper, Trammell sitting quietly in the passenger's seat, Martha suddenly felt detached from the events of the day. The shock tunneled away like she had just left a movie starring herself. The slow-flowing traffic lulled her into a false sense of normalcy. The wipers thwacked a steady rhythm against the steady rain. On Ballard Avenue, she pulled into an empty spot along the curb, killed the engine, and doused the lights.

She reached out and touched Trammell's hand before he could open the car door. "Let's sit a minute."

She tried to focus, to figure out whether or not to tell Trammell about the key, to make sense of all that had happened in the past twelve hours, but fatigue muddled her mind. Pieces didn't fit together, information was missing. Hewitt had obviously left the key for her to find, but so far, it wasn't unlocking anything. He knew she would hoist the responsibility of figuring it out on her shoulders and carry it around like Atlas until the world came to an end, heir or not. That she might be heir to his estate only added to her confusion. It was like trying to put a puzzle together with a blindfold on. Rolling her aching shoulders, she yawned and sat up straight. She squinted through the windshield at the old brick building to the right. One more sign of Ballard's gentrification—the marine alternator repair shop was now a "Guitar Emporium, Fine Stringed Instruments." The store was dark, but below it lights from the basement windows reflected off the wet sidewalk in silver arcs that coruscated with the rain. A sign with the words *Ballard Gazette* had an arrow pointing toward the basement.

Trammell glanced at her. "Aren't you being a little paranoid?"

"Being paranoid is the best way to stay safe." Her eyes continued to sweep the night. "People get tired, they get careless. That's when an attack comes. Creeps don't usually send an invitation."

"You'll have to tell me sometime how you seem to know so much about creeps."

"No, I don't."

Trammell was quiet for a moment. "Do you think Hewitt is still alive?"

Finally. A hint of sadness in his voice. He sat staring straight ahead, darkness hiding his expression. "No," she said quietly. "I don't think so . . . but what I think and what I know are two different things. Right now, I'm proceeding like he's alive and in trouble."

"If they're still looking for something, why would they kill him?"

"Good question." A movement at the basement windows caught her attention. "I just saw a shadow move across the light in your office."

"Mac's supposed to meet me here. We're on deadline."

In an instant, all the windows went black. Darkness swallowed the pools of light on the sidewalk.

"Whoa." Trammell already had the door half open. "Those lights are on different switches. That had to be the breaker."

Tall and athletic, Trammell covered the distance between the car and the stairwell in half a dozen strides. As he started down the steps, he turned back. Martha was on the sidewalk, following him. "There's a back door," he whispered, pointing. "You'll see the garbage cans. Be careful." He disappeared.

"Don't go . . ." But her words echoed off the empty space. She turned and sprinted toward the back of the Guitar Emporium. The rain-slick sidewalk went downhill. Martha swung wide around the corner as Jonesy had taught her. It was deserted. Then gunfire split the silence in two. She stopped short, slipped, and fell hard to one knee. Adrenaline launched her back to her feet in a single motion. She skidded to a halt at the edge of the alley behind the building. The gunshot had come from inside the building. She glanced around the corner and pulled back. No one in sight. She waited, then inched around the corner toward the garbage bins. A second gunshot, this one closer. She needed to get to the door.

She hadn't taken three steps when a shadow appeared from the door well. Black ski mask, gloves, and clothing reflected no light. All she could discern was a flip of hair extending below the mask. That and the gun that he swung from point to point with a two-handed grip. No extra motion, no sign of hurry, just deadly efficiency. A professional. He leveled the gun at her. She ducked behind the garbage bin as the *crack crack* of two shots blasted the brick wall behind her. Shards of brick and mortar cascaded onto her head. She rolled through a puddle to the recycling bin and came up in a crouch, ready to spring with the next shot. None came. Long seconds passed. Silence. She peered around the bin. The shadow was gone. She quickly scanned the back of the building. When the lights blinked back on, she was instantly blinded.

And her backlit silhouette made a perfect target. She dove for the door well, slipped through the open door, pulled it softly shut, and threw the dead bolt. It locked with a satisfying click. She wasn't about to give the shadow an opportunity to double back and surprise her from behind. What she didn't know was if he had a friend inside. Lights or no.

She was in some kind of supply room. She crept past metal shelves with reams of paper, toner cartridges, and old computer monitors, an old water-stained carpet muffling her steps. A door was ajar, a slit of light shining through. She dropped to her stomach. People seldom looked low when holding a gun.

A swift glance into the next room revealed neither a second gunman nor gunfire. All she saw was Trammell crouched over MacAuliffe who was lying prone, not moving, eyes closed, blood covering one side of his face. Relief swept through her when she saw the faint rise and fall of his back. She sprang up and rushed to join them.

"Is there anyone else?" she asked, her eyes darting from corner to corner. Partitions and half-walls blocked too much area for her to be certain the room was safe.

"I don't know," Trammell whispered. He looked up nervously. "Molly and Benji. I don't know where they are."

Martha punched 911 on her phone and handed it to Trammell. "It's the police. Give them the address and stay on the line. Who're Molly and Benji?"

"They work for me. They should have been here, too." Then he was talking to the 911 operator.

Martha dropped down beside MacAuliffe. The blood flowing into his beard was from a scalp wound on the side of his head, a ragged tear in the skin. She rolled him onto his back; his ashen face now stared straight up. She patted him down and found no other wounds. The gunshots must have missed him. She hated to think of Molly and Benji. MacAuliffe took another breath, this time accompanied by a groan.

"He's not shot," Martha said. Trammell relayed the message to the police. "It looks like he got busted over the head. We'll need an ambulance."

Trammell nodded and conveyed that to the operator. "One person hurt. Maybe others."

Staying low and moving quickly, Martha swept through the room, rounding each corner and partition with caution, ready to strike without hesitation. A desk had been searched, papers scattered about, drawers pulled out and left open. The monitor showed a Word document frozen on the screen. She moved on.

In the bathroom, she was met with wide-eyed fear. Molly and Benji sat on the floor, bound back to back beside an industrial sink, a broom and mop beside them. Their panic increased until she began stripping the duct tape off their mouths, reassuring them that the police would be there shortly. Under the duct tape, each of them had had a rag stuffed into their mouths. She removed the rags, and asked, "Are you hurt?"

"I'm okay," Benji said, his voice hoarse, defiant.

"Fuck no!" Molly screamed. "Oh my god. Oh my god." Her tightly curled auburn hair shook. "That bastard had a gun! What about Mac? Is he alright? Is he dead?"

"He'll be okay. Are you shot, hurt?" Martha asked.

"No! But I could've been! "

Martha nodded and glanced at the duct tape that held their feet together. No point telling Molly just how lucky she was. No point trying to get her to stop screaming either. Zip ties bound their hands and bound the two of them to each other. Someone hadn't expected to find two people waiting for him. He only brought enough zip ties for one. She had no way of cutting them.

"The police will be here soon." Martha said. "Your hands aren't turning blue. He may have left a fingerprint or something on the duct tape. You'll be fine. Just hang on."

She left them bound in the bathroom, Molly still screaming. Martha ignored her.

Back in the office, Martha found MacAuliffe sitting on the floor against the wall, his eyes closed. Trammell knelt beside him, kneading his hands, as if to get the blood going. Steadying him with quiet talk. His head whipped around when she came back.

"They're okay," Martha said, "Molly and Benji. They're in the bathroom."

"You left them there? Molly's screaming her head off."

"They're tied up, but they're not hurt. The police'll want to check for prints."

"You left them tied up in the bathroom? Fuck the police."

Trammell's lanky frame uncurled like an erector set come to life and he strode away.

Sirens screamed in the distance. Martha dropped to one knee and took MacAuliffe's hand, laying a finger against his wrist. His pulse was faint but steady. She found a tissue on the desk and began wiping blood off his face.

His eyes opened and shut again almost immediately. "You?"

Martha wasn't sure if it was a question or an accusation. Her voice quiet, she asked, "You okay? No, of course not. Stupid question."

"Once wasn't enough for you tonight?" His tongue flicked out and lingered on the blood that covered his lips.

"Don't. Let me get you cleaned up a little. There's blood everywhere." She gave his hand a squeeze and tried to lighten her voice. "This time, it wasn't me. I'm not that messy."

A brief smile was immediately replaced with a grimace. "What'd they hit me with, a falling crane?"

"Nah, probably a gun. You're lucky twice tonight. He could have shot you instead."

"Tell my head that in the morning. Oh, Jesus, that hurts."

"Sorry. Just trying to clean it up a bit. It'll be like a bad hangover."

"Yeah, but without the pleasure of getting drunk first." She smiled, while pressing gently to stop the flow of blood.

Flashing lights suddenly filled the half-windows. Seconds later, two police officers stormed into the office, vests on, guns drawn, moving in a fill-and-protect pattern, one leading, one covering. "Hands up," they commanded. Martha and MacAuliffe raised their hands. MacAuliffe's hands didn't go very high, but they were up, visible and empty. One officer paused beside them. Short and squat, she stooped to assess the seriousness of MacAuliffe's injuries. Speaking into a shoulder mic, she requested an ambulance.

"Anyone else here?" the officer asked.

"Three in the women's bathroom," Martha said. "A woman and two men."

"Injuries?"

"None."

The woman nodded to her partner and some silent communication flicked between them. The man took the lead. The woman had taken her first step when her radio crackled. Both officers immediately came to a halt. She responded, "Initial entry is clean. Two people, one injured. Request backup. Continuing sweep."

With that, the two officers began moving again through the building.

"The others?" MacAuliffe managed. He shifted, sitting a little straighter against the wall.

"They're okay. Molly and Benji were tied up in the bathroom, but they're not hurt." Martha daubed at the wound again and wiped more blood off his face, focusing on his right eye and the right side of his mouth. She grabbed more tissue. "What happened?"

"I stopped for sushi on the way in." He paused, shut his eyes tight, and grimaced. "The door was unlocked. I called out. No one answered. I assumed . . . they had gone out to eat. Benji's not good about remembering to lock up. I was working at my desk . . . final edit on a story. Went back to the fridge for a beer. We keep it in the storeroom. Opened the door. Lights went out. . . . Last thing I remember."

MacAuliffe closed his eyes and groaned. His skin was ashen. He was going to hurt tomorrow.

"Which means someone was wearing night goggles or they wouldn't have been able to see you well enough to clobber you on the head," Martha said.

"Probably not your everyday burglary."

"Probably not."

Two more of Seattle's finest arrived with guns at the ready, eyes and hands working in unison, snapping from point to point. Dark vests covered their torsos. Martha and MacAuliffe raised their hands again. One officer scanned the entire perimeter, stepped back to the door and flashed a thumbs-up. Two paramedics hustled through the front door, one carrying a large medical kit. He hurried over to MacAuliffe.

Martha eased to one side. She was about to step back into the supply room when, supported by Trammell, Molly entered the room and caught sight of the bloody MacAuliffe. Rushing toward him, she dropped to her knees. "Oh, Mac," she wailed, "oh, my dear Mac. God, he's been shot. Someone do something."

The paramedic deftly slid between her and MacAuliffe. He signaled to one of the police officers, and said, "He's in good hands now, ma'am."

Molly tried to take MacAuliffe's hand, but a police officer stepped in and took Molly under the arm. He gently led her to a chair in the foyer.

More police officers swarmed into the office. The short, blocky female officer ordered them to secure the perimeter. Gathering evidence could wait. Martha saw "Corvari" on her nametag. "Officer Corvari, you might want to call in Detective Eric Metcalf," she said. "This is probably related to a case he's working on."

"What case would that be?" She had already turned toward her shoulder mic.

"The Hewitt Wilcox disappearance."

Corvari relayed the message to dispatch. Martha continued, "Lance Trammell, the tall guy over there, came in the front and I went around to the back door. A guy dressed in black with a ski mask was just coming out. He took a couple of shots at me. I can show you where."

"Were you injured?"

"No, he missed."

"Okay, give me a minute here."

Martha stepped back and found herself suddenly alone. Trammell was talking to a police officer. One paramedic continued attending to MacAuliffe. The second knelt before Molly, holding a needle up to the light. A clear liquid squirted from the end. The cops all moved with a purpose. Martha found a chair and hunched over her knees. Whoever trashed the houseboat must have known Hewitt had talked to Trammell. But who? And how did they know? If they knew Hewitt had approached Trammell, they must know Hewitt had contacted her. Maybe Trammell was right about the Mormon Death Angels.

She glanced at MacAuliffe. The paramedic had placed a couple of large square gauze pads on his scalp and was unrolling a bandage to hold them in place. Had MacAuliffe been lucky or had someone only meant to knock him out? If so, why the shots in the office?

"Okay, you wanna show me where he took these shots at you," Corvari said, approaching Martha. She had holstered her gun. The bulletproof vest hid any semblance of a figure.

"He must have been wearing night goggles," Martha said, as they moved to the back door. "He threw the breaker before smacking MacAuliffe over the head. The shots definitely came after the lights were out. And when he came out the back door, he held the gun like a professional."

"A professional thug? Someone must have been really disgusted with that sex column."

Martha allowed herself a brief smile. A cop with a personality? In a long day of "just the facts, ma'am," it seemed out of place—and welcome. "I doubt it. Trammell was probably the intended victim. MacAuliffe just got thirsty first. He went into the back for a beer."

Outside they were greeted by rain that pelted against the building. Martha pulled her coat tight around her. A poncho-clad cop stood up near the sidewalk where Martha had first rounded the corner. A second officer stepped out of a doorway one store down. The policewoman snapped on a flashlight and called out to each. They acknowledged her and resumed their positions.

"I came around that corner where the officer is standing," Martha began, pointing. "The man appeared in the doorway about the same time. Mostly just a shadow, dressed in black. Wearing a ski mask. He had his gun raised with two hands when he appeared. I dove for the garbage container. I heard two shots and felt the debris fall down on me. I rolled behind the recycling bin. Then, he was gone, down the hill toward Shilshole Avenue."

"How do you know it was a guy?" Corvari asked.

"No hips. He had no hips, and he moved like a guy."

Corvari nodded. She lifted the top of the recycling bin, peered in with her light and closed it again. She scanned the brick wall with her flashlight, pausing at two pockmarks where crude ovals of fresh red clay contrasted with the faded exterior. She lowered the beam to look behind the recycling bin and ran it back up the wall to look at the pockmarks again.

"Okay, I'll have forensics get on it," Corvari said. "But I hate to rain on your parade, ma'am. Either the guy wasn't a pro or he was just trying to scare you. Both those shots are easily a foot over your head. And you're a big girl. They're not wide or low. Just two shots in exactly the same place. There's only a couple of old pizza boxes in the recycling bin. He could have shot through the plastic if he intended to hurt you. I'd say the dude was trying to scare you. Give himself a chance to run like a bunny through the bushes."

Martha remembered the deliberate way the man came through the door and swung the gun toward her. She hadn't stopped to consider whether he was aiming at her or over her head. Just two shots and no more. Like MacAuliffe, she wasn't dead because the gunman didn't want her dead. It was only vanity to think otherwise.

"You're probably right," Martha said, shaking her head. "I also heard two shots that came from inside the office. After the lights flashed off, but before he came out of the building."

"That's why our sweet Molly Brown thought her friend had been shot," Corvari said, nodding.

Inside, they found the bullet holes in the ceiling above the spot where MacAuliffe had lain unconscious on the floor. Corvari ordered the area cordoned off until forensics arrived.

"You're sure this was after the lights went out?" she asked.

"Positive."

"Which means the writer dude was already unconscious and the two kids were bound together in the bathroom."

"Just more fireworks?"

"Or he needed to practice with his night goggles on."

Trammell approached them as they were looking at the ceiling. Fatigue lined his thin face. Dark stubble now covered the area around his goatee. He said to Corvari, "The guy over there said I should talk to you."

"And now you're talking to me."

"I think I found why the guy was here. My workspace has been searched."

"I saw that. Okay, let's go take a look. Anything missing?"

"I'm not sure yet."

Martha watched Trammell lead the policewoman back through the maze of partitions. Molly sat sobbing quietly on a small sofa near the office entrance, her head on Benji's shoulder, her eyes closed. He had thrown an arm around her. A police officer knelt in front of MacAuliffe, scribbling a note. Martha slumped to the floor beside him.

"How you doing, James?"

"Shitty," MacAuliffe said. "Like a garbage truck just ran over my brain."

"Make sure Molly knows where they take you so she can visit."

"As if I haven't already had enough fun tonight. Maybe I'll call you instead. You can come punch me in the kidney and we can share some laughs."

Martha smiled and squeezed his hand. "Take care, James. Be safe."

"Yeah, backatcha."

With the help of the paramedic, MacAuliffe grunted to a

stand. He limped toward the front door, giving Benji a fist bump on the way by.

"And don't forget to have them take a look at that leg while you're there," Martha shouted out.

He turned back, and through his beard, she caught a glimpse of a tired smile. But it was a smile all the same.

SEVEN

At six o'clock, Martha groped for her squawking alarm and slipped back into a troubled dream. Images rose on a dark sea, people and places all gathering together in no logical pattern: Hewitt with his long white hair swirling in the current; her sister Rachel, radiant and alive, hovering above the water, a wingless angel; a bloody Uncle Walt peeking in at the edge of her dream like a voyeur. Waves crashed on a desolate, rocky shore that loomed in the background.

Her eyes blinked opened. Crashing waves were replaced by the ringing of her phone. Before she could throw back the covers, the phone went silent. A sloth-like lethargy took over, and she remained motionless in the warm bed. The solid lump that was Beatrice purred under the covers near Martha's feet. Her favorite spot. Stroking Beatrice with her toes evoked an even more throaty purr. Under her grandmother's down quilt, made for harsh winter nights in northern Michigan and blessed with a Chippewa prayer, the world beyond her bed held no appeal.

Fragments of the dream flitted in and out, soon to be lost, she knew, to the waking mind. Rachel and Uncle Walt slipped from her grasp like a handful of seawater. When Hewitt's image faded into the depths of the ocean, Martha bolted upright. Her sister and Uncle Walt were both dead. Across the dark room, her phone lay on the dresser. A faint beep indicated a new message.

In a panic, she tossed back the covers and thumbed to the new message. She recognized the number immediately—the private number of her boss, Ben Matthews. She didn't realize she had been holding her breath until she let out a long sigh. But relief quickly gave way to dread. She glanced at the clock. Six thirty-nine. She had texted Ben a couple of hours ago, then texted Crystal, figuring Ben wouldn't know how to retrieve a message even if he saw it there.

Martha hit the callback button. Ben answered immediately. "Martha, we go into conference on the McGwire trial in fifteen minutes. Hang on a sec."

A Corelli cello concerto replaced his voice. She cursed under her breath. Joel McGwire had hired the firm to clear himself of corruption charges. McGwire was richer than God, but not quite as wealthy as Bill Gates was. At age eighty-four, the parking lot baron and real estate developer faced the bleak possibility of spending what was left of his life in jail. And he expected CH&N to prevent that from happening. Ben Matthews was personally overseeing the case and had selected Martha as the lead. Hewitt's accusations of selling her soul flitted through her mind. Jury selection started in three weeks. Martha and her CH&N team were not ready, as Matthews knew very well.

He came back on line. "Sorry about—"

"I'm not able to make the meeting, Ben," she interrupted. "Ronnie's been involved from day one. Ask him to lead." Also a junior associate, Ron Belle was bright, ambitious, and ruthless. He would play it like a fireman rescuing a baby from a burning building. "He knows the case, Ben. I need a few days off. Something urgent's come up."

Martha liked Ben and was beholden to him for her present success. He had been fair and tough, counseling in private, supportive in public, increasing her responsibilities with each successful case. Her growing salary and the promise of an office with a window overlooking Puget Sound reflected her value to the firm. But that didn't mean the company owned her.

"Yeah. I got your text this morning," Matthews said. "Crystal said it was family. Everything okay? Are you back in Michigan?"

Matthews routinely worked sixty to seventy hours a week and expected his juniors to work even more. Getting time off was akin to winning the lottery. CH&N had even reserved a private office for junior attorneys to use if sick—the quarantine room. More than once, Martha had isolated herself there.

"No, I'm home in Seattle. It's getting ugly, Ben. I finished my second interrogation with the police this morning at three a.m. I don't know what's going on, but it seems I'm a prime suspect in a missing person's case. I have to take a few days off to sort this out. I tell you this in strictest confidence. Please extend my personal apologies to Mr. McGwire."

Matthews' voice softened. "A suspect? Jesus! Of course. Take the time. I was just calling to get the password to your computer. Crystal's not in yet. Is there anything you need? I can assign someone to represent you."

His response surprised, even humbled her. No guilt, no lectures, just understanding and support. She said, "That's not necessary, Ben, but thank you. I just need some time."

She gave him her password.

"It's Thursday, Martha," he said. "I'm covering the McGwire meeting this morning. Check in with me by Monday."

"Of course." Martha paused, "And thank you, Ben. I appreciate it very much."

"You just take care of yourself, and call me directly if you need anything. You know my private number."

Martha slumped back on the bed and thought about burrowing back between the sheets, but she knew there would be no more sleep. Already her mind whirled with unanswered questions. She ate half a stale muffin, the remains of yesterday's hurried breakfast before leaving to meet Hewitt on the pier. Several cups of coffee, brewed strong, provided no new insights into what had happened to Hewitt. She kept coming back to Trammell and the Mormon Death Angels. Could they really exist? What did Hewitt have and where was it? Would the key unlock that mystery?

Donning yoga pants and an old sweatshirt with the sleeves cut off at the elbows, Martha shoved the sofa against the wall. She unrolled a yoga mat on the Persian carpet and began stretching. Body and muscles soon flowed to the rhythm of her steady breathing. Eyes half-closed, she coaxed her body into harder and harder positions. A touch of perspiration formed across her forehead.

Fifteen minutes later, she stopped mid-pose, kneeling on the mat, one leg back, her back straight, an arm forward. Her eyes popped open in frustration. Halfway into her routine and still her mind roared. The only thing flowing up her spine and out the top of her head were questions. Foremost among them—what on earth was Hewitt trying to tell her with a torn postcard of Pete's Supermarket and a mysterious key wrapped up with fishing line? It was the next question that had her bringing her hands together in an abrupt *"Namaste."* Why would a gunman purposely shoot over her head? Answer one—he wanted her alive. Answer two—he'd be back.

She rolled up her mat. Yoga had become like methadone to a

heroin habit. Before yoga, she had been addicted to the violence inherent in Shuto Kai karate, kendo, and t'ai chi ch'uan, gaining power and confidence. And power in a former victim was a dangerous thing. At some point, Martha realized her hunger for power was overtaking the spiritual quest. So many principles of yoga and the martial arts were the same—grace, beauty of movement, the strength of character—but yoga was devoid of violence and its power was only over oneself. Something she desperately needed.

Today, however, what she needed was a good old-fashioned fight on the *tatami*. And if she was the target of some crazed Mormons, all the more reason to dust off a few skills.

She stood up, and as she poured a bowl of milk for Beatrice, she glanced out the kitchen window across the lawn to the big craftsman house on the bluff, with its perfect view of Shilshole Bay Marina, Puget Sound, and the Olympic Mountains. A perfect view of what had taken all her available finances. Today, she knew, post-home mortgage loan scandal, she would never qualify to buy the house. But a few years back, with three percent down and a regular job—even if a junior lawyer's salary wasn't what the loan officer had expected—the bank was more than happy to give her a loan. Each raise at CH&N made that mortgage a little easier. And one day—maybe when she made partner—she could afford to live in her own house.

Still worth it, even if it meant living in an apartment above the garage while renting out the main house—most recently to a visiting Dutch scholar at the University of Washington and his family. Karl and Iris Heiden had been renting the house for nearly two years. The Heidens' three girls—twelve-year-old Olivia, her little sister Lilith, and baby Josephina, with her perpetual smile—had been welcome additions to Martha's extended family. She remembered their birthdays, surprised them with trips out for ice cream, and had them up to the garage for a girls' slumber party when their parents had traveled to Portland for a convention. Olivia had even christened the garage with a new name. "Someday, Marta," the young girl said in her rapidly improving English, "I too will live in carriage house. Like a princess. Like you. Only I will have horses. I will always ride them every day. And I will have my prince."

Since then, it had been the Carriage House. Though Martha was still waiting for her prince.

Before Martha bought the property, the garage had been a place to tote things in that never came out. The size of a small barn, it combined the lingering smells of oil, dust, and mold. Turning the loft into an apartment had taken all her after-work hours. One year, she had rewired the building so breakers didn't pop every time she turned on her hair dryer; the next it had been hanging the drywall, a project that had forced her and Beatrice downstairs among the cars for most of the summer. New thermopane windows now looked over an undeveloped ravine and a grove of large cedars, a view she loved. The summer before, she had laid the bamboo floor; the natural grain glowed yellow-gold in the evening light.

Only recently had she allowed herself the luxury of thinking about the completed project. Soon, her tool belt and nail gun and compressor could be put away. A mill in south Seattle had replicated the craftsman molding from the 1907 house, and she was in the final stages of installing baseboards and door and window trim. With the end of restoration in sight, she had begun to think of the Carriage House as home.

She set the milk down, and Beatrice roused herself from sleep. Martha showered and dressed in a cream silk blouse, a lightweight charcoal cashmere sweater, and black jeans. Hoop earrings and a simple white gold necklace finished her attire.

She glanced in the mirror and liked what she saw—delicate cheekbones and a high brow, a gift from Gran and her Native American heritage, and the one blue and one hazel eye. She had long since stopped worrying about her oversized nose and small breasts. She stroked a brush through black curls that fell to her shoulders. Boots added two inches to her six-foot frame.

The Pineapple Express showed no signs of letting up on the rain, so she chose her black raincoat and an umbrella with a carved duck's head handle, a gift many years ago from Hewitt. Like so many of his gifts, it was both playful and practical. "How serious can a corporate attorney be," he had said, "if she carries an umbrella with a duck's head?" She loved the playfulness that Hewitt had brought to her life, and always carried the umbrella if the forecast called for rain. Was that fun now gone? She refused to believe it.

And it was practical. After nearly sixteen years in a city known for rain, she was still amazed that a true Seattleite wouldn't be caught dead with an umbrella.

She grabbed a duffel bag from the bottom of the closet and was then joined on the steps by Beatrice, another morning ritual. Beatrice always stayed home until Martha left for work, then out she went to mouse the ravine and prey on local songbirds. Her electronic collar let her roam in and out of the Carriage House, while keeping out raccoons and neighboring cats. Choosing the front door instead of her custom-made cat door, Beatrice waited for Martha to open it. Martha performed her duties without comment. As she stepped outside, she caught the flash of a cat's black rump disappearing into the bushes. Beatrice immediately took off in pursuit. "You be careful," Martha yelled. "I don't have time to run you to the vet right now."

The cat paid her all the attention that cats are wont to pay.

Martha selected the Mini Cooper again today. The Lexus

was fine for chauffeuring clients around town but it handled like a tank. The '57 T-bird had been lovingly restored to its original mint condition by her oldest brother just before he went off to do ten years in the penitentiary for turning the family cabin in the woods of Michigan's UP into a meth lab. The T-bird didn't come out unless the sun was shining, which meant it was mostly in the garage.

Driving toward downtown Ballard, she heard her phone chime. The number wasn't familiar.

"Martha Whitaker," she said.

"It's Metcalf. I wanted to make sure everything's okay at home."

"Yes, it is, Detective, thank you." She waited for the real reason for his call.

"I had a patrol unit swing by a couple of times last night, and they reported nothing suspicious in the neighborhood."

"I appreciate your concern. Or were you checking to see if I was planning to skip town?"

"Both," he replied matter-of-factly. "Still, you need to be careful until we can figure out what's going on. And don't make any plans to leave town."

"Thank you . . . I guess."

"Okay. Call me if anything seems strange or unusual. And please, be careful."

Before she could reply, the police detective had hung up. Well, at least there had been a hint that he was starting to believe her.

At nine o'clock, parking along Market Street was still available. Martha pulled the Mini Cooper in in front of the Nordic Heritage Gift Store and Delicatessen. It was the only place in town she could buy lutefisk. She shipped the Norwegian delicacy back to her father a few times each year.

But today she stopped instead next door, where a sign read
Gustafson's Lock and Key Shop. A doorbell jingled as she entered. It smelled musty, like old people and nursing homes. The
cramped space had two walls lined with every key imaginable.
Facing the back wall, an old man hunched over a workbench,
his age-spotted hands busy on a grinder. He turned and eyed
Martha through a pair of safety goggles. "How may I help you,
miss?"

She held up the key from Hewitt's pill bottle. "I was hoping
you might be able to identify where this came from."

He approached the front counter. It took him a couple of
strides to straighten up completely, which brought him to her
height with her boots on. Uneven white stubble covered most of
his creased face.

Martha laid the key on the counter.

Instead of looking at the key, he stared into her eyes. "Heterochromia iridium," he said, "now that's a rare condition. Passed
on through the maternal gene, I believe."

"Yes, it is," she said. "Most people don't know that."

"I'm not most people." His smile showed small yellow teeth.
Blue lips hinted at circulatory problems. "And a nose straight
from royalty. The Hapsburgs, perhaps?"

"More like King Olaf from Norway, many times removed on
my father's side, probably through some illicit affair."

"Ah, the vanity of youth," he said, his blue eyes sparkling
with life. "Kings don't have illicit affairs. They are king. As I am
king of keys." He held up the key, a short silver barrel with in-
dentations and protrusions on one end. He rotated it in the light
a couple of times. "And this isn't even a challenge. Life abounds
with disappointments. It's the key to a Brinkman's safe, usually
goes with an electronic code. They're quite common, available
at most any office supply store. Either the L70 or L80 model."

He handed back the key. "Usually, people come in with a safe but no key, and I can help them. You come in with a key but no safe. With that, I can be of no assistance. There're probably a million of them. I'm sorry."

Martha pocketed the key. Her fingers worked its fluted edges. "You've been a great help," she said. "Thank you." There was no way she could keep this from Metcalf. She placed the key back on the counter. "Is this something you can make a copy of?"

"If it's a key, I can make a copy of it. Now whether I should is quite another matter."

She reached for the key. Gustafson stretched out a hand, palm up. "Give me half an hour."

"Thank you so much. I'm going to visit Mr. Yamamoto. I can be back in an hour."

"I'm closed for lunch from eleven to one," he said. "And my nap. I have to conserve my energy. I'm teaching Scandia folkdance tonight at the Nordic Heritage Museum."

Martha returned to her car just long enough to grab the duffel bag. At a nondescript door tucked between a credit union and a burger shop, she turned and bounded up a flight of stairs. Across an open *tatami* floor, a middle-aged Asian man sat behind a desk. He glanced up from a laptop and then rose, moving toward her with the slight waddle of a man thick in the chest and legs. The left ear was missing its upper half. As always, he was dressed for work, his white *gi* cinched tight around his waist with a black belt. The bars showed he was a ninth-level black belt. Bare feet extended below loose white pants. Several inches shorter than Martha, he greeted her with a low bow. "Miss Whitaker, it's been too long."

Martha returned the bow, dropping even lower, no easy task given their height difference. "Mr. Yamamoto, my apologies. I hope the *sensei* forgives me."

"There is nothing to forgive."

"Would you have time for a private lesson?"

"I would be honored. Please prepare yourself."

In minutes Martha returned wearing her *gi*, tied securely with a black belt indicating her rank of the sixth level, *rokudan*. Her hair was held back in a French twist. Her morning yoga, while unsuccessful in quieting her mind, had properly stretched tendons and ligaments. She was as flexible as a whip. Yamamoto was nowhere in sight. She bowed before stepping on the *tatami*. In the center of the mat she sat down and quickly settled into the *zazen* position, her arms extended. She closed her eyes.

Yamamoto was the seventh master under whom she had studied. He was the most skilled, but also the most reluctant to teach her. After their second or third lesson, he had asked her to sit on the bench with him. On one *tatami*, a younger *sensei* led a class of small children in the basic footsteps. Two adult men had replaced Yamamoto and Martha on the second *tatami*, and they sparred with a grace that stopped just short of violence. First- or second-degree black belts, Martha guessed.

"Why do you fight, *senpei*?" Yamamoto said, never taking his eyes off the children.

"To learn from you, *sensei*."

"With respect, Miss Whitaker, that does not answer my question. Why do you fight?"

In time, she answered, "So I will never be a victim again."

"That is too easy. Your skill is already there. But you know that. You have had good masters. You have trained long and hard. You are lethal—an efficient fighting machine. But you know that also. I am wondering why I should become your teacher. So why do you fight?"

No answer came to Martha this time.

"Someone has hurt you badly, I know. It is common here to see anger—especially in women—but never have I seen it as intense as I see it in you. Do not let this become your white whale. That's a journey few people return from."

The children hopped and stepped, the men kicked and blocked and twirled. And Martha's mind seemed blank. Finally, she said, "Could you help me find my way back?"

"No, only you can do that." But he laughed and jumped up, telling the children to stop. "*Yame.*" He turned. "Thank you, Miss Whitaker. Now I have a purpose. Maybe I can give you the skills to help your return journey. That will be a challenge for me, as well."

"*Kawate*," Yamamoto said, and Martha felt the heavy pole being laid across her wrists. The session began.

She twisted out of the *zazen* and spun away from the center of the floor, grasping for the pole as she moved. She came up empty-handed. Her leg shot out but caught only a ruffle of fabric. Yamamoto slapped the pole at her leg but she had jumped smoothly to the side. The counter became her move and she snapped a punch at his head. He palmed it aside. The second punch, the real purpose of the move, grazed his cheek as he arched backwards. An opportunity lost, she knew, and she wouldn't get many of those fighting Yamamoto.

For fifteen minutes, they moved across the *tatami*, attacking and counterattacking, blocking and avoiding. Martha's shoulder muscles began to ache in a long dull burn, and her legs wanted to collapse. She could hear Jonesy screaming at her to breathe and let the pain go. The body will take so much more than we think it will. The tide of her breath centered her and brought a crystalline clarity as she moved back toward the center of the mat.

Yamamoto tossed the pole aside and intensified the pace. They moved faster, legs bent lower, each circling for an advantage. Beads of perspiration dripped down her face and her breathing became ragged, no longer under control. Now her height became her disadvantage, and she squatted to maintain as low a center of gravity as possible. Yamamoto launched a series of battle punches, but she stepped through them with a double circling hand, prepared to move over both wrists and dump him to the mat. But he had slipped past her. He dropped to one knee and, before she could twist away, brought her to a backbreaking bow over his thigh.

Martha's entire body relaxed, a signal that she accepted her defeat. He released her. They bowed to each other, her bow again lower, as was correct for a pupil to her master.

"You might benefit from the *Basai Dai kata*," Yamamoto said.

She acknowledged this with a nod. Their sessions on the *tatami* were usually like this—short, intense—but always followed up with time for her to work alone. The ritualized motions of the *kata* simulated a series of fight moves against one or more opponents. It was akin to a meditative dance, if done properly.

And so she began. Her tall, lean frame moved across the *tatami* with a fluid grace, the ritualized steps bringing the understanding of her power as she punched tight air and swirled with a whistling kick. Sweat poured down her face as she moved from corner to corner like a ballerina bent on destruction, first high, then low, twirling her legs like a windmill, a hand motionless before the fatal stab.

And as she reached the end of the *kata*, she achieved the real reward, that quiet center where there was only herself. And the power she could choose not to use.

Breathing hard, she bowed herself off the *tatami*. Yamamoto was on the same bench against the wall, hands on his knees. On either side of him sat a student, probably teenagers, one a tow-head boy, the other an Asian girl. He patted each on the knee and told them to go stretch in preparation for their lesson.

Martha approached. "Thank you, *sensei*."

"It is always a pleasure to work with you," Yamamoto said. "It challenges me. I like that. But you were distracted today, Martha. It leaves you vulnerable."

"Is that so bad?" Martha said.

"In a fight, yes." Yamamoto bowed in farewell. "In life, you will have to decide for yourself. But that is why we are here."

EIGHT

This time the key shop smelled of burnt metal and dust and old people, but the old key-maker was nowhere in sight. Martha froze. Alive from her workout with Yamamoto, she would almost welcome encountering someone other than Gustafson walking through the door. No sound came from the shop. She had her phone out ready to punch in 911 when she saw the original key and the copy on the counter. The dust cover was on the grinder, and the safety glasses beside it—signs of an old man too trusting to lock his doors. She leaned over the counter, was relieved not to find Gustafson lying there in a pool of blood, and put her phone away. Under the keys was a note scribbled on the back of a receipt.

> Having a bit of a lie down. No payment owed if you'll join me and my wife at the Sons of Norway Ball in July. Remember, those born of the passion of the king may someday ascend the throne. Good luck with finding your safe. Harold Gustafson

Martha pocketed the keys and scribbled on the bottom of the note, "I'll consider it. Thank you." She slipped two twenties under the receipt and wondered how James MacAuliffe was feeling this morning. She hoped they had given him some good drugs.

Outside again, she checked each doorway, each window. No one seemed to care that she stood rooted there in the rain. Still, someone out there knew about the houseboat. And Hewitt's visit with Trammell. They had to know about her. She ducked into the Norwegian delicatessen next door—out of habit, maybe just for comfort—and stood back from the door watching the street. No one appeared or stopped or changed direction. Finally, she turned into the deli. It was as empty as the key shop except for the clutter—an intersection of tradition and kitsch that Hewitt had always delighted in—Dale of Norway sweaters stacked beside Klogg mugs and plastic Viking and Valkyrie figurines. Hewitt would hobble around in a Viking helmet while she ordered the lye-soaked lutefisk for her father.

Hewitt . . . his absence made the store seem all the more empty. A sadness crept over her at the times that they would never again share. Fifty years separated them—and didn't make a bit of difference. "I'm an old soul and so are you," he had said once while they were trolling for salmon off Jeff Head. As his downrigger snapped to attention, he added, "We've both seen too much, you and I."

And so they had.

Hewitt reminded her of the Norwegian grandfather she'd never met—a miner in the copper fields in the UP back when that grueling job paid a decent wage. Because of Gran's stories, Olaf Thornson was as alive to Martha as if she had known him all her life. Back when her own father was the hellion of the third grade class, Olaf had dropped dead at the bottom of a mineshaft. Remarried to the staid and stern John Whitaker, Gran never stopped missing her first husband. "How my Olaf could kick up his heels and dance!" she'd say. "Laughed and danced and played the fiddle and drank and smoked and talked as if life would end tomorrow. Which for him I guess it did."

And so, too, Hewitt—laughing and talking and dancing and smoking dope as if life would end tomorrow. Which for him, now, maybe it had.

Hewitt's infectious spirit had been the perfect tonic for a young woman who took after her Grandpa Whit more than she cared to acknowledge. Alone and lonely in a new town, she had been drawn to Hewitt's intellect and sense of play, a perfect counterpoint to her own sober take on the world. She had accepted Hewitt's friendship, relieved—and surprised, at first—that it didn't have sexual undertones. A willing fishing partner and able listener, he slowly elicited her life story—but only when the salmon weren't biting and the waves were gentle on the Sound. He listened patiently to the bits and pieces until, eventually, the pattern emerged like a tapestry on a loom. He listened without condemning; he understood her demons. She shared things with him that no one knew but Gran. Hewitt had been confessor to her sins, absolving her, understanding her, reassuring her. "We're peas in a pod," he had once said. "Wounded warriors home from the front. Except you went back and finished your battle. I never did. I'm proud of you for that. I only wish I had your strength and determination."

When pressed for his own battle, he looked away. "It was a long time ago, my dear. Let's leave ancient history alone on a day like today."

Sky as blue as a Dutchman's pants arched overhead as they trolled the underwater rise between President Point and Point

Jefferson. A soft breeze created a golden streak of shimmering water from the morning sun. One eight-pound coho already lay gutted and iced in the cooler.

"Sometimes it helps to talk about it," Martha said. "I know."

He kept his gaze fixed on distant Whidbey Island. "And re-open old wounds of a love destroyed?"

"Or heal old wounds."

When he turned, his brow had tightened over his hawkish nose. His words rolled like the thunder from the pulpit of the righteous. "I have bled enough over those sordid tales in which Achilles lost his Patroclus, in which Romeo lost his Romeo. I shall not give them the satisfaction of shedding more blood. The avenging angels can burn their fucking wings in Hell before they will get that satisfaction from me."

The vehemence of his pronouncement drove Martha back into the captain's chair, her hands balled into fists, her legs braced. Who was this roaring madman in the boat with her?

Then she saw the tears rolling down the creases of his aged face. His shoulders slumped and his face relaxed and suddenly he was just a grieving old man.

She relaxed, reached out, and drew him close, a daughter comforting a father. "I'm so sorry, Hewitt," she whispered.

"No," he said, stepping back from her embrace. "I'm the one who's sorry. You didn't deserve my anger. I'm so sorry." He wiped his cheeks with his jacket sleeve. From a jacket pocket, he pulled out a folded paper towel and blew his nose. A weak smile turned into a weak laugh, one still tinged with bitterness. "Seventy years later and I still turn into a blubbering moron. Come, come, my dear, please forgive an old man his moment of weakness. Someday I'll share my tragic tale of youthful infatuation. But not to-day. The sun is out and the fish are biting. Did I ever share with you my secret recipe for preparing stuffed salmon?"

Now, she realized with a jolt, someday might never come. She might never again see him nattering about the Norwegian deli like an ancient Viking, wreaking havoc with a cane for a sword. She might never hear his tragic tale of youthful infatuation or be able to help ease the pain of Romeo losing his Romeo. Was Hewitt really dead? The empty space where he had stood told her she needed to consider the possibility.

But, not now, not today.

A woman stood behind the counter, tapping a pen as if she had a store full of waiting customers. Martha acknowledged her with an embarrassed smile. She ordered two pounds of lutefisk to be shipped to Sault Ste. Marie and included a note that said simply, "Miss you, Daddy. Be well. Love, Marti."

If the silver Audi had been parked behind her, she might not have noticed it. But it was across the street. When she pulled the Mini Cooper onto Market Street, the Audi made an illegal U-turn. That caught her attention. She stayed in the curbside lane for a couple of blocks. The Audi stayed well behind in the center lane.

Just past the Majestic Bay movie theatre, without signaling, she swung a quick right. Moments later, the Audi nosed around the corner. At the Ballard Public Library, its swooping roof of natural grasses now brown and dead, she made another right and then a quick left into the parking lot. The Audi motored past. The driver, a young man, never gave her a second glance.

Five minutes went by, but the Audi didn't return. With a sigh, she released her grip on the wheel and flexed her fingers.

Back on Market Street, she cruised Ballard's shopping district, no sign of the Audi in her rearview mirror. But, sure enough, at the light on 24th, the Audi came to a stop three cars behind. The light turned green and, at the last minute, she switched off her blinker and went straight through the intersection. One car turned, the second didn't. Staying well back, the Audi followed behind her. Her hand went to the gearshift and, for a moment, she considered losing the tail in the backstreets and alleys of Ballard. But if she did, she would be no closer to discovering who was following her and why.

A better idea came to her.

Heading west past the Ballard Locks, Martha began to parallel the Ship Canal. The car directly behind her had turned off. The Audi hung well back as she passed the sailboats moored at Shilshole Bay Marina. Among them was her "yacht," as Metcalf called her small fishing boat. The twenty-three-foot Grady White would be a yacht when her Mini Cooper became a limo. And then she was passing Little Coney's and the boat ramp where yesterday they had pulled Hewitt's empty van from the water. Back to the beginning, she thought. But where was the end?

At the stop sign, she drove straight through to the only entrance and exit to Golden Gardens Park. She had a little greeting prepared if he followed her in. But when the Audi came to the stop sign, it turned right onto Golden Gardens Drive and disappeared under the railroad trestle.

Okay, Plan B. If she was wrong, she would just be a little wet from the rain.

Martha parked, killed the engine and popped the back hatch. She dug out the tire iron. It was a small bar, maybe a foot long, but that worked to her advantage. She ran toward a pedestrian walkway that took her under the railroad tracks, and took the steps two at a time to the upper parking lot. It was empty, the access gate closed. About a hundred yards down the winding Golden Gardens Drive, right where she expected to see it, the silver Audi sat on the shoulder next to the railroad trestle. Facing away from her, it offered a perfect vantage point from which to watch the only exit to the park.

She slid the tire iron up her sleeve. Hugging the embankment, she walked steadily toward the Audi. All she needed was a little luck. He would be expecting her to appear in front of him.

She noted the license plate number and, two strides later, stood beside the driver's window. A quick snap of the tire iron and the window shattered into his lap. She had the bar pressed against his throat and found the gun in his shoulder harness before he realized she was there. She tossed his gun over the car and into the bushes.

"Both hands on the wheel," she ordered. He did as commanded. He was hardly more than a kid; spots of fresh acne dotted his chin. His red hair was cropped military style.

"Talk." She eased her grip just enough to let a little air pass down his trachea.

"Officer Danny Kimble," he croaked. "SPD. Detective Metcalf ordered me. To keep an eye on you. For your protection. After last night. Please. I can't breathe."

She eased the pressure on the tire iron. The kid gasped for air. Martha said, "ID. Show me your ID."

He fumbled for his neck badge. Martha saw his picture, Seattle Police Department, and his name, Danny Kimble.

She released her hold. "Christ, why didn't you guys say you'd be shadowing me?"

Kimble gulped for air. "Why didn't . . . Metcalf tell me you were a psycho bitch." He rubbed his neck. "Fuck . . . where's my gun?"

"In the bushes. Find it yourself. And tell Metcalf I think his little game sucks. Better yet, get the fuck out of here. I'll tell him myself."

Throwing gravel, the Audi squealed around the corner under the railroad trestle and went right through the stop sign at

Seaview Avenue without slowing down.

Back at the Mini Cooper, Martha replaced the tire iron and pulled a small blanket from the backseat. She toweled herself dry and grabbed her cell phone. Metcalf answered in two rings.

"It's Martha Whitaker," she said. "Danny and I just had a little chat. You can send me the bill for the broken window and his gun."

"I'm sorry?" Metcalf said. "I don't know what you're talking about."

"Don't give me that shit, Metcalf. I'm really tired and my fuse is getting really short. Officer Danny Kimble, SPD. You assigned him to tail me. Well, he's now on his way back to mother. Lucky I didn't break his neck."

Metcalf didn't rise to her anger. "Ms. Whitaker, I don't know any Officer Danny Kimble, and I don't have anyone tailing you. What happened?"

Shit. It took her a moment to gather her thoughts; she had time to curse her own stupid gullibility. The kid had been in her grasp. Shit Shit Shit. He didn't even have to break a sweat to get her to believe his cover. Because she wanted to believe it, because she wanted to believe Metcalf was a jerk and that he still considered her his number one suspect.

Like the lawyer that she was, she began relaying pertinent details to Metcalf in sequential order. Facts without emotions. Metcalf never once admonished her for her stupidity. He left that to her.

"I disarmed him . . ." she said, and paused. "The gun! Hang on, Detective."

She tore out of the parking lot. Crashing over the speed bumps, she swung around the corner, punched it under the railroad trestle, and slammed to a stop on the gravel where the Audi had been. It took just seconds to find the gun.

With a soggy tissue from her jacket pocket, she grasped it by the barrel. She had no idea what type it was. She asked Metcalf, "How do you tell if the safety's off?"

"Depends," he replied. "But usually there's a little switch on the left side, just above the trigger, where you can reach it with your thumb when holding the pistol. Up, the safety is on; down, it's off."

Martha gingerly flicked the switch up. The kid had been tailing her with the safety off.

"Okay, I've got his gun. Maybe forensics can find fingerprints or match it to the bullets from last night." Then she described the young man, down to the acne on his chin, followed by the type of car and its license plate. Martha added the exact location so they could check for tire prints and broken glass.

"And Metcalf," she continued, "the kid had a forged ID from the Seattle Police Department. He knew about the shooting last night, and he used your name without a moment's hesitation. You haven't even been assigned to the case for twenty-four hours. Someone's getting information really fast. That might be a good place to start."

"Yes, it would be," Metcalf's tone grew more somber. "But right now I have other pressing matters to handle. What do you know about University Rare Books and Manuscripts?"

"I know that if Hewitt's dead, I own it."

"Then you better get over here," he said. "I need you to identify a body."

NINE

Scattering gravel, Martha punched the Mini Cooper and, like Danny Kimble minutes before her, ignored the stop sign under the railroad trestle. Speeding past the marina, she tried to prepare herself for a body stretched out on the floor of University Rare Books and Manuscripts. A glance at the gun in the passenger's seat reminded her of Kimble's deadly intent. Had he planned the same fate for her? Had Ralph Hargrove, Hewitt's long-time manager, discovered Hewitt's body when he arrived to open the store that morning? She shuddered at what she might find.

Along the way, she dialed Trammell's number.

"Yeah," he said. His voice still carried the timbre of sleep. When she had left the *Ballard Gazette* at three a.m., he was still working with the police to verify what files had been stolen from his desk and laptop. And Metcalf wasn't about to let him leave without a good explanation of why he and MacAuliffe had ignored the "Do Not Enter" tape at Hewitt's houseboat.

"You okay?" Martha performed a last-second turn into the Wallingford Center parking lot. No one pulled in behind her.

"Helluva headache," he replied. "Like someone knocked me out cold last night."

"You'll live. Take some ibuprofen and drink lots of strong coffee."

"You're about as sweet as thorns on a rose."

"I'm improving," she said. "The last guy compared me to barbed wire—must be my winsome personality."

"Yeah. You okay?"

"I'm alive," she said, "which is more than can be said for someone at Hewitt's bookstore."

"The place over in the U District? Who? Hewitt?"

"I don't know yet. Metcalf wants me to identify the body. I pray to God it isn't Hewitt. If it is, that still doesn't explain how his van ended up in Puget Sound."

"Someone hiding evidence?"

"At a public boat ramp?" Martha said. "I don't think so."

"Maybe to keep us looking in the wrong direction while they got out of town."

"Could be. If so, it worked," Martha said. "There's more. They didn't all leave town. I had someone tailing me this morning. When I caught up with him, he claimed to be working for Metcalf and had a Seattle Police Department ID badge. I bought it hook, line, and sinker and let him go. Metcalf said he didn't have anyone following me."

"Maybe Metcalf's lying."

"Why would he?" Martha said, but wondered if Trammell might be right.

"Doesn't want you to know that you're still a suspect?"

"I have no doubt that he still considers me a prime suspect." It suddenly occurred to Martha she could be driving to a crime scene to be arrested for Hewitt's murder. "I just wanted to warn you to watch your back. These guys are after something that they haven't found yet. Which means you're in just as much danger as anyone."

Metcalf and a forensics officer met her at the car. The forensics expert remained at the Mini Cooper to process and catalog the gun, promising to lock the car when finished.

"Detective Metcalf can get in easily enough if he needs to," Martha said in parting.

They exchanged withering looks, but Metcalf didn't say a word as he ushered her through the throng of people pressed against the police cordon outside the store.

University Rare Books and Manuscripts was tucked off University Avenue on a side street. A hint of despair pervaded everything in the area, including the bookstore, which was sandwiched between a tattoo parlor advertising body art and skin piercings and a Pho restaurant already pumping out the aroma of garlic and roasted chilies into the air. Counterculture radicals from the '60s had been replaced by homeless panhandlers, a few students with backpacks, and leather-jacketed punks. The transition had started fifteen years ago when Martha had been a student at the U, and nothing had stopped the slide toward urban blight.

Inside, the store was dim and dusty, with more police officers mingling about than customers at a book signing. Rows of books lined unpainted shelves on three walls. All the requisite categories were there—except Romances, which Hewitt refused to sell. The store had a reputation for the best collection of science fiction and fantasy in the greater Seattle area and maybe on the West Coast. Martha noticed that the cabinets and the cash register were intact. A first edition of Asimov's *I, Robot* looked undisturbed. The really valuable books were never displayed. She had no idea where they were kept. Their marketing and sales happened almost entirely on the web.

There was no sign of Ralph Hargrove. Bespectacled and pudgy, Ralph had been the driving force behind the store's emphasis on sci-fi and fantasy, which in turn was the driving force behind its success. With bookstores closing all over town, University Rare Books and Manuscripts continued to turn a small profit for Hewitt, as she well knew from taking care of his finances during his illnesses. Month in and month out, Ralph deposited a steady stream of revenue into Hewitt's business account, providing enough—with the Pho restaurant—to pay the mortgage and Hargrove's salary, with a few dollars left over. Hewitt always joked that he kept the bookstore open to keep him in latte money.

A chill swept over Martha as she realized suddenly they wouldn't need her to identify a body if Ralph were here. Not if the body was Hewitt. Oh, Ralph, not sweet Ralph. Shy and unassuming, he may have been the gentlest man she ever met. God, let it be a stranger.

Metcalf led her toward the office at the rear of the store, where the flash of a camera exploded like lightening. It was where Hewitt had worked on the "Manuscripts" part of the store's name. A closer look revealed a foot protruding into the doorway. She braced herself, but Metcalf made no attempt to bring her to the door.

His hands worked something—keys or loose change—in the pockets of a well-cut, dark gray suit designed more for the downtown business world than a University District crime scene. His appearance gave no indication that he had been working another crime scene in Ballard a mere few hours before.

"Harry," Metcalf called out. A burly man approached. Wild dark hair touched the shoulders of a faded Carhartt jacket, its shoulders soaked with rain. Except for penetrating brown eyes, his face was hidden behind a bushy black beard. Next to the dapper Metcalf, he looked like a logger from the Olympic forests.

"Detective Harry Callison, Homicide," Metcalf offered by way of introduction. "We're partners on this investigation now. Harry, this is Martha Whitaker, the woman I mentioned to you."

"Ma'am," Callison said, nodding. "I need you to identify our victim, if you can."

A skinny redheaded woman stepped over the motionless foot, a camera slung over her shoulder. "All yours, Detective," she said. "But try not to touch anything. We may have a partial fingerprint."

"Enough to get an ID?" Callison asked.

"Not sure yet."

Callison turned to Martha, his voice surprisingly gentle. "I have to warn you—this is going to be gruesome. You've probably never seen anything like it before. Concentrate on his face, stay no longer than you absolutely have to."

Her mouth went dry. He took her elbow and guided her toward the body.

Martha froze, unable to bring her eyes to the victim's face. Fear hadn't touched her last night when she had been shot at. Now, she couldn't stop shaking. "Good God," she murmured, looking anywhere but down.

It was Hewitt's houseboat all over again. Every drawer pulled out, file cabinet emptied onto the floor, but instead of papers, clothes were tossed around the room. A picture frame had been pulled apart, the backing torn off; stuffing ripped out of a futon covered everything like a foamy layer of snow. The sweet, sickening smell of blood mingled with the stale odor of a locker room.

At Callison's insistence, she lowered her eyes at what she didn't want to see—a body stretched out on the floor. A mutilated corpse. When she finally brought herself to look at the face, she realized it was going to get worse. A police officer knelt beside the body, his gloved fingers touching the elastic band of the men's underwear that had been pulled over the victim's face. They had once been white, now they were red fading to brown from dried blood. At a nod from Callison, the officer rolled back the underwear. Martha gagged at the sight of a penis sticking out of Ralph Hargrove's mouth.

She turned and ran.

When she stepped out of the bathroom, she had washed her face and rinsed the vomit from her mouth. Her stomach still churned, but she thought she could control it. Metcalf stood waiting.

"It's Ralph Hargrove," she said.

"He worked here?" Metcalf asked.

Martha just nodded.

"Looks like he lived there, in the back room."

She spoke in a strained whisper. "Hewitt's, it used to be Hewitt's office. I haven't been here in a while. Maybe two, three years." She gagged again. "Oh, God."

"Okay, steady. Breathe deep, look around." Metcalf's voice was quiet and calm. "When did you last speak with Mr. Hargrove?"

"Yesterday morning." She tried to focus, to blot out the image of the castrated Hargrove. Her stomach lurched again. She tilted her head back and took another deep breath. Oh God, why Ralph? And why mutilate him? Numb and trembling, she wrapped her arms around her body to stop the shaking.

"After Hewitt's van was pulled from the water, I called Ralph. He hadn't seen Hewitt in a couple of weeks. They had lunch. They didn't even talk business. He said Hewitt was fine. It fact, he said Hewitt seemed downright groovy."

"Groovy?"

"That's what he said. Ralph liked those old-fashioned words."

"Groovy. Hardly how you'd describe a frightened man."

"Something must have changed. Don't you get it? Something changed," Martha snapped. "Did you find a safe?"

"Why do you ask?" Metcalf's reply was cool and noncommittal.

"Because the really valuable old books and manuscripts weren't out on display. They have to be kept somewhere. I assume they're in a safe."

"Worried about your inheritance?"

"No," Martha said, keeping her voice even. "I'm worried Ralph walked in on a robbery."

"No, we haven't found a safe." He paused. "What do you know about Mr. Hargrove?"

"What do I know about Ralph? Not much, I guess. Worked with him a little when I was taking care of Hewitt after his stroke. Mostly on finances for the bookstore. Ralph was perfect for running it: knowledgeable on all things literary, hardworking, probably even more frugal than Hewitt, a keen eye for what would sell and what wouldn't. I can only remember one time when he made a bad decision."

"What was that?"

"He bought a first edition, sight unseen, of H. G. Wells' *War of the Worlds* from a collector in Chicago he'd been corresponding with. Turned out not be a first edition. When Ralph contacted the guy about getting his money back, the seller responded with a note that said simply, 'Caveat emptor.'"

Metcalf looked at her, finally arching one eyebrow. "And?"

"It means buyer beware."

"So, he got screwed."

"Yeah, he got screwed."

"Could that have anything to do with his murder?"

"I don't see the connection. It was ten years ago or more. It wasn't that much money, a few thousand dollars maybe. Ralph immediately tendered his resignation. Hewitt just laughed it off."

"He laughed off a few thousand dollars?"

"Hewitt's not motivated by money. He's motivated by love, by an intellectual curiosity, by good food and fine wines, by smart, fun people. But not money. If he has enough, he's emperor of his realm. If he doesn't have enough, he's a miser and a recluse."

"What did you know about Hargrove's personal life?"

"Not much. I didn't know Ralph outside the bookstore. Hewitt told me they were lovers for a short time, but he found Ralph boring. Which he was, frankly, unless you were talking about books. He was harmless, the ultimate librarian nerd. And Hewitt was like most men, gay or straight—he liked his partners young and beautiful and dynamic. Ralph didn't fit any of those descriptions, probably not even twenty years ago. Hewitt said that to help Ralph get over his broken heart, he offered him the job of managing the bookstore. Best decision he ever made."

"The victim was gay?"

"As much as he was sexual at all, I suppose."

"Might explain the castration. What else do you know about him? About his finances, his boyfriends, his habits, any-thing."

"Come on, Metcalf, I didn't know him. We exchanged Christmas cards every year. That was about it. His was always the same—a photo of a row of books and a line that read, 'Books are like having Christmas every day.' He always signed it Ralph Hargrove. As if I might have forgotten who he was. Never any note. I liked him, he liked me. We both liked books and we both liked Hewitt. Ralph was still in love with him, you could tell just by the way he looked at him, but he was too shy to pursue it again. If you call that a relationship, then we had one."

"Could he have been the old man's dope supplier?"

"I doubt it. I don't know. I have no idea where Hewitt got his pot."

"You knew right where he stashed it, but you have no idea where he got it? Really?"

"Yeah, really," she barked. Creases showed around Metcalf tired eyes, but his face was intense, studying her. "Why? You think I had something to do with this?"

"Not necessarily."

She heard the truth behind the lie. "Not necessarily? Why would I want to hurt Ralph Hargrove? You think I'm some kind of psychopath? This isn't about me! Hewitt got mixed up in something he couldn't control. Ralph is probably a casualty of that. Did Trammell tell you about the letter Hewitt brought him?"

"Yeah, he told me some myths and legends from the days of the Lone Ranger and Tonto. Interesting theory. Just doesn't happen to be any evidence. I prefer to look for motive and follow the evidence. So I can pursue some boogeymen who probably never existed, or I can follow a woman who has more toys than someone twice her age, who can't afford to live in the house that she bought so she lives in the garage, whose brother is in jail for pedaling drugs, and whose father has been struggling to pay off medical bills from her sister's prolonged hospice care after her suicide attempt. And this same woman happens to be the beneficiary of Mr. Wilcox's estate, if he should prove to be dead. It's beginning to look like that estate is probably worth a lot. That gives me ample motive, Ms. Whitaker. Now I'm just searching for the evidence."

"You bastard," Martha snapped. "You lousy bastard." She raised her hand involuntarily. Only years of discipline held her back. She took a deep breath and narrowed her eyes. "You've been doing your homework. Well, dig away. We Whitakers like to hang all the family skeletons out on display. Did you also find out that I have another sister who's an alcoholic and spends too much time gambling at the casino, and that our mother abandoned us when I was five years old?" She paused. "Anything else, Detective?"

"As a matter of fact, yes."

She stared hard at him but said nothing.

"Don't leave town, Ms. Whitaker."

Martha started to stalk away, then twirled with one last question. "When was Ralph killed?"

Metcalf looked at her for a long time before answering. "Forensics thinks between five and six o'clock last night. But it'll be up to the ME to give us something official."

"I was with you at that time for our first little tête-à-tête. How do you like being the alibi for your prime suspect?"

"*A* suspect," he corrected. "And I said *about*. By seven o'clock last night, you and your attorney had left the station. Where did you go? You claim to have broken into a barricaded crime scene to look for a cat. An accomplished attorney like you must realize how flimsy that sounds. Besides, just because you didn't handle the scissors that snipped off Hargrove's manhood doesn't mean you weren't involved. Maybe Hargrove walked in when he wasn't supposed to. Maybe you have a homophobic partner who got a little carried away. Didn't like the pictures we found stuffed in his shorts. Forensics thinks he probably bled to death here while they ransacked the office. Yeah, someone cut him, stuffed his dick in his mouth to keep him quiet and let him lie on the floor to bleed to death while they went through his underwear."

Martha fell into stunned silence. When words came, they were a harsh whisper. "You fucking think I arranged this? And the break-in at the *Ballard Gazette* last night, the tail this morning? I suppose I arranged those as well?"

"We'll see if they check out."

"I'm sorry, what?" Martha strode back to face the man. His expression never changed. A smile that might have been a sneer. All cop and all attitude. He continued to jingle his keys.

"You know what I'm curious about, Ms. Whitaker? I'm curious about the gun. I wonder if it's the same gun used last night by this so-called professional who stole nothing, who supposedly shot at you but happened to miss you by a mile. One person got a lump on his head because he wanted a beer from the back room. It's the old magician's trick—create a lot of commotion with one hand to distract attention from the other. But nothing got stolen. Seems odd, doesn't it—tear up a bunch of stuff that won't get you a dime at a yard sale but leave an old book worth about ten grand untouched? Makes me wonder if someone is orchestrating a show for the cops. Now this morning, you call me with some cockamamie story about how you manhandled a kid with a loaded gun, but then this same kid with pimples on his chin deked you into letting him walk away. I'm sorry, Ms. Whitaker, if I'm a bit skeptical. Who is your partner in crime? A lover? One of your upstanding brothers? Someone you picked up on Craigslist? Don't worry, I'll find out."

Martha's voice went deadly quiet. "If you think I made this up, I could give you a demonstration right now."

"You're welcome to try," Metcalf replied with a crooked smile.

"And give you a reason to add assault to your laundry list of crimes? I don't think so."

"Come on. Show me. I won't file charges. I'll just pick you up off the floor. When I file charges, it will be for something much more serious than assault."

"Metcalf, you're beneath contempt." She turned aside. The power not to act was as important as the power to act.

"Thought so. Just like every attorney I know, you're all bluff and bluster and then you run and hide behind your JD and legalese. I've seen your act before and I'm not—"

She sprang in and had his hand out of his pocket before he could react. She bent his wrist back toward the elbow and could have easily snapped it. His first instinct was to escape the pain, a motion that spun him away from her and, in the end, brought his wrist and elbow closer together. She let him do the work of further entrapping himself. He told her where his gun was when his right hand grasped the back of his suit jacket. She palmed it away and tightened her grip. He arched to his toes to escape the pain and she easily unsnapped the holster and removed his gun. With one last twist of his wrist, she released him and handed his gun back.

Metcalf's eyes darted around the room, but the only one paying attention was Callison. The detective smiled at Martha, gave her a nod, and withdrew his hand from inside his Carhartt.

"That doesn't prove a thing." Metcalf rolled his shoulder

and, without bothering to holster his gun, casually dropped it into his coat pocket.

"You're right, it doesn't," she replied. Her anger had dissipated like steam from a release valve. Okay, so she failed the self-control test, but she still took great satisfaction in watching Metcalf shake out his numb fingers. Was this the joy of the bully? Her voice dropped several notches. "But it does demonstrate two things, Detective—one, I could easily have disarmed the guy this morning. It's a useful trick when trying to subdue a three-hundred-pound meth addict on a rampage. And two, that I'm a person of my word. When I tell you I can do something, I mean it. I'm not being arrogant. I'm not playing cowboy. Just honest."

"Here's my word, Ms. Whitaker," Metcalf said. "Money. Follow the money. That leads straight to you. With ample motive and plenty of opportunity. And I will find the means. Trust me."

TEN

Martha charged out of the bookstore. Lined up against the police barricade, the gawkers and bystanders fell silent and quickly parted as she ducked under the tape. No one tried to question her. Except one.

"Martha—Martha, wait."

She turned to see Trammell's now familiar deep-set eyes and dark goatee under the yellow rain jacket. She kept walking, afraid she would lose control again if she were to stop. How could anyone have done this to Ralph? And Metcalf? How dare he accuse her! How fucking dare he! Something horrible was happening, and the prick couldn't see past the obvious. Dogma. He was blinded by cop-school dogma. He wasn't going to find Hewitt if he played this by the book and only investigated her. Fine. So she would find Hewitt for him. If he was still alive. For the second time, doubt began to edge into her thoughts. Martha shuddered at what they might have done to him.

Trammell pushed through the crowd to follow her.

"Martha, come on."

Her long strides forced Trammell to start jogging.

"Just leave me alone," she snapped over her shoulder. "Don't you have a story to write or something?"

"Mac's already done it. Molly found a photo of you on your company's website. It's not great for print, but it'll work."

Martha stopped short. "Don't you dare."

"You were shot at last night, the paper was broken into, and its lead investigative reporter was clubbed over the head. That's big news in Ballard, and I'm a newspaper man." He paused. "You let the *Seattle Times* run your picture about the McGwire case. But you get shot at outside my office, and you're too important to have your picture in the *Ballard Gazette*? It doesn't work that way."

"You, too?" she snapped. "What is this, my life's an open book for everyone to go poking around in?"

"Martha, five minutes on Google gave us more information than we could use. We're not running anything that isn't available to anyone with a computer and a mild curiosity."

"Well, knock yourself out. Go talk to Metcalf. He's got the rest of my life history. You might find something really juicy for your story. I'm sure you'll be interested in his theory that last night was a setup—mine. That I planned it all."

"What? That's crazy. Christ, you're getting soaked."

She ignored the rain. Her hands in her pockets, she felt the fluted edges of the safe key and realized she hadn't turned it over to Metcalf. Damn him all to hell. She wasn't giving it to him now.

Trammell touched her shoulder. "Come on, talk to me."

Martha shook herself free. "Not today. I need to find out what's going on. I need to know what happened to Hewitt. And now, apparently, I also have to clear my own name. I'll be sure to give you first dibs on the story. That is what you're interested in, isn't it, the *story*?"

Beside her again, Trammell said, "Come on. Give me a fucking break. I care about Hewitt, but it's also a story that's worth investigating. I'm a reporter. It's what I do."

"Well, it's not what I do. And it's not how I treat friends."

She was the one who had remained faithful to an eccentric old man when he felt abandoned and betrayed by others. She was the one who had nursed him back to health, fed Dante when he was out of town, showed up with wine and dinner when he was between lovers and feeling lonely. What did it get her? Accusations from people who knew no more about her than what they found on the fucking Internet. The only other person who had remained faithful? Ralph Hargrove. Who now lay dead with his . . .

She shook off the image of the mutilated man. She slid into the Mini Cooper and slammed the door shut. The blanket, still damp from earlier that morning, again served as a towel.

Trammell stopped beside the car, head bent to the window, hands thrust deep into the pockets of his jeans. Martha lowered the window. "It was Ralph, by the way," she said. "Ralph Hargrove. The body in the store. Not Hewitt. I'm sure that's why you drove over here."

"I'm sorry. It must have been horrible."

"Yeah. It was."

"I didn't know him."

"He was a sweet man who didn't deserve to die and sure didn't deserve to be castrated and left there to bleed to death."

"Oh my God." Trammell shook his head. "That's awful."

"Well, maybe you can work it into your story."

She hit the button for the window to roll back up.

"Martha, I am sorry, truly," Trammell blurted out, before the window closed. He added, "Did you know Hewitt may have been a Mormon?"

Her laugh carried the bitterness of rebuttal. "Yeah? He was no more a Mormon than the Pope. He called them the Morons."

"Yeah, okay. Maybe not a practicing Mormon, but eighty-seven years ago one Hewitt Wilcox Chappell was born into a Mormon family in St. George, Utah. He was later excommunicated."

The window slid back down. "How do you know that?"

"The Church of Latter-day Saints. Best genealogical records in the world and available to the public. The paper subscribes to the service."

"Fits right in with your Wild West theory. You go for it, might be a Pulitzer in it for you. I'll just keep trying to find out what happened to Hewitt."

"You can't let go of anything, can you?" he said. "I'm trying to find out what happened to him, too. I've just got different resources and different methods. It doesn't mean I'm wrong or right. Just different. Seems that's an unpardonable sin in your book."

He whirled and strode off, water splashing with every step. Martha watched the slick back of his yellow rain jacket. Couldn't let go? He was right about that. The last time someone had said that had been deep in the woods in Michigan's Upper Peninsula when snow lay thick on the roof of a cabin and some forgotten thaw had left thick icicles hanging from the eaves. She could still see the river, a ribbon of ice covered by its own blanket of snow. On snowshoes, she had followed it in. It would be her highway out.

She was no longer in the Mini Cooper but back on that frozen river, step by step closing in on the cabin, step by step through the grove of firs that surrounded it and kept the bone-numbing gusts off Lake Superior at bay. She could still feel the eerie stillness of the scene, still hear the distant wind, could feel the crust of ice breaking over the powder below as she stuck her snowshoes in a drift by the porch. Could still remember the crack of the door busting open. And there he was. The man seven Whitaker kids grew up calling Uncle Walt.

His beard was longer, more white now than brown. His shaggy salt-and-pepper hair seemed to have a life of its own. Under red suspenders, his plaid shirt billowed out over a growing belly, the sleeves rolled up just enough to reveal the bottom edge of a tattoo that she knew read "Semper Fidelis." Her father had met Walt in boot camp. Wading through the blood and fear and jungles of Vietnam, they had forged a bond that was to last the next forty years. Walt had saved his life. How, she did not know. It was a story her father refused to tell. But when Martha's mother left, it had been Uncle Walt and Gran who stepped up to help look after the kids.

Now he cradled a hunting rifle in his arms.

She slowly removed her heavy mittens and lowered the muffler from her face.

"You?" was all he said. "You ain't welcome here."

For emphasis, he jacked a round into the rifle.

"Rachel died last night."

"Well, that's a blessing for your Pa, I'm sure."

"For you, too, I imagine," Martha said.

"I don't know what you're talking about."

"Of course you do. But her secret didn't die with her, Walt. I know. I survived. We were too young back then to know how to tell Dad that dear old Uncle Walt had raped us. Maybe for Rachel the despair of suicide seemed like the hope of salvation. But not me. I'm still here."

"You're one crazy fucking bitch, you know that?" Uncle Walt rocked back and forth, the gun pointed straight at her. "What the fuck do you want?"

"Call it survivor's guilt, but I swore one day I'd see justice served by bringing you in to answer for your crimes. Today's that day. I'm just sorry I couldn't have done it years ago before Rachel's botched suicide. I had to grow up first."

"You can't let anything go, can you? That was a long time ago."

A long time ago that she relived nearly every day. She almost laughed out loud. "We can leave here together, Walt, or I can haul you out on a sled. Your choice."

It was his turn to laugh, a bitter chuckle. "You never were the smartest of the Whitaker kids, Martha. I ain't goin' nowhere. You seem to forget who's holding the gun. The ice will be breaking up on the lake soon. No one will ever find you. I'll be sure to shed a tear with your Pa."

"Guns are overrated," she said, with more confidence than she felt.

She had called on all her training to prepare herself for this moment. She had been up half the night performing the *katas*, one after another, until she had no more tears to weep. Still she danced. At the end, every muscle sang in anticipation, every lethal point of contact fused into their memory. With the first sweet light of morning, she had entered Rachel's room, brushed out her bed-matted hair, held her cold hand, and kissed her brow. The feeding tube was gone, the oxygen mask hung off the tank. Tubes and tanks had all been pushed aside. Her father sat dozing in a chair by her side. Rachel, eyes closed, face serene. Whether she had found oblivion or peace, it was over. Her last wish fulfilled.

She let her father sleep. She envied him. The troubled sleep of the grieving was perhaps better than the waking dreams of the vengeful, but she couldn't think about that now. Rachel was dead. And now it was time. She dressed for the twenty-below temperatures, found her snowshoes, and wrote a note telling her father she was going to deliver the news to Gran on the reservation. She might need to stay a while. And that she loved him. And Rachel did, too.

And she did go to Gran's. Stopping long enough to tell her the news and trusting her enough to share her plan. Gran puffed deep on a cigarette, tears welling. A hand as wrinkled as a winter apple reached out for Martha's. She coughed, and said, "Only you know what your spirit is telling you to do, Marti. Be safe, my wild one, be safe. The lake can kill you as easily as Walt. I have one granddaughter to mourn; don't make it two."

Martha made the first move. She bolted left. Startled, Walt swung the deer rifle from the hip, but when she pulled up short, turning sideways, narrowing the target, he couldn't stop the heavy rifle fast enough. His shot went wide. A scream came from inside the cabin. She spun and made straight for him as he tried to jack another shell into the chamber. He made it just in time to shoot his big toe off as Martha hit the gun with a well-placed kick. She twisted it away, dislocating his right shoulder in the process. He screamed with the sudden pain. An elbow slammed into his ribs. A shattered kneecap dropped him to the porch like falling lead. But Walt Boudreau hadn't survived Vietnam for lack of courage. A hand snaked out toward an axe beside a stack of wood. Martha broke his fingers with the heel of the rifle, then tossed the gun into the snow.

He had blown the front of his boot off. His big toe still clung to the bloody stump of his left foot by a ligament. Panting, Martha looked at it and said, "Now, I'll have to pull you back to town, you lousy bastard."

He winced and a groan escaped his lips. With cold eyes, he snarled, "I don't think so, cunt."

She kicked him hard in the groin. He succumbed to the pain

and doubled up.

More screams came from inside the cabin. Martha raced inside, found nothing, and headed up to the loft.

A dark-haired girl, no more than twelve or thirteen, stood beside the bed in wide-eyed terror. Not so long ago it might have been Martha. Martha steadied herself against the door jam. It took a moment before she could find her voice. "It's all right, honey," she said, "He'll never hurt you again. Never."

But the girl just stared at her with wild eyes. It was then Martha saw she was handcuffed to the bedpost. She had tipped over a bucket that had obviously been used for a chamber pot. The girl's thin body was draped with a see-through nightie. Sores covered her pencil legs. Martha took a step closer, and the girl jammed herself flat against the wall. Martha stood very still.

"It's okay, LuAnn," she said. "That's your name, right? LuAnn. I saw the poster at the rez. It said you were missing. It's okay. It's all right, honey. I'm here to take you home." She slowly reached out a hand. "Everything will be okay."

Martha knew what a lie that was, but she had lied to herself for so long, stuffing down the pain, that the lie came easily. Still, what she had gone through was nothing like this. The flyer had been posted a month before. A month at the hands of this monster. Oh, God, she hadn't been able to save Rachel. Now she was too late again. Rage and despair threatened to paralyze her. Breathe. Move. Act. The litany to confront her fears brought her back.

She forced herself to speak, her mouth dry, her voice hoarse. "Do you know where the key is, honey?" She pulled a quilt off the bed and recognized Gran's handiwork. She wrapped it around the girl's shoulders and knelt down. She touched the handcuffs. "The key to the handcuffs?"

LuAnn just stared at her with wide, feral eyes.

"Okay, I'll be right back. I promise I'm not going anywhere without you. I promise." The girl started screaming again as soon as Martha's head disappeared down the stairs.

From the porch, a bloody trail led down the steps. Blood on white snow like Japanese calligraphy to where Walt, on his belly, clawed the snow with one arm. He rolled over and his hand rose up holding the rifle.

A long icicle hanging from the eaves turned the sun into a prism of light. Martha snapped it off and flew off the porch, all her rage focused on the monster's face. She reached him just as he shouldered the gun. She drove the icicle deep into his right eye. One last shot exploded wide, missing her by inches. He screamed like an animal in the wild and began to thrash. She rammed the icicle deeper still, into his brain. And then, it was done.

She sat back and then elbowed away from him. But he filled all space. Just like he had at the motel on US Highway 2 outside Superior, Wisconsin, the night everything had changed. With her father recalled to Washington, DC, good old Uncle Walt had offered to drive Martha and Rachel to Gran on the reservation. He carried the sleeping Rachel, still a few months shy of eight, into the room, undressed her and put her into bed. Sitting next to Walt in the dark, Martha ate cold Kentucky Fried Chicken and watched David Letterman. She could smell the whiskey as he inched closer. It started slow, a gentle touch, then a second. Pretending she was a statue, that she didn't exist, didn't stop him from placing her hand on his leg and then on the bulge in his undershorts. That's what people who love each other do, he whispered. You love your Uncle Walt, don't you?

Love him? Of course she did. He was her Dad's best friend. She had grown up with Uncle Walt's bear hugs and thought that love smelled like the tobacco and whiskey the two men shared.

That first time, he made her sit on him. Martha still remembered the shock and pain of him penetrating her. She felt like she had been ripped in half. Over the next nine months, he raped her five more times. Martha was too scared to tell her father, too ashamed to let anyone else know, and too frightened to fight back. Not even when she was old enough to understand what had happened.

Now it was over. He lay still in blood-soaked snow. Her panting began to subside. It was finally over.

She picked herself up and brushed off the snow. She found the key to the handcuffs in the pocket of his work jeans. She ran back to LuAnn.

The next few hours felt like dancing a *kata* underwater. If she had any emotions about having just killed Walt Boudreau, she couldn't find them. All she knew was that he would never brutalize anyone ever again. Martha had planned on justice, but vengeance would do. It touched her with no regrets.

LuAnn slumped to the floor, nearly catatonic, when set free. Martha carried her downstairs, wrapped in the quilt. Warming water over the fire, she bathed the girl, scrubbed the dirt from under fingernails, and cleaned as many of the sores and wounds as she could. She found a comb and slowly began to stroke her tangled hair. All the while LuAnn rocked back and forth, humming a three-note tune. Martha ransacked the kitchen for food and forced LuAnn to eat and drink; forced herself, as well; she needed to refuel if she hoped to pull the girl out of the woods.

Finding none of LuAnn's clothes, Martha bundled the girl in Boudreau's flannels and wool, covering it all with his down jacket. It made her nearly gag, but she had no choice. She laced heavy Sorel boots to her feet. She set scarves and hats and gloves for both of them by the door. When Martha stepped outside, LuAnn found her voice and began to scream again. Nothing Martha said would reassure her, so she just walked out the door with the promise that she would be back shortly.

A path through the snow led to a large shed, nearly hidden amongst the trees. Martha located the wood-hauling sled and inspected the runners and leather harness, cinching up the straps to fit her smaller girth. She slipped into the harness and hauled the sled to the front door. She needed blankets, hides, anything to provide warmth to get LuAnn back across the lake. One old deer hide was stretched and tacked to the wall. She ripped it down and threw it on the sled. She climbed the ladder to the loft. There, she found several more hides and a couple of sleeping bags, strewn about like a nest—and a second chamber pot.

This had to be where Walt hid LuAnn—and who else?— when her father came to visit. Regular as reveille in the morning, her father brought out supplies to Walt on the first of each month. They drank bad whiskey and got drunk. Her father would spend the night, and in the morning, turn the snowmobile down the river toward home. He would never know a young girl was bound and gagged out here.

Fuck you, Walt, fuck you. May you rot for all of eternity and beyond in the lowest regions of hell. For a moment, she wished she could kill him all over again.

Back at the cabin, Martha layered the bottom of the sled with deer hides and two sleeping bags. Beside the door, she piled blankets to go over the girl. A second deer hide, with the hair still attached, would go over it all.

By noon, the sun had faded and heavy gray clouds crept across the sky. She had no choice but to leave before the body was found. She couldn't have stood a night in the cabin anyway.

In the kitchen, she assembled a survival kit in case she didn't make it across the lake before nightfall. Matches, several candles, some kerosene sealed in a Mason jar. She packed them all in a small pot, in which she could melt water if needed. She added firewood, more food, and a flashlight. She found a compass in the gun case. She thanked her stars for a father, a marine, who had taught her a thing or two about survival. The compass would guide them even in a whiteout and keep them alive. She had no intention of being reacquainted with Walt in death anytime soon.

What she did next, she did for her father. Walt was dead. Whatever justice Martha and LuAnn might find would come from that fact. But, just as she had kept her secret from her father, she refused now to see him destroyed by this.

She dragged Boudreau's body into the house. This prompted a long series of moans from LuAnn, now too exhausted to scream. Comfort was not Martha's to give, not now, so she continued her tasks. She wrapped the body in a wool blanket and found his stash of booze in a bottom kitchen cabinet. She dumped first one bottle, then a second on the blanket and onto the floor around him. She scattered the bottles around the floor. Then she soaked it all in kerosene. She took a nip of the last bottle of scotch before pouring it out on the floor. She wiped down the rifle and placed it back in the gun case.

Heavy flakes of snow swirled down through the trees in wide lazy circles as Martha loaded LuAnn onto the sled. A snowstorm could spell death. Martha brushed a flake off LuAnn's nose. The girl showed no reaction. Martha slipped into the harness, picking up her snowshoes from the drift beneath the porch, and hauled the loaded sled back toward the river.

She returned to the cabin. She made a torch from the end of a burning log from the fireplace and one of Walt's wool caps.

From the doorway, she tossed it inside, watched the kerosene smolder for a moment and then ignite. She shut the door. As she shrugged back into the harness, she heard the first whoosh of the alcohol exploding. She never looked back as she began the trek down the frozen river toward Lake Superior. For the next two hours, as the falling snow grew heavier, as the afternoon slipped away and the distance grew between her and the cabin, Martha caught glimpses of the blaze. The old cabin with its dried out timbers and planked floor and cedar-shake roof burned like an offering to angry gods.

At the head of the lake, Martha stopped long enough to eat and drink. She checked on LuAnn who either had passed out or was sleeping. All that mattered at the moment was she was still breathing. Martha brushed snow off the blanket and pulled it back up over the girl's face. Massaging her shoulders did little to relieve the pain. From the edge of the woods, heavy snow was driven in swirls and bursts of white across the ice. The afternoon light disappeared early and fast in the far north, but at the moment it offered enough visibility to take a compass reading on the point of land three miles across the bay.

On the frozen lake, where the wind had blown the snow clear of the ice, her snowshoes were useless. She tucked them into the sled.

Crossing the first hundred yards of the lake was the hardest thing she had ever done. A winter of gales had stacked the ice up along the lee shore of the lake like a broken field of cordwood. Slabs two feet thick rose twenty feet high in places. She tried to retrace her path in, but there wasn't always enough room for the sled. She picked her way around the largest barriers, hauled the sled over the smaller ones, all the time pushing to get through the ice field before the gray skies turned impregnably black. Finally, sweat pouring down her back, she came to the end. Before her lay open ice. She took another compass bearing in the last of the light and began pulling through the gloaming with only the rubber soles of her boots to grip the ice.

But she found a rhythm and soon began to make steady progress. The wind blew at her back—one small gift from the karma gods. Her hands went numb from the cold and she could no longer feel her toes buried deep in her boots. A patch of ice circled her scarf. The sweat down her back had long since grown cold, sending shivers through her body. What muscles she could still feel cried out in unrelenting pain. The leather harness felt like it had burrowed under her skin.

Once, she thought she saw the cabin still burning, dim but visible in the distance. Only it appeared directly in front of her. Had she gotten disoriented and come full circle? She began to panic. Hypothermia was setting in, leaving her judgment in question and compromising her ability to make a shelter even if she was able to make it to shore, something she now began to doubt. It took her three attempts to turn on the flashlight. The compass still pointed in the right direction. She tapped it with the flashlight. The needle moved freely in the liquid. She looked again. Either the compass was broken or there was definitely a light coming from the far shore. Regardless, she set her course for it. Neither she nor LuAnn would survive a night out on the ice. She hadn't brought enough wood to keep a fire burning for an entire night, so she pressed on, all thought melting away as she put one foot slowly in front of the other, jerking the sled, inching it on behind her.

Within a half an hour, she was looking at headlights through the driving snow. Another ten minutes and she had hauled the sled up the bank and onto the shore. There was her car parked at the end of the road. Beside it was Gran's rusty old pickup truck, its headlights beaming bright across the bay, twin beacons guiding her home. Gran slid out of the cab, country music blaring from the radio. She tossed a cigarette into a snow bank and poured steaming hot coffee from a thermos. The old woman showed her strength when she lifted LuAnn from the sled and carried her to the warm truck. Martha stumbled beside her through the snow, grateful to be back, grateful to be alive, grateful she had finally begun to put the nightmare of her life behind her.

Maybe now the wounds could begin to heal. Scars would remain, but life left its scars. Scars meant you had survived.

In the thirteen years to follow, not a day went by when she didn't think of Rachel. Now, sitting in her Mini Cooper, Martha thought about Gran and Hewitt, both now gone, the only two people who knew the full story of what happened that day in the woods.

Smoke in the backcountry had been reported, but when you live off the grid, you die off the grid. Charred bones were discovered amid the ashes of the destroyed cabin a few weeks later. On the first of March. It was her father who found them. He had ridden his snowmobile to the cabin with the month's supplies. He planned to share the grief of losing his daughter with his best friend, only to discover that he had a second funeral to plan. This one he arranged and conducted himself, alone, Marine to Marine, brother to brother. Semper Fi.

Whatever story Gran had told LuAnn's family and the officials on the reservation, it never reached Martha's ears. Whatever story LuAnn had told, it never included her.

Martha still heard from LuAnn White, now Sister Rachel, from time to time. Gran had put them in touch a few years after her return. It turned out that LuAnn was a survivor as well. She found her strength and solace in God and with it the ability to forgive if not completely forget. In a convent in Calgary, she was sequestered from the outside world.

"I am to be officially accepted into the convent next week," she said one day in a phone call. LuAnn asked permission to use Rachel's name. God had chosen that name for her life in Christ. "I would be honored, and Rachel would be, too," Martha had whispered. While she did not believe, she spoke from the heart when she added, "May you always go with the grace of God for this beautiful gift, Sister Rachel. Thank you."

"You can't let go of anything, can you?" A different time, a different state, and different circumstances. Still Trammell was right—the answer was the same today as it had been then—"No. I can't."

ELEVEN

For the third time in twenty-four hours, Martha pulled her car into the tiny parking lot at Pete's Supermarket. Outside, the rain drummed steadily on the roof. She loved the sound of rain, and for a few moments, she sat motionless, listening. And watching. Across the way, barren trees lined the shore and a leafless bramble of blackberry bushes and scrub brush covered the bank. The row of houseboats extended into the lake. Nothing unusual caught her attention.

Remembering the night Rachel died had made her homesick, and she speed-dialed her father. When he answered, she said, "Hi, Daddy. It's Marti in Seattle."

"Do I know another Marti?" came her father's familiar response. It had become a joke between them, and it always made her smile. Only tonight, it was a half-hearted smile. He said, "The Weather Channel shows you been getting soaked with something called the Pineapple Express. You got webs growing 'tween your toes yet?"

A lifetime of cigarettes and drinking had made his voice low and rumbly. To her, it would always be the sound of home. Her voice choked as she tried to laugh. "Not yet."

"Well, just be grateful you ain't home, honey. Colder 'an a well-digger's ass here. We ain't seen the topside of zero in weeks. Lake completely froze over. That don't happen often."

"No, Daddy, it doesn't. Hey, I'm running into a meeting so I can't chat, but I just wanted to give you a head's up. I'm working on a case that's gotten the attention of the Seattle police and the local media. They may be calling."

"Sounds a little more serious than you're telling."

"It's nothing to worry about, but you'd be doing me a big favor if you just told them 'no comment.'"

"No comment it is then."

"Could you spread the word? I'd appreciate it. I don't have time to call everyone."

"No problemo. Hey, thought you might want to know the tribe is advertising for a lawyer. They've got plenty of money these days. Ain't gonna be what you make in Seattle, but probably pretty good for around here. Sure be good to have you back home."

"I'll check that out, Daddy. But, right now, I gotta run. Late for a meeting."

"No comment," he laughed. "Oh, Marti, no need to send any money this month. I'm swimmin' in dough."

"No comment," Martha said. "Love you much." She hung up.

Every month he told her not to send money because he had plenty. Every month she did anyway because she knew it was a lie. He would be paying off Rachel's medical expenses until he died. And working for the Chippewa Nation? She shook her head. Not in this lifetime. Still, her father never failed to offer her a chance to return to the Soo—a one-theater town where the long winter was punctuated by snowmobile races and hockey games. She seldom had a conversation with her father that didn't include the announcement of some fabulous chance to come home.

Home? She had lived in Seattle longer than she had lived in Sault Ste. Marie. Home didn't mean the same to the daughter of a career military man. The only house she identified with her youth was Gran's out on the reservation. Even that had been just a place to land between moves. She always used the word "home" when getting ready for one of her annual visits to the UP. But after a few days there, she felt the urge to return "home" to Beatrice and the Carriage House. Hewitt always laughed that when he agreed to cover part of the down payment, he didn't know he was helping her buy a garage. But the big house was just an investment. Home was the Carriage House with its smell of cedar trees and salt breezes, with its small spaces perfect for a single woman and her cat. If your heart was in two places, did that mean you were home in both? Or home in neither?

She pushed the car door open and splashed through the cold rain to Pete's.

She had the store to herself. A few premade sandwiches and salads remained in the deli case. The sight of food made her realize she was starving. She settled on a spicy tuna roll, a mixed green salad, and a bottle of water.

At the checkout stand, a woman with a perfect tan and blond-streaked hair looked up from her paperwork. "Thanks for swimming into Pete's," she said, and then laughed at her own joke. A nametag identified her as Karen. "Did you find everything? We're having a special today on snorkels and fins."

"Yeah, thanks," Martha smiled. "Say, yesterday, I stopped by and bought a bottle of wine and talked to one of the workers about it. Brownie. Short, bald, mid-fifties or so. I was wondering if he might be in today."

"Maybe I can help you," the woman said. Her voice dropped an octave, her back straightened. "I do the wine purchasing."

For the first time, Martha realized she didn't know what had happened to the 1996 Ruffino Chianti Riserva. She had set it down someplace in the trashed houseboat and forgotten to take it with her after the police arrived. Metcalf probably drank it for dinner last night. What a waste of a good wine.

"No, it was a great vintage," Martha lied. "I just wanted to tell him how much I enjoyed it. It was the perfect recommendation."

"You hear that, Brownie," the woman yelled. A bald head popped around the corner from the produce section. "The lady liked your wine recommendation yesterday. There's hope for you yet."

Before Brownie could give away the fact that he had nothing to do with her wine selection, Martha asked, "Do you have a moment?"

He came around the corner. The cargo pockets of his khaki shorts bulged with cut strings. He dried his hands on the hem of a green Pete's sweatshirt. "Sure."

"She thought you were in your mid-fifties," Karen added, with another of her giggly laughs. "I keep telling you, you should just shave your head completely."

Brownie ignored her as he and Martha walked down the produce aisle toward the racks of wine.

"I'm so sorry!" Martha said. "No disrespect intended."

"None taken," Brownie said, waving it off. "When you're bald at twenty-five, you get used to people thinking you're older than you are. Besides, I'll be forty-seven in a month."

"How embarrassing. I mean, for me, not about turning forty-seven."

"It's fine. It'll give Karen something new to tease me about, and she always needs something." He stopped in front of the racks of wines lining the back wall and cocked his head up at her, then faced the featured wine specials. "How can I help you?" he said.

Martha glanced at Karen, who was busy with a customer. She pulled the torn postcard from her purse. "Yesterday, you wanted to know if I was interested in a postcard of Pete's. I thought it was a little odd, but now I'm wondering if you might have seen the other half of this." He studied the card, as though looking at the Dead Sea Scrolls. She whispered, "Hewitt left it for me. He didn't tell me where the other half was, but I'm thinking you might know."

"Yeah, I do," he said finally. "Come with me."

In the small back office, Brownie perched on the edge of the desk chair. Martha remained standing.

"You know, when Hewitt bought that postcard, he only wanted to pay for half. Said it was all he was going to use. Classic Hewitt." An attempted laugh was choked short. His hands trembled slightly before he steadied them by working the underside of the desk drawer. He pulled out a five-by-nine envelope. A torn half of a postcard was taped where a person might write an address on the envelope. "Hewitt said to give this to anyone who came with the other half. He thought it would be a tall woman with one blue eye and one brown eye. We met before, at Hewitt's seventy-fifth birthday party many years ago, but you probably don't remember."

"No, I'm sorry, I don't. But I've seen you here many time over the years."

"It was a long time ago." Brownie pointed at her half of the postcard. "Seemed straight out of a spy movie. I almost mentioned it yesterday, but you didn't say a word, and he insisted the person had to have the other half of the postcard." He paused.

"Have they found him yet?"

"Not yet," Martha aligned her postcard to the edge of the one taped to the envelope. A perfect fit. So, the key, the torn postcard hidden behind the fake light switch *had* been a message for her. It took all her restraint not to tear the envelope open on the spot.

"It's horrible what they did to his boat," Brownie said. He stared at the envelope, but she made no attempt to open it. He continued, "I mean, we're a pretty tight community down here. It's hard not knowing what happened. We all feel a little more vulnerable. We're worried about Hewitt. We heard they found his van out at Shilshole."

"Yeah," Martha nodded. "I know. Listen, you said yesterday you helped him with a package. Do you remember what it was? Or where he was sending it?"

"He wasn't sending it," Brownie said. "That's the thing. It was something wrapped in brown butcher's paper, about the size of a book. Since his last stroke, he's had trouble with his one arm. We placed it in a Ziploc, gallon size, I remember, then sealed it with duct tape. He couldn't manage the tape, so I did it for him. Sealed it, and then we wrapped it all again in a jumbo Ziploc."

"Like he was waterproofing the package?"

"Sure seemed like it."

"But you don't know where he took it?"

"No, he was all secretive about it. Said it would only get me into trouble."

"He was right. How did he seem to you? I mean, happy, sad, nervous, excited?"

"In a hurry. Like he couldn't get out of here fast enough. Usually, he's full of stories. You know," and his voice dropped an octave, "'You think this is rain? Why there was a time we were rounding Cape Horn in a rain so heavy fish would just swim past us on the deck. Caught enough in my hat to feed the whole crew.'"

Martha nodded. "Yeah, I know. 'Fish couldn't tell the difference between sea and sky.'" Their smiles quickly faded. "Did Hewitt do anything unusual? You know, jump when the doorbell jingled or someone walked by the office door?"

"He made me close the door. He was all hush-hush. And, he did say something strange. 'Now I've taken them over the brink and there's no coming back.'" He added, "I had no idea what he was talking about, and I didn't ask. Now I wish I had. Who's 'them'?" He looked up at her. "Do you think he's . . . do you think he's dead?"

"Yes. I don't know. There's a good chance anyway. But until they find a body, I'm working on the assumption that he's not."

"Anything I can do to help? Everyone's on edge right now. Worried about Hewitt but also a little scared. I always liked the old guy. We don't get enough characters in life. He was one of them. A friend and a neighbor."

"Thanks, Brownie," she said. "You've already been a big help. Hewitt was right. This has gotten dangerous, a lot more dangerous maybe than he expected."

Brownie stood up. Relieved or disappointed, she couldn't tell. He extended his hand. "Let me know if there's anything I can do, okay?" They shook.

Martha let go of his hand. Would he make the same offer if he had just had to identify Ralph Hargrove with his penis stuff into his mouth or had been the one clubbed over the head last night? Who knew why one person runs and another stands and fights—why Rachel had allowed rape to undermine the value of living while Martha had turned it into the white-hot focal point of her soul?

And what would Hewitt do?

TWELVE

Martha slid back into her car and immediately relocked the door, the memory of disarming Danny Kimble still fresh in her mind. She didn't need Kimble or any of his friends performing the same stunt on her. She scanned the area and checked all the mirrors. One of her masters, a diminutive Scot named Bertie Wallace, had emphasized that one moment may be all you ever get to subdue a worthy adversary. Don't flinch. Don't miss the opportunity. You may not have another.

Now, she added her own axiom to Bertie's: You may not live to have a second.

The Mini Cooper sloshed its way through a huge puddle without stalling, and soon she was shooting up the hill toward Eastlake. At the last minute, she decided to head around the south end of Lake Union and turned right on Eastlake. She studied the cars, front and back, making a mental note of each. Nothing obvious caught her attention. Through the Mercer Mess, Seattle's finest example of urban gridlock, traffic crept along at a glacial pace. Only a blue Volvo station wagon still hung behind her from her entry onto Eastlake. The Volvo tank could maybe run her off the road, but it would never keep up with the Mini Cooper in a chase through the backstreets of Fremont or Queen Anne. Stalled in traffic, she scanned the mirrors, vulnerable to a surprise attack on foot.

God, I'm paranoid, she thought. Then remembered Danny Kimble's gun had the safety off. She scanned the surrounding cars and checked her mirrors again.

At Dexter Avenue, she took a sharp right without signaling, which prompted the man in the blue Volvo to honk his horn and thrust an arm at her in the universal salute between drivers, but he continued straight. She drove north, cruising with the slower traffic in the right lane. Her iPhone chimed. Metcalf. She considered ignoring it. In time, she said, "Martha Whitaker."

"Metcalf," he said without preamble.

"Yes?" She pulled onto a side street and brought the car to a halt.

"We found the car that was tailing you this morning," he said. "A rental. It was backed into a corner in a parking garage at Sea-Tac. Driver's window busted in. I've got a team going down there now to see if they can lift some prints or find anything else."

The obvious response remained unsaid. Instead, Martha said, "Thanks for letting me know, Detective."

"It was rented to a guy who called himself Danny Kimble. Had a Utah driver's license to match, home address in Salt Lake City. Danny Kimble turns out to be a police officer there. Only thing is, Danny Kimble's a desk jockey dealing with traffic violations. And he's fifty-six years old."

She refrained from saying he didn't fit the description of the young man who had tailed her.

"There's no record of a Danny Kimble getting on a plane today. He might be flying under a different name, he might still be in town." Metcalf paused. "This doesn't change things, you know. I sent the gun to ballistics to see if we get a match to last night's shooting in Ballard."

"Of course it changes things," Martha replied. A car came down the street behind her. With cars parked along both curbs, there was no room for it to get by. So she started moving again. "Otherwise, why call me? It's another Salt Lake City connection. And the more elaborate the hoax gets, the more likely I'm just telling you the truth."

"What Salt Lake City connections?" Metcalf asked.

"Jesus, Metcalf," she snapped. "The Mormons."

"That's stretching it," he said. "You've maybe moved down a couple of notches on my top ten list, but don't think you've fallen off it. I know you're up to something, you and that Trammell guy. Maybe you should tell me what it is."

"It's simple," Martha said. "We're trying to find Hewitt or find out what happened to him. Am I wrong to assume we share the same objective?"

"I haven't seen either of you in your dive gear yet. That's where you're going to find him. Question is, did he go in on his own, or did someone help him? Who trashed his house and why? Who killed Ralph Hargrove and why? Am I investigating one murder or two? If you know anything about any of this, you need to tell me."

"Anything else?"

"Yeah, why did you instruct your father to say 'no comment'? What are you hiding?"

"Nothing," she said. "I'm shielding the people whom I care about from your personal vendetta against me."

"It's not personal, Whitaker, that's what you don't seem to get. I don't give a frack about you, but I do about the truth. Who dumped Hewitt Wilcox in the water? Who killed Ralph

Hargrove? I can and will subpoena your father if I think he can help me answer either of those questions."

"What's he going to tell you?"

"Well, he seemed to have had no qualms about telling the police about your brother's meth lab. Turned him in, in fact. Sounds like the kind of fine upstanding American I might want to have a chat with. Might know something about his little girl's finances, or maybe he wonders why she's got an offshore bank account in the Cayman Islands. Could be he's concerned about her anger management problem. Maybe his version of your run-in with Gabriel Perconte is different from the one in the court documents. I mean, come on, a starting linebacker for a Pac-12 school misses six games because he got beat up by a girl? Your father might have some interesting stories to tell."

Her voice turned low. "Then fucking subpoena him, Metcalf. Subpoena me, while you're at it. You, of all people, shouldn't find it hard to believe that Gabriel Perconte got his ass kicked by a girl who didn't want to get raped, especially if that girl was me."

"Pretty taken with yourself, aren't you, Whitaker? Well, maybe you'd like to visit Mr. Perconte. He's up in Monroe at the high-security lock-up with some of our other finest citizens. A Bellingham student nurse didn't care for being assaulted with intent to rape, either. But here's the difference. She was willing to testify. She was willing to help us put him away. But you? You had to play vigilante, even if it meant more people got hurt. Look what that got Ralph Hargrove."

His comment, like a punch to the solar plexus, left her stunned. She lowered the window for air. She knew Metcalf was right: she had refused to take Perconte to court because she exalted in her ability to personally exact retribution, in her own power, and was determined to make up for her inability to protect Rachel. She didn't need the courts. She had herself and that was all she needed.

Finally, she found her voice. "For all my hubris, Metcalf, and, yes, I won't deny having plenty, you cannot blame me for Ralph Hargrove's death. It's not fair and it's not true."

"Did you give Hargrove a second call and tell him to be careful? You'd already talked to him once after you'd seen the old man's houseboat. Somebody's looking for something, and you knew Wilcox owned the bookstore. Or did you not want to warn the 'sweet librarian nerd'? Or maybe you knew he was already dead."

Martha lashed out. "Fuck you, Detective. You got anything to back that up, then fucking arrest me. By the time I suspected anyone else might be in danger, I was in your goddamn interrogation cell without so much as a phone. Did *you* call Ralph and warn him? You took great pride in telling me I was suddenly the owner of commercial real estate in the U District. You knew. It's why you kept me waiting for almost four hours. You had your busy bees doing your homework. You found Hewitt's will and pronounced me guilty before you ever stepped into that interrogation room. You had already decided I was after the old man's money. While I sat there getting grilled by you, someone walked in and killed Ralph Hargrove. Another person is dead because of *your* arrogance, *your* misjudgments, Metcalf. Don't get holier-than-thou with me, you sonofabitch. There's plenty of guilt to go around. I suggest you—"

She stopped short. She was shouting at a dial tone.

How dare he blame Ralph's death on her.

Martha slammed the car into gear and darted back onto the street. Her purse tipped over, and the envelope lay exposed. She told herself to call Metcalf back and let him know about the key and the torn postcard. Fuck it. Let the slimy little bastard wait another half hour.

Maybe she still had some work to do on self-control.

The street came to a dead end. A left turn led back up the hill to Dexter Avenue, the only way out. At the street end was a mini park, a patch of green about the size of the Carriage House. She backed into a parking spot, providing her a view of the two streets at the corner of the L-turn. She kept the car running, the warm air drying her boots.

She took the envelope from her purse, studied it, turning it over once. A standard white envelope, five by nine, nothing written on it, front or back. The flap was sealed. The torn postcard of Pete's Supermarket had been taped to the front. The whole package was the thickness of a single sheet of paper. So much for the lost diaries of Brigham Young or Joseph Smith.

Martha ran a fingernail along the seal and withdrew a single five-by-seven photo. A photo she knew well: the impromptu group shot taken at Hewitt's seventy-fifth birthday party—which had doubled as his office retirement party—a dozen years before. Everyone had gathered on the end of the fishing pier next to the Shilshole boat ramp while Hewitt tried out his birthday present—a salmon fishing pole. She flipped the picture over. Nothing. She turned it face up again, studied it from corner to corner. Again, nothing. She rotated the photo in the light. Could you be any more goddamn cryptic, Hewitt? She already had a copy of the photograph, and it hadn't cost her nearly this much trouble to get it.

Was the message in the photo itself?

The Elmer Fudd face of Ralph Hargrove, looking startled by the camera, appeared in the upper right-hand corner. Then, an awkward space between him and the woman to his right, as if he'd had to be coaxed to stand next to her. Martha didn't know the woman he so studiously avoided, but could find nothing of interest about her. Handsome George Garvey, Hewitt's lover at the time, was next, a hand resting on Hewitt's shoulder, a broad smile on his face. Somewhere in his mid-fifties at the time, George was tanned and athletic. For the first time, she noticed his distracted look as he gazed off to the left of the camera. Martha now realized George was just going through the motions. It was shortly after the birthday party that Hewitt discovered his betrayal. It had been the precursor to Hewitt's first stroke.

Martha saw herself on the other side of Hewitt in the back row, smiling, eyes half-closed. Her hair was pulled back off her face; she wore a white cotton blouse, a simple necklace. Nothing seemed significant. On her right was Gary . . . Gary . . . Gary Bell. They had met in Hewitt's class and dated a couple of times before Martha determined he was a colossal bore. He pontificated; she was his audience. He had an opinion on everything and needed no invitation to share. At the end of the second date, he was ready to progress to the next step—sex—and she was ready to use him as orca bait. She told him exactly what she thought of that idea, and him. He'd just shrugged. He had a lot of fish in his pond and wasn't going to waste time trying to land a small one.

Martha exhaled. Whatever message Hewitt was trying to send, she doubted it had anything to do with the narcissistic waste of human potential represented by Gary Bell.

To Gary's right stood Huey, Dwight, and Louis, or Huey, Dewey, and Louie, as they were known—the très amigos of cultural and historical anthropology, each with successful careers in the field. Dwight's was the only black face in the photo. Martha wondered if that was significant. If so, she couldn't fathom why. She still saw Louis on occasion. He lived in Port Angeles and worked as an anthropologist for the Makah Indian Tribe, a position Hewitt had helped him secure. Hewitt had done pro bono work for the tribe for years, but after his heart attack, he had recommended to Duncan Miller, a tribe elder, that Louis take over. That had led to a fulltime job when a hotel developer had unearthed an old Makah village site on the shores of Dungeness Bay. The hotel project had been shut down and Louis hired to work with the excavation team. Sometimes when he got to the city, Louis and Martha would rendezvous for a beer. He usually needed free legal advice, but he always made her laugh, so she thought it was a fair exchange. It had been over a year since they last got together. She knew he had visited Hewitt a couple of times through the years.

A diminutive Asian woman, Yumi Murasaki, stood in front of Gary Bell. The assistant dean of the Anthropology Department at the time, Dr. Murasaki had died of ovarian cancer shortly after retiring, and Hewitt had asked Martha to attend the funeral with him. A beautiful blonde woman of Nordic heritage knelt directly in front of Martha. Martha tried to remember her name, but all she could come up with was the nickname Bonnie Beer, for her fondness for the same. The department administrative assistant, one Annabel Lewis, who claimed Meriwether Lewis as an ancestor, knelt beside Bonnie and scowled as if she would rather be swallowing hot lead. But, as Martha remembered, she always looked like that.

Then came two faces that she had completely forgotten about. They were younger, but it was definitely Brownie and Karen from Pete's Supermarket. Brownie had no more hair then than he did now; Karen had a nice tan. Why would Hewitt give a photo to Brownie to safeguard, when he was in it and probably already had a copy?

That left only Hewitt in the center of the photo. He was turned sideways and smiled for the camera by looking over his left shoulder. He always reveled in being the center of attention. "Enough about you, let's talk about me," he liked to joke—only Martha knew the truth behind the joke. The camera had caught

Hewitt mid-laugh. At that moment, everything was about him. Martha remembered few times when Hewitt seemed as happy.

In the photo, as in real life, he was the perfect Ancient Mariner—long white hair pulled back in a ponytail, white beard neatly combed. In a black turtleneck, he looked the old salt he had been before an interest in crumbling manuscripts and dusty old books replaced his passion for the sea. He was sitting on an impromptu captain's chair—the back of his research colleague Roger Morey, if Martha remembered correctly. Morey's face was lost between Bonnie and Annabel. Hewitt leaned back into George, holding his new fishing pole. Hewitt's exaggerated pose made it look as if he were trying to land a world-record King salmon. The line, however, dropped slack over the pier railing right about where Martha stood yesterday morning in the pouring rain, waiting for the rendezvous that never happened.

Martha studied the shadows and hidden corners and backdrop for something significant. Nothing. Okay, so what *wasn't* in the photo? What was missing? Might there be a message there? The one glaring omission was the absence of Dr. . . . Dr. something Obbert. Of course. Of course he wasn't there. He and Hewitt had been fighting at the time—she remembered it had been about the authenticity of a handwritten note from Abraham Lincoln to Stephen Douglas. Obbert insisted it was fake; Hewitt insisted it was authentic. The spat between the two friends had grown into a major battle. It got personal and ugly, especially on Obbert's part. He accused Hewitt of having less than professional motives. And, at about the time of the birthday party, it had produced a rift between them that had never been restored. Months later, after extensive ink, paper, and handwriting analyses, experts had pronounced the letter authentic.

Jonathan. That was his name. Jonathan Obbert, the third. He had been censured by the university and resigned as dean of the anthropology program. He had been lucky to keep his job.

"Oughta sue the bastard for defamation and character assassination," Hewitt had fumed, even after hearing of Obbert's fall from grace.

"Being right and selling the letter for a tidy profit isn't enough?" Martha asked. "Let it go."

"That's unexpected advice coming from you."

The remark stung more than she wanted to reveal.

Hewitt quickly added, "That was uncalled for and unkind. My deepest apologies, my dear. It's probably wise counsel. Still, it's hard."

In the end, he had followed her advice.

She knew the message delivered with the photo couldn't be about Obbert and his excommunication from the anthropological community. But what was its meaning? Martha looked back at the photo. Hewitt, his laugh frozen in time, still fell back into the arms of Gorgeous George. Ralph still stood off to one side. Huey, Dewey, and Louie still looked relaxed and happy.

Goddamn it, Hewitt, she muttered, what are you telling me? Why all the secrecy hiding a photo that I already have? Come on, talk to me, dude, talk to me in a language I can understand.

THIRTEEN

Martha closed her eyes and heard the rain drum on the top of the Mini Cooper. The car heater began to warm her feet. Damn it, Hewitt, why couldn't you have written a note on the back of the fucking photo, "Call Annabel" or "The bastard GG has the safe." She sighed in frustration and her shoulders sagged. She listened to the rain for a minute more, hoping it might calm frayed nerves and the memory of hurt feelings.

Whether it was for an instant or for several minutes, she didn't know, but what she was sure of was she had dozed off. Her eyes snapped open and she hurriedly checked all the mirrors. Nothing but wet green grass behind her in the small park and soggy bramble to her left descending to a pewter gray Lake Union below. No Danny Kimble approached to repay the favor of a broken window. When she looked forward, her heart missed a beat. A sky blue Volvo station wagon barreled down the street toward her on a head-on collision course.

He who flinches first loses, Bertie had taught her. He who flinches first often dies. Martha didn't flinch.

She jerked the transmission into drive and punched the accelerator to the floor, the wheel hard right. Tires sprayed gravel, and the Mini Cooper responded like a racecar, shooting up the hill. Even with the quick jump, Martha barely evaded the Volvo. It tried to follow her around the corner, but it bounced up over the curb with a thud and came to a stop.

But not for long. As the Mini Cooper climbed toward Dexter Avenue, the Swedish tank regained momentum and charged up the hill after her. She turned right, stomped the accelerator and swerved around two cars before the Volvo made the corner.

She took a deep breath. Thank god she had kept the car running. She had started planning an escape route when another idea hit her. Groping for her phone, she slowed down just a touch, and dialed Metcalf.

He answered with, "Hey, I'm sorry about hanging up on you. I had an incoming I had to take and . . ."

"Save the mea culpas, Metcalf," she interrupted. "Wanna talk to one of the bad guys?"

The blue Volvo was gaining on her.

"What's up?"

"I've got one on my tail right now." The nose of the Volvo kissed the Mini Cooper before she punched the gas, jumping out of reach. "The bastard just hit me."

"Where are you?" Metcalf was talking fast. "I can get squad cars to you in minutes. Tell me where you are."

Martha sped down the hill. When she looked up, she said, "Oh, shit. The bridge is up."

The spans of the Fremont Bridge stood straight up against the gray sky. A single mast crept toward the opening. Cars were stacking up in all directions. Shit Shit Shit. In a moment the Volvo would again be within striking distance. She spun the wheel. Only when she pulled the car out of the fishtail and got the nose headed back up the hill did she realize she must have closed her eyes.

The Volvo now zoomed down the hill toward her. As she looked over, she saw a thin face, intense with ferocity, topped by a military haircut. Left handed, he pointed a gun out the window. Oh fuck! She ducked and almost immediately popped her head back up. Everything seemed intact. Either he didn't shoot or he missed completely.

"Whitaker, Whitaker!" It was Metcalf's voice.

She raised the phone again. "Do you know where the Harbor Patrol offices are on Northlake, by Gas Works Park?"

A quick peek in the rearview mirror showed the Volvo in the middle of a tight, full-speed U-turn.

"Of course. Just tell me where you are!"

She glanced at the digital clock on the dashboard. "I can lead him on a chase for, say, five minutes. By my clock, it's two thirty-four. In five minutes, I'm going to pull into the Harbor Patrol parking lot. If he's not local, he might follow me in. Tell the Harbor Patrol I'm in the dark blue Mini Cooper. The bad guy's in a sky blue Volvo station wagon. Don't get them confused. Oh, and they probably should put on their vests. I think he's already taken one shot at me. Five minutes, Metcalf."

She tossed the phone into the passenger's seat.

A hard right took her up the steep hill toward Aurora Avenue. At the highway entrance, she squealed her tires and flung gravel with great show, and then eased off the accelerator. She heard a pop and glanced back. She had let him get too close, and a gun poked out of the driver's window. This time she knew he had taken a shot at her. She swerved just as she heard a second shot. No glass shattered, no tire blew. Swerving in and out of traffic, she crossed the center line and, for a brief moment, stared at three lanes of oncoming traffic. She blew by a slow delivery truck and swerved back before a black Mercedes whooshed by, horn blaring.

Halfway across the Aurora Bridge, Martha darted across the three lanes, preparing to hop off the highway at the next exit. She glanced at the clock. Only two minutes had gone by. Could she keep this up for three more? She slowed down and cut into the line of traffic exiting the bridge. A van slipped between her and the Volvo. Thank god. The traffic slowed but never stopped. At the first street, Martha turned right and raced down the hill. She skidded through a stop sign, around a corner, and onto Stone Way. Here traffic was heavier and she was forced to slow down, giving the Volvo time to move up behind her. The light at 34th Street was coming up fast. It was red. She looked back and again up. It remained red. The Volvo swung to the right and pulled up beside her in the next lane. The man rested the gun on his left arm and took aim.

She swerved left into oncoming traffic. A car jumped the curb to get out of her way. She passed the cars waiting at the red light and spun around the corner. She didn't make it. The car skidded across the slick pavement and smacked nose first into the curb. The sudden stop brought her full force against her safety belt. She glanced back before her body had completed its whiplash. The Volvo had gone around the stalled traffic on the other side and up onto the sidewalk; a pedestrian lay prone. She jammed the car into reverse. The tires had barely begun spinning when she slammed the transmission back into drive. She bounced over the curb and onto the sidewalk, sparks flying out from under the car. She veered right and pointed the car down the Burke-Gilman Trail.

Two bikers pedaled directly at Martha, heads down, rain

hoods covering their helmets. She blasted the horn. She barely registered their startled faces before they dumped their bikes into the bushes alongside the trail. She sped by, hoping the middle fingers they flashed in response meant they were okay.

No sign of the Volvo behind her. Then she caught a flash of sky blue in her peripheral vision. The Volvo was on a parallel course on Northlake Way, the two cars separated by twenty yards or so. The Volvo vanished behind a building and Martha slammed on the brakes, screeching to a halt. She saw the Volvo flash through another open space and then disappear behind the next building. It never reappeared on the other side.

She darted a glance at the clock: four minutes had passed. She hoped Metcalf had gotten through to the Harbor Patrol. What kind of crazy idea had this been? A steep bank rose on her left, a brushy ditch descended on her right. There was no turning around. She could back out or drive straight ahead, and she knew the Volvo would be waiting. And that was the direction of the Harbor Patrol. With one foot on the brake, she slowly increased pressure on the accelerator.

The digital clock flashed the fifth minute. She had the gas fully down before the brake released. She flew down the trail. A prayer to a God she no longer believed in slipped from her lips. The blue Volvo was again in motion. A few hundred yards ahead, the trail converged with the street. Martha drove straight ahead, bouncing off the trail and onto road, nearly T-boning the blue Volvo as she hit the pavement. The driver swerved to avoid the impact. She quickly veered to the right onto a small side road. No sign marked the dead-end road that terminated at the Harbor Patrol. She could only hope that her pursuer didn't know what waited for him at the other end of their chase. What did wait for them? she wondered. She honked at a white boat of a Buick and bounced through potholes like a skier flying over moguls, the car shuddering with each violent rise and fall, the blue Volvo closing fast.

Ahead, she saw the one-story white Harbor Patrol outstation and a squad car along with several civilian vehicles. She glanced back; the Volvo showed no signs of stopping. Christ, there wasn't a single cop in sight. Oh, you sonofabitch, Metcalf. Out of road, she slammed on the brakes and dove out of the car before it stopped rocking back and forth.

The Volvo was right behind her, barely missing the Mini Cooper as it skidded to a stop. The head with a military hairdo appeared, followed by a gun, followed by his hands and arms. He had barely cleared the door when he yelled, "On this glorious day the Almighty has chosen me to be the hammer to slay His enemies! I am the hammer and may God be my anvil!"

Martha ducked behind the Mini Cooper as the first two bullets thumped into the side of the car. She rolled through a puddle, ready to move again, wondering where to run.

"Police. Drop the gun," came another voice. Two officers stepped out from the brush on the far side of the driveway, guns readied. Behind her, another two stepped from the doorway. Two shots rang out and the man staggered briefly but righted himself. He snapped off a shot. A police officer went down, the second dove to the side. The shooter's attention returned to Martha. She rolled over the hood of the last car in the row and dropped to the far side. More shots cracked around her.

"No earthly power will stop God's chosen!" she heard him shout.

"Vest," shouted another voice. "He's wearing a vest!"

She sprinted for the corner of the office building, only to discover the building extended out over the water. Wood siding splintered high over her head from a wild shot. In one stride, she crossed the dock and dove headfirst into Lake Union.

Silence. And a cold so harsh and sudden it took her breath away.

A bullet zipped through the water a foot to her right. Still she swam. She had noticed a patrol boat moored at the dock right before she dove. She prayed she could reach it before she needed to breathe.

The hull appeared overhead, black against the gray surface. The silence of the water was replaced with the sound of blood pounding through her brain. One, two, three more strokes. Martha surfaced on the far side of the hull, gasping for air. The gunfire had ceased. She expected to see the Hammer of God striding down the dock and prepared to dive again. She had been cold before. This was superficial cold, not the mind-numbing hypothermic cold that would follow in a few minutes. She could ignore it. She dove just as she heard her name.

She surfaced a second time. She heard Metcalf calling, "Whitaker! Damn it, lieutenant, get someone in dive gear, now. Whitaker!"

"I'm okay," she called. It came out weak, through a mouth half full of water. She kicked hard and her head rose well above the surface. This time she yelled, "I'm okay. I'm okay."

"Where are you, Whitaker? It's Metcalf."

She pushed off from a piling back into open water and waved. "Here! Right here."

She struggled to keep her head above water. The weight of her clothes dragged her down, and the bone-numbing cold overrode the signals from her brain to her legs to kick harder. Metcalf and a uniformed officer sprinted down the dock, holstering guns as they ran. Metcalf thrust his arms into the water and grabbed her extended hand. The second officer grasped her other hand, and together they hauled her out and plopped her onto the dock.

Martha curled into a ball, folding her arms around herself, clutching her elbows tight against the trembling. Something broke loose and spun away inside her, leaving her sick with a nameless fear. Oh Lord, she murmured silently. A plea, but not a prayer.

FOURTEEN

Officers hovered around Martha as if she had been the one shot. She was dressed in the blues of a Seattle police officer. The pants were too tight in the hips and too short in the legs, but it beat sitting around in the Harbor Patrol office in dripping jeans and a soaked cashmere sweater. She pulled the blanket draped over her shoulders tight around her chest. A cup of coffee warmed her hands and her insides. It was fresh and brewed strong.

One ambulance had already come and gone, rushing a wounded officer to Harborview Hospital. A slug, missing his protective vest by millimeters, had blown out his shoulder. There was no hurry for the second ambulance that sat parked in the driveway, its lights and engine off. The Hammer of God lay beside the Volvo, his blood washing away in the driven rain. A bullet to his left temple had ended any chance of getting information from him.

From the bits and pieces that she overhead and what little Metcalf told her, she was able to fit together what happened. The Hammer of God had staggered from repeated shots that found their target but had not brought him down. Taking the body shots had caused more than one of his shots to go wide. Twice he returned fire with the police and then immediately refocused on her. When she disappeared underwater, he had jumped back into the Volvo. He had shot out the tires of the patrol car and had the Volvo in gear when the bullet that killed him found its mark. He was dead by the time the car crashed into the side of the Harbor Patrol office. No one knew who fired the fatal shot. For officers more accustomed to being boat jockeys than a SWAT team, it was probably better that way.

When they rolled him out of the car, it was clear how he had withstood the fusillade of bullets. Under his black leather jacket, the Hammer of God wasn't wearing a bulletproof vest. He was wearing bulletproof body armor. It caused quite a stir among the officers. They paused to stare at it, more interested in the armor than in the dead man who wore it. Probably carbon fiber, they agreed, lightweight but immensely strong. In a design taken from the knights of old and updated with modern materials, overlapping panels at the shoulders, waist, and hips acted like hinges and extended the protection over his groin and upper arms. It would have been the envy of any police unit in the country. If they had access to it, which they didn't. This kind of body armor was available only to the elite units of the military. The Hammer of God had been very well connected.

They found no ID on the body, none in the car.

"Yes, I'm fine," Martha assured the Harbor Patrol officer who sat down beside her. He nodded. It was the same man who, with Metcalf, had pulled her from the lake. His leathery face was creased from sun and wind. He wore a blue stocking cap; his police jacket was soaked through from rain.

"Is Lieutenant Lolich here?" Martha asked, glancing around.

"No, he's not, ma'am. His wife is ill, and he's taken a few

days off. I'm Lieutenant Frank Lane. I'm in command today."

"I'd like to thank you and your officers for saving my life."

"You're welcome. I'm proud of the way my men responded. Lucky we had a patrol boat in, or the outcome might have been different. I'm glad you're not injured."

"How many of your men were hurt?"

"One shoulder wound. He'll survive, if the good Lord and the fine doctors at Harborview have their way." The hint of a smile tugged at the corner of his creased mouth. "And one busted ego. One of my younger officers took a shot to the chest. His vest did its job, but the impact knocked him flat on his back. The shooting match was over before he realized what had happened. It won't be something he lives down any time soon." The man paused. Intense blue eyes stared at her without flinching. "But the real question is, what did you do to warrant the attention of a psycho wearing body armor no one has seen outside of the Middle East?"

"I'd like to know the answer to that myself." It was Metcalf, in a borrowed blue police shirt, untucked at the waist. He pulled up a chair.

"I wish I knew," Martha said. "Somebody thinks I know more about what Hewitt was doing than I do." She let her fingers feel the warmth of the cup before taking another sip. "Thanks for coming through, Metcalf. I can't tell you how much I appreciate it."

Metcalf nodded.

"Did you get a hold of Trammell?"

He nodded again. "He's fine. There's been no sign of any more trouble. He's at his office. The whole staff is there. I sent a couple of squad cars to ensure he stays safe."

"Any chance I've moved off your top ten list now?" Martha asked.

"If I had ten people, yeah." Metcalf ran a hand through his dark hair. Two imp horns remained standing. "As it is, I'm not sure I have anyone on it at the moment except maybe our Hammer of God. Or the people he worked for."

"I'm sorry," Lane said, quietly incredulous. "People don't get chased all over town and shot at by a paramilitary madman without someone having *some* idea what's going on."

"I have this friend, he's really been a surrogate father to me," Martha started. "His name is Hewitt Wilcox. He lives on the last houseboat over by Pete's."

Lane nodded that he knew the boat. As Martha recounted the events of the past thirty-six hours, starting with Hewitt's missed rendezvous at the fishing pier, she leaned forward, her hands clasped together as if in prayer. Telling the story allowed her to catalog events, like organizing note cards in a file, while trying to make sense of something that right now made no sense at all. Metcalf complemented her account with details of the break-in at the *Ballard Gazette* and the disturbing shift the case took that morning with the discovery of the emasculated body of Ralph Hargrove. The perps were searching for something important, but no one knew what it was.

Martha knew she was about to ignite a firestorm. She decided this time it was better to face it than run away. Like setting a backfire, she thought. She drew a breath. "And Hewitt left me a key, wrapped with half a torn postcard." It was close enough to the truth.

"What key?" Metcalf interjected.

"A key to a safe."

"So that's why you asked about a safe at the bookstore. Why didn't you tell me this before? What the frack, Whitaker? I knew you were holding out on me."

He was right, of course, but she refused to let the accusation go unchallenged. "Because I didn't know what it was until this morning. I was going to tell you earlier today, but you were too busy accusing me of being some criminal mastermind. When I tried to tell you, you hung up on me. Remember? Your ears were a little too sensitive to hear the truth, as I recall."

"I had an incoming call," he snarled.

"And I'm going to be the next Pope."

"Both of you stop!" Lane commanded. The lieutenant was accustomed to having his orders obeyed. He nodded toward Martha. "Please continue."

"Hewitt left me this key." With a look at Metcalf, she added, "I only got it yesterday. I didn't know if it had anything to do with this. I still don't, for that matter. This morning I talked to a locksmith, and he said the key goes to a Brinkman's safe, an L70 or L80 model. It requires the key and an electronic combination to open. Hewitt forgot to put that part down for me. According to the locksmith, there are only about a million of them in the country."

"Oh, great," Metcalf muttered.

"And the torn postcard," Lane said, ignoring Metcalf. "I gather that was important, too?"

"A torn postcard?" Metcalf said. "What was he doing, reading spy novels?"

"Probably," Martha answered, ignoring his sarcasm. "le Carré is his favorite."

She told them how she located the second half of the postcard and what was inside the envelope. "There's nothing on the photo that I could find. It's just a picture of a few friends taken years ago at his seventy-fifth birthday party. I might have missed something, but I did get a little busy right about then."

"Where's the photo now?" Metcalf asked.

"In my car."

"The key?"

"In my jacket pocket, hanging in the women's bathroom. Unless it fell out during my dip in the lake. Then you'll know where to find it." She didn't mention the copy tucked into a little pocket in her purse. "You're welcome to both."

"That's so nice of you, Whitaker. Thank you. Jesus fracking Christ, I could put you in jail right now for withholding evidence in a murder investigation."

"I wasn't withholding anything. I didn't know it might be evidence until about an hour ago. I've been a bit preoccupied since then, in case you missed the news flash."

Lane acknowledged the silent nod of an officer and stood up. He was short and wiry, balanced like an aging welterweight waiting for the bell. "Okay, forensics is here. I want that body out of my parking lot." He paused and looked hard at both of them. "You two bicker like school kids. Which is really boring for the grownups. So, get over it, both of you. Miss Whitaker, you *were* withholding evidence. You know it, I know it, and Metcalf knows it. Turn everything over now, tell us everything you know or think you might know. And let us do our jobs. If you meddle any more in this affair, I'll personally escort you to a cell."

He turned to Metcalf. "Detective, you've got a job to do, and you should start doing it. You've got some people to track down, a safe to find, and a car to get dusted and examined by forensics. It sounds like someone thinks Mr. Wilcox was getting too close to a story they didn't want known. You ought to be harassing Miss Whitaker less and spending more time finding out what the heck is going on. If any more of my men get shot because of you, Detective, you'll be wishing you had never heard of Frank Lane."

Lane zipped his jacket and turned to Metcalf again. "I assume you've got someplace safe where Miss Whitaker can stay until you get this resolved."

Metcalf sat back in a pout. "With my budget, I'll be lucky to get permission for her to stay in your guest room."

"Mildred would approve, I'm sure, but we both know that's not necessary." Lane leaned forward, his voice low. "Son, I've had it with your can't-do attitude. I thought the SPD was made up of folks with more mettle than that. Some religion-spouting psycho wearing body armor drives up to my front door and tries to kill this woman. If that's not worth the protection of the Seattle Police Department, then I'm working for the wrong people."

The room went quiet. Metcalf slid farther back in his chair, his arms crossed at his chest. Officers in blue uniforms, mostly Harbor Patrol officers, inched in closer. They had Lane's back and he had their respect, an even harder thing to earn. Metcalf knew it, as well.

"Thank you," Martha said to the lieutenant. "But I can't afford to go into hiding right now. It's not just Hewitt. I'm involved in a big project at work. I've got to be there. I know how to be careful."

"It's not just your safety I'm worried about," Lane said. "It's the public's safety. I have one officer who's already in the hospital. God knows who else is in the hospital or in the morgue because the Hammer of God didn't care if he ran them over or drove them off the road. I will *not* be responsible for a civilian death because you're too important to miss a little work." To Metcalf he added, "Time to cowboy up and find Miss Whitaker a room."

"Yes, sir," Metcalf said, nodding his head, as if that would help him believe his own words.

"Please, Lieutenant," Martha started.

He cut her off. "I'm sorry. Did you think this was a request? It's not. Either you'll accept our protection, or you'll get it in a jail cell. And, I can assure you, Miss Whitaker, the food will be much better outside our jail than in. Your choice."

"Could you at least be the one to call my boss and tell him?" Martha hoped the comment might lessen the tension. The ramrod straight Lane showed no reaction. She sighed. "All right, Lieutenant. I'm grateful for the offer and accept your protection."

"Good choice, Miss Whitaker," Lane said. "And, yes, I would be glad to speak with your boss."

A phone call from Lieutenant Lane might save her job for a few days. But would it give them time to find out who was the Hammer of God?

FIFTEEN

Homicide Detective Harry Callison drove Martha to the Carriage House in an old Chevy Malibu that smelled like every half-finished meal he had ever eaten. They took the scenic route through half a dozen Seattle neighborhoods. Three Dick's cheeseburgers provided Callison with a pre-dinner snack and an excuse to examine everyone who pulled into the parking lot after them. His full beard and broad weightlifter shoulders reminded her of Brutus from the old Popeye cartoons. Finally, he set a course for the top of the hill in Ballard.

No new insights came to her on the drive, only more questions without answers. Oh, Hewitt! Damn you! She mourned his loss and cursed his cryptic messages.

Her house came into view, and so did two squad cars parked outside the main house, lights flashing through the growing twilight. A uniformed officer in a rain slicker was visible in the front yard, his head bent low as he searched the edges of the house with a spotlight.

She thought she'd vomit. Callison snapped a look in her direction. All she could say was "Oh my God." All she could think of was the Heidens. Fear gripped her as she conjured up the images of the girls. No, no, not the girls.

Callison parked down the street and told her to stay put and keep her head low. "The keys are in it if you need to move in a hurry. I saw you can handle yourself, but be careful. There's enough horsepower to leave your panties behind if you step on it."

He unsnapped his Seattle Mariners jacket as he walked toward the house. The two or three minutes he was gone was more than enough time for Martha to imagine the ghosts of the three tow-headed Heiden girls holding hands with Ralph Hargrove. "No, dear God, no," she whispered.

Callison hurried back to the car, knocked on the window. "Everyone's safe. Come on."

Olivia was the first one to see her. All arms and legs, she loped across the lawn toward Martha and wrapped her arms around her. Her blond hair was spilling out of its purple ribbon, and Martha remembered she had been invited to Olivia's piano recital that afternoon. In imprecise English, thick with the guttural Dutch accent, Olivia said, "Oh, Marta! They snapped Mama's heart. Mr. Bear lost his Mr. Moose and Mama—"

"I'm so sorry, honey." Martha took Olivia's hand. "Let me talk to your mom."

Olivia led her to the kitchen where, with baby Josephina in her arms, Iris stood talking to a police officer, and where every cabinet stood open and every drawer had been emptied onto the floor. At the breakfast nook, Lily was stuffing cotton puffs back into the deflated body of Mr. Moose, whose inseparable companion, Mr. Bear, sat on the table supervising the delicate operation.

Olivia tried to explain, "Mama will make Mr. Moose new heart."

Breathing hard, Martha gripped the counter. A new heart. Maybe it had been Mr. Moose and Mr. Bear in a frilly pink room that led them to conclude this wasn't the home of a single woman, that made them stop short of what they'd done to Hewitt's place. Maybe it had been as simple as reading the mail.

She jumped when Callison tapped her shoulder. "Gotta get moving. There's nothing we can do here. There's two more officers upstairs. We'll have a forensics team out as soon as one's free."

"Please wait—for a minute. These people are my renters and my friends. I owe them—"

At the sound of Martha's voice, Iris turned abruptly from the officer. Her blond hair was pulled back tight, her lips so thin they had nearly disappeared.

"Iris, I'm so sorry," Martha began.

"Sorry? You said this to be a safe neighborhood. Safe? Look at this!"

"They were looking for me, Iris. They thought I lived here. I'm so sorry. I never thought they would—"

"Stop right there." Callison shot a look at Martha and stepped toward Iris. "We're in the middle of an investigation that involves Ms. Whitaker, and we're not at liberty to discuss it. These officers will do an excellent job of taking care of you, ma'am."

"You are criminal, Marta?" Iris asked, her blue eyes wide.

"No, no. Of course not," Martha replied, trying to sound calm and reassuring but failing miserably. "I can't talk about it right now, but the people who did this were looking for me and something I might have. I don't even know what it is."

"I must insist," Callison interjected.

"I do not care what they were looking for!" Iris shouted. "I cannot have this!" She glanced at Lily, still re-stuffing Mr.

Moose. "You understand we must leave."

Martha couldn't promise they would be safe if they stayed. She couldn't promise they wouldn't face some future threat. She said, "I understand. Absolutely. I'm so sorry, Iris."

"I do not understand. They took nothing. They are after you? I am sorry, too, but now we must move."

Martha nodded, but Iris was no longer looking at her. Only Olivia, eyes full of questions, met her eyes.

On the short walk to the Carriage House, Martha fought back tears and wished she had hugged the girls goodbye. She cursed herself and Hewitt and the goddamn Hammer of God and all his goddamn fucking cohorts. Maybe it was just a delayed reaction to nearly being killed. Maybe it was the realization that she would lose the house if she didn't have renters to help her with the mortgage. Maybe it was something more, something deeper. Her carefully constructed world was spinning out of control.

For all her strength and self-reliance, she was helpless to stop friends from disappearing, from getting hurt. Hewitt. Ralph Hargrove. And now the Heidens. A couple of beers and hamburgers on the grill and even cold, stiff Iris would start adding contractions to her stilted English. And the girls! Loving and open—just like their father.

She led Callison up the stairs to the Carriage House and switched the lights on, expecting to see everything she owned strewn about the bamboo floor. It was exactly as she had left it that morning: breakfast dishes in the sink; her laptop, its top closed, on her desk; the rolled yoga mat in the corner. The only difference was the cat. Beatrice lay on the back of the sofa, head up and alert, all her attention focused on the stranger who accompanied Martha into their private living quarters.

"Nice digs," Callison said, sliding his gun back into the shoulder holster. "For a garage. Whowouldathunkit, living in a garage? Apparently, the bad guys didn't."

Martha glanced at him. Nice digs? A tiny apartment above a garage? "They must have just had an address," she said. "They didn't know I rented out the main house."

Which meant they hadn't been following her until today. Hewitt's disappearance had escalated things. But why? Now it was Callison and Metcalf's job to find out.

She pulled her carry-on bag from the closet. She started laying out jeans, slacks, a few blouses, a couple of sweaters, and some cotton tees.

"Who's doing your work?" Callison called out. "On the remodel?"

Martha poked her head around the bookcase that separated the bed from the main living quarters. She said, "I'm doing it myself."

"You own a nail gun?"

"And the compressor. My miter saw and table saw are downstairs in the garage. Why? Isn't a girl supposed to own a nail gun?"

"I didn't say that. We're living in my brother-in-law's basement. Lost our house a couple of years ago. Seems a cop and an out-of-work hair stylist ain't exactly the bank's preferred customers for a loan these days. We got three girls, just like your friends there. Be nice to put up some walls, maybe a small kitchen. Just thought you might have a reference for someone who works cheap."

"Sorry. Try Angie's List." Callison's financial woes didn't concern her. She returned to packing, adding a second pair of shoes. If she could travel through Europe for three weeks with two pairs of shoes, it seemed reasonable to expect the same living in a hotel room. Bras, panties, and socks she stuffed around the edges of the suitcase.

In the bathroom, she looked longingly at her six-foot-long claw-foot tub. Wherever she was going, she suspected a soaking tub wouldn't be in the package. She put together a toiletry case, leaving most of her cosmetics untouched. What was the point of makeup when you were locked in a hotel room?

Beatrice now sat on Callison's lap. He scratched her ears and worked a busy finger under her throat. Martha could hear the rumble of her purr halfway across the room.

"Traitor," she said to the cat, and then sighed. "God, I need to have someone come in and feed Beatrice. Olivia usually does it, but that won't work now."

Martha thought about asking Jody next door, but Jody had the memory of an old person with Alzheimer's. She had used a professional cat-sitting service once when the Heidens were out of town. She fired up her computer to find the phone number.

"Hey, remember, no computer, no Internet," Callison said. "Any good hacker with an iPhone parked on the street could be in your machine in minutes."

"I'm just looking up a number for a cat feeder. It'll take just a second and it's in my contact list. I'm not going online."

"I can have Rebecca—she's my oldest—stop by and feed your cat."

Martha didn't even glance back at him. "Yeah, right. Things must be pretty slow down at the precinct if you're coordinating pet services."

"It'd give her a chance to visit your cat. My wife's allergic to cats and dogs, so she can't have a pet. And Becca is always looking for ways to make a buck. But, if that's too fucking weird for you, knock yourself out. Only use the yellow pages or my phone."

For the first time Martha looked at Callison as something more than a cop with a gun. "I'm sorry," she said. "That was childish. It's been a stressful day. I don't want to impose, I know you're busy."

"It's no problem. We're close, and Becca loves cats."

"Thank you, Callison."

"That wasn't so hard, was it?"

Martha refrained from offering the first comment that came to her lips. Instead, she offered a weak smile. "Let me show you what to do."

In a nook beside the kitchen, Martha had built a cat house with room for food, water, and a litter box. She stared for a moment at the food dish, certain she had filled it this morning. It was empty. "Getting to be a little pig, aren't you, B.?"

The cat rubbed against her leg. She added a second dish for dry food, and filled both. She explained to Callison how to care for Beatrice.

She packed up her computer, slid it into her briefcase, and handed the bag to Callison.

"I'll log this in downtown with your cell phone," he said. "They'll be safe."

"I'd feel better if it was with me."

"But we wouldn't."

"What am I supposed to do all day?"

"Lots of things. Watch TV, write letters to your family, read *War and Peace*. Whatever. Just don't go online. No email or texting, and definitely no cell phones. The temptation will be too great if you're holed up for more than a few days."

Martha grabbed her best rain parka from the closet. "Okay, Callison, if you're going to be my chauffeur, let's go."

Only he wasn't her chauffeur.

They walked past his Chevy Malibu to a new black Ford

Explorer with dark-tinted windows that waited at the curb. So much for being inconspicuous. But the Seattle Police Department had heard enough of Martha's opinions, so this one she kept to herself. The passenger's door on the SUV popped open as they approached. Callison lifted her bag into the back, but kept her briefcase. Martha slid into the car.

Lance Trammell helped her find the seatbelt buckle in the dark.

SIXTEEN

The week that followed proved to be one of the most difficult of Martha's life. Shut off from the outside world, devoid of information, unable to work, and powerless to act, she felt stripped of all that defined her as a person. She also discovered she didn't always like her own company. Meditation brought little peace. Yoga helped, but not much. On day three, when she had the front room to herself, she pushed the hotel furniture against the walls and performed the *kata*s from beginning to end, reveling in the chance to move with violent grace. Sweat running down her face, she was finally able to forget for a few minutes all the unanswered questions.

When she finished, Trammell was leaning against the doorjamb to his bedroom watching her. Their ever-present police attendant sat on the counter in the tiny kitchenette.

"I think I recognized the punch you knocked me out with," Trammell said.

"Remind me not to get into a fight with her," the cop said.

Martha looked at each of them. She refused to leave the place of inner calm by entering into the endless banter and tiresome quips of people locked up too long together. Without speaking, she went into her own room and shut the door.

She went into the bathroom and stared forlornly at the tub. It was a tub for dogs and dwarves. She could soak half of her body at a time. How she missed her own tub. Hot water to her chin, a few essential oils and a sea-foam of bubbles, she could remain in that special meditative place created by a good workout for another hour or so.

She showered and changed into fresh clothes.

Metcalf hadn't booked them into Motel 6, but it wasn't the Four Seasons, either. The suite on the back side of the Waterfront Hotel on Lake Union looked out at a shrub-covered bank leading to the Mercer Street exit off the Interstate. Lake Union could have been in another time zone for all they got to see of it. All phones had been removed. There were no computers. Clock radios and televisions in each room provided the only links to the outside world.

Once a day for an hour, the exercise room was "Closed for Maintenance," and she and Trammell were allowed to work out, their off-duty police officer standing outside to head off hotel guests who couldn't read. Trammell's routine never varied: he ran a brisk five miles on the treadmill before lifting weights with whatever time remained. Martha had no idea how to use any of the equipment, but boredom and desperation to get out of the room prompted her to tag along.

With a little cajoling from Trammell, she dismounted the exercise bike and agreed to try weightlifting. He spotted for her, hands poised to take the bar if she should waver. She was surprised to find how weak she was in the upper body. All her strength was in the long, sinewy leg muscles of a dance master. After that, she joined Trammell every day at the weight machine. She liked the way the workout made her newfound muscles ache.

On the fourth day, she looked up from the bench and into his face. He didn't notice her studying him. Sweat from his own workout glistened on his brow. With high cheekbones, a strong nose, and a broad forehead, he resembled an underfed Roman emperor. The thinness in his face left him just short of looking gaunt and a little sad.

"You look so serious, Trammell," she said. "What are you thinking?"

He looked away. She thought he might be blushing.

"Come on, you can tell me. What?"

He turned back. "I was thinking I've never spotted for anyone as lovely as you."

"Well, thank you. I don't get to hear that every day." She grasped the bar again and began another set of reps. His hands scrambled back to their protective position. "Is there . . . is there anyone special that you . . . you spot for?"

It was probably the first personal question she had asked him.

"Yeah, she's called the *Gazette*. With the paper, I don't even have time for a cat."

The bar came down. Martha rested for a moment with it inches off her chest. "Cats are . . . low maintenance, thank, God. But I understand . . . the problem."

"You?" he asked.

To avoid answering, she pushed up again. "No." It came out more as a grunt than a word. "I'm not keen . . . on the idea of an office romance and they're about . . . only people I see these days."

"Yeah, I know what you mean. Mac's not really my type."

She rested again. "There's always Molly."

"I don't think I could stand the drama."

Martha started her last lift. She tried to talk. "What's . . .

behind . . . the Hammer . . . of God?" Every muscle in her arms quivered as she reached the peak and held the bar straight up. She sucked air in ragged gasps. She tried to set the bar back in the support, but her arms wouldn't work. They couldn't go any farther up and they wouldn't come down. "I think . . . I'm stuck here."

Trammell eased the bar onto the overhead support. Martha felt her arms collapse with fatigue. When she could move again, she sat up, and Trammell tossed her a towel. Her arm trembled as she tried to catch it. "I could perform the entire set of *kata*s and my arm wouldn't quiver like this."

"You're using new muscles. That's a good thing." He hesitated, then sat down on the far end of the bench, and studied her. Uneasy under the scrutiny, Martha looked away. Trammell continued, "'I am the hammer and God is my anvil.' It's the language of the religious fanatic to justify his own brand of terrorism. Seems the Islamic extremist doesn't have a monopoly on religious fanaticism. 'I'm doing God's will. God has given me permission to rape and pillage and murder.' It's a story as old as religion."

"You're still convinced the LDS is behind this?"

"No, I'm convinced someone with strong LDS connections believes he's doing God's will. It may lead to the Avenging Angels. It may just lead to a Mormon fanatic. But I haven't seen anything so far to make me change my mind."

The next day, returning from their exercise hour, they found Corvari waiting to replace their guard. The police officer that had led the investigation at the *Ballard Gazette* was out of uniform, but Martha recognized her linebacker's body and pretty smile. Trammell learned her name was Bess, short for nothing, just Bess Corvari, a few generations removed from Corsica, which made her French, not Italian as everyone assumed. She soon became a regular in the three-person rotation for guard duty. She also seemed to be the only one pleased to be there.

"The overtime's been fantastic," Corvari said one day. "I'll have all my Christmas bills paid off in two paychecks if they keep you dudes in iso a bit longer. And I'll have all my Christmas cards written in another day or two."

"Christmas was a month ago," Trammell commented.

Corvari acknowledged his comment with a shrug.

Martha fretted about work. Metcalf assured her Lieutenant Lane had kept his promise and personally called her boss. Being the target of an assassination attempt seemed to have convinced Ben Mathews to excuse her from the McGwire trial. She wondered if the Heidens had moved out and if Beatrice was okay. She worried about money. She had a couple of months of mortgage payments saved, but if she didn't find new renters soon, she faced the same fate as Callison with the house. She felt sidelined: at work, in finding Hewitt, in life.

Metcalf was the only one allowed to brief them on the investigation. From what Martha could tell, there were no new developments. Most days they heard nothing from the detective. "It doesn't do any good to hide you guys if all they have to do is follow me," he said.

"Danny Kimble knew you were the lead detective within twenty-four hours of you getting the case," Martha reminded him. "They're getting information from someone, and they're getting it fast."

On the afternoon of day five, Callison stopped by, looking even scruffier than before. He was wearing the old Carhartt jacket and hadn't trimmed his beard since the last full moon.

But he had a wide grin on his hairy face when he announced Christmas had arrived. He came toting a box filled with books and movies and crossword puzzles, a couple of Sudoku books, even a jigsaw puzzle and a backgammon set. A Costco-sized box of popcorn perched on top. He had set out the collection box at work—"Donations for the Terminally Bored," he had called it. Whatever was dropped in, he delivered, including a paperback copy of *War and Peace*.

He didn't or couldn't offer any details on the investigation. But he did have a personal question for Martha. "Do you think Beatrice might be pregnant?"

"If she is, I've got a vet who owes me my money back," Martha said. "Why, what's the matter?"

"Oh, Beatrice seems fine. She and Rebecca have really hit it off. I now have to take a book to read because Rebecca will spend an hour brushing her after doing the chores. I hope that's okay?"

"Detective, what's the matter with Beatrice?"

"Nothing that we can tell. It's just that she's going through twice the amount of food as you told us. And she doesn't feel like she's getting fat or anything. She's just eating a lot. Rebecca weighed her last night: thirteen pounds, maybe thirteen and a half. Does that sound about right?"

"Yeah, she was just shy of fourteen at her last checkup." Martha paused. "But I don't own a scale."

"Rebecca brought one from home."

The next day, Metcalf arrived with take-out Thai for lunch. Between bites of curry scallops, he informed them he had managed to track down several people lined up in the birthday photo. Gary Bell. Huey, Dewey, and Louie, Karen and Hector Brown. Hector? No wonder everyone, including his wife, called him Brownie. None of them had any idea why Hewitt selected that photo. Except for the Browns, none of them had seen or heard from Hewitt in ages. Brownie had related the details of assisting Hewitt with the package and guarding the envelope with the photo until Martha arrived.

"Do you think he might be holding something back?" Metcalf asked.

Martha didn't have a clue. Brownie and his wife had been friends with Hewitt for a long time, obviously, but Martha hadn't remembered meeting either of them until the week before.

When asked, Bonnie Berkowski and Annabel Lewis were as baffled as Brownie. Annabel, from her position as the department's admin assistant, had been a great help in tracking down most of the students. Handsome George Garvey, Hewitt's ex-lover, apparently had transitioned from wet Seattle to sunny Palm Springs. The police there were looking for him.

"Maybe the photo was a feint," Trammell said. "A misdirection to keep people from looking someplace else?"

"Then why all the secrecy around it?" Corvari offered from the kitchen.

Metcalf ran his hand quickly through his hair. "And why would Hector Brown expect Whitaker to be the one to claim it? He said Wilcox had expected her to come in with the second half of the postcard. I think we just don't know what the message is yet."

Metcalf had expanded his search, talking to everyone on the dock, Hewitt's former colleagues at the university, the business owners near University Rare Books and Manuscripts. He checked all of Hewitt's phone calls. Nothing.

Whatever Hewitt had been up to, he hadn't shared it with anyone.

"What about the safe?" Martha asked.

"*If* he bought it in Washington within the past ten years,

we've narrowed it down to a possible eight to nine thousand units. We can't realistically expect that to lead anywhere."

"Surely, you've gotten some evidence from the crime scenes," Trammell said.

"Yeah? Well, maybe you can tell me what," Metcalf snapped in reply. "Each break-in was the same—quick and dirty, nothing stolen, nothing fenced. The only eyewitness is Martha, who got a glimpse of a man dressed in black with a flip in his hair. We didn't get much in the way of fingerprints. Forensics has a partial from the back office at the bookstore, but it doesn't match anything we have on file. I'm wondering if that might be another case altogether—a frustrated lover, an abused boy, something that would explain the castration. The timing just happened to be coincidental."

That theory was greeted with utter silence.

"The Volvo had to be registered to someone," Trammell offered. Martha could see the journalistic wheels start to turn.

Metcalf nodded. "We tracked it to a couple from Vancouver, BC. They reported it stolen to the RCMP from their condo in Whistler. The Washington plates belonged to a car in Lynden, so we figured that's where he crossed the border. But none of the agents remembered talking to anyone who fits the description of the Hammer of God. And what was he doing in Canada? It's not like he couldn't have stolen a car here."

"The man had no ID, but he must have had fingerprints. What about DNA? I mean, there must be something. I can't live the rest of my life in this goddamn hotel." Trammel stood up and started pacing.

"Have you sent divers down at Hewitt's houseboat?" Martha asked. "If he was waterproofing a packet, that would be a logical place for it to be."

"Harbor Patrol checked it out. Nothing." Metcalf stood up

to leave, his lunch mostly untouched. "Oh, and ballistics reported the bullets from the gun at the Harbor Patrol site didn't match
the bullets we found at your office."

"And the Hammer of God didn't have enough hair to have a
curl under a face mask," Martha said. "Neither did Danny Kimble for that matter. At least two people are still out there."

"Bingo," Metcalf said. "Which is why you have to stay here
a while longer."

"You make it sound like we have an option," Martha said.

Corvari offered a smile and a nod. The smile would remain
sweet as long as they didn't try to leave. It also wouldn't hurt to
have her around in case the unfriendlies, as Metcalf had started
calling them, made an unexpected visit.

"Oh, a couple of personal messages. I almost forgot," Metcalf said. "Lance, your partner said to tell you that the paper got
out this week without a hitch. Maybe the finest edition yet."
There was a pause followed by a long "Um." Then, "I was wondering, are the questions to the Sex Doctor real?"

"All of the questions come from our readers," Trammell said
with the assurance of someone who had answered the question
a million times before. "Finest edition yet. Mac's jerking my
chain."

"You said you had a 'couple' of personal messages," Martha
said, when it looked like Metcalf was headed to the door.

"Oh, yeah. Your boss called Lieutenant Lane who called me.
Seems he doesn't want to talk to a mere detective."

Martha ignored this. "And the message is?"

"He met with someone named Gorky or something like
that. And, you're not to worry. He's taken over the case himself."
As if to himself, he added, "Maybe he'd like to take over my case,
too. That would be nice."

"Thanks." Martha understood the words, but not the message. Ben Matthews had met with Mr. Göksu? She could only guess that getting Ben involved with her pro bono work for Göksu had been the subtle work of Crystal. 'Mr. Göksu is here to meet Martha, what should I do?' Never mentioning that she had called him to come in, in the first place.

The door had barely closed behind Metcalf when Corvari approached them from the kitchenette. An open UDub hoodie revealed a gun in a shoulder holster. Thick, solid forearms and biceps suggested hours in the weight room. Her short blond hair was matted from a motorcycle helmet. If Corvari considered it a bad hair day, she didn't comment on it.

"Metcalf's such a prick," she snorted. "The Sex Doctor? He believes those questions are real? You must be feeling really confident right now."

Trammell pushed back his chair and disappeared into his bedroom. The door slammed shut.

"What's got his knickers in a twist?" Corvari asked.

"A week shut up in a hotel room would be my first guess. Or you offended him. I think he may be the Sex Doctor."

"Really?" Corvari mouthed the word more than said it. "He seems so normal. I never would've guessed." She turned back to Martha. "You know, word around the office is you cleaned Metcalf's clock pretty good last week."

Martha measured her words carefully. "I wouldn't say that. I demonstrated how a girl could disarm a person with a gun." She knew only one other person had seen the demonstration. Was Callison purposely undermining Metcalf's authority, or was it just gossip around the water cooler?

"Maybe you could give me a few tips," Corvari said. "You know, disarm someone with a gun without having to shoot them. The paperwork is horrible if you have to shoot someone."

"Sure," Martha said. "Heaven forbid we should have any

more paperwork in our lives."

Corvari stood up and started pushing furniture out of the way. "You don't know what paperwork is until you've been a cop."

"Or a lawyer."

"Yeah, there's that." She looked around. "Well, let's do it. Unless you want to read more *War and Peace*. But I can tell you how it ends. I saw the movie. I swear, was there ever a Russian who wasn't tortured and depressed?"

"You got that right." Martha stood up, shaking out muscles and ligaments and tendons. "Besides, in an hour you'll be too sore to move, and I can go back to reading my book. Unless Trammell and I decide to just walk out the door."

"Oh, I understand that you could do that now if you wanted. It's just that you'd have to do it over my dead body."

"And god forbid the paperwork." Martha smiled for the first time in a week.

SEVENTEEN

On the ninth day, Trammell and Martha rendezvoused over dinner. They seldom ate together during the day, but they had gotten into the habit of sitting down together late in the day to share a meal. He had decided again on fish and chips, cole slaw, and a beer. Martha ordered the special—macadamia-crusted halibut, garlic mashed potatoes, and tiny asparagus spears. Trammell declared asparagus in January to be an abomination before man and God.

"Just think of the carbon footprint it took to ship asparagus from Chile," he argued. "Maybe we shouldn't have asparagus and tomatoes and strawberries all year round."

The inclusion of strawberries was directed at Corvari, who had declined to join them because she had a late dinner date. But she didn't think it would spoil the rest of her evening if she had a piece of strawberry torte.

"Oh, get off your soap box," Martha laughed. "Where do you think your fish came from? My money's on farm-raised Atlantic cod out of Canada. And what exactly are we supposed to eat in the winter? Turnips and rutabagas from the root cellar? If we only ate locally, we wouldn't eat a fresh green from November to April. There's not a commercial fish caught within a hundred miles of Seattle anymore. At least I can go out and catch my own fish. When we're out of here, I'll take you salmon fishing and prepare you a sunset dinner of grilled salmon so fresh and moist and tender that the gods and Corvari will fight to join us."

"You're on," Trammell said.

An exaggerated handshake led to a pushing and pulling contest. Martha could have taken him any time, but she liked the sense of play after so many days of seclusion.

"Lookit, Bess," Trammell yelled. "I'm lasting longer than you did."

"It's not a bronco riding contest, you nitwit," Corvari said, shaking her head. "Even I could've kicked you in the balls by now."

A knock at the door, and Corvari was instantly on guard. She held a finger to her lips, and moved to the peephole. "Yes?"

"Room service for two," came the response.

Corvari recognized the voice. If the answer had been anything else, she would have had her gun out and Martha and Trammell would be diving for their respective bedrooms. As it was, they stepped aside to remain out of sight. Moments later Corvari reappeared pushing a cart stacked with silver domes. She announced, "Dinner is served."

Tired of eating at the coffee table, Martha had set the small table. Place mats, cloth napkins, forks, knives, and spoons all properly arranged. It wasn't much larger than a bar table, but if they packed tight and kept their feet tucked in, it accommodated the three of them.

"Chardonnay, Bess?" Martha asked, pouring herself a glass.

"If only." The officer looked at the table. "If we had a candle, this would be a regular romantic dinner for three."

In a moment, Martha returned from her bedroom. She lit a tea light. "I had hoped there might be a bathtub for real people. Foolish me."

"Thank you," Trammell said, a couple of bites into dinner. "This is nice. 'Small cheer and merry welcome makes a merry feast.'"

"Shakespeare?" Martha asked.

Trammell nodded with a smile. "You're getting better."

"No, you're just predictable." She sampled her halibut. The cooks were getting better. The fillet was still moist. Martha asked, "What did Metcalf mean today when he said 'your business partner'? I thought you owned the *Ballard Gazette*."

"I'm the publisher and editor," Trammell said. "Mac's a partner in the business. But his idea of being flush is having enough money to pay his moorage and buy an extra latte. He wants to write, I want to make money and do good journalism. He's the romantic idealist; I'm the pragmatist. We make a good team. God knows, he doesn't need me to put out the paper. He needs me if he doesn't want to go bankrupt in three months. If this Hewitt story ever develops, he'll be the one to write it."

"Okay, I've got a question," Corvari said. "Who's the Sex Doctor?"

"When you start telling me what Metcalf tells you in private, then I'll start sharing some of my secrets," Trammell answered.

"Well, some of us find it disgusting. I know what you told Metcalf, but you've got to be making those questions up."

"Every one of them comes from readers." Trammell's voice took on an edge. "There's nothing illegal. What two consenting adults do in the bedroom is none of my business or yours. A number of folks seem to have forgotten that simple courtesy."

"Would you be so high and mighty," Corvari countered, "if it didn't sell papers?"

"Absolutely. And since when did profit become a dirty word? The Sex Doctor helps keep us afloat, no question. If I kill the Sex Doctor because you're offended, I'd probably kill the *Gazette* and all the good stories we print. Freedom of the press, remember? It's our only check on the power brokers in government or business or the guy leading a religious sect. Lose it and we lose our freedom as a people. And because of that freedom, you," he glanced at Corvari, "have the freedom not to read it."

Whoa. MacAuliffe wasn't the only romantic idealist at the *Ballard Gazette*. Martha said, "That doesn't sound like the first time you've given that speech, Trammell."

"Sorry. I get a little worked up on the issue."

"No apology necessary, dude. I'm a big girl," Corvari said, taking another bite of strawberry torte.

Trammell turned to Martha. "You sounded pleased when Metcalf said your boss was helping out on one of your cases."

"Did I?" Martha asked. "Yes, I suppose I was. Surprised and pleased, I guess. It's a pro bono case I'm working on. He didn't have to step in. The firm has no responsibility for it. The client's a poor immigrant who could never afford Carey, Harwell and Niehaus, or any attorney for that matter. I heard about his situation from a friend. And doing pro bono work doesn't hurt, come promotion time."

She realized how that sounded, and while true, it wasn't the reason she had taken on the Göksu case. How did people like Trammell wear their hearts on their sleeves? It was such an invitation for disappointment, even betrayal. Still, she wondered why Ben Matthews had agreed to meet with the grieving father. He was a senior partner. There were no more promotions coming for him. Martha glanced around the table. "How's that strawberry torte, Corvari?"

"You ain't getting off that easy, honey. I understand about

attorney-client privilege and all, but you can tell us something."

"He's from Turkey," Martha explained. "Makes almost nothing. He has an only son, the pride of a very proud man. A group of punks beat the kid up one night, thinking he was the next Islamic suicide bomber. He's not Arab, not even a Muslim. He's a Persian Christian. But, to a bunch of thugs, it didn't matter. Now the kid's in a coma and going to spend the rest of his life on a ventilator with a feeding tube, and he has enough lines hooked up to him to bankrupt the family. I'm trying to get them help to cover medical expenses for who knows how long—weeks, months, even years."

"God, that's horrible," Corvari said.

"Yeah," Martha agreed.

Trammell stared at her, as if looking directly into her soul. She was afraid he would find it lacking. She said, "It's not all altruism." She paused a moment, and thinking she might choke on the words, she added, "My sister lived for three years in a coma. It nearly killed my father, and it cost him everything he had to keep her alive. I didn't want to see that happen to another family."

She didn't move.

Trammell reached out and squeezed her hand. "I'm sorry. I didn't know."

"Can't even fathom how it must be every time you see that poor boy," Corvari said, pushing back her chair. She patted Martha on the shoulder. "And it's a hell of a lot better than being the Sex Doctor and telling us how fucking patriotic you are because of it."

Martha gave a weak laugh. She slid her hand out from under Trammell's.

"Hey, come on," Trammell said to Corvari, with faked chagrin. "That's not fair."

"Get used to it," Corvari said. "Life's not fair, in case you hadn't heard. Just ask Martha's client."

Martha curled up on the sofa, *War and Peace* open on her lap. Corvari was right—the Russians were a tortured, depressed lot. Mass butchery and endless war offset by moments of individual heroism. Did one really make up for the other? She glanced at the back of the book: only seven hundred pages to go.

Corvari washed up the few dishes not returned on the dining cart, humming quietly. Martha recalled how her grandmother had always hummed when working. A series of soft sounds and flowing melodies. As a little girl, Martha decided Gran had too much joy trapped in her body, and she released the excess by humming. Martha had tried to hum like Gran, but it felt unnatural, like when the sun and moon were in the sky together. She always thought it was because she didn't have enough joy.

Now she wondered if Gran had hummed to release some of the sadness that haunted her.

Trammell sat on the floor, his back against the sofa, hands clasped behind his head, headphones on his ears. A black-and-white image of Frank Sinatra talking to a young Angela Lansbury flashed across the television screen. A half-empty bowl of popcorn was nestled in Trammell's lap. His long legs were crossed at the ankles, displaying socks with thin spots on the heels. Martha felt a sudden longing to slide down beside him. It had been so long since anyone had held her, since she had felt strength that wasn't her own. She hated the vulnerability, but that didn't change her desire to reach out and touch another human. What if she took the lead? Would he understand that it was more about her than about him, that she was feeling weak and scared and lonely, that she needed some kind of reprieve from the sadness that haunted her?

Only then did it occur to her that he might be feeling weak and lonely and scared, too.

A commercial flashed on the screen in a kaleidoscope of garish colors. Trammell jumped up, and noticed her watching him. "Want a beer, a glass of wine, while I'm up?"

It took her a moment to decide. He showed no impatience as she stared at him. Tall and lithe, motionless but with an athlete's natural grace. She saw him differently now. A true romantic hiding behind the guise of a pragmatist. "Yes, that would be nice. There's a Merlot open."

She continued reading, sipping her wine, and occasionally pausing to study him. Twice she made up her mind to ease onto the floor beside him. The third time she worked up the courage to move. She set her book down and slid off the sofa. His eyes were closed, his breath steady and shallow. He was sleeping.

She nudged him gently. His eyes popped open. "You're sleeping, Lance. Go to bed."

He sighed and got to his feet, rotating his neck and shoulders. When he looked down at her, he remained still for the longest time. She waited for an invitation to join him, a signal—a beckoning hand would have been enough.

When the invitation didn't come and he had closed the bedroom door behind him, she remained on the floor, her hand pressed against the warmth of the carpet where he had been.

EIGHTEEN

Her morning workout completed, Martha assumed the *zazen*, her arms coming to rest upon her knees. Her fingertips touched. She counted her breaths in and out, one two three four. An image of Hewitt entered the flow of her mind chatter, followed by the mystery of the photograph on the dock, then the key and the photo again. Then Trammell. With each new interruption, she refocused on her breathing, one two three four.

Finally, she reached the quiet center of her soul and stayed there.

She heard a knock at the door. "Come in."

Charles Dennison entered the bedroom, the only guard who arrived for his babysitting stint in his work blues. Martha didn't know if he had just come from his shift in a patrol car or thought the uniform lent him authority. He needed it. Maybe five foot six and a hundred and fifty pounds, scrubbed fresh, he looked more like an intern pretending to be a police officer. He held out his cell phone and said, "Metcalf."

"Thanks." She took the phone, still seated on the yoga mat.

"This is Whitaker."

"I hope it's not too early," Metcalf said.

"Not at all." She waited.

"We've identified the shooter."

A long paused followed. She remained silent. If he wanted to parse out information like a miser, she could wait.

"His name's Piter deVries," Metcalf said.

"No one I know," she said.

"He was forty-six. Originally from South Africa. It came in this morning from Interpol. They had his prints on file."

"South Africa?" Martha eased off the floor and onto the corner of the bed. "What was he doing in Seattle chasing me?"

"We're not sure yet. But he's got an interesting history. A white supremacist. Left South Africa in 1992. Paramilitary. Worked for a private security firm from Arlington, Virginia, and earned a lot of frequent flyer miles—mostly to Africa, some to the Middle East. Sierra Leone, Mozambique, Egypt, once to Germany, Iraq, Iraq again, Kuwait, Sudan, you name it. There's more, but you get the picture. His only prior entry into the US was five years ago. He arrived on a British passport, stayed four months, entering and exiting through Reagan International in the other Washington. I've spoken with US and Canadian Customs. No record of a Piter deVries entering Canada or the United States in the past five years."

"He was a mercenary?" Martha said slowly.

"That's what it looks like. We're still tracking down information about him, but I thought you should know. This probably means we're going to have to get the feds involved. They have a lot of resources that I don't."

"Of course." Martha had no idea what it meant to get the feds involved, but access to resources sounded good. "Thanks, Metcalf."

The line went dead.

Dennison had stepped out of the room, and for a moment Martha was tempted to dial her father just to chat for a few minutes about the weather in the Soo and the thickness of the ice on the lake, about how the nieces and nephews were doing at hockey or dance. Nothing and everything.

She walked out into the common room.

"I'm sorry, the exercise room is closed to you today," Dennison said. Trammell was in the kitchenette in a gray T-shirt, sweat pants, and running shoes. He slowly lowered an orange juice carton and stood there with his empty glass.

"You're joking, right?"

"I'm not, sir. I'm sorry. The hotel is full this weekend. There's a boat show across the street. The hotel won't close the exercise room for you to use."

"Christ." Trammel slammed the glass down so hard it broke. He left it there, and with his hand bleeding, stormed back into his bedroom.

"Middle of a boat show, huh? That was good planning on your part," Martha said, handing the phone back to Dennison. She shrugged and walked away.

"Yeah, we probably didn't plan on all the leads drying up as soon as you two were off the street. Should've rented by the month."

"What does that mean?" Martha whirled to face him.

"Seems pretty simple. Nothing's happening. Seems a little strange. But what do I care? I'm getting plenty of overtime."

"Implying what? What's Metcalf told you?"

"Metcalf hasn't told me anything. Hard not to notice, though. You and the dude hole up and everything stops. Like turning off a tap. Just be glad you're not at the Blue Light Motel. But I can ask Metcalf to book you a room. Need a hour? Two?"

For the first time, she looked closely at Dennison. She wanted to wipe the smirk off his face. Instead, she whispered, "You little prick."

"Any time."

Martha spun away rather than give in to the temptation. She returned to her bedroom, slamming the door behind her. She rolled up her yoga mat and tossed it into a corner. She yanked the duvet cover across the bed, and stripped out of her clothes. A smart-ass cop. And a mercenary? A fucking mercenary. What kind of trouble had Hewitt gotten himself—and her—into?

At the moment, she didn't care. They were stuck in a hotel. Tensions were mounting. The cops were getting nowhere fast. Going on ten days and they had dug up the name of a dead mercenary. That felt like small progress. And the cops were beginning to talk. Leads had dried up? Dennison had been pretty clear about who he believed was responsible for turning off the tap. Once again, she was being targeted. Metcalf had to be behind the talk. Christ, she needed to get out of here, mercenary or no.

She dialed up the temperature on the shower until it was scalding hot, turning her skin pink, opening every pore. Scenes flicked through her mind, like a montage of silent images from a home movie. This time she let the reel play—Hewitt working a sockeye off the stern; Hewitt struggling along the hospital corridor, his pale butt exposed by the hospital gown; Hewitt smiling as he rounded everyone up for the birthday photo.

And the image of the dock on that wet dawn two weeks ago now—the rendezvous that never happened. Same spot. The wharf of good times and bad. The wharf . . . the wharf—then it hit her. It was the place, not the people! The message Hewitt was sending in the photograph was about the location. That's why he took such pains to waterproof the package.

Her hair still soapy, she wrapped herself in a robe and found

Dennison in the living room watching CNN. He jumped up. "Everything okay?"

"Can you call Lieutenant Lolich at the Harbor Patrol?"

In a moment, she was talking to Lolich. "Whatever Hewitt was trying to tell us, I think the answer is under the Shilshole fishing pier. Can you have your divers check?"

She explained where they might find it. Lolich asked several questions and finally assured her he'd have a diver on the way within the half hour.

Hair rinsed and blown dry, dressed in a white silk blouse and black jeans, Martha stood in front of the mirror. Her thick, dark eyebrows arched over her mismatched eyes. She brushed her hair, and with a flip of the hands, she let it fall to her shoulders. The blouse was clean and pressed. The hotel had done a decent job. When they got their laundry back, Martha learned that Trammell did own more than one black mock turtleneck. He owned a stack of them, all identical, and three pairs of jeans—also identical. The sartorial imagination of . . . well, of a newspaper man, she decided, but it did make those morning decisions about what to wear a lot easier.

When she knocked on his bedroom door, she held a small first-aid kit that Dennison had requested from the front desk. Trammell answered the door dressed in jeans, absent the turtleneck. Solid shoulders, not wide, but toned from the free weights, narrowed to nice abs and a trim waist. He had the clean, well-scrubbed scent of someone just out of the shower. He wore no jewelry or watch. A washcloth was wrapped around one hand.

"Let me fix up your hand," Martha said, stepping uninvited into his private sanctuary. It looked like a boy's room—the curtains closed, the bed unmade, dirty jeans and turtlenecks tossed in a corner, a jumbled stack of books, magazines, and papers piled on the nightstand.

"Let me put a shirt on."

"Don't have to on my account. It's your hand I'm worried about."

He stopped and looked at her. "Okay."

He perched on the bed and held out his hand. Martha sat beside him. She removed the bloody washcloth and looked at the cut. Blood still oozed from a deep puncture wound. She wiped it clean with the washcloth and ripped open an alcohol swab to clean it. While she tended to his hand, she told him about her conversation with Metcalf about the South African mercenary.

"I also talked to Lolich," Martha added. "I think Hewitt was telling me with the picture that it was the place, not the people in it. Lolich is sending divers back out to the pier."

"Interesting. Makes sense. Let's hope they find something," Trammell said. "I'm gonna go postal if I don't get out of here."

"Join the club."

"Plus, I'd really like to go to that boat show. I know Mac is over there right now, dreaming about his next boat."

"MacAuliffe's a boater? My opinion of him just soared."

"He lives aboard an old Cal 27. It's got about as much room as your car. I'd really like an update on what's happening at the *Gazette*."

"It'll be fine. He can't lose all your money in a week. Haven't you ever gone on vacation?"

He thought for a minute. "Not for more than four days since we started the paper."

"Four days? Even I can beat that."

Martha daubed the wound with an antiseptic, folded a piece of gauze, and placed it on the cut.

"I've been thinking about what Metcalf told you about the deVries guy," Trammel said. "It makes sense."

"How does it make sense?" Martha tore off a piece of tape.

"Think about it: Mormon men have to do two years of mission work all over the world. DeVries could have connected with them in any number of places he's been in the past twenty years. LDS is a natural for a white supremacist with a religious bent. Of course, official church doctrine doesn't allow bigotry, just like they'd never admit to the existence of the Death Angels. But look at the senior leadership councils—the First Presidency, the Quorum of Apostles, the Quorum of Seventy—all that. White men, every last one of them. Not a woman or a black face among them. If you fled South Africa because you despised what Mandela did, you might find a warm reception from certain members of the Mormon Church."

"And if there's any truth to Hewitt's theory about the Mormon death squad," Martha said, "a white supremacist professional mercenary guy might get some extra attention."

"Exactly. DeVries wasn't on a suicide mission. I bet he fully expected to accomplish his job and get out alive. He was already back in the car when he was killed. Cops, paramilitary are trained to take body shots and his body armor covered all vital organs except one—the brain. Was his mission to kill you or just scare the living shit out of you?"

"I thought his intent seemed pretty clear," Martha said.

"But that's what we thought the night they broke into the *Gazette*. Only the facts didn't line up. When the Hammer of God pulled into the parking lot that morning, he didn't know you'd set a trap for him. The Harbor Patrol doesn't even have a sign on that road. He probably figured God would protect him from the infidels. If he hadn't taken a bullet to the head, who knows how things might have turned out? He didn't have any other life-threatening wounds."

"And I'd be dead," Martha said. "They've escalated things.

They're not trying to scare the messenger any more—they're trying to kill the messenger. They think we know something that we don't, something they don't want anyone else to know."

Trammell looked at Martha and then down at her hand. "Are you going to just hold my hand or you going to put that tape on?"

"I haven't decided yet. Why?"

"No reason. Take your time."

NINETEEN

Gray light slipped around the edges of the curtain. Martha lay on her back, remembering the slow circles Trammell had traced on her shoulders and back with his lips, taking forever to undress her, a forever that surged with rising tension and growing excitement. His hands had caressed her through the silk blouse, his lips explored the smooth skin of her neck. When he eased the blouse off her shoulders, she wanted him to reach around and cup her breasts. Still he hesitated. He was in no hurry to rush his pleasure or hers, which was a finer pleasure in itself.

She had sighed then and sighed again now at the memory. A smile crossed her face.

Lovers had been few through the years. Learning the difference between the horror of rape and the joys of making love had been a slow lesson to learn. For a long time, she had feared her own sexuality as much as she had feared Walt Boudreau. The first time she experienced tenderness and pleasure in lovemaking had left her breathless. Now, Trammell had shown her there were so many new worlds still to explore.

Beside her, she heard the soft rhythm of his breathing. He dozed on his side, his back toward her. She ran her finger in light circles over his shoulder. He stirred, and she replaced her finger with her lips. It was time to return the pleasure.

When the knock came at the door, they were still intertwined, their breathing just starting to return to normal. Martha bolted upright. It took a moment for her to call out, "Yes?"

"Metcalf. I'd like to talk to you guys for a minute if you think you could put on some clothes."

"Just a minute," she responded.

Before rolling off Trammell, she touched his lips with hers, lingering long enough to feel him getting excited again. Reluctantly, she slid off him. Trammell rose, got dressed, and slipped out the door. Donning jeans and her blouse, she wondered why Metcalf was here so early. She didn't dare hope that they were about to be released.

In the living room, Trammell stared out the window and Metcalf paced, cell phone to his ear. Dennison stood motionless in the kitchen. Only then did Martha realize they had a visitor: Lieutenant Lolich from the Harbor Patrol. His eyes were half-closed, his hands intertwined over a generous stomach. Against his dark suit, his tie was a burst of autumn color captured in silk.

"Sorry to keep you waiting, Lieutenant," Martha said, joining him on the sofa. "I didn't know you were here." Glasses made his eyes appear larger than they were. A puffy face and dark bags under his eyes gave him the appearance of a man who had had too little sleep for too long.

"We suspended the search for Mr. Wilcox a couple days ago," Lolich started. "Nature will take its course, and if the body is in Puget Sound, it will surface. I'm sorry."

Martha nodded, barely able to mumble, "No one mentioned it. I understand."

Metcalf snapped his phone shut and turned to Lolich. "Forensics found nothing of note in the van. Just a cane wedged between the seats. Otherwise, everything you'd expect but nothing else." To Martha, he added, "But your suggestion led us right to the package Mr. Wilcox had hidden."

A bundle wrapped in brown paper rested in the center of the coffee table. Trammell edged closer to the table. Martha leaned forward. Only Lolich seemed in no hurry to get to it. He produced a copy of the photograph from Hewitt's birthday party. A thick finger pointed to the new fishing pole and traced the fishing line that came off the end. At the spot where it went over the edge of the pier, he stopped. "Right there, my officers found a fishing line tied to the railing. On the other end of the line was this package. They didn't even need to go in the water. They just pulled it up. The outer wrapping was a black garbage bag with a ten-pound fishing weight inside. That's what held it down. It was covered with silt, and with it being black we didn't see it the first time through the area."

Martha flashed back to that rainy morning wait for Hewitt. Her fingers had plucked that line like a guitar string. It hadn't been an illegal crab pot, after all. Hewitt's packet had been right in front of her the whole time. She just hadn't been smart enough to realize it.

"So what is it?" Trammell asked. He was by now perched on the edge of his chair.

"We were hoping you might be able to tell us," Lolich said. "Detective Metcalf and forensics have examined it. On the surface, it's easy: it's a collection of old letters and documents. But, from your dealings with Mr. Wilcox, we thought you might have more insights as to what it all means. Forensics found fingerprints on the wrapping and we're tracking those now. It was a crude but effective waterproofing technique. Everything was still dry inside."

He folded back the brown wrapping. "First, there's a short note; it was written on the back of Mr. Wilcox's electric bill."

He handed it to Martha. She recognized Hewitt's tight, back-slanted script. The note was brief: "Martha. If you find this, it means I was unable to deliver to Lance Trammell, 'Ballard Gazette.' My profound gratitude, as always, if you'd do so. Forever think of me w/love, as I shall you. Your humble servant. HW."

"Forever think of me w/love, as I shall you" was all Martha could see for a moment. Hewitt knew that if she received his note, they would not be meeting again. She had delayed her grief. Now at the sight of his hurried words—and the finality of his message—everything collapsed. She tried to neither stop nor hide her tears.

Lolich handed her a handkerchief, but otherwise gave her little time to reflect. He turned the note over and said, "There are eight documents in all, dating from 1838 to 1876. Each has a protective tissue top and bottom, with a piece of stiff cardboard separating them. A piece of wood—forensics suspects it's a common cutting board—kept everything flat."

Trammell reached out, but Lolich quickly said, "Please don't touch."

He donned a pair of latex gloves. The first tissue had "Samson Avard 1838" written in pencil on the upper right corner. Lolich lifted the tissue paper, revealing a single sheet of paper. It was as yellow as an old man's teeth, the handwriting faded to a ghostly gray. Creases where the paper had once been folded into quarters were still visible. The upper left-hand corner was missing.

"This is the letter Hewitt showed me," Trammell said. Without touching the paper, his finger traced the lines and he read aloud:

Nov 7 1838
Brother Port

May this find you secure in the blessings of Jesus Christ, Son of our Almity Father. In these troubled days the Almity will bless and keep his childrin in the House of Israel safe from the wrath of Gentiles. the childrin of God shant stand by meek before the unholy perscutors. The Holy Profet of Zion has blessed his People with a vison from the Almity. The mighty Jehovoh, has told the Profet that you, Brother Port, must be the sword of Zion in battle agin the Gentiles of Mo. The Army of Israel shall bring the Lord's wrath upon His enemies and those who would have us gone from this Earth. May you, like Saul before the Philistines, bring fury and vengeance down upon there leader so no brother of Zion need ever feare the hand of the Unholy. With God as yer shield and his Son as yer sword, may you smite him dead & let Satan take his soul to burn forevr in Hell.

My blessings to Sarah first among yer blessed wives and yer ma.

Yer brother in the Almity God
Sam. Avard

They sat silent after Trammell had finished reading.

Finally, Martha said, "So this is what the Hammer of God thought I had?" She glanced at Trammell, and added, "And what he wanted to keep from you."

"What about this letter would incite someone to such extremes?" Lolich asked.

"Hit men and death squads," Trammell said. "Hewitt came to me a couple of weeks ago with this letter and said he had the evidence to prove the Church's involvement in the assassinations of its enemies. He wanted to know if I was interested in the story."

"This doesn't prove anything," Lolich said.

"I agree, but Hewitt claimed to have other incriminating documents. Mostly circumstantial evidence, I'll admit—like this letter—but they linked the Church with the Avenging Angels."

"But how does this even tie in with the church?" Martha asked. "A good defense attorney could rip that theory to shreds. First, how do we know it's even authentic? Second, who's 'Sam. Avard'? Then, it's the language of the illiterate and the zealous. Certainly, Joseph Smith and Brigham Young were not illiterate. And last, even if it was authentic, it's still not coming from church authorities, just a member of the church."

"As far as authenticity, I had only Hewitt's word, but this was his profession, so I trusted him. Based on his information, I was able to do a little research. Brother Port was a guy named Orrin Porter Rockwell, a known gunman. The Mormons were still in Missouri in 1838; Smith was still alive. Some historians believe Rockwell was responsible for at least seventeen murders. Probably more. Samson Avard ran Joseph Smith's private security detail."

"It's still a big leap," Lolich said, "to say this implicates anyone of knowing about or leading a vigilante death squad."

Trammell leaned forward as he spoke. "True. This letter wouldn't implicate Smith or anyone else. But, Hewitt claimed to have other evidence that, when put together, could mean only one thing: someone was ordering the Avenging Angels to do these killings. Some people claim the death squad still exists today. Krakauer touched on it in *Under the Banner of Heaven*, but couldn't find any conclusive evidence. Maybe with these documents and Martha's experience with the Hammer of God, we've finally got our proof."

"But Samson Avard was denounced and excommunicated by Joseph Smith," Metcalf said. Everyone stared at him. "Come on, you're not the only ones who can use Google. I did some checking on your cockamamie theory about the Death Angels in the Wild West. Avard turned state's evidence against Smith and couldn't throw out names and accusations fast enough. Trying to save his own neck from the noose, most likely."

"Sure, that's possible," Trammell said. "But first, this letter purports to have been written before Smith's denouncement of Avard; second, some of Avard's claims may have been true; and third, it was only one piece in a chain of evidence that Hewitt compiled." He turned to Lolich. "What's next?"

Lolich carefully turned over the Avard letter, then a piece of protective museum paper. On the next tissue was written "Emma Lee 1857." He turned the tissue over. The paper was smaller than the previous letter, though just as yellowed, the ink just as faded. A jagged tear ran down the left side. The handwriting was neater, the lines straight, the cursive more ornate.

"This one looks more like a page from a diary," Trammell said. He studied it before reading aloud.

Aug 24 '57 yng John still ailing with the dysentry looking pale and to weak for chores. asked our Heavnly Father for a blessing to be bestowed upon our son thru sister R. one child this month has slipped the bondage of earth to find Paradise with our Lord and our hearts cannot take two. tomato patch and corn healthy but deer et most of the peas. John will build bigger fence maybe mete for table. mete would be good for we now have nine hungry mouths to tend to. blessed with surprise visit from Ste George visitng the flock thru all of Deseret after recevin blessings and instruktions from the Eldest

Ste. children heared his wisdom and strength from God when he led prayer for our humble dinner for God hast delivred His enemys into the hands of the just & riteous amongst us. after dinner the Gen. and John walkt the orchard lookin at apple crop. apples the deree aint et looking boundiful-- praises to the Lord. John preparing to leve on job for Elders taking Wm. and Orrin and Mary's boy B. will be gone several days but taking rifles to hunt game and no need to provision w/ mete just flor and coffee and tack. I included pares for I know Wm

The single page ended mid-sentence.

"So, now deer have joined the death squad?" Metcalf mocked.

Trammell flung himself back in his chair. "Christ, man, you still don't get it, do you? In 1857, over 120 non-Mormons were killed when their wagon train was ambushed in southern Utah. The Mountain Meadow Massacre. It was made to look like an Indian attack. Years later, a guy named John D. Lee said Brigham Young had directly ordered the attack. Of course, Lee, like Avard, was discredited and excommunicated. I don't know the exact day of the massacre, but if you go back and look, I'll bet you'll find this diary entry from Emma Lee was written shortly before."

"That's reading an awful lot into some settler's diary," Metcalf said. "At best, it's circumstantial. At worst, it's a wild accusation with no evidence."

"Of course, it's circumstantial. But you put enough of it together and it starts to tell a story. Come on, Metcalf, be a detective. Who's Emma Lee? One of John Lee's wives or daughters? He's visited by the General, Saint George Smith, who has a message from the Elders. And who's the chief Elder? Brigham Young, of course. And the message is, 'God has delivered his enemies into the hands of the just and righteous amongst us.'" Right after the General's visit, John Lee and several others took their rifles and left. Then there's the massacre. Coincidence? What the hell do you think this might refer to? For that matter, Metcalf, what the hell do *you* think is going on here? So far it looks like you've produced nothing except the name of the Hammer of God. You're so stuck on proving that Martha's after Hewitt's money that you're blinded by what's right in front of you. I've been stuck in this goddamn hotel room for eleven days now and I'm fucking tired of it."

"That's not what it looked like this morning when I got here," Metcalf said. To Martha, he added, "What's that say about you, Whitaker?"

"You goddamn prick," Trammell leapt up, reaching for the detective.

No one had noticed Dennison enter the living room. But he was quick. He stepped between the two men. The hand that reached for Metcalf was now behind Trammell's back, and the little man in blue had the much larger Trammell on his tiptoes.

Then Dennison was on his toes. In an instant Martha had his other arm in a lock. "Let go or you won't use this arm again for months," she hissed in his ear. She twisted his wrist and pulled it higher up his back. Dennison released Trammell. She shoved Dennison away. He instantly twirled and sent a foot flying toward her head. The push and bad footwork left him off balance, and she palmed the kick aside. She was about to drop him to the floor, a palm to break his nose, but pulled her punch, and snapped, "Don't even think about it."

The entire scene had happened in a flash. Her instinct to protect Trammell came with no warning, no thought. Lolich and Metcalf were on their feet. She and Dennison stood facing each other, two fighters alone in the ring.

Lolich centered his portly frame between them. To Dennison, he snapped, "Step back. That's an order, son." Turning to Metcalf, he commanded, "Detective, you will refrain from making any further crude and derogatory remarks to these people."

Metcalf muttered something that might have been, "Yes, sir." Louder, he added, "But she was assaulting a police officer in the line of duty."

"A fact we shall overlook this one time . . ."

"It wasn't the first time," Metcalf muttered.

"Do not interrupt me, Detective." Lolich wagged a finger at Metcalf. "If you continue to provoke them—and me—with your unprofessional behavior, you'll be lucky to find a job working night patrol at Tent City. Or I shall stand aside and ask Miss Whitaker to clean your clock. Which she has already done, or so I've been made to understand." Turning to Trammell and Martha, he said, "I'm sorry. Did either of you get injured?"

Trammell shook out his hand, but he said, "No, I'm okay."

Martha shook her head.

"Oh, goodness," Lolich sighed. He searched his back pocket but found nothing. He cleaned his glasses on the end of his tie. In a voice that was almost a whisper, he said, "What have we become? As if I didn't have enough to think about right now."

Martha pressed up beside Trammell and stared down at the papers. "Lance, is this something you can print? Is your story here?"

For a long time, Trammell looked at the papers, now in two neat stacks on the coffee table. Finally, he shook his head. "I need to be one hundred percent sure they're authentic. That was Hewitt's role in this. If they're forgeries, the paper would be fucked. We wouldn't survive."

"But Hewitt left them for me to give to you. You've already seen one letter. You talked to him. What else do you need?"

"I need to speak to whoever authenticated them. There's no

documentation here—you know, what'd we call it in class? The Letters of Authenticity. I need those. Without them, all I've got are some old papers."

Martha nodded. "Well, Hewitt's certainly not the only person who's qualified to determine if these are real or not. We've just got to find the right person."

"Yeah, you're right. If we can stay alive until then."

"If we don't get these published," Martha said, "we'll always be looking over our shoulder for the next Hammer of God. Print the story and the church will go into damage control, but they'll leave us alone. Hurting us would only prove the case. I'll pack my bag."

"I'll join you. Share a cab?"

Metcalf interrupted their tête-à-tête. "Don't even think about it. You're both staying put."

"Then arrest us." Martha threw the words at him like punches. "Because you sure as hell can't stop us otherwise." She glanced at Dennison and bowed. "*Rokudan*," she said, and like a *sensei* to a prideful pupil, she added, "And master of the eight gates of t'ai chi ch'uan."

"*Nidan*." He bowed lower in return, a second-level black belt before a master. To Metcalf, he said, "I'm sorry."

"Please, both of you. We can't guarantee your safety unless you're here," Lolich said.

"Lieutenant," Martha said, "I quit the Catholic Church because I didn't believe in Purgatory. Now I'm living it. You and I both know you can't hold me against my will without charging me with something. Read me my rights, or let me go."

"Detective?" Lolich looked at Metcalf.

"I don't have the manpower to protect them out on the street." He shrugged. "If Dennison wants to press charges, I'm happy to arrest them."

Dennison shook his head. "And further my humiliation?"

"Fine," Metcalf said. "If Whitaker thinks her ninja act is better protection than the SPD, let her go. Have a nice day. Just don't sue us for your funeral expenses. And frankly, ever since she went off the grid, there's been no more activity. Every lead has dried up. Curious, isn't it?"

Lolich ignored this veiled accusation, but Martha didn't. She glared at Metcalf. So he was the one talking. He smiled at her, a goad, a challenge. Power was having the control not to act. Finally, she turned away.

"It's not right. I know it's not right," Lolich said, as Martha and Trammell disappeared into their bedrooms. Brushing Dennison aside, Metcalf was gone, the door slamming in his wake.

When Martha and Trammell walked out of the hotel and into a wet day, the porter who had opened the door invited them to return soon. For a moment, they paused, blinking despite the gray-covered sky. Martha inhaled deeply of the fresh air. She wanted to wash her face with the rain. But, there are nightmares that don't go away with the day. The fear that had prompted her to accept police protection in the first place resurfaced in the cab ride back to Ballard.

TWENTY

Sometimes the best place to hide is out in the open.

The taxi dropped Trammell off at the *Ballard Gazette*. The driver waited while he and Martha walked into the office. They found MacAuliffe by himself in the production room reviewing Molly and Benji's draft layout. This would be the first of eight to ten renditions, all of which would be developed, tweaked, and discarded over the next two days. He looked up from the computer screen when he saw them.

"So, they finally let you guys out of the asylum," MacAuliffe said, with a warm smile. "Did they find someone?"

His long blond hair and his beard had been clipped short. A strong aquiline nose was centered on a broad, intelligent face. With a little grooming he was rather handsome. Stitches and a thin red seam about four inches long ran from the top of his head to his right ear.

"They didn't let us out," Trammell said. "We left. And not without a fuss. And, no, they don't have anyone yet."

He gave a brief recap with the promise to fill in the details later. "Maybe on the boat, if you've got room for a guest?"

"You've seen my boat," MacAuliffe said. "It's pretty cozy. I don't mind, if you don't."

"I've got a taxi waiting," Martha said. "What dock are you on?" He told her, and she promised to stop by later.

Back at the Carriage House, without her laptop and phone, Martha felt alone and isolated. Beatrice was nowhere to be found, but she had food and water. The litter box was clean. Callison had done the dishes. Otherwise, the house was exactly as she had left it. She found the key to the main house and walked through the backyard. The windows were dark, the driveway empty. She unlocked the back door and was surprised to see a row of winter coats hanging in the mudroom. Boots of varying sizes were lined up against the wall.

Martha opened the door from the mudroom to the kitchen and called out, "Anybody home? Iris, Karl, it's me, Martha."

Only the echo of her voice answered.

Evidence of the kitchen having been trashed was gone, as if the break-in had been part of a bad dream. In the kitchen, cereal bowls were stacked in the sink; a milk carton sat on the counter. From the small breakfast table in the corner, Mr. Moose and Mr. Bear watched her with brown button eyes. Mr. Moose looked like he was recovering nicely. Martha hadn't considered what it might take for the Heidens to find a new place to rent. At least it meant another month of income. The phone sat on the counter. She removed it from the cradle and dialed Callison's number.

"It's Martha Whitaker," she said.

"You okay? I've been expecting to hear from you."

"Everything's fine. I take it you heard we left the hotel."

"Hard to miss that one. The choirboy got yelled at for letting you walk. Personally, I would have arrested you and let you spend a couple of nights with the drunks and streetwalkers.

Might change your mind about life in a hotel room. But it wasn't my call. It is now, though. Metcalf's no longer lead. I am. As if I didn't have enough to do. What's up?"

Martha went through her list: cell phones and computers for her and Trammell; copies of the documents. "And if it's okay, I was wondering if Rebecca could continue taking care of Beatrice for me?"

"Not going home?"

"I'm not sure, but this way I won't have to worry."

"Can do, but Whitaker, I want to know where you land. The SPD is still the best protection you've got."

"Did Metcalf tell you 'the unfriendlies' were getting information about what the police were doing almost as fast as it happened?"

"What do you mean?"

Martha related the story of Danny Kimble. "Doesn't it strike you as odd they got to Hewitt's houseboat, the newspaper, Ralph Hargrove, and my renters ahead of the police? Hewitt's houseboat, maybe. But the paper? And Ralph? How did they know Trammell and I had met? Where did they get that information?"

"That's a serious accusation. If it were true, why didn't they try something at the hotel?"

"I'm not making accusations, Callison. I'm letting you know why I'm reluctant to tell you where I'm going. And I don't know why they didn't come to the hotel. Something doesn't add up."

"Don't be foolish, Martha."

After a moment, she said, "Do you have to tell Metcalf where we are?"

"I'm not negotiating with you on this. I'll do what I think is right."

After a long pause, Martha said, "I'll think about it and let you know when you come by with our things."

Martha circled the Mini Cooper. No sign of bullet holes. The paint job was flawless. The body shop had placed all her personal items in a bag before detailing the car, inside and out. The umbrella with the duck's head handle stuck out of the bag. Near the bottom was a tube of lipstick she had been missing for weeks. Tucked between the pages of the owner's manual was the envelope with Hewitt's ripped postcard taped to it. She pulled out the umbrella and the envelope.

The car purred as she joined traffic heading across 85th. Tempted to punch it through a yellow light, she resisted and eased to a stop. Tires screeched behind her, and in the rearview mirror she saw the angry face of a man throwing up his hands. She stopped at the nearest Safeway, browsed the aisles, and occasionally dropped items in her basket. Near the deli she glanced at her watch and set the basket down. At the back door, she popped open her umbrella and crossed the street. The Number 48 bus was just arriving. Hopping on, she rode it back, getting off one stop beyond the house. Her umbrella again open, she hurried past the main house like someone wanting to get out of the rain. All seemed quiet around the Carriage House. She dashed in, grabbed a tote bag and a business suit, and tossed them in the Lexus. She drove around the corner and down the hill, parked the car, and caught the Number 48 back to the grocery store. Her basket still untouched, she purchased the items, took out cash from the ATM, and drove home in the Mini Cooper, parking it in the garage.

Dusk came early on the overcast winter afternoon. Martha set the light timers for four hours in the evening, beginning at six o'clock, and for two hours in the morning. Brushing her teeth and changing into clean clothes had to substitute for the bath that she longed to take. She jotted a couple of notes. With no computer and no phone, there was little to do except wait. She took a deep breath and willed herself to be patient. Callison's copy of *War and Peace* felt heavy as an anchor, but she forced herself to open the book.

She must have dozed off because suddenly Beatrice lay curled in her lap. She didn't realize how much she had missed the cat. Each stroke of her fur brought forth a purring that vibrated through her lap. It was like she had never gone. But, Martha also knew that for Beatrice, any warm body would do. Was that what Trammell was to her, just another warm body to cling to when she was feeling lonely and scared? Was that all she was to him?

Voices came up the stairs. She rose, still holding the cat, her whole body tensed until the voices became distinct enough to make out the conversation.

"I think Beatrice eats so much because she's lonely." It was a young girl's voice. "Maybe I could stay with her."

Martha recognized Callison's voice. "Beatrice will be fine, honey. You're not old enough to stay here by yourself. Besides, you have to go to school, so she'd be alone all day anyway."

"Maybe Beatrice could stay in my room."

"And you and I would be looking for a new place to sleep." Suddenly his voice changed; it grew short and sharp. "Back downstairs. Get to the car. Remember what we talked about?"

"Yes, sir," came the timid response.

Martha called out, "It's okay, it's me, Martha. I'm alone. Door's open." When no response came, she added, "Room service for two."

Callison entered, pistol drawn. He glanced around and holstered his weapon. He assured his daughter it was safe to join them. His arm on her shoulder, he made introductions. Rebecca was tiny standing next to her father. Brown hair was pulled back into a ponytail. An elfin face and ruddy cheeks still showed some baby fat.

"Pleased to meet you, ma'am," Rebecca said. She held out a soft hand. They shook. "I think Beatrice is lonely."

"That's why I'd like to have you keep looking after her," Martha said. "I can see you're doing an excellent job. Her fur is beautiful. You must be brushing her every day."

Beaming, Rebecca nodded.

Callison was having another bad hair day, though he had shaved his neck and cheeks since she had seen him last. His Carhartt was damp from the rain. He eased a couple of briefcases off his shoulder, setting them on the floor. "Here's the stuff you asked for. I put copies of the letters in your briefcase."

"Thanks." She handed him one of the notes. "Here's where I'm staying, but please don't spread it around. You understand why. Do I have you to thank for my car?"

"I just delivered it. Lieutenant Lane had it repaired."

"Well, thank you both," Martha said. She turned to the girl, "Rebecca, this note's for you. Plus, I want to pay you for the work you've done so far."

Rebecca's interest in money overrode petting Beatrice. She counted it out, stopping a couple of times, as if she was remembering her numbers. "Wow, Dad."

"That's too much," Callison said. "Rebecca, you have to give—"

"That's what I pay my regular cat sitter," Martha interrupted. "And she doesn't do nearly as good a job."

Callison and Martha sat opposite each other at the table. The detective peppered her with questions about her relationship with Hewitt, about this "Death Angels" theory Metcalf had scribbled in the files, about what wasn't in the files. Who was Piter deVries, and why did he think a few musty old letters was worth killing her over? And who's Danny Kimble? That had barely been a footnote in the files on the day Ralph Hargrove was murdered. Martha sat patiently through the questions, knowing it was how she would handle taking over a case.

"Do you think Hewitt might have faked his own disappearance?" Callison was jotting notes in a small spiral-bound notebook. He looked up, his dark eyes holding hers.

"Yeah, it's possible," Martha replied.

"If he was scared, is he the kind of guy who would run away and let you take the heat?"

The question brought her up short. Finally, she said, "Maybe. Hewitt never made any bones about being a coward. Said he learned it in the war. But he would never knowingly put me in danger." She paused. "Why? Do you think he might have run?"

"The Harbor Patrol hasn't found his body yet. I need to explore all possibilities. If he went underground, where would he have gone?"

Martha shook her head. "If I had any idea, I'd have already gone to find him."

"No idea? None?"

"He joked sometimes about finding a cabin where television, the Internet and cell phones, and everything else that he detested couldn't reach him."

"Did he say where that might be? Mountains? Beach? Close? Far? US? Foreign? Anything?"

"Callison, it was a joke. He usually said it when he read how cell phones had reached some tribe in the jungles on the upper Amazon."

"Many a truth was told in jest."

No amount of prodding or cajoling or rewording of the question changed her answer. Finally, she snapped at him, "Callison, I don't know, okay? If I did know or if I even had an inkling of where he might be, I'd tell you. Browbeating me won't change the fact that I just don't know. I think he's probably drifting in Puget Sound. Christ, I thought you were a fucking homicide detective, not a missing persons cop."

Immediately, she looked over at Rebecca who hadn't looked up from stroking the cat. Beatrice lay stretched out with her belly in the air. Martha could hear her purrs rumble across the room.

"Sorry," she said.

"Time to go, honey," Callison said to his daughter. "Beatrice will be here tomorrow. Wait for me at the door. I have to talk with Ms. Whitaker for minute."

Rebecca skipped to a stop in front of Martha. "Do you have another cat?"

"No, just Beatrice."

"But why's all the food's gone but she's not getting fat?"

"I don't know, Rebecca, but that's a problem for another day. And thank you again for taking such good care of her."

"You're welcome. And thank you for the money. My mom says I need new shoes. I know just which ones I want."

Rebecca hummed the tune from *Frozen* as she disappeared down the stairs.

Callison's dark eyes bore into Martha. His voice low and harsh, he said, "I *am* a fucking homicide cop. Most homicides are pretty straightforward—a gang fight, a drug deal gone bad, a husband who finds the neighbor fucking his wife. But this doesn't pass the sniff test. Something's not right. When I first got out of a patrol car, I worked Fraud. White-collar assholes think they're smart. They pile layer upon layer of bullshit to hide their tracks. So I would dig down through all that bullshit until I could find them with their pricks in their hand. This feels more like that than a homicide."

"Tell that to Ralph Hargrove."

"Oh, don't get fucking pedantic with me, Whitaker. You're too smart for that. Of course it's a homicide. That's why I'm now in charge, not the choirboy. But why was Hargrove killed? And what's all the helter-skelter about with secret agent tricks and mercenaries and fake B&Es? It feels like someone's piling on the bullshit. It doesn't make sense—yet."

The evening had turned to night. Callison had no more questions. Martha had no more answers. They stared at each other for a minute, then Callison pushed himself away from the table.

Martha rubbed noses with Beatrice, and said, "So why are you eating all the food?" The cat was as forthcoming as Hewitt was with her secrets.

Soon, Martha made her way down the stairway. She entered the garage, adjusting the two briefcases, the straps slung in an X across her chest. She walked across the garage and slipped out the back door into the dark.

A trail opening appeared in the hillside bramble that was Beatrice's favorite hunting ground. Martha gasped as a motion caught her eye. A black cat darted down the trail. Had Beatrice come out with her? She pictured her curled on the back of the sofa, taking Martha's farewell with barely the twitch of a whisker.

She followed the path on its winding route down the hill, the ground slick with mud. Twice she stopped to listen, standing patiently in the rain, the hood of her rain jacket thrown back so she could hear better. The trail ended at the street near where she had left the Lexus. She waited in the shadows. When she finally emerged, she walked past the car once and doubled back only when she felt positive no one was watching it.

She rendezvoused with Trammell by pulling her boat up to the transom of MacAuliffe's sailboat. She easily held the boats apart with a hand on the stern rail of the sailboat and rapped on the hull. "James, you there?" she called out, quickly adding the password from the hotel, "Room service for two."

MacAuliffe popped his head out of the companionway.

"Everything okay here?" Martha asked.

"Just another perfect day in paradise," MacAuliffe said, looking over her boat. "A stink potter? And I was growing so fond of you. Oh, well, no one's perfect."

Martha smiled. "Ask Trammell if he'd like to go for a boat ride."

She motored around the breakwater, the only boat out on a dark, drizzly night. The dodger broke the wind and kept the rain off. From the tiny galley, Trammell handed up a slice of pizza, followed by a beer. She accepted both gladly. The boat rocked gently on an incoming tide. At Meadow Point she pointed it east into Richmond Bay, motoring slowly through the night. Halfway to shore she eased the boat into neutral, and they drifted with the current.

Trammell stood in the cabin with his head and shoulders out the companionway so he wouldn't have to slouch. The galley light behind him had him in silhouette. "Mac's doing the genealogy research for me," he said. "If we can find the lineage of the Avard or Lee families, it might help us backtrack on the history of the letters. By tomorrow, I should have some more names to add to the list. That'll free me up to go over to the U. I've got an appointment with one of my old archeology professors, Dr. Davidson."

"Good. I've had a new thought. Maybe we don't have to have the documents authenticated. Hewitt was ready to turn the letters over to you, which means he'd already done it. He wouldn't have been willing to certify them as legitimate without

Letters of Authenticity. The records have to be somewhere. I'm a signatory on his bank accounts. If he paid for the letters with his own money, I should be able to find out. Maybe you could ask the prof who I should be looking for, a company, an individual. We also should find out if they've added new testing procedures since we were in school. Spectral analysis, shooting it with laser beams, whatever."

"Good idea," Trammell said. "I thought I'd make some more copies. Ask Professor Davidson to study them for any historical inaccuracies. If he can't, he probably knows someone who can."

"We can't forget about the safe. Hewitt included the key to the safe because it was important."

"How are we going to find it if Metcalf and an entire squad of detectives can't?"

"He must have given us the clues." Martha smiled at him. "We're just not seeing them yet. My beer is empty, kind sir."

"At your service, ma'am. More pizza while I'm at it?"

"That would be most gracious of you. Thank you."

When he gave her the beer, she touched his hands. He still wore the bandage on the palm of one. They were thin and bony, the veins prominent. Yet those hands could be so gentle, with the lightest of caresses. She released his hand and smiled again. "Thanks."

He nodded, watching her for a moment. He flicked off the galley light and carried their pizza up to the cockpit, settling down under the dodger in the portside captain's chair. With the diesel idling, the boat rode up and down on an incoming swell. Lights dotted the hillside of North Beach and Blue Ridge, the reflections glimmering off the water, reflections broken and distorted by the steady drizzle.

"It's nice to breathe without being afraid of what's behind me, what's around the next corner, or hiding in the shadows,"

Trammell said. "I don't know how you manage."

"It's mostly an act," she said. "I've spent a lifetime training myself not to become paralyzed by fear. I was for a long time."

"You're always in control," he said. She couldn't tell if that was a compliment or a criticism. Maybe a little of both.

"This morning I wasn't," she said.

The current had carried them toward shore. She could see the dark line of the beach beginning where the reflections stopped. She engaged the transmission, pointed the boat north, and gave it a touch of throttle. In a couple of minutes, she put it back in neutral and turned around in the cockpit. Her eyes remained fixed on the hillside where affluent Seattleites raised their kids and walked their dogs, drank their lattes and denounced conservative politics as if it were a disease. Where they listened to classical music over candlelit dinners, while discussing Chihuly glass and the sorry state of the public school system. All with their backs to the picture windows overlooking a vista more beautiful and profound than any they would find on the four hundred channels at their fingertips.

Martha had pursued this community and joined it willingly, seeking to separate herself from a past in which a can of tuna, a package of noodles, and some cream of mushroom soup fed a family of eight. The first new dress she had ever owned had been for her first communion. What a waste that had been. She wondered at times if the moral compass set by Gran and a loving, hard-working father had gone askew. But then she reminded herself that she lived above a garage, that Mr. Göksu was her most valued client, that silk and diamonds held little value other than what the person wearing them brought with them.

She wondered what Trammell was seeing as he looked back at the hillside. A life he aspired to? A prison he'd escaped from? A life he would never have if the next assassin was successful? Or was he staring at the hill to avoid looking at her? He was strong and fit and scared to death. That made them alike. Just because fear could be controlled didn't mean it didn't exist.

Martha checked the surrounding water for any moving lights, found none. They were a black boat on a black sea, invisible to the world, outside of time, the universe theirs and theirs alone; here fear didn't scare her, but her passions did.

Trammell came to her, lifting her face with his hands, pulling her toward him. There was a moment of shock at the chill of his hands. They warmed as they caressed her body. He kissed her, long and languorously. His arms wrapped her, knotting behind her back. She pushed him away and began to remove his clothes there in the cockpit. Was this the well from which her fears sprang? She was on the verge of something magical, and someone was trying to take it away from her.

TWENTY-ONE

The role of power attorney came as naturally to Martha as slipping into a business suit. Every junior lawyer at CH&N attended mandatory in-house seminars with euphemistic titles, such as "Cross-Examination Techniques" and "Maximizing Witness Discovery Information." Among themselves, they called it "attorney charm school." The seminars focused on what they didn't teach a person in law school: how to use direct eye contact and modulate the timbre of the voice—a whisper can be more threatening than a shout; how even slightly aggressive body posture immediately puts people on the defensive; how interruption is your friend—do it often; how short, demanding sentences force attention and demand a response. And, most of all, how silence is golden. Use it like a sledgehammer to emphasize your point. People hate confrontation, but they loathe silence.

Few people were skilled at deflecting a head-on assault from someone trained at attorney charm school. Mr. Andrew Togaard, branch manager at the credit union, was not one of them.

In her charcoal-gray wool suit, hair pulled back tight against her head, a crisp white blouse buttoned all the way to the throat, Martha leaned forward and dropped her voice. "I'm sorry . . ." She made a point of looking at his business card, though she already knew the name on it. "I'm sorry, Mr. Togaard. I understand the bank's policy. But you must have misunderstood me. I'm signatory on three joint accounts with Hewitt Wilcox. I have every right to access that information. But I need information that predates the most recent six months."

Martha let silence fill the space between them. Although well cut, his suit jacket was tight across his chest. Togaard was about her age, which made him ancient compared to his employees. Finally, he repeated, "I'm not denying your right to the information, ma'am. I'm saying that to get back records, your request needs to be submitted in writing and—"

"And the response time is two to four weeks," Martha interrupted. "I don't have that much time. Either you can help me or I can come back with a subpoena delivered by the Seattle Police Department."

"There's no call for threats. I don't make the—"

"It's not a threat, Mr. Togaard. I am merely outlining my next course of action. In fact, it may be better for Detective Callison and me to attend to these matters at the offices downtown. You should inform your boss that Harry Callison, a detective with the SPD, and I will be at his office within the hour with a subpoena for the information."

She pushed Callison's card across the desk. "If you have any doubts, you may call this number for confirmation. Time is of the essence, Mr. Togaard. We both know you can access those records with a couple of clicks of the mouse. This is more important than I am at liberty to tell you. I ask that you make up your mind."

She stood up, buttoned her jacket, and picked up her briefcase. She saw him sizing it all up, figuring what the consequences might be if she and an SPD homicide detective arrived at his boss's office with a subpoena. Was it a bluff? He would know only if he picked up the phone and called Callison.

Waiting, Martha caught a faint whiff of diesel. She breathed deeply—definitely diesel with a little bit of the musty odor that pervaded everything on the boat. She smiled at the memory of sleeping spooned with Trammell in the tiny bunk. Rather than return to the dock, they had spent the night at anchor off Richmond Beach, motoring in with the dawn.

The branch manager pushed the card back at her. His voice was cold. "What do you need, Ms. Whitaker?"

Martha removed a set of folders from her briefcase and began laying out paperwork. "I'm a signatory on these three joint accounts with Hewitt Wilcox. This document indicates I have legal power of attorney for Mr. Wilcox. And this is why I'm here."

She laid a newspaper clipping on top of it all. It was just a few paragraphs from the *Seattle Times*, under the headline "Retired Professor Missing, Feared Drowned."

"Please feel free to make copies of these documents for your records. Mr. Wilcox is missing. Information has come to light that his disappearance may be related to his business activities. To assist in this matter, I have been asked by the police to review his bank accounts to see if anything in his financial records might help direct their investigation."

"To start, I need the past two years of records on these accounts. I also need to know if he had any other accounts with you—for example, a safety deposit box or another bank account. I know he didn't use electronic banking or an ATM card. He wrote checks and made deposits and withdrawals in person. I need copies of those checks. I may need to see the originals, but for now, the copies will do."

"If at any time you have questions about my veracity or need information that goes beyond bank policies, you may call Detective Callison."

Martha sat down in the chair opposite Togaard and crossed her legs. He leaned forward, examining the documents one by one, ending with the three joint accounts. He typed something into his computer, studied it for a moment, and said, "It will take me a couple of hours to process all of this. Would you like to wait, or come back?"

"I'll come back." She rose and looked at her watch. "Say, eleven thirty. Thank you for your assistance, Mr. Togaard." She handed him a card. "Here's my number if you need to contact me."

On the dock outside Hewitt's houseboat, Martha hesitated. The police tape prohibiting entry had been removed. The helm's-wheel gate hadn't properly latched, and it banged with the wake of a landing floatplane. The engine roar was audible in the distance. There was no hint of morning sun, only a steady drizzle. Martha looked down the empty dock and back again. She took a deep breath, stepped through the gate and onto the deck. She unlocked the door.

Little had changed since she had last been here—nearly two weeks ago now, she realized. The houseboat still resembled the aftermath of a drunken brawl, except now there was a faint white powder on most things. Residue from the search for fingerprints.

Where to start? Defeat swept over her. Take it one step at a time, she chided herself, item by item. Still, it took a moment before she pulled a hanger from the heap on the floor, removed her suit jacket, and hung it in the empty closet. One of Hewitt's old shirts, its sleeves tied in a knot around her waist, served as an apron over her wool skirt. The houseboat had been without heat since the break-in and the damp winter air sent a chill through her bones. She found a wool sweater and put it on. Lingering scents of marijuana and old person emanated from it. She wondered if there was some afterlife where they might meet again, where Hewitt would assure her that he had lived a long and happy life, that he was okay with the way things had turned out. Martha didn't believe it for a minute.

She unearthed a portable heater from a midden of books and clothes and cushions, righted it, and turned it on. The coils began to glow. The blue tarp still covered the broken sliding glass door where Trammell, lying half in and half out of the houseboat and had provided an introduction they wouldn't forget. At the desk, she leaned down and began sorting the papers strewn about her feet, unsure of what she was looking for, trusting that she'd know it if she found it.

A thought came to her, and she used her phone to Google the phone number she needed. A voice like tires on a gravel road answered, "Gustafson's Lock and Key Shop, Sven Gustafson speaking."

"Mr. Gustafson, it's Martha Whitaker." She paused, and added, "The woman with the heterochromia iridium eyes."

"Ah, yes, how pleasant to hear from you again, Miss Whitaker. Did you find your safe?"

"No, but that's why I'm calling. You said the Brinkman L70 and L80 models were opened with a key and a combination number. What is the combination number?"

"That varies with every safe, of course." Before Martha could explain herself, she heard the rasping that might be interpreted as a laugh. "It's a simple five-digit number, my dear. You turn the key, punch in the right sequence of five numbers, and "open sesame"! Good enough to keep the casual thief out."

"And are the safes small enough to be portable? I mean,

could you move one, yourself?"

"With a long enough lever, I could move the world." The locksmith cackled. "But I'd probably call my grandson to move it for me. I would suggest he bring a hand dolly. He would ignore me, of course, and just pick it up. Kids."

"Thank you. You've been a big help. Again. Be well."

"'Well' is a relative term when you're eighty-two, Miss Whitaker. But I can still dream of being twenty-seven and having you accompany me to the Sons of Norway Ball."

"I may just take you up on that, Mr. Gustafson," Martha said. A faint smile crossed her face. Dancing with Gustafson at the Sons of Norway Ball would cause a few heart palpitations among the white-hairs. Maybe it was time to honor her Norwegian roots a little more.

She resumed sorting papers, adding one more thing to search for—a five-digit number.

Warranties for everything from the television to a ten-dollar bedroom clock were dumped in a pile, together with an empty folder that said "Warranties." Martha shuffled quickly through them for information on a Brinkman safe. Nothing. She shoved them back in the folder and hung it in the bottom desk drawer. Telephone bills, utility bills, and moorage bills were separated and filed. She organized the phone bills in reverse chronological order. On a note, she wrote, "Review phone bills."

Copies of the bookstore ledgers showed that Hewitt had trusted Ralph Hargrove to handle the store accounts, making deposits and payments, buying books and pricing them. Ralph wrote and signed his own paychecks. Every month he mailed copies of the checkbook ledger to Hewitt. When they arrived, Hewitt had told her to file them without so much as a glance. "Ralph'll call if there's a problem," he had said. "Man's a miser when it comes to my money. I'd sell that damn store if I thought

Ralph could get a job anywhere else." When she saw what Ralph was paying himself every two weeks, she understood why he had been living in the store's back office, socks and underwear hung up to dry on an improvised clothesline. Had that been Ralph's or Hewitt's miserliness? The bookstore had a steady revenue stream throughout the year, spiking with the holidays and tapering off in summer months when most of the university students were gone. Hewitt certainly could have afforded to pay Ralph more than what was in the ledger. Had he known Ralph had taken up residence in the back of the store? She doubted it.

She set the ledgers aside. She would compare them with the bank statements when she picked them up from the bank. A glance at her watch showed she had an hour yet.

The monthly bank statements were at the bottom of the pile. She organized them, noting they went back only to the previous year, with June and July missing. Was that significant? The last statement was for December, which made sense. Where were previous years? Filed away? Thrown away? Stolen? Skimming the statement, she saw Hewitt wasn't broke, but he also didn't have a pile of cash. She set them aside to compare with the bank records. A search through the dwindling heap of papers didn't produce a checkbook.

To her note she added, "Look for investment accounts— IRAs, CDs, etc." And "Stop checks."

Next came a year's worth of credit card statements, again with June and July missing. What had Hewitt been up to in the early summer? She knew he often traveled in the summer. Had someone else been picking up the mail? Had he never received the statements? She made a note, "Check accounts for Ju/Jy activities."

She dialed Togaard's number. When he answered, she said, "Mr. Togaard, Martha Whitaker. I forgot that Hewitt Wilcox also had a credit card with the bank. Could you access those statements for me, as well?"

"I already have."

"Thank you. Did you find any investment accounts? CDs or IRAs? Anything like that?"

"No, but I'm still searching. The copies you requested are printing now. They should be ready in a half an hour or so."

"Thank you. I appreciate your help on this. Oh, and—"

But he had already hung up. One of the consequences of playing power bitch was people tended not to be chatty.

When you own your home, don't drive, rely on rabbit ears for your television reception, and eschew any technology developed post-1975, you don't need a large filing system. Martha thought she had come to the end of Hewitt's business records when she uncovered a stack of information on the Seattle Gay & Lesbian Association, including a photo from the *Gay Pride News* of Hewitt dressed as the "Fairy Santa" for the annual holiday party.

With the memory of his lover George Garvey's infidelity still working like a canker in his mind, Hewitt had asked Martha to be his date that year. The post-party party took place in a dark pub on Capitol Hill. Hewitt remained in his role as the Fairy Santa, dispensing naughty gifts to all the good little gays and lesbians. One of his helpers was a six-foot-two, two-hundred-pound dyke with hardware poked into many different body parts. Dressed in an elf's costume that ended in a garter belt and high heels, Santa's helper took an immediate interest in the tall, dark-haired stranger on Santa's arm. Out on the dance floor the Elf circled Martha like a pike preying on a minnow. Martha found herself responding, cheeks flushed, heat gathering in her belly. As the song ended, the Elf had pressed hard against her and kissed her with an animal hunger. The *click click click* of the

Elf's tongue stud against her teeth hit Martha like a bucket of ice water. The Elf took the news that she had tried to hit on the one straight woman at the party with grace and good cheer.

"If you change your mind," the Elf said, "just ask around for Julie B. Folks will know how to find me."

Julie B. Martha still found herself flattered and embarrassed by her attention. She located the folder labeled "G&L Assoc" and placed all the papers back in the desk drawer.

A well-worn manila folder with no label was next in the pile. Inside was just a single photo, a blown-up copy of an old black-and-white picture. Nothing was written on either side. It must have been a small picture to start. It had been blown up until it was grainy, the image fuzzy. Two young men stood in front of a barn. An open barn door created a black background to frame them. Part of what looked like a full hay wagon was visible on one side. With straw hats pushed back on their heads, they were laughing, arms slung over each other's shoulders. One had long hair that touched his shoulders. His shirt was open halfway down his chest, the sleeves rolled up. A bandana was knotted around his neck. The other man, boy really, pencil thin and handsome, was half-turned toward the man with the long hair.

Martha looked again. "Oh, my god," she whispered. It had to be Hewitt sixty, no, maybe seventy years ago—a teenager, but she was certain it was him. She peered at the grainy photo. She recognized the face, the thin, hawkish nose, the curve of his mouth when he laughed. He wasn't just turned toward the man, he was gazing at him adoringly. She remembered the conversation out on the boat. Someday he had promised to tell her the sordid tale of youthful infatuation, how Romeo lost his Romeo. Now "someday" had come. Hewitt wasn't here to tell the tale, but this longhaired man must have been his Romeo. Why else would he save this blown up photo?

224 Jeffrey D. Briggs

She carefully returned it to the file and placed it in the desk drawer. It took her a minute to recover from this most intimate intrusion into a life, a time she didn't know—a life and a time lost forever.

Sheaves of magazine pages slipped to the floor as she picked up the next folder. Recipes, predominately for salmon and crab. And there on the top, Hewitt's "private recipe for crab-stuffed salmon." She didn't know whether to laugh or cry. She could hear him in the Carriage House kitchen, preparing the dish, instructing her like a spy whispering in the dark. Queen Victoria had asked for the recipe and been denied. The secret had almost gone down with the *Titanic*, but among the seven hundred souls who survived was the galley mate who had prepared the dish for the Astors' private dinner party that fateful December night. Decades before, Hewitt had learned the recipe directly from the *Titanic* survivor, and he now shared it with her. In a voice as solemn as a high priest, he made her take a binding oath that she would reveal it only once—to a worthy successor, maybe her heir, a child he yet hoped to spoil like the grandchild he would never have.

The real tradition, of course, was that of the sailor weaving a tall tale.

How could he have vanished? A tear slid down her cheek.

She slowly folded the crab-stuffed salmon recipe and slipped it in her briefcase.

In the last folder, she discovered the missing June and July statements. Phone bills, moorage bills, credit card and bank statements were all there, as well. Invoices were all marked "Paid," but not in Hewitt's tight, backward scrawl. The handwriting was straight up, more cursive without being ornate. There was a slash through the stem of the 7.

Someone else had paid his bills in June and July. Who? She

backtracked through time. She didn't remember Hewitt being gone, but she had been working on the Palmeiro case, with barely enough time to go to the bathroom between research, team meetings, interrogatories, and discovery. Days and weeks blended together.

If Hewitt had been gone then, what about his cat? She remembered watching Dante in September, but she was positive the cat hadn't stayed with her during June and July. Hewitt hadn't mentioned anyone new in his life, and Hewitt was never shy about being in love. All too often he had sworn off men only to fall in love again, infatuation and lust assuring him he had found his soul mate at last. Still, he was in his eighties, in failing health, with enough scars around his heart from broken relationships and dead friends and lovers that Martha believed him when he said this last time that he was done with love.

Her phone rang. She located it under a folder on the desk, and said, "Whitaker."

"It's Lance. You doing okay?"

"Yeah." She hugged herself with her free arm. "But it's hard. Everything holds a memory. If it doesn't, it's got question marks all over it. Who would've thought that I'd laugh and cry just finding a Christmas party flyer, an old photo, a recipe, all with memories or questions?"

"It's how we grieve, Martha. It's perfectly normal. Give yourself that." He paused. "Listen, I found something I thought you should hear. It's from one of the letters that Lolich brought. It's from one Nancy Pace to 'Mama E,' dated February 26, 1870 . . . blah, blah blah, here it is: 'Do not believe rumors about my Eli. He been as willing as the next to meet his God. Only for Eli this blessed meeting come sooner and not by his own hand. He was sacrificed for doing as he was told by that scoundrel who sits on the throne of our beloved Prophet. Sacrificed for the ungodly deeds of the Elders. B. Young come all the way out to our ward and told Eli to be the Hammer with God as his Anvil, and together they could beat back the Gentiles from grabbing Deseret country. The Howland boys and that vagrant Dunne sneaked up from the canyon like spies of Satan, only they smacked up against the righteous hammer, my Eli. But the generals of the Army of Israel have agin forsook their foot soldiers, and Eli was laid upon the altar of the Lord so their hands looked clean.'"

"That's almost word for word what Piter deVries was shouting when he came out of the car," Martha whispered. "And this goes back as far as 1870?"

"Yeah. And here's another thing. When Joseph Smith and Avard Samson first created his private security force, it was called the Army of Israel, aka, the Danites. Now, at the time of this letter, some thirty years later, Brigham Young has replaced the martyred Smith, the Mormons have moved from Missouri to Utah, and yet there's *still* a reference to the 'Army of Israel.' Coincidence? I don't think so. This Nancy Pace seems certain that Brigham Young is involved in the plot and had her husband killed to keep it quiet."

"So who's Nancy Pace?"

"Mac tracked her down this morning through the church's genealogy records. The nineteenth wife—don't say it, Martha— the nineteenth wife of John D. Lee, the man behind the Mountain Meadow Massacre, was a woman named Emma. That was her diary account that Lolich brought to the hotel. So, one of John D. Lee's other wives was a woman named Rachel Woolsey, and Nancy was their daughter. Then Nancy married this guy Eli Pace."

"Nineteen wives? You've got to be kidding me."

"Martha, now's not the time."

"That'd keep him busier than Secretariat at stud."

"Maybe that was the point. But it didn't prevent him from having time to plan a raid against a wagon train of settlers passing through the area. Before he disappeared, Hewitt suggested I research John D. Lee. When Lee came under federal scrutiny for the Mountain Meadow Massacre and was excommunicated from the church, both Rachel and Emma remained faithful to him. They both thought he'd been set up by church Elders to take the fall. Lee was still alive when this letter was written, living in exile in southern Utah, but in a few years—'74, I think—he'll be turned over to the feds and executed, calling out Brigham Young with his dying words. Literally."

"But that wasn't enough to implicate Young, I take it?"

"It's easy to discredit anything a man says who's facing a firing squad."

"But it doesn't mean it wasn't true."

"Which is what Hewitt suspected. He was building a case of circumstantial evidence. If enough of it adds up, it may point to the truth. Another incident he discovered involved Lee's son-in-law, Eli Pace. In 1869, it's believed that Eli Pace, husband of Nancy, killed three non-Mormons. He mistook them for federal agents looking for Lee. But they weren't feds. They were three men from the John Wesley Powell expedition down the Grand Canyon! Two brothers named Howland and a guy named Dunne."

He paused, as if consulting his notes, and continued. "In January 1870, Eli Pace died under suspicious circumstances. It was eventually ruled a suicide. Now a month later, in February 1870, Nancy Pace is writing Mama E, telling her not to believe what she's heard, that, in truth, Brigham Young, or B. Young, as she calls him, had ordered Eli killed so as to deflect another federal investigation."

"So, one more piece of circumstantial evidence implicating

Brigham Young with the Mormon Death Squads," Martha said. "Something that somebody would like to keep very hush-hush."

Silence hung between them until, finally, Trammell asked, "Anything new on your end?"

"Nothing as juicy as what you've got," Martha said. "It just some oddity that I can't quite pin down. There're no records of Hewitt doing any business on the rare manuscripts, no files, no notes, no records of any kind on any historical documents. There're just personal accounts and information. Ralph was living in the back office at the bookstore, so Hewitt wasn't working there. He left eight documents—the letters and the diary pages—so he was obviously still working. But where was he working?"

Martha glanced about the houseboat. "I've still got a lot to sort through." She paused. "You doing okay?"

"I'm fine here, though everyone's getting tired of Molly insisting all the doors be kept locked."

"Yeah, well, they didn't get tied up in the bathroom at gunpoint. Don't get careless just because it's inconvenient."

"Backatcha. Gotta run, but I wanted to let you know one other thing." The pause was heavy, as if Trammell couldn't find the right words.

Martha was sure he was about to say Hewitt's body had been discovered.

"Mac found something else during his genealogy search: Eric Metcalf is a practicing Mormon."

She sat back, stunned. Finally, she nodded her head. So many things began to fall into place.

TWENTY-TWO

Togaard had left the bank records with his administrative assistant and disappeared. Martha wrote out an authorization to suspend all activity on Hewitt's checking account, signed in triplicate for each stack of copies, and ignored the middle-aged woman rolling her eyes over the top of her reading glasses. "Will there be anything else today, Ms. Whitaker?" she sighed. Martha understood who had been assigned the tedious task of compiling all the paperwork. She smiled and thanked her.

Back at the houseboat again, she stopped at the sight of a Pete's Supermarket grocery bag beside the front door, tucked out of the rain under the eaves. Inside, she discovered a hot dish of homemade macaroni and cheese, a Caesar's salad and a loaf of hard-crust bread. Surely, it had to be from Karen and Brownie, but there was no one on the docks, no one waved from a window to take credit for this hospitality. But Hewitt had a whole community of friends and neighbors here who had been touched by his disappearance. The aroma of the mac and cheese triggered memories of Gran, who always believed comfort food was the surest way to help you find your way when your faith in God wavered.

In the kitchen, Martha found an unbroken plate and some cutlery, washed them and dished herself a scoop of mac and cheese, a little salad and the heel of the Pugliese bread. In the far corner, she saw Dante's food remained untouched. The cat door was working properly, but still no sign of the damn cat.

The houseboat still lay in shambles—except the desk. She had placed files back in the drawers, righted the chair. It wouldn't be the first time she ate lunch at a desk. Between bites, she examined the bank documents. First, she focused on the business account. Ralph's handwritten ledger matched line for line with the account for University Rare Books and Manuscripts. Ralph had reconciled to the dollar, if not quite the penny, every month. Deposit records from the bank corresponded to deposit lines from the ledger. Ralph had made daily deposits. The smallest one was for $17.34—the Saturday after Christmas, Martha noted—and the largest for $2,822.19—the Saturday before Christmas. The best revenue days coincided with a notation on a rare book being sold: a signed first edition of *Dune*, a first edition of Mark Twain's *A Connecticut Yankee in King Arthur's Court*. Skimming the totals, Martha figured the store was bringing in an average of about $400 a day with periodic spikes that coincided with a rare book sale.

Outgoing expenses appeared straightforward: utilities, electricity, and phones. The check duplicates were all in Ralph's handwriting. To The Richard Hugo House, $500, with the memo saying "poetry slam sponsorship," and $1,000 to 826 Seattle, with the note "donation." Dozens of small checks were made out to individuals, all with the same memo, "Books." One check for $115 had the note "Bradbury—Wicked—1st" written on it.

Checks to Costco, an office supply store, and a mailing service all seemed in line with doing business. Every two weeks, Ralph paid himself $1,500 by check. He wrote himself a check for $1,000 right before Christmas, with the note "Bonus per HW." Each month, Ralph transferred everything over the six months operating expenses into Hewitt's checking account.

Nothing seemed out of the ordinary.

Martha's five-month stint as Hewitt's bookkeeper had familiarized her with his personal finances. She quickly identified that four deposits were still made each month directly into his account—Social Security, a small retirement check from the University of Washington, and rent payments from the two tenants who shared the building with the bookstore. All direct deposits, just like she had set it up. Ralph's deposit of the bookstore funds was the fifth deposit each month, regular as clockwork.

Through two years' worth of statements, only eight other deposits were made. All were for under $100 except for two, and both of those had come in during the past six months. In May of last year, Hewitt had deposited a check for $1,734, and in October a check for $1,254.89. Martha searched through the copied transactions from the bank. The first one was a personal check from Mitch Adair. The memo line had the word "reimbursements" scribbled on it. The second check was from a bank, drawn from the account of the Estate of Margaret Cunningham. Again the memo just indicated "Reimbursements." Martha had no idea who either Mitch Adair or Margaret Cunningham was.

She found a second check from Mitch Adair for $89 with the memo "Symphony Ticket."

The houseboat rolled and Martha tensed. She slid her chair back, ready to move. The houseboat surged and dropped again. The distant sound of a floatplane idling back its engine drifted in from across the lake. She waited another minute to be sure no one was using the floatplane's wake to camouflage their arrival, before returning to the checkbook ledgers.

His moorage payment and the mortgage payment for the bookstore property occurred on the first and fifteenth of each month, automatic payments, just like she had set it up. The rest of Hewitt's personal expenditures turned out to be a chaotic mess. Monthly statements didn't balance with the checkbook ledger, check numbers were out of sequence, a couple were missing altogether. Martha flipped through the check copies: drugstore, phone bill, Pete's Supermarket. Checks for as little as $6.82 and as large as $213.52. She paused at a check written to Mitch Adair for $73. She pulled it out and set it aside.

It didn't take her long to find what she was after: a check to the Institute of Forensic Anthropology for $3,892, with a memo noting "Dr. June Povich," and a second to the University of Washington's Quaternary Research Center for an even $5,000, with a memo designating it a "donation." The two checks had depleted all the extra money in his checking account, resulting in an overdraft charge for his moorage payment. Thank god she had set up overdraft protection for his accounts or his houseboat might have been cut adrift in Lake Union given the demand for the prime end spot on the dock. Martha pulled the check copies, placed them on the desk, and glanced around the floor. All the files had been reordered and placed back in the desk. None included any business invoices. Strange that Hewitt would pay $3,892 without an invoice. Reflecting on that for a moment, she decided it wasn't strange—for Hewitt.

Flipping through the check duplicates, she found a second check from eighteen months prior to the Institute for Forensic Pathology, with the memo "Dr. June Povich." Around the same time, there was a record of another donation to the UDub's Quaternary Research Center.

Martha ran a hand through her curls in frustration. She pushed back her chair and searched the houseboat for remaining files. She found none. No invoices, either. For that matter, the houseboat offered up no direct sign of Hewitt's work on the old manuscripts. He had hidden eight rare documents on the bottom of Puget Sound, and yet, here at home and at the bookstore, there was no evidence the documents existed.

After killing Hewitt, had his enemies swept up all evidence of his involvement in authenticating the rare letters? Martha doubted they could have been that thorough. The wreckage looked more like a quick and dirty search for the package Lolich had found in the water under the pier.

Did Hewitt have an office someplace else?

Then another thought occurred to her. A quick reexamination of the three bank accounts confirmed her suspicion: thousands of dollars paid out and not a penny of income recorded for Hewitt's work on the rare manuscripts. Was Hewitt researching and documenting old manuscripts for the LDS as an altruistic gesture? A gift to the Morons, as he called them? It made no sense. Did he have another bank account someplace else? Was he hiding money in the mattress? Unlikely, if he was writing $6 checks to Pete's. A missing office, missing income, a missing safe, a missing Hewitt. They couldn't all have been washed away with the outgoing tide.

The best way to deal with all the uncertainty, Martha decided, was to have a second helping of mac and cheese. Someone had used a nice four- or five-cheese recipe, and given it some tang with a liberal sprinkling of cayenne pepper. Toasted breadcrumbs on top made a satisfying crunch. She paced amid the debris while eating. The first edition of Cotton Mather's book lay near the bottom of one pile. She righted a bookcase and set the leather-bound edition on the shelf. Black spots of mold appeared along the bottom edge of the three-hundred-year-old book.

Sorting through the rubble of the living room, she found an upside-down frame under a pile of books, its glass and gilded frame broken. Two letters were displayed in the frame, both copies: a Letter of Authenticity and a letter containing the once-familiar scrawl of "A. Lincoln" in a short, congratulatory letter to Stephen Douglas for defeating him in 1858 for the Illinois senate seat. Hewitt had sold the original letter to the same Chicago collector who had screwed Ralph over the H. G. Wells first edition.

"Why that asshole?" Martha had asked.

"Let's say he paid a little more than it was worth," Hewitt said. "Caveat emptor."

With a pile of unpaid medical bills—even after Medicare—and a meager income, Hewitt had welcomed the unexpected windfall. A miser when he had no money, Hewitt was generous to a fault when he did. Ralph had received a bonus for finding the letter tucked in between the pages of an old Sandberg biography of Lincoln recently dropped off at the bookstore. Hewitt then tried to give the last of it to her to help with the down payment on the house. She had argued for him to put the money in a low-risk investment CD.

"You're the best savings account I have," he laughed. "You're high interest, my dear. I know who's going to take care of me when I'm old."

"You're old now," she said.

"And who takes care of me? You! But I plan to get older and when I do, I need you to be there, not a pile of money."

They settled on a five-year, low-interest loan. She paid it back in two.

Martha looked at the broken frame and dropped it back to the floor. The Letter of Authenticity had vindicated him and helped her buy the house, but she still wondered if it had been worth the price—Dr. Obbert's friendship. It also reminded her that the Mormon documents were meaningless without those Letters of Authenticity, something Hewitt well knew. He had told Trammell the documents were ready to be published. Hewitt would have included the letters unless he couldn't get to them on short notice. So where were they? In the missing safe?

She added LOAs to her growing list of missing items. From her briefcase, she pulled out her laptop and booted it up. Within seconds the air card found a satellite signal. She googled "Institute of Forensic Anthropology" and "Povich."

A recent conference in Phoenix, Arizona, at which Povich had presented a paper on "Analyzing Inks in Forgery Cases" to the Criminal Forensics Association of America, popped up. The second link was for the anthropology staff at Arizona State University. She was surprised to discover the name "Dr. June Povich" under a man's photo. At least it wasn't Shirley, Martha thought, and returned to her search. The third link was for the Institute of Forensic Anthropology's homepage. Two clicks and she had a phone number. Three rings and she had a person asking, "How may I direct your call?"

"Dr. June Povich, please," Martha said.

A prolonged silence told Martha this conversation was not going to unfold the way she had expected.

"Who's calling, please?" came the disembodied female voice.

"Martha Whitaker in Seattle, Washington. It's regarding a payment to Dr. Povich and the Institute from a couple of months ago."

"I will transfer you, please hold."

Canned music droned on and on, until Martha thought she might have been forgotten. Finally, another woman's voice said, "Dr. Lewis. How may I help you?"

"This is Martha Whitaker in Seattle, Washington. I'm an attorney representing the estate of Hewitt Wilcox. I'm trying to reach June Povich regarding a job he did last summer for Dr. Wilcox. I cannot find any accompanying Letters of Authenticity. I was wondering if Dr. Povich could reissue them. Without the letters, the documents in question have little value to Dr. Wilcox's heirs."

Another prolonged silence. "Dr. Lewis?" she said.

"I'm here. I'm Dr. Povich's assistant. He sent the letters out some time ago. I can verify the dates if you'd like."

"Thank you, but somehow the letters have been lost, and I need Dr. Povich to reissue them so the heirs of Mr. Wilcox's estate may put them on the market if—"

The woman interrupted her with the blunt, "I'm sorry, but Dr. Povich is dead."

Alarms clanged inside Martha's head. "May I ask what happened?" She remembered to breathe. "I ask because Mr. Wilcox has disappeared under suspicious circumstances, and it may involve the documents in question."

The hesitation on the other end of the line informed Martha that Lewis was either reluctant to discuss the matter or had been advised not to. "It looked like suicide, but now the police are questioning . . . school wasn't in session. He . . . he often worked from home so we didn't think anything of not seeing him for a few days. . . . His housecleaner found him." Her voice started to break. There was an audible sob. "But something wasn't right. Things were missing, little things, but things I knew he had in his desk, in his home safe."

"Such as?" Martha wondered. "Money, jewelry, valuables?"

"No, no, he kept a log at his desk to track the work he was doing from home. That was missing. Work papers were gone and an old diary he was analyzing for ASU."

"When did all of this happen, Dr. Lewis?"

"Right after New Year's."

"So sometime in the past three or four weeks. I assume they did an autopsy?"

"Death by strangulation, consistent with hanging."

"But nothing else?"

"My God, there didn't have to be anything else," she wailed. "June was seventy-one and didn't weigh a hundred and fifty pounds. I could have hung him from a light fixture if I had caught him by surprise."

"I'm sorry," Martha said, her voice quiet. "I know this is difficult. I'm just concerned about some of the similarities between the death of Dr. Povich and my client, Dr. Wilcox."

The sobbing was faint, as if the professor had covered the receiver with her hand. Martha waited, then asked quietly, "Did you know Dr. Wilcox?"

"I've met him a few times over the years. June introduced us at a conference."

"Did you work with Dr. Povich on the documents from Dr. Wilcox? It would have been sometime last year. There were at least eight of them and they were all from the middle of the nineteenth century. Letters or journal entries from the Mormons living in Utah at the time."

"No, I didn't. I was doing field research when Dr. Wilcox brought them down. June told me about them, but I didn't see them. I don't think there were eight of them, unless Dr. Wilcox sent them in different batches."

"Why's that?"

"June said he was working on a couple of letters for Dr. Wilcox. He wouldn't say 'a couple of letters' if there were eight. But I know he received documents from Dr. Wilcox on a pretty regular basis, so they could have come in over a period of time."

"You say Dr. Wilcox brought the letters down. Did he usually deliver the documents in person to Dr. Povich?"

"Not always, but on occasion. It was an excuse to get together and talk shop and maybe go out. They enjoyed each other's company."

Martha flashed on the image of Ralph Hargrove, dead, his genitals stuffed in his mouth. "Were they lovers?"

"It was none of my business."

"I understand. Do you know anything about the Letters of Authenticity?"

"I could find the dates they were issued, get you copies, but I can't reissue the originals. The documents would have to be analyzed all over again."

"But they were issued?"

"I'm sure of it."

Martha had one last question. "When was the last time you remember seeing or talking to Dr. Wilcox?"

"I called him a couple of weeks ago with the news of June's death. As a courtesy, mainly, because I knew they were friends. But, also, because he had another couple of documents with the IFA that June hadn't authenticated yet. I wondered if he wanted me to finish the job for him."

"What did he say?"

"He was pretty shaken by the news of June's death and said he'd get back to me, but not to do anything for the moment. God, now you say he's dead, too?"

"Missing," Martha said. "Presumed dead. Under suspicious circumstances."

When she rang off, Martha hit Callison on her speed dial. The police officer picked up on the second ring. She informed him of the checks written to the Institute of Forensic

Anthropology and the Quaternary Research Center, and how he might want to expand his investigation to include the recent death of Dr. June Povich, a professor of forensic anthropology at Arizona State.

Sitting back in the chair, Martha tried to calm her pounding heart. Now, at least, she knew what had scared Hewitt so much. He had seen the Death Angels coming for him next.

TWENTY-THREE

The afternoon daylight had nearly disappeared when Martha closed her umbrella outside the main entrance to Johnson Hall, a four-story brick building on the University of Washington's old campus. To the west, clouds towered black and ominous. She shivered, but not from cold.

From the direction of Red Square, a tall, lanky figure strode toward her in the now-familiar yellow rain jacket. Each step splashed water against his worn jeans. No one seemed to be following him, no shadows lurked in doorways. He bounded up the steps, two at a time, and wrapped her in a tight hug.

"You okay?" Dark eyes widened with concern. Water dripped off his hood and onto his nose. Gaunt and unshaven, Trammell looked like a refugee.

She remembered her text: "Found nother body. If still at U, meet Johnson Hll 4pm." She said, "I'm fine. I should've been more clear."

Trammell pulled open the heavy wooden door to Johnson Hall. "Why are we here?"

Scanning Red Square, Martha didn't answer. A student in a

hoodie sprinted through the rain toward the Suzzallo Library. A man in a trench coat strode up the main path from Drumheller Fountain, his face hidden by a black umbrella. He carried a briefcase and wore black boots. High-top boots, well polished. Military boots. A hard shove propelled Trammell through the open door. She jumped in behind him. Military Boots kept marching toward Red Square, his pace chewing up the rain-soaked path.

She turned and saw Trammell pressed against the wall, ready to move at her signal. To his unspoken question, she said, "Probably just jitters. You okay?"

His shoulders relaxed. "Fine. I trust your instincts." Trammell smiled. "And you didn't knock me out this time."

More than the smile, Martha saw the intensity of his gaze. Without questions or bravado, he had reacted to her actions, he had followed her lead. Trust was such a precious gift. She didn't know if she had earned it or deserved it.

They moved up the steps together and started down the empty hall. "I still don't get why we're here," Trammell said.

"In the past eighteen months, Hewitt wrote four checks, two to the Institute of Forensic Anthropology and two to the Quaternary Research Center, here in Johnson Hall." Martha stopped at a building directory. "Third floor."

On the elevator, she continued, "I don't know if they're related. The check memo said 'donation,' but each time there was a check written to the IFA in Tempe, there was a second check written to this research facility. Right after New Year's, the professor Hewitt was working with in Tempe was found dead. A suicide. Only his closet colleague doesn't believe it for an instant. I only hope we don't find the same here."

After a half hour wait, Martha explained the situation for the third time, this time to the Center's director, a large, slovenly man with the sartorial discretion of a dirty laundry basket. Through thick glasses, he gave her a look of bewilderment. But he didn't get to be the director by being entirely clueless. Pressing a button, he said, "Gladys, would you join us for a moment?"

A petite woman with a shocking mane of short, snow-white hair listened to Martha's fourth explanation about the check donated to the Quaternary Research Center. Gladys didn't even glance at the check. "Of course. It's a gift from Dr. Wilcox for work that Dr. Martoni did for him. It's funny you should ask. I just talked to a guy named Metcalf from the Seattle Police Department. He was asking about the same thing."

"Metcalf?" Martha managed to remain calm. "Could you tell us where Dr. Martoni's office is?"

"He said he was following up a lead."

"Maxine Martoni?" the director asked.

"Yeah, Max," Gladys said. "Do you know another Martoni? Dr. Wilcox worked frequently with her." She turned back to Martha. "Her office is over at the Burke Museum, but she uses our labs, mostly for carbon dating and spectral analysis. If payment for those services comes in under a donation it's easier to keep the money in the program without upsetting our budget." She glanced at her watch. "They don't close for another fifteen minutes."

"Thank you." Martha hurried toward the door.

"You said they worked together a lot over the years," Trammell said, turning back. "How many times, would you guess?"

"Oh, ten to twelve, maybe more," Gladys said. "Professor Wilcox was always generous with his donations."

Martha and Trammell jogged across Red Square and past the towering west façade of the Suzzallo Library. The tall stained-glass windows cast multicolored hues into the dark evening. Martha ignored the rain. Trammell pulled up the hood of his rain jacket. "Christ, I'm tired of this shit," he said, the breaths coming easily as he stayed beside her. "I've got moss growing down my back."

"Some sunshine would be nice," Martha replied. "And I would love to go snorkeling in warm water."

She pulled up to a fast walk. Her legs felt like lead. God, how could she sustain a half hour workout with Yamamoto but not a five-minute jog? Streetlights made pale halos of the drizzle. Nothing seemed more appealing and more remote than sunshine. Hawaii maybe. Cabo San Lucas. Anywhere but here. Would she invite Trammell to join her? The fact she even entertained the thought surprised her. Together, on a vacation?

Of course. A vacation. It had been right in front of her the whole time and she hadn't seen it. She stopped short.

Trammell turned on his heels, his eyes darting from building to building. "What?"

"I think Hewitt had a new boyfriend," Martha announced. "A guy named Mitch Adair. Money went back and forth between them on several occasions, as if each had to pay his own way on a vacation, on a date to the symphony. It was right in front of me, but I didn't see it until now. Who's Mitch Adair?"

Lights from the Burke Museum of Natural History and Culture were visible ahead. In the distance, headlights zoomed in and out of view along the arterial that ran through the U District. Trammell and Martha climbed the steps two at a time toward the museum's main entrance. Halfway up, they were greeted by a carved orca whose proportions were life-size, except for an exaggerated dorsal fin. A movement behind it brought Martha to an abrupt halt. Trammell froze. Someone who hadn't been there seconds ago was hurrying off in the opposite direction. Trench coat, black umbrella, briefcase. Martha didn't need to check for the black military boots.

"That guy—either he's following us or is one step ahead," she said.

The man vanished behind a giant Douglas fir in a grove of trees. Trammell broke into a run. His silhouette popped out of the trees at the street. Without hesitation, Military Boots darted between oncoming cars. Horns blared. Trammell hit the street right behind him. A long, loud squeal of brakes followed.

Racing to catch up, Martha saw Trammell tumble over the hood of a car and drop out of sight. She had nearly reached the street when he popped up on the far side of the car. Traffic came to a screeching halt. The driver of the car came out shouting and waving his arms. They ignored him. The night had swallowed Military Boots whole.

Martha glanced back at the well-lit museum. "Lance, come on," she yelled, gesturing at him. She ran back and together they charged up the steps.

"You okay?" she shouted, though he was right beside her.

"Yeah," he gasped.

The lobby was empty except for the tall skeleton of a hooked-beak raptor. The tiny gift store was deserted. A sign on the front counter listed the rates for entry, but no one was there to take payment.

"Hello," Trammell called out, his voice booming. "Anyone here?"

The echo bounced back off walls and glass. Martha peeked over the counter, half afraid of finding another Ralph Hargrove sprawled out on the floor. Nothing. No signs of a struggle. Papers were neatly stacked, the cash register was closed, and a padded chair was tucked under the counter as if the last person had left for the day.

"Check the basement," she whispered. "Be sure to check the bathrooms. I'll check the main floor. Yell if you find something."

Trammell split off. Martha dashed across the lobby to the Burke Room. With chairs neatly stacked against the walls, the conference room was deserted. She threw open closet doors and looked behind a lectern.

Returning to the lobby, Martha stood motionless beside the "Terror Bird of Brazil." An eerie stillness pervaded the place. Museums were never completely empty. There were always clerks and docents and maintenance people, even when no patrons filled the floors, but no noise filtered through to the lobby, no footsteps coming or going, no distant voices. The place was a mausoleum.

The floor sparkled from the overhead lights and it took her a moment to realize the glass on the Northwest Native Treasures display case had been shattered. An empty hole glared at her like a witch's eye. A placard indicated a Gwasila tribal mask was missing. A second empty space caught her attention. A Tlingit knife was gone. Was this a robbery? A dozen other items remained untouched. The mask and dagger could have fit into Military Boots' briefcase.

Martha ran into the first room of exhibits. A prehistoric whale skeleton stared at her with its empty eye sockets. She sprinted on, nearly overturning a display case of fossilized crabs. She caught it before it crashed to the floor.

Then she saw the blood. The crimson trail led to an inert body propped up against the leg of a giant mastodon. The Gwasila tribal mask covered the face, and blood gathered in a puddle around the body. The carved bear-head handle was the only visible part of the missing Tlingit dagger—it protruded from the person's chest.

The person was small and light and completely unresponsive. Martha laid the body flat and flipped the wooden mask off, coming face-to-face with another kind of mask, the death mask of an Asian woman, her eyes closed, her mouth set in the same exaggerated "Ooooh" as the Gwasila carving.

TWENTY-FOUR

The flashing lights turned patches of her bloody suit brown. Martha leaned forward on the lobby bench, rubbing her bloody hands like Lady Macbeth. Trammell sat beside her, but she had shrugged off his attempts at comfort. She had been so close to preventing this murder, so close to discovering what was behind this whole nightmare.

She glanced up. Callison stood at the center of a group of police officers clustered in the lobby—some in uniforms, Metcalf in an expensive suit, many in civilian clothes. Everyone was talking. The flashing lights and din of voices made it feel like a night at the carnival.

Out of the group, the short, squat figure of Bess Corvari chop-stepped her way toward them.

"Hey, guys," she said. Out of uniform, she wore a faded University of Washington hoodie with frayed cuffs and a pair of low-riding jeans. "Callison's undermanned, so he called me in to work with his Homicide team. I need to ask you some questions. I'll start with you, Martha. Lance, give us some space. Just not too much."

Martha answered Corvari's questions in a monotone. She took her through the course of her afternoon—the bank, the conversation with Dr. Lewis, the visit with the director of the Quaternary Research Center, the phone call from Metcalf—not hesitating on details, not offering opinions.

Corvari paused at the mention of Metcalf. "Our Metcalf? From the SPD?"

Martha never looked at the policewoman who had just shared nearly two weeks of her life. She just nodded. Corvari tucked the notebook into the back pocket of her jeans and said, "Let's get you out of that jacket, honey."

Corvari removed her hoodie and helped Martha out of her ruined suit jacket and then her blood-soaked blouse, using her bulk as a protective screen. Martha submitted to her ministrations. Corvari pulled Martha's ebony hair out of the sweatshirt and announced, "Well, you have plenty of room to grow into it."

Martha peered at Corvari as if seeing her for the first time. Her throat felt like sandpaper as she rasped, "Thank you, Bess."

The policewoman stood there in a simple white T-shirt, as nonchalant as if it had been the middle of summer instead of winter. For the first time, Martha noticed both arms were completely covered in tattoos that stopped abruptly where the cuffs of a long-sleeve shirt would be buttoned. She wore a gun in a holster in the small of her back.

"Don't worry a New York second about that," Corvari said. "I've got more UDub hoodies than Trammell has turtlenecks." She paused. "You're gonna be okay, honey."

Dr. Martoni was dead. Dr. Povich was dead. Hewitt was missing, presumed dead. She had blood on her suit and her hands. She could purchase new suits. Blood would wash away with soap and water. She would sleep tonight, and she would wake up in the morning still trying to figure out what was going on. The only sleep left for the good professors and her long-time friend was the final one that awaited everyone.

Someone was sobbing, and the volume suddenly increased. It was one of the museum employees Trammell had found tied up in the downstairs bathroom. A couple of uniformed cops were taking statements.

"It's the same MO as the newspaper," Martha said. "Remember he tied up the nonessentials in the bathroom?"

"Yeah, I remember," Corvari said.

"He was wearing black military boots. You might be able to find some foot prints."

"Yeah, we're on it." She paused. "But you're sure the lady said Eric Metcalf?"

Martha again only nodded.

Corvari strode over to Callison, still at the center of the group. Separating him from the rest, she spoke to him for a moment. Martha couldn't hear the words but knew what Corvari was saying. Metcalf, Eric Metcalf. Callison towered over the younger woman by a head. The muscles on his neck bulged. He listened for a moment, and then spoke through clenched teeth.

The detective whirled away, and Martha caught a glimpse of Metcalf suddenly left standing alone with Callison. They spoke for a moment, the tension between them obvious, even if Martha couldn't hear the words. Arms akimbo, Metcalf shook his head and snapped a last comment. Metcalf pivoted and stomped toward the door. His eyes met Martha's for an instant. They were full of rage.

Callison was yelling at someone and pointing toward where Martha had found the dead anthropologist. Having overcome her first impression of the brutish detective, she had grown to like him. The "Gifts for the Terminally Bored" had been a gesture of empathy and understanding not offered by any of the other officers, including the very likable Corvari. Despite his scruffy appearance, Callison had a professionalism that was missing when Metcalf led the investigation. Still, he was playing catch-up late in the game.

She was surprised when, amid the chaos swirling in the museum lobby, Callison approached and sat beside her on the bench.

"You okay?" His voice was quiet. "That's a horrible thing for anyone to go through."

"I'll be okay, thanks."

"Someone's upped the ante," Callison said. "At the newspaper office, Corvari tells me the operation was much the same, but they were just trying to scare you. Now, they're killing people. The guy from the bookstore. Now this. So what's changed?"

"But that's not right," Martha said. "Dr. Povich was the first person killed. That happened before the attack at the newspaper, before any of this started. That's what scared Hewitt, I'm sure. He got the phone call from Povich's colleague and knew his death wasn't a suicide. He understood. He knew they'd be coming after him. He called me to meet on the pier within two days of talking to Arizona."

"Then why didn't he warn Martoni?"

"Maybe he did. Maybe she didn't believe him. Maybe she didn't think it would happen this fast. Maybe—"

"Or maybe he bolted without telling anyone anything," Callison said. "He slithered out the back door, leaving everyone else in front of the firing squad."

"But where's the evidence for that? There's no body, there's no murder weapon. Then there's the trashed houseboat. What makes you think that Hewitt's not dead, and you just haven't found him yet?"

"Maybe all we have is a lot of maybes," Callison said, large hands running through his dark hair until it took on the Einstein look. "What we need is something concrete."

"Did you call the Tempe police?"

"I assigned it to Metcalf. He talked to them, and he talked to someone here at the U. That's why the lady mentioned his name. He was in a meeting with me, Martha, when this was all going down. I wanted to know why no one on this case had ever heard of Povich or Martoni. Someone's not just a step ahead of us; they're running laps around us. I'm getting pretty damn tired of it."

Martha took a breath, working up her courage. "Or they had heard of Povich and Martoni, and they weren't telling."

"What do you mean?"

"Think about it. The unfriendlies are getting information from somewhere. It wasn't twelve hours before Danny Kimble knew Metcalf had been assigned to the case and had himself an authentic-looking Seattle police ID. I'm sitting in an interrogation cell when Metcalf informs me that I'm now owner of a dusty old bookstore in the U District and the building where it's located. Metcalf knew Hewitt owned the building before he made his first accusation against me. The next morning, Metcalf tries to blame me for Ralph Hargrove's death. I call you this afternoon to say check out Povich. You assign it to Metcalf. Less than an hour later, someone in military boots kills Dr. Martoni. What is the one common denominator running through all of this? Eric Metcalf."

"That's a serious accusation," Callison said. "And I don't take it lightly. But the same series of coincidences that you cite against Metcalf, he's holds up against you. What do you think he was just telling me? You're holed up incommunicado for a dozen days under police protection, and nothing happens. You and Trammell take a hike, and people start dying again. That makes a homicide detective pause, even a slow one like me."

"Of course he would. Did you ever consider it might have been a set up? Who fought the hardest against putting Trammell and me in that hotel? Detective Metcalf. He claimed he had no resources, no manpower. He fought with two superior officers about it. Our going into protective custody had to slow his attempt to eliminate all evidence of the documents and the people who knew about them. By the way, did your resident choirboy tell you that he might actually have belonged to the Mormon Tabernacle Choir? He's a Mormon, Callison. Born in Provo, Utah, to a long-standing Mormon clan, graduated from BYU, had his first job as a cop in Orem, Utah. The LDS are quite thorough with their genealogy research, and a couple of minutes on Google fills in the blanks. Someone from the LDS is desperately trying to prevent these documents from seeing the light of day. And it sure as hell looks like they're getting their information from someone inside."

Callison leaned forward, his voice a harsh whisper. "Or someone in a financial crisis thinks these documents are a lot more valuable being sold back to the Church rather than being published in the newspaper. How much would they be worth to the Mormons if they could bury them forever? I have no idea, but that might be an interesting question to ask. And, this same someone is now sleeping with the paper's head dude. Coincidence? Keeping a close eye on him and everything he knows? This someone also lied to me about where she was going to be last night. Imagine my surprise when the Port police informed me your boat wasn't in its slip in the marina. In fact, it wasn't anywhere in the marina."

"Last minute change of plans." Martha snorted with contempt. "Since the police haven't been able to protect anyone yet, why would I be so naïve to think anything's changed?" She shook her head. "So Metcalf's convinced you that I'm the prime suspect here. I thought there was at least one smart cop working this case."

"Seems stupid is a contagious disease, Whitaker. You didn't think we were smart enough to be told about the key and the postcard. You withhold evidence, beat up an officer or two, meddle in a major murder investigation. Framing a cop isn't such a big step from that. And you wonder why we're having a hard time believing anything you tell us."

Having started, Callison seemed unable to stop. He perched on the edge of the bench, his face turning red as he spat out the words. "Metcalf hasn't convinced me you're behind this any more than you've convinced me that a Seattle cop is involved. My job is to consider all possibilities. That means you. That means Trammell. It means Hewitt Wilcox may be dead or he may not be. I don't believe or disbelieve any of it until I've got proof one way or the other."

"You know what else the choirboy pointed out to me? How did our perps know Trammell and his newspaper were involved? You were the only one who had met him. Metcalf had never heard of him until *after* the break-in at the newspaper."

"That's ludicrous, Callison. Check my cell phone. You're the effing police; you can run the records. You won't find any frantic calls the night I met Trammell, you won't find any calls to shady associates. And you won't find any calls to Arizona. I've got nothing to hide. You know where I live. Get a warrant, search it, have forensics dust it for fingerprints. Hell, you don't even need a warrant. You have my permission. Just go for it. But, hell, you've probably already done that anyway. You'll find my prints and yours and Rebecca's. You'll find lots of cat hair and some sawdust. I never heard of Povich or Martoni until this afternoon, and Povich was killed weeks ago. If someone knew about Povich, it was because they'd been investigating Hewitt and who he saw to get the documents authenticated. They probably also knew he had met with Trammell about getting them published." She paused. "And I suppose the Hammer of God was a decoy? I set him up and had him killed so I'd get more of the cut?"

"No honor among thieves," Callison retorted. "Doesn't it seem odd that a bunch of supposed professionals can't seem to shoot straight when they're aiming at you?"

Martha rose, snapping the zipper of Corvari's hoodie up tight to her throat. She offered him her wrists. "It's time to either handcuff me or let me go. I've heard enough of your accusations for one night. Should I call my lawyer? He would love to join us at the table. You might want to ask Metcalf how that went. In the meantime, Military Boots, Danny Kimble, and the masked man are still running free. I wonder who'll be their next target— me? Trammell? Someone we don't even know about yet? This case might just solve itself if they run out of people to kill."

"You're better than that, Whitaker." Callison stood. They stood eye to eye but his bulk made her feel frail, vulnerable. "You can help us, but we're not here to help you in your private investigation. If you find something or have a brain fart in the middle of the night that might be relevant, you tell me and only me. If the old man calls you in the middle of the night full of mea culpas, you call me and only me. If one of the creeps comes visiting in the middle of the night, you don't kill him; you call me. Otherwise, if you don't want to go back into lockup, stay out of my fucking investigation. Take Trammell and go check into a beach cabin under an assumed name or something. But tell me where you're going, and then be there. I will check."

TWENTY-FIVE

Martha stormed out of the Burke, only to run into Metcalf standing under the wide overhang, a cell phone pressed to his ear. Hard-won restraint kept her moving despite a fervent desire to push his nose out the back of his smug face. She charged down the stairs past the carved orca, afraid of what she might do if she hesitated.

"Martha, wait," Trammell shouted.

She spun around. He had followed her out of the museum, and now shrugged into his rain jacket.

"Trammell, hold up a sec," Metcalf called out.

Martha continued down the sidewalk. In a minute, Trammell came jogging up beside her.

"Did he tell you to watch your back?" Martha snapped, eating up the sidewalk in long, hurried strides.

"Yeah, he did—but he said 'you guys be careful.' It was pretty specific. 'You guys.' Gave me his cell phone number if we need to contact him directly."

"Did he tell you that he's got Callison thinking that I'm behind the break-in at your office or that I'm sleeping with you just to keep an eye on you? Which, of course, means he still thinks I'm behind Hewitt's disappearance, the murders, all of it."

"Matter of fact, he didn't. Didn't sound like that at all. Actually said 'good sleuthing' about finding Povich. Of course, he didn't say thanks or anything else remotely civil. But, it is Metcalf, after all. *Is* that why you're sleeping with me?"

"Fuck you, Lance."

"Come on. It was a joke."

"Yeah. Hilarious. A woman's dead, I'm covered in blood, the police think I'm responsible. Ha ha. Take the stand-up routine elsewhere. I've got work to do."

"Martha, I'm sorry." Trammell reached for her hand, but she pulled it away. "We've come this far together. Let's finish it together. Besides, how do you know that's not why *I'm* sleeping with *you?*"

She rolled her eyes, but this time when he clasped her hand, she let him.

For a few minutes, they walked side by side, through the puddles, across the wet grass. They were true Seattleites, walking without an umbrella in the rain as if God's tears didn't fall on them.

Parked at the ramp to Hewitt's houseboat, Martha and Trammell sat quietly, alert to any movement in the shadows. Lights from Pete's Supermarket spilled out into the night. Her anger had been replaced by a quiet determination. If Metcalf's cynicism had now infected Callison, then she would clear her name herself.

She glanced at Trammell. He too studied the darkness for any hidden threats. With him, she felt the slaking of a long thirst. Yet, she still found herself hesitant to reach out to him. What was she afraid of? Loss of freedom? Maybe just loss. The blood on her jacket could just as easily have been Trammell's. When he rolled over the hood of that car.

Martha turned off the car. Her growling stomach told her it had been a long time since her small lunch. She nudged Trammell. "Watch my back. I'm going to buy a bottle of wine to go with dinner. They carry a nice Pinot Noir."

She grabbed her briefcase and splashed her way toward the store. Inside, she headed to the back and stopped in front of the store's best wine selection. Karen Brown, the sleeves of her Pete's sweatshirt rolled up to her tanned elbows, was kneeling, stocking a new shipment. She looked up with tired eyes and smiled.

"Oh, hi," she said, rising. "Any word on Hewitt?"

Martha shook her head. "I'm sorry."

Karen nodded. "Did you get the hot dish I left on the houseboat? Thought you might need a little comfort food."

"Oh, that was you! Thank you so much. We're going to go finish it right now. I saw you carried the Beaux Freres Pinot Noir from Oregon. I thought it'd go nicely with the mac and cheese."

"Nice choice." Karen checked the shelf, moved a couple of bottles, and then turned. She yelled toward the open office door. "Hey, Brownie, you sell the last Beaux Freres Pinot?"

A voice came back, "Yeah, last night. To Kat and Nat."

Turning back to Martha, she said, "I've got a nice Et Fille Pinot Noir you might want to try. It's light, but the flavor is still intense. It's what we drink at home."

"Then it's what we'll drink."

Brownie popped out of the office in a pair of khaki cargo shorts, his spindly legs covered in white long johns and ending in wool socks and Gore-Tex hiking boots. He buried his hands deep in his pockets. He said, "Any news?"

"No, nothing new," Martha lied, trying to emphasize it with a weary smile.

Karen shook her head. "My goodness, what's it been, two weeks now? What are the police doing?"

"It's January, the water's cold, and we've had some big tidal flushes with the new moon. They can't make . . ." She trailed off.

"How can the police have nothing?" Brownie said. "His car's found in the Sound, someone's ransacked his boat, and they have nothing?"

"Oh, they do," Martha said. "Me. I'm the person with the motive. I inherit Hewitt's estate if he dies. The police have practically accused me of orchestrating Hewitt's disappearance. None of it's true, but why let details get in the way of a good theory?" She paused. "You don't remember anything else that Hewitt might've said or anything he might've hinted at when he was here?"

Brownie's head glistened as he shook it. "Nothing. I've been over it with you and a Detective Metcalf and some guy named Callison. Told them I helped Hewitt package up a bundle, which they knew because my fingerprints were all over it. That he scribbled a note on the back of that postcard. I mean, I don't know anything else."

Martha leaned close. "Scribbled a note. What note?"

"On the back of the postcard."

"There was nothing written on the card when I found it in the houseboat."

"Then it must have been on the other half, the one he taped to the envelope."

"Oh, Christ," Martha muttered to herself. She had dropped to one knee and was searching through her briefcase. She flipped through pockets until she found the white envelope with half a postcard of Pete's Supermarket taped to the front. Once she had made the match of the two halves of the postcard, she had been anxious to look at what was inside the envelope, but had never looked further at the part taped to the envelope. Now, she found an edge and carefully removed it.

Karen and Brownie went still, as if afraid to breathe. Martha turned the card over and read aloud: "Turn, Beatrice, O turn your holy eyes upon your faithful one who, that he might see you, has come so far."

Several seconds of utter silence followed her reading of the line. Fucking Hewitt, Martha raged to herself. Another goddamn cryptic message to decipher when what she needed was a straightforward pronouncement.

Brownie said what they were all thinking. "What the hell does that mean?"

A long-ago memory came to her. Hewitt had used the line when Martha arrived at his houseboat with two black kittens nestled in a shoebox. Nearly identical, brother and sister. Hewitt kept the brother, named him Dante, and Martha took home the sister, Beatrice, the two cats forever linked with the line which she now recited, "Turn, Beatrice, O turn your holy eyes upon your faithful one who, that he might see you, has come so far. Out of grace, do us this grace; unveil your lips to him, so that he may discern the second beauty you have kept concealed."

"It's from Dante," she said. "The angels in the Earthly Paradise are asking Beatrice to show her face to Dante."

Brownie looked at her as if she had just escaped from the asylum. She added, "Dante, the Italian poet from the Middle Ages, not Hewitt's cat."

But it referred to the cat, Martha was sure. She read the line again. How could Beatrice the cat turn her eyes upon her faithful Dante? Only if Beatrice came to Dante. Or, if Dante came to her. But Martha hadn't been able to find Dante despite searching for him on at least three occasions. And, if she found Dante, why would it matter if Beatrice beheld him? Martha looked up.

Could it be? It had to be.

She glanced at the Browns, "I'm sorry, I have to go. I think I know what it means. I mean, I don't have any idea what it means. I just think I know where we have to go to find out."

The goodbyes were short, the Et Fille Pinot Noir forgotten.

Martha navigated back toward Ballard. A Tom Waits tune played on the radio. The steady *thwack thwack* of the windshield wipers supplied the rhythm for her thoughts. She explained to Trammell what little she could guess: Hewitt was delivering a message through Dante, something only Martha would understand in case the postcard was discovered by someone else.

"But I thought you couldn't find the cat," Trammell said.

"I don't think I was looking in the right place," she replied. "If Beatrice is supposed to turn her holy eyes on her faithful one, then Dante the cat needs to be where Beatrice the cat is. And that's at my place."

"In Ballard?"

"Yeah. Hewitt and I adopted a brother and a sister from the same litter. Hewitt had just come through cancer treatment and was having a hard time. He was feeling blue. A dog wouldn't have worked because he didn't have the strength to walk it. So I went to the pound and found these two rescue kittens. They weren't more than six or eight weeks old. Hewitt named them Dante and Beatrice. He kept Dante, and I have Beatrice, as long as I continue to open cans of food for her every day."

Trammell was silent for a time, watching the dark road pass. Finally, he said, "Which means Hewitt must have dropped Dante off at your place sometime before he disappeared. And he wouldn't have done that unless he knew he wasn't coming back."

Martha nodded. It could only mean Hewitt was afraid

he'd be killed, or he planned to run away. All he had and all he would ever have was the here and now—his books, his lovers, his friends—and he had every intention of holding on to them like a captain on a sinking ship. Whenever faced with the stark reality of his own mortality, he had a favorite quote. She glanced at Trammell's dark face silhouetted against the passing lights. "Do you know who said, 'Do not go gentle into that good night / Old age should burn and rave at close of day / Rage, rage against the dying of the light'?"

"Dylan Thomas."

"I think Hewitt's alive. He didn't believe in going gentle into the good night. He didn't go gentle into Puget Sound. And no one drove him into it either. I think he ran away."

"Because he wouldn't have left you Dante otherwise?"

She nodded again. "Hewitt took great pride in being a coward. He always joked the best way to face danger was to use your legs. To run away."

"Where would he run to?"

"I don't know. It's the same thing I told Callison. Someplace remote, someplace where he could be an eccentric old hermit."

Lady Gaga came on the radio. Martha punched in a new station. A Boccherini violin concerto gave them space to think.

"But sometimes danger gives a person courage," Trammell said. "Even a coward."

"It's possible, I suppose, but I don't think so."

"He'd just run away and leave you and his bookstore manager and Dr. Martoni and God knows who else to face these creeps? That certainly fits my definition of a coward."

"Or he didn't know they'd come after us. Maybe he thought they were only after him, and if he disappeared, things would die down. Maybe we'll get some answers when I get home."

Behind them, she could make out nothing but headlights.

She made a last-second turn onto a residential street and slowed down, keeping an eye on the rearview mirror. She wound north through several blocks packed tight with cars. No one followed. She merged onto a different arterial and resumed the trip toward home. They drove the rest of the way in silence, accompanied by "Autumn" from Vivaldi's *Four Seasons*.

Martha drove past the house, circled the block, and went down the hill. She pulled into an alley and parked in the deep shade of a garage and an untended hedge. "There's a flashlight in the glove box."

They walked back to the street. Farther down the hill, the distant lights of Shilshole Bay Marina lined up in rows as straight as a runway. At the trail entrance, Martha slung the strap to her briefcase over her shoulder and said, "Stay close. It'll be muddy." She shined the flashlight on the ground and began scrambling up the hillside, taking the switchbacks without slowing down, moving around puddles when she could, walking through them when they covered the trail. Corvari's sweatshirt was soon soaked, and Martha along with it. Trammell slipped once, cursing under his breath. Martha paused while he regained his balance.

At the top of the ravine, she came to an abrupt halt, and Trammell ran up against her back. She whispered, "We're here. That's my place to the right."

The garage was dark, but a light shone from the Carriage House living room. Nothing stirred. The only sound was the patter of rain falling on the metal roof of the garage.

After a couple of minutes, she whispered, "Let's go."

Like prowlers, they scurried across the yard to the shadows of the garage and crept along the wall. Martha was about to turn the corner to the front of the garage and the door to the stairwell when something in her peripheral vision caught her attention.

It came from above. She looked up at the trees. Not a branch stirred. She realized a light reflecting off the trees had suddenly gone out. Voices and footsteps were coming down the steps. She pressed tight against the wall. Trammell followed her lead.

The door opened, and Martha heard the lyrical voice of Callison's daughter, Rebecca.

"But it's not right, Mama," the girl said.

"What's not right is your being out so late, young lady" came a mature woman's voice in response. "Do you have the key?"

"Yeah. But Daddy can't help it when he has to work late."

"We seem to have our roles mixed up here, sweetie. I'm the one who's supposed to say that. This was not one of your father's better ideas. This lady lives in a garage and we live in a basement. I'm not sure which is worse."

"But I can buy all my school clothes now, all by myself. I have my own money." The girl paused. "Something's wrong with Beatrice. I just know it, even if you don't believe me."

"Honey, Beatrice is a cat. She's fine. She's still eating; she's still using her cat box."

"But she wouldn't come out, and Daddy said I was supposed to tell him if anything unusual happened," Rebecca insisted.

"I don't think Beatrice hiding in the laundry basket is exactly what he had in mind."

"But she ran away when I tried to brush her. That's not like Beatrice. She likes me."

"I'm sure it's all fine, honey. Come now, it's late and tomorrow's a school day."

Martha heard the snap of the lock and footsteps on the gravel as they walked away. She poked her head around the corner of the Carriage House.

Something rubbed against her leg, and Martha nearly jumped into Trammell's arms. She glanced down and saw Beatrice, soaking wet from a prowl through the woods. She picked her up and kissed her pink nose. The cat's sandpaper tongue licked Martha's nose.

"So you've been taking care of your brother? Well, I think I know where he's hiding."

Martha put the cat under her sweatshirt and rubbed her vigorously. She waited until she heard an engine start. Lights flashed on and a car pulled away from the street. With Beatrice under her shirt, Martha unlocked the door. She felt, more than heard, the familiar, comforting rumble of the cat purring against her rib cage.

Martha led Trammell up the staircase with the small beam from the flashlight. "That was Callison's daughter. And his wife, I presume. Rebecca's been feeding my cat."

"That's another way of keeping an eye on things, I suppose," Trammell replied.

Martha stopped at the top of the stairs. "You think so? Would Callison expose his daughter to that kind of risk if he thought something might happen here?"

"No one would suspect it."

"Really? People are getting killed and he uses his daughter to monitor my place?" She paused. "And me?"

"He's got to think she's not in any danger, but he might be using her for information."

"But everyone in this case is in danger."

Before he could answer, she pushed open the upper door and released Beatrice from her sweatshirt. The cat scampered across the floor, disappearing in the dark room. She didn't turn on any lights. Rebecca or her mother had overridden the timer when they had turned off the lights. Martha disappeared into the bathroom. In moments, she came back, cradling two black cats.

"Lance, meet the missing Dante," Martha said, lifting the

head of the second cat. "He must have followed Beatrice in through the cat door. Her collar unlocks it, and little brother must've scooted in right behind her. That's why Rebecca thought Beatrice was going through so much cat food. She's been feeding two cats. I owe her more money."

She sat on the sofa, petting Dante until he started to purr. "So what message are you delivering for Hewitt? What message can you deliver with a cat? Or is the cat the message?"

"Maybe it's both," Trammell said, perching on the edge of the sofa. "Check his collar."

Martha's fingers ran around the collar, finding nothing except his nametag. She turned the beam of the flashlight onto the metal tag.

"Here's our message." She unsnapped the collar and handed it to Trammell, directing enough light in his direction for him to read:

4 Ebenezer Lane
Tropic, UT 98117
37° 36' 43.20
112° 8' 24.00

"What the hell?" Trammell said, holding the tag up to study. He turned it over. On the other side was only the word "Dante."

Martha stared at her soaked skirt and muddy shoes. Where the hell was Tropic, Utah? And what did that have to do with Hewitt? Was it one more connection with the LDS? She was getting fucking tired of Hewitt's games. Did he think they were in a John le Carré thriller? Petting Dante, who had been delivered to his Beatrice in anticipation of this exact moment, Martha felt toyed with, manipulated.

Trammell interrupted her thoughts. "Something isn't right.

What's your zip code here?"

"98117," Martha replied.

"Which means it's not the zip code for Tropic, Utah. The other numbers look like GPS coordinates."

"We use them all the time when we're fishing." Shooing Dante from her lap, Martha pulled the laptop from her briefcase, fired up the machine, and within seconds had entered a search for "4 Ebenezer Lane, Tropic, UT."

"Well, the zip code for Tropic, Utah, is 84776," she said. "It's a small town in the south-central part of the state. Population about 500. But that's not a known address. Give me those GPS coordinates."

Trammell read them to her. She typed them in and started a new Google search. In a few seconds, a dot in the middle of nowhere appeared. She pulled back on the image. "It's someplace west of Tropic. It's either on the edge of or right inside Bryce Canyon National Park."

Google Earth provided a different view. Trammell stared at it for a moment. "Looks like nothing but a white blanket."

"High-country snow," Martha said. She zoomed in closer on the coordinates, and cliffs and canyons began to take shape amid the ever-present white. She zoomed in until the satellite image broke up into too many pixels to retain its focus. She zoomed back out. They stared at the image for a long time. Finally, Martha said, "That shadow could be a rooftop."

"It could be most anything—a rooftop, a snow-covered rock, a dip in the earth." He glanced around. "Where's your bathroom?"

Martha directed him toward the bedroom and handed him the flashlight. "We better keep the lights off." And she added, "Put the seat down when you're done."

When he returned, Martha was busy typing. After a couple

of minutes, she looked up and said, "I've booked two tickets in the morning to Las Vegas. It's closer than Salt Lake City and it's a more logical place to run and hide. I guess we'd better figure out what Hewitt wants us to find in Tropic, Utah."

Martha awoke once in the night, with Trammell's arm draped across her shoulder and a cat curled on either side of her feet. She was warm and comfortable spooned up against his body. Cool marine air blew in from the Sound. Trammell snored softly. At their feet, Dante rumbled in accompaniment. She listened for a long time, wondering if some unusual sound had awakened her. She heard only Trammell's breathing and the cat's raspy purr. Maybe they were the unusual sounds. The sounds of peace.

TWENTY-SIX

The next time Martha opened her eyes, a dark shadow loomed over her, black against the night. She spun away from the shadow, hitting the floor with a thud. Instantly, she was up, in a defensive crouch, her heart racing.

"Martha, it's me. Sorry. Didn't mean to startle you."

"Oh, God," she sighed and collapsed back on the bed.

He leaned down and kissed her. "That's all I wanted to do. I'm going to run down to Mac's boat. I have some clothes there, and I need to tell him what's up."

She struggled upright. "What time is it?"

"Nearly six."

She stretched long and slow like Beatrice beside her. But he was right, it was time to get moving. "Use the back door in the garage," she said. "I'll come down and lock it behind you. Go down the trail, the way we came in last night. Take your phone so you can call me when you get back. The car keys are on the table."

"Thanks, but I need the run. I don't think it's even a mile. I won't be gone long."

"Okay, but be careful. Don't forget your phone." She paused, remembering last night. "And thank you for . . . for everything."

In the dark, she couldn't see his face, but she knew he was smiling, too.

In the kitchen, Martha sat listening to the familiar sound of coffee gurgling. It would be an hour before dawn broke, but she didn't dare risk a light. The Carriage House was dark and cool as a cathedral with its vaulted ceilings and exposed beams lost in the shadows. Now, it felt like the relic of a cathedral, cold and abandoned by people and time. She cherished her solitude, but now it felt empty, incomplete.

The cream in the refrigerator had spoiled. She threw out the first cup of coffee with the curdled lumps in it. A can of condensed milk provided an emergency backup. She powered up her laptop. With a couple of clicks, she had a new purple and gold Huskies hoodie ordered for Corvari. She gave the Seattle Police Department as the delivery address. She typed in the next Google search: "Mitch Adair" Seattle.

Her first clue was in a link to the *Seattle Gay News*. The lead story featured a photo caption: "Santa's elf, Mitch Adair, gives away presents at this year's annual Pride Foundation Christmas party." Martha clicked on the photo to enlarge it. Short and slightly pudgy, Adair made a good—if aging—elf. Under his elf hat, he had gray hair clipped short and glasses as round as his face. A neatly trimmed salt-and-pepper beard compensated for a weak chin. She didn't recognize him, but from the checks going back and forth between them, Hewitt and Mitch Adair had to have something more than a casual acquaintance.

She sensed she was closing in on the journey's end. The address in Tropic, Utah, had been left for her to find. Would she find answers at the end of the snow-covered road or just more questions? Would she find Hewitt alive and hiding out in a mountaintop cabin? Or, would she be too late? Again.

Maybe she was wrong. Maybe Hewitt really was drifting in the Sound, his bloated body waiting to be washed ashore on the edge of the next winter storm. But the feeling that Hewitt was alive had settled over her. Tropic, Utah, was the key.

The high mountains of southern Utah could not be taken lightly in winter. She created a task list:

- Cash
- Snowshoes—rent from REI
- GPS from boat
- Chart/map

Then she returned to her search for Mitch Adair. One link took her to the Seattle Pacific University magazine *Response*. An article from the previous summer carried the headline "Professor Emeritus Mitch Adair updates readers about making a difference even after retirement." A small photo showed Santa's elf—minus the costume. Martha opened the article and began to read:

Finding Happiness Among The Poor
By Dr. Mitch Adair

It's been a year since I wrote about leaving my SPU family and my quest to live on less, give more, and be content with what God has entrusted to us. After the death of my dear mother, I sold my house, shed myself of the encumbrances of modern technology, and undertook a journey of self-discovery, a journey that has taken me to the slums of New York City and Calcutta, on a pilgrimage to the Holy City of Jerusalem, and to the remote regions of southern Utah.

Now it has brought me back home. Last month, I began volunteering at the Seattle Union Gospel Mis-

sion, where I feed the hungry and homeless five nights
a week, witnessing a small miracle with each meal I dish
out.

A sanctimonious do-gooder. Martha shook her head and
skimmed the rest. Santa's elf had retired eighteen months ago
from his position as a philosophy professor at Seattle Pacific
University. Nowhere did he mention why he was in the remote
regions of southern Utah. Neither did he mention anything
about family—wife or partner, kids, or traveling companions.
Only the death of his "dear mother." Remembering the check
that was drawn on the "Estate of," Martha was pretty sure her
name was Margaret Cunningham. On this spiritual quest, Mitch
Adair seemed as alone in the world as Martha felt sitting at her
kitchen table.

She raised her eyes and stared out the window. Another pewter dawn was breaking in the eastern sky. Her mind took her
down along the Ship Canal, where SPU's small campus was a
combination of green lawns and brick buildings and stately old
trees. It was a Christian university and apparently not a place
where a gay Christian would want to discuss his other volunteer
activities, like being Santa's special helper at the Pride Foundation Christmas party.

Google identified five Mitch Adairs in greater Seattle. Martha ruled out the ones under fifty years old, which left her with
two phone numbers and addresses. It was almost seven o'clock.
Too early to call? Fuck social niceties. The first address was someplace near Capitol Hill, the heart of the Seattle gay and lesbian
community. Martha dialed. A loud beep answered, followed by a
recorded message saying this number had been disconnected or
was no longer in service. Maybe it was the house he had sold last
year. The second number belonged to a Mitch Adair in Bothell, a

suburb on the shore of Lake Washington, north of Seattle. After four rings, she was asked to leave a message for Mitch, Helen, Jamie, or Suzie, or she could shout out a hearty *woof woof* for Simon.

She hung up and closed the laptop.

Typical of the way the world works, Martha was lathered up in the shower when her phone rang. It was Trammell, back from his run to the marina. He waited at the top of the trail for her to come down and open the back door to the garage. Wrapped in a towel, suds in her hair, she scurried down to the garage, leaving wet footprints across the cold concrete floor. When she opened the door, his eyes grew wide as she let the towel fall like a petal from a rose.

TWENTY-SEVEN

Martha snapped the phone shut, cutting off an irate Callison in mid-sentence. She glanced up and saw Trammell standing on the far side of the luggage carousel, watching the suitcases go round and round. A large bag filled with snowshoes and winter gear lay at his feet. His small carry-on with extra black turtlenecks and jeans rested on top. His eye caught hers as she approached.

"That went about as well as expected," Martha said, crowding in beside him.

"Didn't like our leaving town without telling him first?"

"Among other things."

Martha saw her bag coming around the carrousel, the handle marked with a pink breast cancer bracelet. She reached out and grabbed it. The airport was a cacophony of flashing lights and blaring sounds—it was Las Vegas, after all—and at least three security guards stood within fifty yards of them. Would Callison try to stop them? Was he already on the phone to airport police?

"I still think it was a bad idea," Trammell said.

"I promised," she said. "But it'd probably be best to get out of here as soon as possible."

They made their first stop minutes after leaving the airport—to purchase sunglasses, something neither of them had thought to pack—but otherwise they drove straight on, Trammell at the wheel. Interstate 15 stretched like an endless concrete ribbon to the northeast, rolling through brown hills and around red mesas and barren ravines. Remnants of dirty snow could be seen in the crevices of the north-facing bluffs. The sun set in a dazzling display of reds and oranges as they passed from Nevada into Arizona. When they pulled off the Interstate at St. George, Utah, stars had started to peek out through the black fabric of the eastern sky.

Trammell fueled the Ford Explorer and cleaned the mud-splattered windows. They decided to fuel themselves, as well, and agreed on a diner next to the gas station.

Between bites of meatloaf sandwich, Trammell said, "St. George was one of Brigham Young's winter homes. It's named after one of the early apostles, George Smith. He was a brother or cousin or some relative of Joseph Smith's."

Martha nibbled at her fries as he talked, enjoying the sound of his voice. "So how do you know that? I mean, to me, St. George is just the name of a city on the map."

"When Hewitt first came to me with his story of having some pretty strong evidence of the Mormon Death Angels," Trammell responded, "I started researching the history of the LDS—background for the story. Plus, it would help me determine if there really *was* a story or if it was just something in Hewitt's imagination."

"So what do you think now?"

"There's definitely a story here. We just don't know what it is yet. Do we finally have conclusive evidence of the Mormon Death Angels? Or is someone just afraid we have the evidence, someone who's spinning fantasies out of an innocent series of letters and events?"

Martha raised an eyebrow. "I don't understand."

"On the drive up, I was thinking of my brother John," Trammell started. "You were sleeping. Gave me time to think. John would love it here. Desolate, no people, no civilization. He's a schizophrenic and lives like a hermit in a little trailer deep in the woods on the Olympic Peninsula. He won't stay on his meds because he's convinced they're a form of mind control—you know, Big Brother kind of stuff. My dad and I take turns checking on him. But, each time I go, I don't know who I'm going to find— the happy John or the paranoid John, the depressed John or my brother John. One time I showed up in a white shirt, and he thought I was the guy from the fun house coming to take him back to the hospital. He took a couple of shots at me with a rifle. Good thing he's a bad shot."

Trammell offered a wan smile. "I don't wear white shirts anymore when I go to see him. Anyway, they're all real. They're all a part of John—the delusional and the coherent, the brother who loves me and the maniac with the rifle."

Martha touched his hand. "I'm so sorry. I didn't know." It seemed completely inadequate.

"You had no reason to know," Trammell said. "It's not something I talk about a lot. It just is. I stopped trying to make sense of it a long time ago and just tried to accept it. It wasn't easy. I was so angry. Angry at a God I didn't believe in, angry at John for not taking his meds, angry at my parents. But I had to let it go or I'd drive myself crazy. John is John, it's not right or wrong or good or bad. It's who he is. A paranoid schizophrenic who can't always distinguish reality from delusions.

"So, I was wondering if we might have the same thing going on here. John thinks I'm going to cart him off in a straitjacket, so he tries to shoot me. Maybe someone thinks the documents implicating the Elders of the LDS are real, so they're taking their shots at everyone who might expose them. It doesn't matter what the truth is, or that the solution is more extreme than the damage that could come from the documents themselves. They believe we're trying to put the church in a straitjacket. It doesn't matter if it's true, only that they believe it's true."

"Killing in the name of the one true God," Martha said. "Sounds like the history of the world."

The clear night brought out the Milky Way, sweeping like a celestial cloud of diamonds across the black sky. As her father had taught her, Martha found Orion's belt and saw Canis Major chasing the hunter through the night. She wondered if Trammell's father ever took his two sons stargazing. She glanced over, but Trammell continued to doze, his head propped at an awkward angle against the window. There was so much about him she didn't know. The thought of finding out both frightened and excited her.

Snow banks began to appear alongside the road. They were climbing in elevation. By the time she pulled off I-15 at Cedar City, the snow was a couple of feet deep, the headlights catching drifts of powder blowing across the road. The lights of Cedar City disappeared in her rearview mirror as she drove east along Highway 14. In the first twenty minutes, only one other car passed, giving the headlights a flick when Martha forgot to dim hers. The landscape was lost in the dark; all she saw were snow banks and the stars overhead.

"Where are we?" Trammell asked, suddenly sitting upright. He flexed his neck and rolled his shoulders.

"In the middle of nowhere," she replied. "Have a nice nap?"

"I feel like a boa constrictor's wrapped around my neck.

How you doing? You must be exhausted."

"Nah, I've a sky full of stars to keep me awake and the snow reminds me of home."

Trammell gazed out the window. "The stars remind me of Neah Bay."

"What's in Neah Bay?" Martha turned off the radio.

"My dad. We had a cabin there when I was a kid, and we'd spend weekends fishing and beachcombing and hanging out with kids from the reservation. He said the only way he could go back to Boeing every Monday morning was his weekends at the beach." Trammell squinted out the window. "The snow looks deep."

"Probably a couple of feet." A comfortable silence settled over them. The road was straight, the pavement dry, and she reached out and found his hand in the dark. Finally, she said, "What's your dad do now?"

"He took an early retirement and moved out to Neah Bay permanently. It puts him closer to John."

"He must worry about him a lot." She hesitated before adding, "I'd like you to take me to Neah Bay. Meet your father. Maybe your brother."

"I'd like that, too." Trammell said quietly.

"What about your mother?"

"She died a couple of years ago. Breast cancer. She beat it once when she was in her early forties. She wasn't as lucky the second time."

"I'm sorry."

"So am I. I miss her a lot. I saw you had a pink bracelet on your luggage."

"My grandmother. In a lot of ways, she raised me." Martha offered something akin to an ironic laugh. "She was a heavy smoker her whole life. We expected lung cancer to kill her, but instead it was breast cancer."

"What about your mother?"

The car was warm and dark, his voice, gentle. It felt like she was in a confessional talking to a priest. She said, "I don't remember much about her. She left when I was little. I went to my first day of kindergarten, and when I came home, she was gone. We never heard from her again. My dad was a lifer in the military—Marines—so he packed up seven kids and sent us to live in the Upper Peninsula with his mother."

It was his turn to say, "I'm sorry." He took her hand in both of his. "At the hotel, you mentioned your sister. What happened?"

For a long time, she didn't say anything. Finally, she started. "My dad's best friend was a Marine buddy from Arkansas named Walt Boudreau. We called him Uncle Walt."

Over the next hour, in the dark, warm confessional of the car, she told the story she had never told anyone but Gran and Hewitt. Beginning to end. All of it. Hiding nothing about what she had done. When they crested a hill and the few night lights of Tropic, Utah, came into view, she finished with, "I'm only sorry I didn't do it earlier, when there was still time to save Rachel. But I wasn't old enough or ready enough."

Trammell held her hand. Neither spoke for a long time. She took comfort in the fact he didn't immediately pull away. "I can't imagine—" he started, but the rest of the words lingered unsaid. "How could—" She could see him struggling, looking off into the dark. His hand on top of hers felt like an anchor in a storm. He brushed her face with his fingers. "God, how awful. I'm so sorry. Raped, watching your sister slowly die, killing the person responsible for it. Jesus, nothing can ever be completely good or innocent again. Nobody deserves that."

They sat in the warm car in silence. In time, he added, "Thank you for being honest with me. It helps me understand."

He continued holding her hand. Still, she knew, the deepest level of honesty could often exact a price.

Snow lay thick over the neighborhood yards of Tropic, Utah, a blanket under which they would hibernate until spring. Few lights were on. They passed a hotel and a bed-and-breakfast, both dark, driveways buried in unplowed snow. The storefronts of Main Street were all dark for the night except one: the Bryce Valley Inn.

Trammell checked them in under the names Kirk and Mary Gibson. Only Callison knew where they were, but it didn't hurt to be cautious.

TWENTY-EIGHT

In the morning, Martha saw Trammell watching her as she dressed. He sat up in the hotel bed, his chest bare, his eyes following her every movement in the hotel mirror. She paused and stared back at him. Their eyes met and she smiled.

"You're beautiful when you smile," Trammell said.

"When I smile?"

"Well, I mean, you're beautiful all the time, but there are times when you'd make angels blush."

"I like that." She laughed. "I'd like to hear more, but it must be over the breakfast table. I'm starving."

By eight o'clock, Martha had the Ford Explorer in four-wheel drive heading through town. The stores on Main Street were still closed, with few signs that the town would be open that morning. They drove past a city park with an old log hut in it. Sunrise broke pink and red against the mountains and mesas to the west. Dawn moved down the slopes of the mountains as the sun inched its way higher in the east. The valley was soon bathed in a bright sunshine that carried no warmth.

Martha donned her sunglasses. Trammell navigated from the passenger's seat, a road map and a topographical map spread out across his lap. He had powered up Martha's GPS and compared it to the built-in unit on the rental vehicle. Their coordinates matched.

The road out of town was bare and dry. They passed white clapboard houses and a couple of singlewide mobile homes, one with a wooden deck slanted at an odd angle. On the edge of town, the windows of the Bryce Valley High School were lit, teachers busy preparing for the school day.

For the first mile or two, Martha studied the rearview mirror as much as the road ahead. No one followed them out of town. They passed a farmhouse and outbuildings set back from the road. In the corral, shaggy horses and donkeys huddled together, heads down, as if in a rugby scrum. The last field gave way to rolling hills of Ponderosa pines and tall scrub brush poking out of the deep snow. Ahead, Martha could see the rugged ravines and coulees like ribs of white corduroy leading to the mountain slopes that would eventually ascend to the rim of Bryce Canyon National Park. Someplace between here and there, she would find Ebenezer Lane. It appeared on none of their maps, but the GPS coordinates put it someplace in front of them.

The pavement ended and they continued along a gravel road. A snowplow had cleared a one-lane swath, pushing the snow up high along the banks. Headlights appeared around a corner, and Martha pulled over as an old truck rumbled past without slowing down. From under a baseball cap, the driver nodded and raised a hand. Martha waved back as he disappeared into the rearview mirror.

They drove another mile or so and stopped at a sudden clearing in the Ponderosa pines. A pair of tire tracks led off the road. In the distance was what might have been a house, maybe a shack. The wood siding hadn't seen any paint in recent decades; the metal roof was mottled green and rust. An old John Deere tractor with a snowblade sat parked in the front yard. Smoke came out of a stack in the roof. A dog beside the tractor barked as Martha slowed.

Trammell checked the coordinates off the GPS and studied the topo map. "This isn't it."

In another mile, they came to the end of the road, having seen no other lanes, paths, or goat trails running off the gravel road. The snowplow had created a turning basin at the end, and Martha swung the Explorer around and parked as far off the road as she dared. She let the car run as Trammell again compared the GPS coordinates with the map. "It's still west of here and a little south," he said.

His finger traced a line along the map. "This may be a path. It looks like it winds in the right direction, but it doesn't seem to intersect with the road."

"Or it could just be the creek bed," Martha said.

"Or the creek bed may be the path. Let's find out."

They scrambled up the snow bank at the end of the road, slipping back a step for every two they gained. Atop the bank, they saw the valley floor ceased with the road. From here, the sides narrowed sharply into a canyon. Martha searched the rugged terrain for anything that might be a path. On one side, hills cut by deep ravines lay buried in snow; on the other, red bluffs soared straight up, too steep for snow to gather. Wispy clouds showed over the top of the distant canyon rim, several thousand feet over their heads.

"We might as well hike in a little ways," Trammell said. "There's nothing here."

"God, why would anyone live here?"

"This isn't where they lived. They settled back in the valley where they had water, farmland, grass for pastures. This is where folks like John Lee and Eli Pace hid when government officials came asking about the deaths of too many infidels. This is where they hid the second and third and nineteenth wife and a whole passel of kids while the first wife offered coffee and cookies to the feds investigating rumors of polygamy."

They scrambled back to the Explorer and pulled out snow-shoes, heavy winter boots, down jackets, wool hats and mittens and scarves. Slinging on small backpacks, they headed out.

Within a hundred yards of ascending the first hill, Trammell fell twice into the deep snow. Martha pulled him up the second time, brushing snow off him. "Lift your feet higher than normal. Walk with your legs a little farther apart to keep from tripping on the edges of the snowshoes. You'll get the hang of it."

And he did, soon taking his turn breaking the path. He crested a ravine and paused, looking down. When she came up beside him, he said, pointing, "I bet that's our trail."

Undisturbed snow, about the width of a country lane, snaked between the pines and up the canyon. Martha pulled off her mittens and plotted their location on the GPS. "If it's not Ebenezer Lane, it's at least heading in the right direction."

They hiked for an hour up the canyon and paused. Leaning on an exposed rock, they ate power bars, shared some nuts, and sipped water. Martha plotted their course again. "We're still on track. We've gone about a mile, maybe a mile and a half."

"In an hour?"

"On snowshoes, in deep snow, I'd say we're making good time." She retied the strings of her wool stocking cap under her chin and stood up. "Come on, let's get moving before the sweat starts to freeze."

After a second hour of hiking came a second break. There

had been no decisions about their course. The snow-covered path was clear, winding its way steadily upward through the pines. Martha brushed a loose strand of hair off her cheek.

"Whiter than new snow upon a raven's back," Trammell said, reaching out and brushing the snow off her hair, letting his hand linger on her face.

"A raven?" she said. "Really? Not particularly flattering."

"Shakespeare," Trammell said, kissing her. "*Romeo and Juliet.*"

His lips were cold, and she took it upon herself to warm them.

Her task complete, she checked the GPS coordinates against the latitude and longitude numbers from Hewitt.

"We're almost there," she announced. A breeze feathered her hair against her cheek. She glanced up and saw a thin cloud layer now covered the sky. "Let's keep moving in case the weather turns."

They were almost upon the cabin before they saw it. They rounded a switchback and paused to catch their breath. The path continued upward, but Martha realized after three or four heavy breaths that she could see the outline of a cabin tucked back into the shadows of the trees. The GPS coordinates matched. In anticipation, Martha glanced at the roof, half expecting to see smoke curling up from the rock chimney. Nothing. No tracks disturbed the snow that lay all around the cabin. Two windows on the front were shuttered and a porch roof heavy with snow was all that kept the front door from being half buried. Two chairs and a bench made from roughhewn boards sat undisturbed on one side of the porch. The cabin, made of the same roughhewn planks and aged to a silver-gray from the harsh mountain weather, was deserted.

All of Hewitt's clues had led her here. Only now she realized

she had expected to find him hiding in this isolated mountain re-
treat. Was this another dead end? If not here, where? Was he really dead? She slumped against a rock; her heart sank with despair.

As if reading her mind, Trammell said, "I'm sorry. Come,
let's see why Hewitt brought us here."

They walked straight across the snow onto the porch, where
they unstrapped their snowshoes and stomped snow off their
boots. Above the door was a hand-carved board that read "4
Ebenezer Lane."

Trammell leaned his snowshoes against the side of the cabin
and asked, "Where do you suppose he keeps the key?"

Martha placed her snowshoes beside his and grasped the
door latch. The door creaked as it swung inward.

"How'd you know that?"

"You're such a city boy," she replied. "Besides, there's no lock.
Probably only locks from the inside."

Martha stood in the doorway for a moment to let her eyes
adjust. She figured the whole cabin might be twenty by twenty
feet, all in one open room, with a couple of curtained doorways
in the back wall. To her right, under one of the front windows,
was a wooden bench with shoes, slippers, and a pair of boots
tucked underneath. Beyond that, an old sofa and a couple of
Mission style chairs circled a rock fireplace. A blue cowboy coffeepot rested on a stone hearth. Other than the chimney, the
entire wall was one extended bookshelf, full. An Indian rug hid
more of the roughhewn planks that made up the floor.

On the opposite side, centered under the other front window, was a small table with four chairs neatly tucked underneath. From there, the kitchen ran back against the side wall.
A shuttered window was centered over a stainless steel basin on
the countertop. All its storage, both above and below a waist-
high counter, was open shelves that appeared nearly full. A small

wood-burning stove occupied the back wall.

Trammell stood beside the table. He angled a sheet of paper to catch the light coming from the front door and read, "'Dear Visitors. Welcome to our mountain home. We hope it provides you with a safe haven from a winter storm or shelter from a summer squall. Please treat it with the respect and courtesy with which you would like someone to treat your home. The Owners.'"

"Where do you suppose Hewitt keeps the firewood?" Trammell said, putting the paper down.

"Probably out that back door."

Trammell disappeared, and she continued her search. She opened one of the books, an autographed first edition of Zane Grey. A second book was also an autographed first edition Zane Grey. Dozens of Zane Grey books lined one section of the bookcase. No doubt all were autographed first editions.

Martha pulled back the curtain leading to a back bedroom. There was just enough room for bunk beds, a knotty pine dresser, and a few open shelves. A lantern sat on one of the shelves and a second hung on the wall beside the bed. The second room was another bedroom, this one with a high double bed, a few more open shelves, and another lantern. The bed was made, topped with a hand-embroidered quilt of brown and green and yellow diamonds, an autumn quilt. Both bedrooms were maybe ten feet square. The height of the bed seemed odd to Martha, until she realized it would be easier for the post-stroke Hewitt to crawl in and out of a higher bed. Then she remembered the trail leading to the cabin. There was no way he would have managed the hike in, even if he only came in summer. She lifted up the quilt and saw the bedposts had been raised about six inches on wooden blocks.

She also saw a Brinkman L70 safe.

When Trammell returned, he poked his head through the curtain and found Martha sitting on the floor in the bedroom. He carried an armload of wood. Snow clung to his boots and pants. She had found matches and the soft yellow glow of one of the kerosene lanterns emanated from the floor beside her.

"I'm going to start a fire to warm this place up," he said. "I also found the outhouse. Frozen solid, by the way. And an outbuilding with an ATV in it. Nice little rig. If we stay until the snow melts, we could ride right out of here. There's enough wood in the shed to last the winter. And when you go to town for supplies, you can use the snowshoes that look like they were made for Brigham Young himself. What're you doing?"

"I found the safe. The key fits."

"Holy shit. Finally." He set the wood down and knelt beside her.

Martha glanced over at him, nodding. "The ATV, that's how Hewitt got up and down the hill. But who hiked out the last time?" She exhaled in a deep sigh. "The key fits, but I still don't have the code."

"It's your zip code."

She rolled her eyes, and said, "What else did you find out there, some of Hewitt's pot?"

"No, serious. Try your zip code. Hewitt gave you the lat and long and a five-digit number that's not the zip for Tropic, Utah. He was giving you the number to the safe."

Martha punched in 9-8-1-1-7 and the safe gave a beep followed by an audible click. She twisted the handle, and the door opened.

"And you thought I was just along for my brawn." Trammell stood up. "I'll get that fire started. It looks like we might be staying for a while."

TWENTY-NINE

artha adjusted the lantern wick until it gave off a steady yellow glow. On top of a stack of papers and books in the safe was an envelope addressed to her in Hewitt's familiar scrawl. Taking a deep breath, she opened it, leaned back against the bed, and stretched her legs out. The letter was dated late September, nearly five months earlier. Before the snow began to bury the mountain cabin, long before June Povich was murdered. She began to read:

My Dear Martha:

If you are in possession of this letter, it means the worst has happened. Either I'm unable to communicate with you or, more likely, I am dead. Ashes to ashes, dust to dust. I suppose it doesn't really matter how, though I have often dreamt that death would visit me at night, right after I've fallen asleep in the arms of someone I love. I suspect, however, that's not what happened.

You see, my dear, I have been going down an increasingly dangerous path these past several years. If, on my death bed, I've had a chance to relay all of this to you in person, please show patience to an old man. More likely, however, I never had the chance to tell you what it is that I pursue—and more importantly, that growing to know and love you as the daughter I never had has been one of the pure joys of my long life.

Since I retired, I've continued my interest in history and archeology through a new avenue of study—my own life and the lives of my immediate family. This line of inquiry has led to startling revelations about my family, revelations that have grown increasingly dark the deeper I've pursued them.

But first, a little background, some of which you may know, much of which you don't. I was born Hewitt Wilcox Chappell into a Mormon family from southern Utah. I was the youngest child of my father's fourth wife, Mary, nee Wilcox. With four wives, all with fertile loins, my father, Ebenezer Chappell, spread his seed abundantly. I won't bore you with the entire family tree, but suffice to say at one time Chappells populated much of the valley.

I hope you can imagine the difficulties of being a gay man born into a devout Mormon clan in the first half of the 20th century. The Elders and Saints didn't have room for us in their pathway to heaven nor on this earth. For years, I knew that I was different; I didn't know what it was that made me different nor what my soul ached for.

My early education and the blossoming of my life came in the arms of a young itinerant farmworker. Enter the magical world of love. Some might call it nothing more than newly discovered lust. But it changed everything—and me—forever. His name was Eric Wain, or Eric the Red, as I called him, for his flowing red hair. He appeared on the farm one autumn day offering to help with the harvest, having hitchhiked up from Oklahoma.

So, she'd been right. The young man with flowing hair in the grainy old photo—Eric Wain, Eric the Red—was Hewitt's Romeo.

Tall and handsome, with the grace of a willow tree in the breeze, Eric the Red initiated me with tenderness, passion, and an uncontrollable hunger. But we lacked the discretion that common sense demanded in a Mormon community in the 1940s. An older sister from my father's second wife stumbled upon us one afternoon in the barn in, shall we say, flagrante delicto.

My father whipped me within an inch of my life. Eric wasn't so lucky. My cousin, Judd Wilcox, was summoned, and within hours, Eric disappeared from my life forever. There had always been rumors about cousin Judd. It seemed when the church needed something unpleasant done, Judd would disappear for a while. Only later did I come to understand how Judd Wilcox was just the latest member of my family to function in this capacity.

Within days, at sixteen, with infected scabs still crisscrossing my back and buttocks, I ran away from home, lied about my age to join the Navy, and sailed off to fight the Japanese—never to return to these brown hills scattered with Moron ancestors and relatives. Or so I thought. But, decades later, I was drawn back to the land of my forefathers. In part, because I inherited this small family cabin in the mountains, a place that held fond memories of my mother and my older sister and brother; but more importantly, because I had to find out what had occurred the day Eric Wain disappeared.

Romeo had lost his Romeo. Martha wondered if Eric the Red had been beaten and dropped at the edge of town, told to never return. Or if something more sinister had transpired. Either way, for Hewitt, his first love had been snatched away. His first love had become his first loss, his first broken heart. It had also told him who he was—a gay man with the capacity for love. Had that memory festered all those years like the scabs across his back? Martha read on.

> I believe that cousin Judd was a member of an elite and ultra-secret vigilante group in the Mormon church. They're sometimes referred to as the Death Angels, but in the past they have gone by many names—the Danites, the Army of Israel, Young's Avenging Angels. Fear and terror are their main weapons, but death is one of the commodities in which they deal.
>
> I found Eric's body a couple of days later by following the vultures. He had been thrown down a ravine like yesterday's garbage, left as carrion for the wolves, beaten senseless, his face unrecognizable. Only the flowing red hair told me it was Eric. Such pain and suffering for such a gentle soul. All because of me! Because of ME!
>
> In the middle of the night, I buried him in the meadow beside the pool in the creek where we first made love. That meadow was his final resting place, and the place where I buried part of my soul. I washed his face and his hair as best I could, wrapped him in one of my mother's finest sheets, and dug his grave deep so the wolves would not dig him back up. I did all that I could to ease his journey onward. But it was never enough— not for me.
>
> You passed Eric's grave on your way in, my dear, if you followed the creek bed. I call it Eric's Meadow. Each spring when the wild flowers bloom, I know he is smiling at me, forgiving me. If only I had been able to forgive myself.

Martha let the long letter fall into her lap. Hewitt had written this letter to keep his promise that someday he would tell her the story and to seal their connection. Brutal past to brutal past. How do you get beyond it? Someday was upon her, and she couldn't reach out to him in comfort and shared grief. She forced herself to keep reading.

The night I buried Eric Wain, I knew I could never worship nor believe in a God who would allow such a gentle soul be so brutally slain, all in the pursuit of love. But with each spade of dirt, with each scab on my back that reopened and bled, I became convinced that such a God could not exist, that these were just the actions of evil men who hid behind words of faith and the ignorance of the faithful to justify their evil deeds. You'd think I might have felt guilt, given my upbringing, but instead, I embraced my homosexuality.

By dawn, I was gone from Bryce Canyon, leaving my first love, my family, my faith, my name behind. And a good piece of my heart. A long-distance trucker headed to Seattle brought me to my new life. The Navy, anthropology, the University, and eventually you, my dear, awaited me on the end of that long truck ride. It was only after hearing your story about how you overcame fear and faced your abuser that I found the courage to revisit this heinous crime from my past. While I share your need for justice, I do not share your skills. So I used my own well-developed abilities: forensic anthropology. I vowed to expose this long line of horrible people for the deaths of Eric Wain and all the other innocent victims they have claimed through the years. And there have been many.

I studied the public records and nearly everything that's ever been written about this secret society within a very secretive church. I was firmly convinced of its existence, but needed proof that would withstand public and peer scrutiny. After my sister died and left me the cabin, I brought my research back to Bryce Valley. I found old family diaries and long-forgotten letters.

At first, I kept my research quiet. I was just Hewitt Wilcox, an eccentric old professor digging up family histories. The Mormons love their history, so people were willing to talk to one of their own, sharing stories and letters and old family Bibles. Hewie Chappell and Eric Wain had long been forgotten in Bryce Valley.

But the more I researched, the more I felt like Luke Skywalker. The dark force is strong in my family. John D. Lee and Eli Pace, my cousin Judd, and my grandfather Harry Chappell—all of whom populated my family tree—have direct connections to this secret group of Moron vigilantes. Could I bring balance back to the family? Could I avenge the death of an innocent man? Could I bring light to the dark side? You showed me how these things might be possible.

I shall not bore you with all the details, my dear. Suffice to say, if you research the Mountain Meadow Massacre and the fate of the three explorers from the John Wesley Powell Grand Canyon expedition, you will begin to see what men with blackened hearts will do when commanded to deliver the vengeance of God. And to this list you can add a young itinerant farmhand named Eric Wain.

As I get close to going public with it, I'm afraid my research is drawing unwanted attention and may be becoming known to the Church Elders. Over the years, I sold documents to the Church for which I had no use, but which were of interest to their archives. It provided a little working capital to continue my research and rewarded my colleagues who have been my eyes and ears in the community. I realize now that it was a mistake. If you're reading this, you'll know that someone must have ascertained the direction I was headed.

I had hoped to have everything ready for my weapon of choice—publication—by next summer. For verification as to the authenticity of these documents, I called on Dr. June Povich, a forensic anthropologist from Arizona State University, and Dr. Maxine Martoni, a University of Washington anthropologist. Their credentials, I believe, are above reproach. I have leads on a few more documents that will substantially strengthen my case, and Drs. Povich and Martoni have documents that they need to finish authenticating. I dismissed the notion of a scholarly publication—I'm well beyond that phase of my life—in favor of a more populist venue. I plan to offer a former student of mine, Lance Trammell, publisher of the *Ballard Gazette*, first option on the story.

I have kept my colleagues in the dark about my intent to publish my findings and believe they might be resistant to the idea of depriving them of financial reward for selling the documents to the Mormons. But I believe that publication is the only way to expose this dark chapter of the LDS, and I cannot justify betraying Eric's ultimate sacrifice in return for 30 pieces of silver.

If you are reading this at 4 Ebenezer Lane, it likely means that my hypothesis on the existence of the Mormon Death Angels has proven correct. Either I am their latest victim or am afraid I will be and have gone into hiding. If you are reading this, then I must have found a way to communicate with you. I also hope to have had time to protect you from their attention, but you are hardly the coward I have so often been and if they threatened you, I have faith that with your strength and intelligence you will know what to do.

My dear Martha, I cannot, of course, tell you what to do with this material if it is now in your possession. Nor can I anticipate the threat it may pose to you or to those around you should it become known that you possess it. My dying wish is that you take it to Mr. Trammell for publication. If you feel unable to for safety's sake, I understand completely. I have done my part. If I am dead, the decision is entirely yours. You may think of it as mere revenge for Eric, but I believe it goes beyond that—exposing something many have tried but failed to expose before—the sinister secrets of the LDS church.

There will be no pause in the march of the universe if my findings remain unpublished. You may think it a just revenge. Yet I believe no person will have quite the same thoughts about the LDS church should this dirty little secret be brought out of the darkness into the light.

The cabin, commit it to fire, if you'd be so kind. I am the last Chappell of the polygamist clan, each with a cabin on Ebenezer Lane. Numbers 2 and 3 Ebenezer Lane have long since turned to ash. As once before near a frozen lake you found fire a step toward closure, may you begin reconciling with my death as the cabin flares into flame and dies down to ash.

I have named you Executor of my estate and my sole heir. There is only one condition: if Dante outlives me, he is to reside with you and Beatrice until the end of his natural days. All the proper documents, signed and notarized, are in my houseboat. I did not involve you with drawing up of my Last Will & Testament only because I wished to avoid the fight your protests would invoke. You'll find them in a file named such in my desk at home.

Dearest Martha, I have been blessed to have known

and loved you. I only wish to have eternity to savor the joy and happiness you have brought an old man in his declining years. May you continue to be a woman of grace and conviction, blessed in life and blessed in love.

As always, your most humble and respectful friend and servant,

Hewitt

Martha sat without moving for a long time, trying to come to terms with one more person gone from her life without the chance to say goodbye, without the chance to tell him she loved him. Maybe she had been wrong about his disappearance. The premonitions of his death were there the moment she saw the waters of Puget Sound lapping over his van. She glanced at the letter again. It was dated September 14, over four months ago. Yet Hewitt had given no indication of his fears when they were carving pumpkins for Halloween or eating Thanksgiving turkey. No mention of it when they gathered at the Carriage House for their Christmas gift exchange; said nothing when she dropped a bottle of Jean Milan Carte Blanche Brut off for New Year's. The certainty that she would find her way to 4 Ebenezer Lane and find his farewell letter left little doubt that he had seen this end. And she realized now that his cryptic messages were meant both to protect her in their secrecy and to lead her to the *Ballard Gazette* where she could finish his work. How could he ever imagine all that was to come?

She sank to the floor and rocked back and forth. For the first time, she mourned the loss of her friend with tears.

When Martha came out of the bedroom, she carried the stack of papers and leather-bound books. Trammell's shadow covered the small table. He was outside, removing the shutters from the windows. Light streamed in.

Illuminating the smoke that started to pour out of the fireplace.

Martha dumped the papers and books on the table and rushed over to it. She stumbled on the Indian rug, catching herself just before she fell headlong into the flames. She found the damper and gave it a quarter turn. The smoke immediately rose up the chimney. The flames shot up with the infusion of fresh air and began to crackle and pop as the wood began to blaze. Coughing, she fanned the smoke away.

Trammell stepped back inside. "Wow, seems like a lot of smoke."

"You forgot to open the damper," Martha said, struggling to control her coughing.

"Of course. Sorry."

"Open the doors. It'll air out in a few minutes." She stepped back from the fireplace, relieved at being thrown into action even if just for a moment. In the kitchen, she found the latch for the window and pushed it out. Trammell opened the backdoor, and cold winter air began to swirl through the cabin before funneling toward the open door.

Martha turned toward the cupboards, examining the shelves. "Flour and yeast. We could make bread. Sugar. Soups. Peet's coffee, French Roast. Nice choice, even if a little stale. And half-a-dozen cans of condensed milk. Top Ramen. Haven't seen that since I was in college. Enough beans to give gas to all of Tropic. Pasta and marinara sauce in a can. I can make dinner."

"That would be nice." Trammell took a package of freeze-dried mushrooms from her hand and set it back on the shelf. He glanced at the papers on the table. "Whoa! What did you find?"

"Your story." She paused and touched the letter and finally added, "And a long farewell letter to me. And that maybe Metcalf was right all along."

"To you? He knew this was going to happen? What do you mean about Metcalf?"

"That maybe I'm responsible for all this. Hewitt got the idea of looking into the history of the Mormons from me. He knew about Uncle Walt, what I did. Said it inspired him to seek justice—or revenge—for a crime that happened a long time ago. It's all in the letter."

"Hey, you know you're not responsible for whatever Hewitt's done." Trammell reached out to touch her but she pulled away.

"Yeah, I know that. But, at the moment, it doesn't make me feel a whole lot better with, what, how many people dead? Is Hewitt one of them? It would seem so from his letter. 'Ashes to ashes, dust to dust.' He knew he was traveling an increasingly dangerous road. And that I set him on it."

"You no more set him on it than I did because I was willing to publish the story. It's not my fault. It's not your fault."

"I fucking know that." She blinked and blinked, desperate to hold back more tears. She failed and they came in a flood, a small sob. This time when Trammell reached out, she let herself be drawn in, burying her face in his shoulder, letting his arms pull her tight. "I couldn't protect him anymore than I could protect Rachel."

"It's not your job to protect everyone."

"Oh, shut up. This isn't about reason. Just hold me for a minute."

For a minute, and then a second, and a third, she took comfort in his strength, in his silence. He would have remained there as long as she needed him. Then she rubbed her eyes against his shoulder and extracted herself from his embrace.

"Seems he expected me to make it here," she said.

"Anything you want to share?"

"Basically, your working theory is correct. He was researching the Death Angels. He asked me to give you the story. I'm sure you've got enough now for that Pulitzer."

He reached out to her. "Hey, you know that's not why I'm here."

"Yeah, I know." She gave his hand a squeeze. "But it's still true. You might as well take it." She nodded toward the stack on the table. "I'd like the letter back when you're done, but the rest is yours. There's the Chappell family Bible—Hewitt was born Hewitt Wilcox Chappell—a genealogy tree, a collection of letters and three old diaries, and six of the eight Letters of Authenticity, signed by Povich and Martoni. Apparently, they were still working on the last set. No wonder they were killed. Take a look. I'm giving it all to you. Hewitt had to suspect that Povich's death wasn't a suicide. He couldn't have known about Martoni." She turned away from the papers and took down some pasta and marinara sauces from the shelf. "I can make spaghetti. I might even remember how to make bread. What do you say we stay here tonight?"

Trammell looked at the material stacked on the table. "Sure. There's plenty of firewood. And no shortage of food. Why not?"

"Go look at the stuff; I know you can't wait. I'll take care of things here. We'll be warm, we'll be comfortable. We're off the grid. It should be safe. No one but Callison knows we're here. Read Hewitt's letter first. It'll give you an idea of what he was doing."

While Trammell sat reading, Martha stoked the fire. Soon, they had both removed their wool hats and down jackets. Martha returned from outside carrying a kettle of snow, stomping snow off her boots on the porch. Trammell looked up from his reading and exclaimed, "4 Ebenezer Lane. It's not an address, it's a sick joke. This was Mary's cabin, the fourth wife of Ebenezer

Chappell. Just like there was a 2 and 3 Ebenezer Lane." A few minutes later, he said in dismay, "Fire? He wants you to torch the cabin?"

"Do you blame him?" Martha glanced up briefly from lighting the oven.

Soon she was up to her elbows in flour and yeast and water, trying to remember the right combination from the Saturdays when Gran made bread for the week. Mostly, Martha's job had been to knead the combination of ingredients, which she now did, pounding it with an unnecessary vigor and rocking with the rhythm of it and all the questions going through her head. Why hadn't Hewitt informed her of what he was up to? Why hadn't he come to her for help? Why all the clues? Why not just tell her outright? She could have helped him; at the least, she could've protected him. That's what family is for. Her hard-won self-reliance railed against the idea that he thought it was she who needed protection. That's why he hid the truth. With the bread rising in the warmth of the cabin, Martha heated up some soup and opened a packet of freeze-dried apples and a box of crackers. She cleared a space on the table and sat down beside Trammell.

"Spaghetti's for dinner," she said. "This is just a little something to knock the edge off."

"'Small cheer and great welcome makes a merry feast.'"

"Let me guess. Shakespeare?"

Trammell didn't need to answer. He picked up his spoon. Stubble had grown across his cheeks and neck over the past couple of days, a shadow that did nothing to lessen the contentment on his face. "A bowl of canned soup to a starving man in the wilderness is a veritable feast. And I mean that literally—we're certainly in the wilderness out here, I'm starving, and this is a feast." Trammell paused, before adding, "He loved you very much."

"Yeah, well, he had a funny way of showing it."

"Maybe he was trying to protect you. He clearly understood it was getting dangerous."

"What he needed was someone to protect *him*." She couldn't let go of the anger—of the sense that had she helped him, he might be here with them, finishing off the canned soup.

"At eighty-seven or ninety-two or whatever Hewitt was, do you really think that? Isn't that when you go out of your way to *not* put the people you love at risk?"

The afternoon continued to cloud over, and soon it began to snow, soft lazy flakes, swirling in slow motion. Martha sat for a time on the front porch and watched, her hands buried in the warm pockets of her down jacket. It was a Hollywood version of a snowstorm, not the driving blizzards she had known as a young girl in the UP, when whiteouts and blowing drifts made moving about perilous for the inexperienced and experienced alike. Fresh snow started to fill in their tracks up to the cabin, like a blanket of peace. Yet Martha knew how quickly that could change.

Like life, she supposed. For the first time in days, she wondered if she had a job to return to at CH&N. Corporate Darth Vader, Hewitt used to call her. What did it matter now? Or the Death Angels, for that matter. She wished Trammell well in pursuing Hewitt's Death Angel story, but she didn't really care anymore if it was published. And with it the danger. Hewitt was gone. Drifting at sea or alive and hiding. Either way, it was just one more hole in a heart full of holes.

Was it a heart that Trammell could help mend? For the first time in years, she was intrigued by the possibility, afraid of being vulnerable, knowing that she must be. The depth of Trammell's eyes and his often sad face captured her imagination as much as they held her in reality. Having driven herself to succeed, she appreciated his intellect and his drive to make the *Ballard Gazette* one of the forerunners of alternative weeklies. The sensation of his gentle touch left her shivering.

As did the touch of a breeze against her exposed skin. The weather was still changing. Snow drifted down from one of the Ponderosa pines that surrounded the cabin. She stood up, her feet a-swim in Hewitt's oversized sheepskin slippers. Maybe there was a real storm coming yet.

Stripped down to a T-shirt, Martha nested on the sofa in front of the fireplace with Zane Grey's *Riders of the Purple Sage*, skimming more than reading. Trammell continued to work by lantern light at the small table, occasionally looking her way and voicing his appreciation of Hewitt's research or the well-documented thread of his work.

The blue enamel coffeepot, now full of water, hung over the fire; her bare feet warmed near the red-hot embers. Zane Grey had no more use for the Mormons than Hewitt had. Maybe that explained the collection of first editions shelved here in Mormon country instead of in Seattle. Hewitt must have wanted reminders of his hatred every time he came to this lonely stretch of southern Utah.

Could she burn the books? Commit the cabin to fire, as he requested? Yes, she decided, yes, she could.

The spaghetti was tolerable; the bread was awful. She had used too little yeast or it had gone too long past its expiration date, and she had baked it too long. But Trammell scraped off the outer layer of charcoal and devoured the hardtack with the enthusiasm of the starving.

The meal finished, Trammell said, "Let me do the dishes."

"Let's leave them," Martha said. "I'm just going to burn them all tomorrow."

"You're going to do it?"

She pushed her plate away and shrugged. "It's what Hewitt wanted. And what am I going to do with an old cabin in southern Utah? It's not like Hewitt's coming back, and I have no interest in returning. Not with its sad history. Besides, I like running water and a bathroom with a flush toilet, thank you very much. We found what we were searching for. We can carry it out easily enough. We know the why and the what, we just don't know the who. That's up to Callison and his team to find out. There's nothing here I can't live without. If burning the cabin is the dying wish of an old friend, I can do it."

"You think Hewitt's dead?"

"He's either dead or wanting us to think he's dead. I can give him that peace."

"But if he's not, he could come out of hiding if we make these papers public."

"That will be his choice. But if you publish this, he has no reason to return here."

But Martha did wash the dishes.

Trammell stretched his long frame out on the sagging sofa, his stocking feet sticking out over one end. He flipped through only a few pages of a Zane Grey before he was snoring, softly at first, then with the regular deep-throated rumble of someone hard asleep. She was content to let him sleep, watching him, listening to him.

The fire had burned low, the coffeepot steamed on the embers. Outside, the wind howled around the eaves. Inside, the quiet of the cabin was disturbed only by an occasional crackle from the fireplace or a long snore from Trammell. She slid into Hewitt's oversized slippers and stepped out onto the porch. Her breath blew away. Driven snow stung her face and she hugged herself. Nothing was visible past the first few feet of the porch. She loved a good old-fashioned winter storm.

Maybe they wouldn't be leaving tomorrow.

Wrapping a towel around the handle, she carried the kettle of hot water toward the kitchen when she again caught her foot on the Indian rug, this time nearly falling headfirst into the sleeping Trammell. Catching herself, she quickly brought the pot back to balance without spilling any water.

She added another log to the fire. Mixing boiling water and snow to fill a basin, she stripped naked and knelt beside the fire as if in prayer. The light of the fire turned her skin a honey yellow. Her dark curls were tinted with gold. The first touch of a hot, wet washcloth against her skin was as profound as a lover's caress. It prompted an audible sigh. Slowly, she began to give herself a bath.

"Fresh strawberries, the Musée d'Orsay, and Raymond Chandler novels."

Martha startled. Trammell's eyes sparkled in the firelight. She didn't know how long he had been watching. The thought of this man taking quiet pleasure from watching her bathe pleased her. "What's that?"

"You looked so sad. It was just a reminder of some of the joys in life."

She smiled. "Thank you."

He struggled against the sagging sofa until he sat upright. "Would you like some help?"

"A woman doesn't take a bath in front of a man if she doesn't want him to help."

"There is much I need to learn," Trammell said, bowing his head and taking the washcloth from her. "I must ask for your patience until I complete my education."

She nodded, bowing like a master to a student.

THIRTY

Martha stood at the cabin window. After six o'clock and still no hint of dawn. Snow continued to fall in thick flurries, driven by gale winds. Tracks leading to the cabin were long gone. A foot or more of snow had drifted onto the porch deck. They wouldn't be going anywhere today.

She pulled Trammell's turtleneck up over her face against the cold. It had been the first thing she could find to put on in the dark. It smelled of him and wood smoke. No, being snowed in wasn't the worst thing that could happen. She pictured him buried deep in the cocoon of the hand-made quilt. How the man could sleep—in the car, on the sofa, all night without so much as turning. If she got three solid hours with another three of tossing and turning, she considered it a restful night.

When she tripped on the Indian rug the third time, firewood thumped across the floor, and she followed it, sprawling on her hands and knees. Cursing aloud, she got to her feet. Red embers still glowed in the hearth from the wood she had added in the middle of the night. She tossed some kindling on, added a couple of logs, and turned the damper back to wide open. As the flames started to flicker yellow and bright, she peeled the rug back and immediately saw the problem—a hatch in the floor that led to a crawlspace under the house. One edge of the panel was raised half an inch. She slid the square section of floor aside and looked through the hole.

In the growing firelight, she could see that the cabin sat three or four feet off the ground, higher than she thought. Had it been a hideout for Mary and the kids when federal agents scoured the mountains for polygamist families? The dirt floor was packed hard and dry. Time, even a century or more, wouldn't pack the earth that hard unless something or someone went down there a lot. With no plumbing and no electricity, why would someone need to get down into the crawlspace on a regular basis? Was it a root cellar? She lit a lantern and lowered it through the hatch. Rough-hewn lumber, little more than barked logs, made up the floor joists. They rested on a foundation of interlaced red rocks, held tight with packed mortar. Down the center ran rocks stacked as pillars for the mid-section of the joists. In one direction, the texture of the earthen floor changed to clods of dirt and loose soil. She raised her head and looked behind. The loose dirt was under the kitchen. Doing a one-eighty around the hatch, she stuck her head back down the hole.

She saw it immediately. A row of crude cabinets hid the rock foundation underneath the fireplace. She dropped through the hole and grabbed the lantern. The crawlspace was empty except for the cabinets. Toward the far end, back under the bedrooms, she saw a break in the red-rock foundation. It took her a moment of squinting in the dim light to realize it was a small door to the outside, hidden outside by snow at the back of the house.

She crawled toward the cabinet doors, brushing spider webs off her face and hair. Four compartments, each with double doors made from timber planks with wooden toggle latches, lined the wall. On the front of each was a neat piece of masking tape. Martha held the lantern up and read "1830 & Extras," "1840," "1850," and "1860 & 70."

Martha undid the latch, and the door for "1830 & Extras" eased open on its own. The cabinet was maybe five feet long and two feet deep, small enough to hide a small child, large enough to hold plenty of potatoes and onions. It went from the dirt floor nearly to the floor joist. A single shelf divided the cabinet into equal parts top and bottom. Whatever its original purpose, now it was being used for storage.

Sealed Mason jars lined the top shelf in rows, each containing something that wasn't canned peaches or stewed tomatoes. A gallon jug rested on top of several Ziploc bags. The bottom shelf contained two wooden boxes, one larger than the other, several containers, one of which was ammonia. A mortar and pestle sat off to one side.

She left the lantern burning and crawled back up into the cabin. Shivering, she dressed in front of the fire, warming her back and then her front as she pulled on wool socks, jeans, and a sweater. She donned her fleece vest and slipped into Hewitt's oversized slippers. She tugged the wool hat with floppy ears over her head for protection from the spider webs. She added wood to the fire and lit a second lantern.

A blanket from the sofa and the second lantern went on the floor beside the hatch. She dropped back down in. With the blanket as a ground cover for the frozen earth, she began to explore the cabinets in earnest.

Two quart-size Mason jars were labeled "1830." She unscrewed a lid. Her nose told her it was something burned. Her fingers confirmed that they were two nearly full jars of black ashes. Labeled jars sat on the opposite side of the shelf—two jars each of "Tannic Acid," "Iron Sulfate," and "Gum Arabic." Oh, God. The uniqueness of the ingredients jogged a latent memory from one of Hewitt's lectures. Gum always struck her as an odd ingredient to put in ink to make it flow better. Hewitt had assured the class that one could neither chew Gum Arabic nor stick it under their desks. For centuries, it had been a key ingredient in ink, until they stopped using it around World War II.

Was Hewitt making ink?

A creeping fear pricked the periphery of her mind. She sat back, hugging herself. It couldn't be. There had to be another explanation.

She found a jar of "Logwood," another of "Indigo," which was almost empty. Ink coloring, obviously, at least the indigo. Behind a mortar and pestle was a small scale. Behind that, an old flat iron. She flipped open the lid of a small wooden box. In it were several old iron quill pens.

She grabbed the gallon milk jug, unscrewed the top, and sniffed: gasoline. The ATV was in the back shed. Trammell had showed it to her. He had even started it up. So why was the gasoline in the crawlspace? She moved the lantern away from the container.

She screwed the top back on and set the jug aside. The first Ziploc bag contained a fat, leather-bound journal, held shut by a large rubber band. When Martha removed the rubber band, it snapped. On the first page, Hewitt's tight, backwards scrawl started at the top of the page.

July 24, 1944
My dearest Eric,
	Sitting alone in the dark—lights are turned off in the mission at 8 o'clock as part of the war effort—I turn again to you for solace and comfort. I couldn't live at

home after what they did to you, but now, it seems, I cannot live with myself. I am alone and lonely in this strange city. I despair of ever being whole again. I see you in the crowds of young men going off to work in the plane factories. I see you at the market where I trade my labors for a piroghi and an apple. Just a glimpse and I turn and run, only to fumble through an apology to some unsuspecting soul. I cannot sleep. I am haunted by your face—the face I found in the ravine, my dearest, not the beautiful one I remember touching and kissing. I spend my days rememorizing every line and touch and feel of your cheeks, those sky blue eyes, the silken touch of your hair, that wispy attempt to grow a mustache— remember how I called it your "dirty-face look"?—all in hopes that it will be that face that visits me at night. But each night it's the crushed jaw, the bloody face, the broken teeth, the missing eye. . . "Why?" Why, why, why? Because I loved you? Because some evil men found that love abhorrent and used God as their excuse? Their vengeful God. How men can be so cruel, I do not know, but I promise I will become whole again and I promise I will never forget you and I promise I will do all that I can to make this right.

The letter continued on, but Martha began to flip through the journal. Daily entries were recorded during most of that first year—Hewitt finding work on the docks in Seattle, making his first friend, lying about his age to join the Navy—all told as if they would soon be read by his lover and confidante. She sensed the easing of Hewitt's despair, the renewal of hope.

The entries stopped for a period in the late fall, and when they resumed, Coxswain 4th Grade Hewitt Wilcox had been assigned to the Naval shipyard in Bremerton. He was aboard the *USS Idaho* when it sailed for the Pacific, a young, frightened coxswain whose job was to drive shore boats into some of the bloodiest battles in the war. Now, the diary entries to Eric the Red read more like prayers to a God he no longer believed in. Protect me, watch over me, soon I will join you.

With the assault on Okinawa, all entries stopped again for a period, and when they resumed, they had turned Eric into a father confessor, forgive me for I have sinned. His Higgins boat bombed, his commanding officer and most of the crew dead, Hewitt had spent three days hiding in the surf behind the wreckage of his boat, too afraid to move. Sometime later he wrote,

> From the wreckage, I watched the dead float by as if on parade, eyes open and unseeing. Unwittingly, but guilty nonetheless, I had driven these young men into a typhoon of steel, to their deaths, ferrying their souls to the underworld, just as I had you, my love. Just as I had delivered you. Your name for me should not have been Achilles, but Charon. In the brief interludes between bombs, I heard the shouts of the wounded, crying for mercy, begging for help. I didn't have the courage to try to help.

Martha closed the book and looked away. On the boat, a long time ago, she remembered him saying Achilles had lost his Patroclus. It hadn't been a throwaway line, but their secret names for each other. She tried to imagine the pure hell of lying in the surf for days, young and afraid, hoping for rescue, waiting without hope. No images or metaphors or words came that would help her understand. Hewitt had never talked about his time in the war. Like her father had never talked about Vietnam. Like how she never talked about Walt Boudreau for years. Some things were too terrible to share even with friends and loved ones. All that we hope to forget is what we most remember. She shivered—from the cold seeping through the frozen earth into her bones, and from how little she knew about the people she loved. But what was the price of silence?

She skimmed the pages. Hewitt treated 1945 like one long journal entry to his dead lover. Few dates appeared. The pen turned to pencil and back to pen again. References were made to being back in Seattle, being mustered out of the services, taking his first lover since Eric's death—a hurried, unsatisfying affair.

Martha adjusted the wick and the lamp glowed bright again. She flipped through the journal pages. The entries became less frequent, and sometime in the early '60s, the entries had dwindled to once a year, each dated July 12. On the anniversary of his lover's death, every year since, Hewitt wrote Eric Wain a love letter. She turned to the end of the journal. The notebook full, loose sheets of paper were stuffed in between the last page and back cover. A few months prior, Hewitt had written his last annual letter.

> It was 70 years today—70 years and the memories are as fresh as the day we parted—my arms still warm from your embrace, the sweetness of your lips still lingering on mine, that crooked smile having just graced its blessing on me. Time has not diminished my love for you. Soon, my dearest Eric, I shall have the retribution I have promised you. This year or next, my work will be complete.
>
> You would be pleased with my new lover. The gentleness of his soul reminds me so much of you . . .

Retribution. Such a powerful word. But did it mean justice or revenge? She placed the leather journal back in the Ziploc bag and set it aside for further reading by the fireplace. She rubbed her thighs and then her arms, glancing back over the Mason jars, the materials for making ink, the jugs of gasoline.

In the stack under Hewitt's journal were sheets of paper, parchment-like, all different sizes, all blank, maybe an inch thick in all. Some had ragged edges, others were neat and perfectly cut. Many had brown edges, as if they had been sitting in Granny's attic for the past century. The next Ziploc contained a second leather-bound book, its pages blank. The last Ziploc contained a loose-leafed collection of letters and diary entries, all written in different hands, all dated in the 1830s—weather, the state of the crops, someone named Eliza getting married in Spring-field, Wilbur breaking his arm in a fall off that damn—excuse my language, Ma—wild mustang he bought from Lone Tree, the drought-damaged crops, fear of reprisal in the border towns for hanging the Lakota horse thief.

Nothing remotely connected the letters to any secret societ-ies as far as she could tell, no mention of the church, or of illicit activities, or of the Elders or Joseph Smith. Just news, gossip, complaints, and longings. Just families keeping in touch with families.

So why had Hewitt hidden them away in the crawlspace un-der a jug of gasoline? She looked at the packet of blank papers, then over at one of the jars of ashes. His lectures on "Fakes and Frauds" came back—one of his most interesting classes—and so did his recounting of the White Salamander letters from Mor-mon forger Mark Hofmann. Paper from the time period, he'd told the class, was readily available and could be bleached clean and pressed with an old flat iron heated in a fire. Ink was a sim-ple formula that anyone could reproduce in their kitchen sink. A chemical analysis dating the ink could be confounded by in-cluding ashes from documents from the proper timeframe. She glanced at the flat iron again, the careful labeling of materials by date, the ingredients for making ink.

She fought against the evidence in front of her as she rifled through the remaining cupboards: "1830 & Extras," "1840," "1850," and "1860 & 70," each with much the same items, minus the jars of "Tannic Acid," "Iron Sulfate," and "Gum Arabic." There was another jug of gasoline and two of something else, maybe kerosene or lantern oil.

Maybe the documents in the safe were the only ones important to his investigation into the Death Angels, and these were just "extras," saved because they might still be useful if not particularly relevant to his research. But blank papers? Ashes? The ingredients for ink?

No. No. No. Not Hewitt, not the man she knew and loved. Yet, why else would he have hidden them away in the crawlspace under the cabin? Why no mention of them in his long letter? Not so much as a "By the way, my dear, you'll find some less valuable documents under the cabin." He didn't want her to find them. That's why. No wonder he wanted her to set the cabin on fire. Burn the cabin, burn the evidence. God. He'd even put the gas and kerosene there to make sure it all exploded in a blaze. He had planned to come back. Must have. Otherwise, why hadn't he destroyed the cabin himself? One thing for sure, if he couldn't make it back, he knew she would do it for him. Unwittingly. The lie was hidden under the veil of friendship.

Thoughts flashed like images juiced on too much caffeine.

He must have developed a method of aging the documents without the ink cracking, one of the telltale clues that upended Hofmann's long-running hoax. Or were Povich and Martoni, his resident experts, in on the scam?

Emma Lee and Nancy Pace Wilcox. Of course. People the church would have no other information on because they weren't important in the history of the saints and elders. That's why Hewitt's documents didn't include anything from Joseph Smith or Brigham Young. They were too well known, the fraud easier to detect.

He had already sold documents to the church. If they were forgeries, experts could compare the style and handwriting of the incriminating documents against those. Forgeries confirming forgeries. A carefully laid out plan. A forgery scam to discredit the LDS.

"My God," she whispered.

"Mormon Death Squad Confirmed" the front page headline in the *Ballard Gazette* would declare. And even if they were later discovered as forgeries, retractions and apologies would be forgotten or ignored. Questions would remain. The damage would be done. And it would destroy Trammell's reputation.

But Trammell would just be one more in a long list of casualties. So Hewitt could have his retribution. It wasn't about justice, it was about revenge. It hadn't been for money or power. Or to reveal the truth. It was revenge, pure and simple. For Eric Wain. For being ostracized, cast out for being gay.

She slammed a cabinet door. He had lied. Lied to her! Used her. Betrayed her. Nearly gotten her killed. And what about Ralph Hargrove, Povich, Martoni? And Lance? All sacrificed for what? For *what*? For a lie. A goddamn lie. A goddamn fucking lie!

First, she had been fucked by Walt Boudreau; now she had been fucked by Hewitt Wilcox Chappell, her closest friend, a man she looked up to like a father.

She slammed the cabinet doors again and again, cursing him with each breath, cursing him over and over.

THIRTY-ONE

Martha sat slumped on the blanket, staring dully at the cabinet door hanging askew on a single hinge. Broken glass from two Mason jars, shattered on the frozen earth, reflected light from the lantern like crystals beside a fire. Each sharp shard pierced her heart anew with Hewitt's betrayal. How could he? How could he? She rocked on the floor as if she had been punched in the stomach, his betrayal washing over her in waves of nausea.

Above her, a floorboard creaked, just once, then nothing. There was no purpose in delaying the inevitable. She called out, "Lance, I'm down here."

The only response was a second creak of the floor, then silence. Her first reaction was to panic. Then she went still and quiet. Her senses strained to catch a sound, a shadow, a smell. It came as a hint of cold air wafting down the floor hatch. It meant a door was open. It meant they had company.

The image of Trammell, stretched out under the autumn quilt, oblivious to the waking world, came to her. She silently grasped two unbroken Mason jars and removed her wool hat and set it on top of the first jar and balanced that jar on the second one. She sidled toward the hole in the floor. As she raised her hat through it, she called out again, "Lance, I'm over here, I'm down—"

The glass exploded in her hand on the crack of a pistol shot. Martha scrambled backward, slamming her head against a floor joist. The wool hat lay beside her foot covered in ashes, the yarn frayed from the bullet hole. Blood dripped from her hand. She had been cut by a shard of glass. Not painful, all fingers worked. Trammell must have heard the gunshot. He was trapped in the back bedroom.

She grabbed the larger glass shards, flinging one at the cabinets, then a second, which smacked the wooden doors of "1850." More followed. Each made a solid thump farther down the wall. Blood beaded her fingertips. She quieted her breath. All she could do was wait. Seconds ticked by like lifetimes. She crouched under the floor joist, back from the hole, poised to spring, ready to kill, not yet ready to die.

She first saw the shadow creeping forward, falling across the floor joist opposite her. All she had left were a couple of glass shards. They would have to do. She prepared to toss them at the wall. Suddenly the shadow spun and cracked off two more shots.

Martha propelled herself out of the hole, yelling "NO!" and driving her shoulder through him, as he turned, knocking him back into the fireplace. The gun popped off one last shot. Hot ash lifted in a gray cloud. He screamed as she pushed his head into the flames. His red hair began to blaze. Right before she snapped his neck, she recognized the pimply face of Danny Kimble.

She tossed him to the floor and grabbed his gun. "Lance," she screamed. "Lance!" She burst through the curtain and ran straight into the mattress. The impact bounced her back. "Lance, it's me."

The mattress dropped, revealing the naked Trammell.

"Good thinking," she said. "Get dressed. I'm sure he didn't come alone."

Two doors, two exits.

Trammell yanked her down. A spray of bullets fluttered the curtain and splintered the back wall. Low to the floor, Martha heard more bullets thud into the heavy planks near her head. She prayed the old timbers were up to the task.

"You know how to use that thing?" Trammell panted.

"What?" Martha mouthed.

"The gun. Know how to use it?"

"No clue." She had forgotten she held it in her hand.

He grabbed it from her, extended his arm into the doorway and squeezed off a couple of shots. Everything went quiet. Now the unfriendlies knew they were up against someone who could shoot back.

"Where'd you learn that?" Martha let herself breathe.

"First-timer's luck." He poked his head around the corner, and ducked back just as a shot splintered the doorjamb. "He's at the front door. Christ! The cabin's on fire. The fireplace. Jesus! Hewitt's papers! I gotta—"

"Leave 'em, they're not important!" Martha tossed him his pants and a sweater.

"Are you nuts?" He hopped on one leg, trying to pull up his pants. "Why do you think they're shooting at us? It's about those papers. If we lose them, the bad guys win."

"Trust me! Forget them. They're not important. We stick together. I've got an idea. Any bullets left in the gun?"

"No fucking idea."

"Let's hope."

Trammell fired a couple of shots, and they charged out of the bedroom with the mattress as a shield. He kept firing until the gun clicked empty and he tossed it aside. Four steps and they were at the floor hatch. Trammel dove through the growing flames into the crawlspace below. Flames licked Martha's slippers as answering gunfire hit the mattress. She staggered when a bullet slammed into her shoulder. It punched the breath out of her and she dropped through the hole like a sack of grain.

Burning embers followed her down, one in her hair. Trammell was there, arms under her shoulders, dragging her back against the wall then smothering her hair with his hands. She blinked to clear her eyes. She struggled to think. Move, she told herself, move. It's only pain, move through it, she heard Jonesy say. Move! Control it or it'll control you.

But it was Trammell. "Move, we have to move." His eyes dropped to her shoulder. "Oh, God, Martha, oh God."

She glanced down. Her left shoulder was covered in blood. She could move her arm, though she wanted to scream when she did. Still, her fingers curled. Her breath was jagged but she could breathe.

"I'll be okay." Her attempt to speak came out as little more than a hoarse whisper. "Far back wall, under the bedrooms, there's a door. Go, go."

Trammell didn't move. "We go together."

She thrust one of the lanterns at him and shouted, "Goddamn it, go."

From the open cabinets, she grabbed the two gallon jugs of gasoline, twisted the tops off. With her good arm, she pitched one up the hole toward the kitchen. She sent the second toward the fireplace. In seconds, an explosion rocked the centuries-old timbers of the cabin. She heard a scream from above. Mid-scream, a second explosion shook the cabin. Someone had ventured too close too soon, hoping to follow them down the rabbit hole.

Trammell had kicked out the crawlspace door by the time she got there and had pushed it into a wall of white snow until he could get his hands outside, then began furiously scooping snow back under the cabin. He turned. "Get some of that on your shoulder. It'll slow the bleeding. Pack it tight."

Smoke filtered into the crawlspace. Martha coughed. The heat intensified. Embers were drifting down through seams in the floor. The fire roared above them. In minutes it would be through the floor boards. Timbers and planks dried for a hundred years were going up like a tinderbox. The snow packed against her shoulder turned red. Pain knifed through her.

Trammell broke through. He poked his head up and dropped back down. He raised it again, this time taking a longer look. "I don't see anyone, but that doesn't mean they're not out there. The shed's to our right."

"Get to the shed."

"We'll be trapped again."

"And you're in your bare feet. Where we going to go anyway? The mountains? We can't stay here. Just go for the shed. If anyone shoots, drop into the snow and crawl."

It took Trammell another minute to create a big enough hole in the snow for them to crawl out. Martha held her shoulder and was nearly overcome by smoke. He went up and out, reached back, and yanked her up by her good arm. Pain screamed through her body.

They plunged mid-thigh into snow, wading as if in slow motion, expecting more shots to erupt. All they heard was the roar of the fire. Steam rose from what was once the snow-covered roof. The wood shakes would go in seconds. They made it to the back side of the shed. Trammell poked his head around the corner, then waved Martha forward, and pulled the door open against a foot of fresh snow.

Martha followed him into the shed. She kicked off Hewitt's oversized sheepskin slippers. "Get these on. Now. Don't argue." With her good arm, she snatched the old snowshoes off the wall and tossed them to Trammell. "Figure out how to make these work." Some kind of old horse blanket was folded up in the corner. "Wrap that around you like a coat."

Trammell stood motionless. "I'm not leaving you."

"Don't be stupid, Lance." She didn't have time for this. "We got one pair of slippers between us and no coat. I'm hurt. You're the runner. You've got the best chance to get out of here. Get back with some help. I have a better chance of dealing with anything here than you do. We don't know how many there are."

"Even if you survive, you'll freeze to death before I can get back."

"There'll be plenty of fire to keep me warm for a while. Get to town and get back. The police will have snowmobiles."

Snowmobiles? She looked at the ATV, glanced around the shed. Behind the woodpile? Outside in the snow? Her eyes drifted up to the rafters. "Help me get up top."

"What are you going to do?"

"I'm going to wait. Start the ATV, rev it high, and then run. Go out the back, loop far out around the cabin before turning back toward the trail. Look for their snowmobiles out on the trail. They had to come up on machines. They didn't walk in this morning through the storm."

"But you can't ride out of here on a goddamn ATV. You won't get five feet in this snow."

"They don't know that. They'll think it's a snowmobile. If anyone's still out there, they'll have to come check it out. And I'll be ready. It may give you time to get out of sight."

"And they've got really big guns, in case you've forgotten."

"Have you got a better plan to get us the fuck out?"

He remained silent and motionless for a moment. Then shook his head and muttered, "Fuck, fuck, fuck. Okay, come on." He hoisted her up between two rafters.

"I'll leave the door open," he said, looking up at her. "Light's still in the east. You might see a shadow first, but fuck with this snow, you might not. If you're over the door, right against the wall, they'll have to look straight up to see you."

"Exactly," she said.

He began strapping the snowshoes around the slippers. He looked up at her. "This is a really shitty plan, Martha, really shitty." He grabbed the horse blanket and stood with one hand on the ignition for the ATV. His dark eyes held her. "Be here when I get back."

"Yeah. Just make sure you do get back."

"I love you."

He turned the ignition before she could reply. The engine sputtered to life, and he revved it once, twice, three times, until it roared in the small shed. Clomping away in his snowshoes, he disappeared out the door.

Martha straddled two rafters, her back against the wall. The loss of blood and the sudden loss of adrenaline left her lightheaded. She was afraid she would faint. She forced herself back to the present, wrapping her good arm around a rafter to brace herself. "Ignore the pain" seemed like such a great idea until someone put a bullet in you. She tried to keep pressure on the shoulder wound. Blood oozed through her fingers and dripped onto the snow drifting through the door, bright red splotches of betrayal.

They'd come soon, they'd come running. For all they knew it was one of their own. With snowmobiles, they could have left Tropic at dawn this morning.

·If they knew where to go.

Martha refused to think about that betrayal. She had been so wrong about so many things. Survive the mountain and then deal with the rest, she told herself.

What would she have said in response to Trammell's "I love you?" She didn't have an answer, but those three words seemed to be the only thing right now that was true and genuine and worth living for.

She looked down. Another splotch of blood fell to the snow. She smelled the burning cabin. Over the roar of the ATV, she tried to clear her mind. Either they'll come or they won't. It was out of her control; all she could do was react if they did.

His shadow arrived first. Arms extended, a two-handed grip on the gun. The noise from the ATV muffled the bullets, if there were any, until one hit something vital. The ATV chugged a couple of times and died. Martha, pressed tight against the wall, prepared to drop between the rafters. But she needed him to take another step. *Just one more step, you bastard.* The gun shifted—left, right, fast. The figure looked down and saw the blood. He started to look up. He took one more step.

Martha dropped. Both feet drove into his back. He sprawled out face first. The gun flew from his hand and skittered across the dirt floor. She rose and sprang at him as he reached for the gun. She stomped on his fingers and kicked it out of reach. He lunged up and she drove the heel of her bare foot into his knee. It snapped backwards, and he screamed in pain, dropping to his other knee. A hand reached toward his boot—for a knife or a second gun, she didn't know or care. His nose broke with a loud crack when she kneed his face. With her good arm, she grabbed his searching hand and twisted it behind his back until she heard the shoulder pop. He howled and went limp.

"Who sent you, you fucking bastard?" she yelled, her knee

on the back of his neck, ready to break it with the slightest downward pressure. "Who sent you here? It was all for nothing, goddamn it, don't you know it was all for nothing?"

"He said you'd be a tough bitch."

Martha snapped her head up. Outside the shed door stood a monster, half his shirt and hair scorched, eyebrows gone, one eye swollen shut, left check and forehead blistering and flame red. The other half of his hair ended in a little flip just below his collar. The gasoline surprise hadn't killed him. Not yet anyway. One hand tried to steady the one holding the gun. Both hands trembled. Still the barrel never left its target—her.

"So we meet again, asshole," she said.

He offered a lopsided grin. "But this time, it's for real, darling. No make-believe. Get up. Without breaking his neck. Where's your boyfriend?"

Martha stood up, raising a hand. She could only bring the other one waist high. The prone man below her rolled to his side, gasping and moaning.

"Long gone," Martha said. "With all Hewitt's papers in his backpack. It's just you and me now."

The man laughed, or tried to. It came out as a wheeze. He winced and blinked his one open eye, as if trying to stay focused. It was a missed opportunity, Martha knew; she might not get another.

"We'll catch him."

"You won't get off this mountain alive."

"Yeah? I'm the one with the gun."

"I've heard that before. You and your buddy here won't get a hundred yards in this snow. Your snowmobiles are disabled, by the way, except the one Lance is on right now."

His eyes darted back over his shoulder, but before Martha could move, they flicked back. His hands still quivered, but the gun remained on her. "You're bluffing." He shook the gun at her. "Where's the old queer hiding?"

"If I knew, I wouldn't be on this godforsaken mountain."

"Unless he sent you. This isn't exactly the kind of place you just stumble on. We know he's talking to you somehow. Tell me where he is and I'll let you walk."

"We both know that's not true, so let's not pretend."

"Don't you get it? We want the fag, not you. We had a deal and he's trying to break it. Thought he could protect you by bringing in the police. Clever move to drive his van into the water." What might have been a laugh came out a grunt. "But we got it figured out."

A deal? Protect me?

"That's why you had to kill Ralph," Martha said. "That put your man in place."

The unburned portion of his lip curled in a sneer. "And let him know we're very serious about him delivering on his promise. We're running out of time, and I'm running out of patience." He steadied the gun. "We need to have a little chat with the old man."

"You're running out of time, all right. I told you, I don't know. Shooting me won't change that."

Martha glanced over his shoulder. With a crackling explosion, flames shot through the roof of the cabin behind him.

"There are no Death Angels." She spoke quickly and turned slightly, bringing her good arm toward the gunman. "It's all a forgery. But you know that don't you? You're part of it. Even the Hammer of God was quoting a forged letter—how ironic."

"That poor prick actually believed God and some high-tech body armor would save his ass. The bastard had a death wish, you ask me. He was just supposed to put a little fear of God in you so you'd get the old queer to get back in the game. Like the night at the newspaper. Oh well, bigger split for the rest of us."

"So you were going to sell the forgeries to the church and Hewitt took them to Trammell instead."

"Shut up. The only thing I want from you is the old man. Tell me where he is or you'll never see your boyfriend again. We've spent too long laying the groundwork for this. We've been getting old documents for him for years, and all he's given us is peanuts along the way. A little here, a little there. Big score's coming, big score's coming. Well, this is the big score."

She slowly flexed her fingers. "You don't think the LDS will know the stuff is forged?"

"They haven't yet, honey. The old man was good, very, very good. Fooled the church. Fooled his buddies. Even got them to sign off on a signature for Abraham fucking Lincoln. Had it framed, I hear. I'll get my money alright, and once I do, you think I give a fuck what the church figures out?"

"So this was the last haul, the big haul. Only, Hewitt never intended to sell it. He didn't get cold feet. He planned to publish it the whole time. He was after revenge. Retribution." She snarled the word. "It's all he wanted. Revenge. And you played right into his hand. You became the Death Angels for him. How much more convincing is it that the Mormons had a secret team of assassins if everyone who's touched the documents ends up dead? You and your buddies couldn't've played the part any better. He set you up and you were just too fucking greedy to see it. You got played. Just like we did."

"*You* might've been played, honey, but we weren't. The old pussy didn't think anyone would get hurt, but we thought the church might pay more and bury the forgeries faster if it seemed a little more real. We just upped the asking price by eliminating a few queers."

"You fucking bastard."

The man in the shed groaned and shifted to a sitting position. The other man's eye left Martha for just a second. In that instant, she jabbed-stepped hard to her left, planted her foot and spun in the opposite direction. The gun swung with her first step and he fired, drilling a bullet into the side of the shed. He fired again. The gun kept swinging away from her.

"NO!" Trammell came around the back corner with the old snowshoe raised like a club. "No, you fucking bastard, not her."

The gunman fired. Trammell staggered but kept coming. Martha lunged at the burnt man. He fired again. Missed again. He screamed when she drove a short jab into the burned side of his face. It spun him, and she kicked his leg out, dropped to a knee, grabbed the back of his collar with her good arm and yanked him down. When he landed, he hit hard across her leg, just as he was supposed to do. With a little more help, his spine snapped. She felt it and heard it. He went limp and she flung him off her leg and into the snow.

She rushed to Trammell, who had dropped just short of his intended target, arms flung out in a final grasp, his mouth still open with a desperate scream. She lifted his face. Blood poured from a chest wound. She started packing it with snow.

"Goddamn it, Lance, you stay with me now." She was shouting and crying and packing more snow against his chest and holding it tighter until it oozed red between her fingers. "Lance, stay with me, and we'll get you out of this."

His eyes opened, eyes she had gotten lost in, eyes she wanted to stay lost in forever. He stared at her for what seemed an eternity. His words were faint, spoken between heavy wheezing. "Strawberries. The Louvre. Shakespeare," he gasped. "Don't forget." He struggled for breath. His eyes opened one last time, and he whispered, "I love you."

Before she could answer, he was dead.

THIRTY-TWO

Martha held Trammell until an uncontrollable shiver wracked her body. She held him awhile longer. Finally, she eased his head to the snow and tried to stand up. She stumbled, felt the world spin and fell. It was time to move or give up. But she could not move.

"Help." The voice was weak, almost inaudible over the roar of the fire. "Don't leave me here."

Inside the shed, the man—it must be Military Boots—was crawling toward her. Blood trailed from his limp leg. Under his snow pants, there had to be a compound fracture, bone protruding through skin. She had no trouble getting to her feet this time. In the outbuilding, the gun she had kicked away in the struggle was only a few feet from him. She felt its heft. The rough texture of the grip caressed her palm. Her fingers played with the cold trigger. She pointed it at the man's head. Imploring eyes begged her to shoot, not to shoot—she didn't know; she didn't care. But they pleaded with her in a way that words never could. He sagged to the ground and closed his eyes. Beyond him, snow had already started to cover Trammell's ashen face. For a long time, she stood there trying to make up her mind. Finally, she turned and heaved the gun far out into the snow and walked away.

"Don't leave me here, please," the man moaned again.

She ignored him.

She stripped the dead man of his half-burnt winter coat, his boots, and gloves. Underneath, he wore a wool sweater. She took that, too. Pain shot through her as she slid it over her head. She nearly passed out. She left one arm empty, and cinched the dead man's belt around her body, strapping her wounded arm hard against her side. Her breath came in jagged spurts.

She bent to kiss Trammell one last time. Lips touched again, her tears spilling onto his unblinking eyes. Oh, to live in a fairy tale where a kiss, a tear, could bring the dead back to life.

But she wasn't in a fairy tale and he remained motionless on the ground.

She recovered the snowshoe he had intended to use as a weapon. A snowshoe against an experienced gunman. To protect her. Chivalry died hard, but it died all the same. She found the other snowshoe behind the shed, along with the horse blanket. She took both. No tracks led from the shed toward the woods. A hole had been dug into the snow. He had stretched out on the blanket, staying out of sight and waiting.

Goddamn you, Lance Trammell, if you had just listened to me, we'd both be alive right now. But would she? The gunman had missed his first shot only because Trammell's snowshoe charge had distracted him long enough to allow her to get within reach.

Martha stood as close to the burning cabin as she dared, letting her wet, bloody clothes dry, eating snow to rehydrate and letting the fire warm her. Her shoulder throbbed, each beat of her heart a reminder of the wound. She kept glancing at the overcast sky, hoping, praying the tower of smoke would bring a helicopter down over the cliff or up from the valley. Nothing filled the sky except more snow. Nothing filled her mind except the memory of Lance Trammell.

The roof collapsed into the burning cabin. She stepped back to avoid the falling embers. The motion of the first step seemed to propel her into action. She wrapped the horse blanket around her shoulders, strapped on the old snowshoes and began to walk through the now gently falling snow.

Martha rode out of the mountains on one of the gunmen's snowmobiles.

Within a quarter mile, just out of sight over the first ridge, she had spied the machines tucked back into a grove of Ponderosa pines. The trail out was easily identifiable by the tracks the gunmen made on the way in. Snow had rounded the edges and started to fill them in, like an ancient footprint in the mud, but there they were, her bread crumbs out of the mountains.

A teenager sneaking out to light a smoke found her lying in the middle of the road in front of Bryce Valley High School. The snowmobile, still running, lay overturned in the ditch.

This began a series of events of which Martha remembered little.

The local volunteer EMT, recognizing the gunshot wound and shocked by the amount of blood he found after opening her jacket, requested an emergency evac to the trauma unit in St. George. In the helicopter, Martha regained consciousness long enough to whisper to the paramedic, "One other still alive. Hurt bad. Follow the smoke up Bryce Canyon."

It was enough. The smoke, once spotted, acted like a beacon to the helicopter pilot and the paramedic. She remembered waking enough to look at the man on the stretcher beside her.

Remembered wondering if she'd regret not having killed him when she had the chance. His eyes opened to slits as she stared at him. For a moment, she thought she was looking at the face of Danny Kimble. Her wandering mind returned to the notion that she had already killed him. Was she supposed to kill him again? Fear came over the man's face when he opened his eyes enough to realize who he was traveling with. Martha closed her eyes and had the odd thought that this wasn't how she expected to take her first helicopter ride.

When she opened her eyes again, she saw a man sitting in the chair beside her bed. Thickset and clean shaven, he wore a uniform of olive and brown. His Smokey the Bear hat rested on a nightstand. Gray lined his temples. Reading glasses sat perched low on a bulbous nose. He saw her move and looked up from the paper he was reading.

"Martha Whitaker?"

"Yes." Her voice was hoarse, her throat dry.

"I'm Officer Ike Thomas with the Utah State Patrol. I'd like to ask you some questions."

She closed her eyes again, but when she opened them, he was still sitting there, still waiting. She answered as truthfully as she could. She didn't embellish, she didn't rant or rave, she didn't lie. The only thing she omitted was the final act, which she had only begun planning. Every time he backtracked or asked the same question again, she gave the same answer, told the same story, omitted the same future ending. Officer Thomas had the annoying habit of nodding his head with every other word, as if she were speaking in iambic pentameter and he was keeping the beat. Unwanted, uncalled for, her memory spurted out Trammell's line, "Now join your hands, and with your hands, your hearts." For now, his name would only bring a silent emptiness, a silence that, she knew, would begin to fade until it was forever out of reach. She began to cry softly. Officer Thomas left the room. When he returned, her tears had dried, and he started all over again with the same questions.

Martha figured she had at least one night of being safe, one night before she needed to start looking over her shoulder. Would he come down from Seattle to finish the job? Would he wait until she returned? Or was there yet another person from the forgery ring that she hadn't accounted for? She had to be ready. But she figured she had one night. She was too exhausted to think of anything more.

But that night, when the nurse came in at two a.m. to check her vital signs, she found the bed plumped up with pillows and Martha on the far side, dozing on the floor, no longer certain she had even one night.

Morning brought intense sunshine streaming through the east windows of her room and another visit from Officer Thomas. This time, an FBI agent, who looked like a Mormon missionary with his short hair and ill-fitting black suit, accompanied him. Another lengthy interview covered much of the same ground as they had covered the day before. Martha gave the same answers.

The FBI agent stepped out, and Thomas gathered up his papers. "We've posted a guard outside your room."

"To keep me in or to keep others out?" she asked.

"Both, for now," he said. "Been in touch with Seattle. A Detective Callison confirmed much of your story. Seems he's not real happy with you at the moment. But the younger Reichart, that's the young man they brought in with you, is starting to talk. We found what was left of his older brother in the ashes of the cabin. Found another by the shed with his back broken. Right where you said he'd be. The Reichart boy is talking, but he doesn't know much. It was his brother's gig, or so he claims."

"Guilty conscience?"

"Maybe." But his snort indicated he didn't really think so. "More likely he's gettin' all cooperative because he wants to avoid the death penalty. Seems they matched a fingerprint of his to a murder scene in Seattle. At some bookstore?"

Martha nodded, torn between not having killed him when she had the chance and grateful that she didn't. "Did he mention who his Seattle connection is?"

Officer Thomas looked at her for a time. His continued silence told her they hadn't identified the Seattle connection. Military Boots must not have known.

It didn't matter; she knew.

He had to come after her. She remained the one person who could tie it all together.

But how could she get out of here? Even if she sneaked past the security guard, she had nowhere to go, no way to pay for it. Her wallet, with all her money, credit cards, and ID, had gone up in flames. As had her cell phone. She had no idea where her laptop might be, or the rental car, for that matter. And would it matter? Would she be strong enough to protect herself when he came for her?

She sat up, waited for the lightheadedness to pass, and then stood, grateful that her arm was in a sling strapped tight to her body. She started simply, moving and flexing muscles: neck, one shoulder, one arm, fingers clenching and releasing, clenching and releasing, one leg, then the other, then toes. Each move hurt. She felt exhausted, but she did it all again. Two days before, she had been in prime shape. It hadn't disappeared with the bullet wound. The wound was painful, but the doctor said it was clean, the bone intact. It wouldn't kill her. One arm, one shoulder was incapacitated, not the rest of her body, not her mind.

She cinched the sling tight to her chest and placed her feet on the floor. Slowly breathing in and out, she tried to quiet the pain, but there was some pain the drugs couldn't mask.

The nurse came in. "Honey, back into bed. I need to take your vitals."

As the nurse prepared to leave, Martha asked, "Could I make a long-distance phone call?"

The nurse nodded, gave her the code to get an outside line, and disappeared.

"Crystal, it's Martha," she said, when her assistant answered. It took several minutes to assure her she was all right, that the doctor said it wasn't a serious wound, well not serious for a gunshot anyway. Apparently, the Utah State Patrol, the FBI, and City Hospital had been in contact with the office. Rumors and worries and innuendos were flying fast on the cubical grapevine. Nobody knew anything, but everyone was talking about what happened to the Ice Queen. Martha again tried to assure her. "Crystal, I'm okay, really. Now, I need your help."

A fitful night sleeping on the hard floor on the far side of the bed had left her reserves nearly empty. The nurse had woken her when making her rounds, only to find her hand captured in a grip that could easily have broken her wrist. The woman shook her hand and said, "What's wrong, honey?"

Martha just stared wide-eyed, as if the nurse were a burnt-faced monster. Her soul felt empty, her body a husk that continued to take each painful breath only because she had a task left undone.

Before ten o'clock the next morning, FedEx delivered a package for Martha Whitaker. The deputy on guard outside the door checked the iPhone, opened the laptop, looked inside the package, and shrugged. Martha signed for the package, and sort-

ed the contents: $2,000 cash, a company credit card, and pho-
tocopies of her driver's license and passport, kept on file at the
office in case of emergencies.

She blew the amazing Crystal a mental kiss. Also inside the
packet was a sealed envelope. Martha recognized the sloppy
scribble of her boss, Ben Matthews. A letter of reprimand? More
likely, her termination letter. Today, it didn't matter. She tossed
it back inside the package, unopened.

The day dragged on, followed by a night that made the day
seem short. The oxycodone did wonders in knocking the edge
off, but how would she manage without it? She started palming
every other one, preparing for when they would stop dispensing
them to her every three hours.

A second FBI agent, whose bedside manner contained all
the pleasantries of a slap in the face with a wet mop, grilled her
on how she knew the documents were forgeries and how she
managed to subdue three gun-toting perps with little more than
a smile and . . .

"Over twenty fucking years of intense training," she snapped.

In the twilight, the lights in the parking lot came on, one by
one. Snow clouds in dark, towering stacks had passed through
in the afternoon, leaving a few inches of fresh snow behind.
Along the western horizon, a sliver of deep red foretold a reprieve
from the next storm system. Officer Thomas' knock startled her
and she spun around. He stood with his wide-brimmed hat in
his hands. In his pleasant baritone, he said, "Didn't mean to scare
you, ma'am."

Her smile felt forced. "Officer."

"I wanted to let you know, we transferred the Reichart fellow
up to Salt Lake, and all the FBI agents with him, thank the Lord
Almighty. We think we'll get a signed confession from him if his

damn attorney—no offense intended, ma'am—doesn't kibosh the deal. Life without parole in exchange for a full statement and future cooperation. Seattle PD was happy as a bull in rut with the confession. They're sending some detective named Metcalf. You know him?"

Martha nodded.

"Anyway, wanted to let you know we're releasing the guard. You're free to go whenever the doc clears you."

"Thank you, Officer Thomas," Martha said. "When is Metcalf due to arrive?"

"Sometime in the morning, I suspect. Is there a problem?"

"No, no problem at all."

L ess than an hour later, Martha walked out of the hospital. She figured she had only minutes before they discovered her empty room. She carried a plastic hospital bag with a hospital toothbrush, her arm sling, and Crystal's package. She tucked her left arm into her jeans pocket, hoping it made her less conspicuous than a woman in a white sling. Outside, her breath vaporized into frozen crystals. She passed the first two hotels she came to and checked into the third. In an hour, she took her belongings and walked out the side door.

One car pulled over. The passenger's window slid down. The driver leaned over and asked how much it would cost for a little company. She offered to break his neck if he didn't keep moving. She walked a mile before checking into a different motel, giving a fake name and paying cash.

Still, she slept on the floor, on the far side of the bed. Nightmares were her only visitors.

S t. George roused itself in fits and spurts. She called a cab, and said merely, "Airport." For the rental car agency, the copy of her driver's license and the company credit card were all the ID she needed. By nine o'clock, she was driving down the highway in a rented Subaru. Northbound Interstate 15 stretched out like a snake winding through a canyon as she began the long journey home. Road signs announced the exit for Cedar City and Bryce National Canyon. With each familiar sign, Trammell was there, asleep in the car, just as before, stars shining above them like a queen's tiara in the black sky.

And now she was returning home, where someone was about to learn what the wrath of an avenging angel was really like.

The rolling hills alongside the interstate were the front range to the Tushar Mountains, with the snow-covered dome of Mount Belknap visible in the distance. Towns she had never heard of and would never visit clicked off the miles. Eyes on the rearview mirror, she exited for gas. She drained the last of her coffee, washing down four ibuprofens with it. The gas station attendant was a chatty sort, tilting his cowboy hat back to reveal a handsome face and yellowing teeth. Leaning close, she smelled cigarettes and laughed at his flattery. No, she didn't get thrown from her horse, but she touched his hand and laughed some more. Did he, by any chance, know a good place to stay in Salt Lake City? Not some dive now but, you know, something with a little class? She desperately needed a massage and a manicure; she wanted a real steak, not some overcooked piece of leather. After thanking him but declining his offer to provide the massage, she accepted his recommendation for the Grand Spa at the Great America Hotel. She plugged the name into her phone and confirmed the directions were correct. She paid for the gas, more coffee, and a ham sandwich with the company credit card.

Twenty miles down the road, she made a last-second exit at Santaquin. One car followed her, but it soon turned off toward the city center. She found US Highway 6 and began to backtrack south, until at Delta the road merged with US Highway 50. She turned west. Once, she stopped amid the barren, rolling hills to down another four ibuprofens and empty the rest of the coffee onto the dirt shoulder. The frozen ground turned to mud and she lathered some across both front and back license plates on the rental car. She looked up and down the road and across the barren white landscape. She was the only living thing in sight.

Martha drove ten hours, stopping only for gas and bad deli coffee and snacks, all paid for with cash. Before entering a place, she removed her sling, donned a stocking cap, and tucked her hair up inside. On the lonely stretches of highways, the ache in her shoulder kept her awake and she had time to think and cry and grow angrier and think some more. Most of her thoughts were about Trammell, but occasionally, they strayed to her friend, Hewitt Wilcox Chappell. A forger and a liar. Even if he hadn't meant anyone to get hurt, he had still run and hid when people started getting hurt. Still hiding behind the wreckage in the surf, just like he had so many years ago at Okinawa. She envisioned him at some remote beach cabin in Moclips or Copalis, listening to the surf roll in while people died and she and Trammel fought for their lives. He had tried to protect her? He hadn't done a very fucking good job, if he had tried. Did he think leaving her his estate made up for putting her in danger? Christ, he may as well have killed Trammell himself. All for a lie—a lie he had been living and hiding the entire time that she knew him. He had ruined Obbert's career for a lie, and would have gladly done the same to Trammell. And he had asked her, "the daughter he never had," to be his messenger. The betrayal was worse than the bullet wound. Far worse.

Once, she pulled off to the side along a stretch of highway that even angels had abandoned. She walked around the car, shaking herself awake, and squatted to pee. Back in the car, she opened the glove box for the bottle of ibuprofen. She remembered how Trammell had used the glove box of the rental car to collect his receipts, all neatly paper-clipped together, so careful to tally his expenses, so he could repay her upon a return that now would never happen.

He didn't want to be beholden to anyone; he needed to pay his own way. Like Hewitt's friend, Mitch Adair. Adair had gone off to find God and came back a more spiritual man for the experience. What had Hewitt gone off to find? Nothing but revenge. And where was Adair now?

She thought she knew where to start looking.

Miles turned under her wheels. Sunshine turned to darkness and still she drove, one hand on the steering wheel, the other strapped hard in the sling to her side. She stopped only for gas, coffee, to pee—the essentials of life on the road. Eureka, Nevada, population 1,013, slipped by, Cold Springs still another fifty miles ahead, nothing in between but high-country desert. No lights, no cars, not another soul in this forsaken spot in the universe. Which suited her just fine.

A little after midnight, the lights of Reno appeared on the horizon, a corrupted haze of yellow against the flawless night sky. A small casino outside of town provided a cheap room and a late dinner of overcooked Salisbury steak covered with canned mushrooms. Martha ate it all.

Back in her room, she found the single strand of her hair undisturbed in the door lock. She stripped naked, cleaning her shoulder where the wound had oozed during the long day. Her shoulder throbbed like a bass backbeat in time with the pounding of her heart.

She slept on the floor, curled up in a fetal position. The nightmares didn't come until nearly morning.

In her shopping cart, she had a bathing cap, double-sided tape, gauze pads, an antibiotic cream, medical tape, a small purse, and an electric barber's kit. She was studying the wigs, trying to decide if she wanted to be a blonde or a redhead when her phone rang. She recognized the number and almost ignored it. Finally, she answered, "Whitaker."

"It's Metcalf." There was a long pause. "I'm sorry about Trammell."

"Yeah, so am I." She didn't offer anything more.

"I was wondering if we can meet."

"Where are you?"

"Salt Lake City, the Grand America Hotel."

"I hear it's a nice place."

"I know you heard that." Again, silence. "I was worried about you, okay?"

Martha didn't respond.

"Whitaker, I'm sorry you're hurt," Metcalf said. "And I'm sorry Trammell got killed. But I'd still like to meet with you. Even with Reichart's confession, there are still a lot of unanswered questions. Like, do you know where the old man is?"

"No," she said. "Do you know how they found us?"

"Where are you?" was his reply.

She didn't like his answer. She didn't offer one of her own. "Okay, tomorrow afternoon in the hotel lobby. Five o'clock."

"You'll be there?"

"Yeah, I'll be there," she lied. "I'll talk to you and only you. If there's so much as a hint that you're lying to me, I'll break your neck. And this time I won't hold back."

"I'm one of the fracking good guys, in case you forgot," he snapped.

"And I'm fucking Florence Nightingale. Five, the hotel lobby."

She ended the call. We'll be meeting soon enough, she thought, tucking her phone in the back pocket of her jeans. She decided she didn't need a wig after all. She picked up a second pair of sunglasses and a small flashlight, and checked out.

Sharing the parking garage with Target was a Best Buy. She loaded her stuff into the car. Fifteen minutes later, she walked out of Best Buy with a new Nikon camera, multiple lenses, an extra battery, a car charger, and an extra sixteen-gig memory card. At the last minute, she had decided to include a cheap phone with her purchase. She had the number activated before leaving the store.

The last stop was a thrift store she had passed on the way into town. Located in an old grocery store, it was advertising post-holiday sales, and Martha quickly found what she wanted. A mannequin was dressed in some of the best women's fashions the store had to offer: a tight-knit cashmere sweater, $17, a matching gold necklace and bracelet, $21, a gray wool skirt that was modest enough for work, $12.

She bought it all, including the mannequin.

Martha stood in front of the mirror for a long time before making the first cut. One blue eye and one brown eye stared back at her. Black tresses, in places wavy, in other places tightly curled, framed her fine features and long nose. She touched her hair—so personal, a tangle of mystery and identity. She flicked the clippers on, took a deep breath, and raised her good arm. Clumps of long, curly black hair drifted to the floor. Once started, she worked quickly, making cut after cut until all of her hair lay piled at her feet.

Again she fixed on her image in the mirror. A stranger in all but the eyes stared back at her. The bald head could have been that of a Buddhist acolyte. It could have been, from a sideways glance, the pate of Lance Trammell. It could have been the skull of an assassin.

The look pleased her.

Heading north out of Reno on US Highway 395, she soon entered California. Next to her, Manny was doing fine, the seatbelt/shoulder harness holding her motionless figure securely in the passenger seat. Martha's ebony hair, taped and glued to the bathing cap, hung limply against the black cashmere on Manny's shoulders. Manny desperately needed to see a hairdresser, but it would have to do. Dark sunglasses hid her blank eyes.

Holding the instruction manual against the wheel, Martha began to read how to use her new camera. Before entering Interstate 5 outside of Mount Shasta, she pulled off at a scenic vista and spent a half hour practicing taking photos and movies of the mountain that had lifted its cloudy skirt to reveal its snow-white summit. Just another tourist in awe of nature's splendor. Manny stayed in the car.

Once Martha hit the Interstate, she set the cruise control to eighty and pointed the rented car toward home. Outside of Roseburg, Oregon, her work phone rang. Metcalf. She ignored it. The clock on the car dash read 5:31 p.m. The phone rang every ten minutes for the next half hour. Finally, she shut it off and stuffed it in her new purse and bumped the cruise control up to eighty-four.

THIRTY-THREE

To bait her trap, Martha sneaked out the back door of the garage and followed the muddy trail back down the hill. A brightening in the western sky hinted that the afternoon might offer a reprieve from the winter rains, but for now, a steady drizzle penetrated the woods, the leafless trees offering little protection. Minutes later, she pulled the rental car into the driveway and parked in front of the Carriage House. Without looking right or left or back, she scampered up the steps, calling out, "Beatrice, Dante, where are my kitties? I'm home."

In case they missed the Subaru parked in front of the garage, she went around the apartment flicking on all the lights.

She looked around. Manny, now cut in half just below her slim Barbie-doll buttocks, sat on the sofa, her back to the door. Her newly curled wig cascaded to her cashmere-covered shoulders. She still wore her matching gold necklace and bracelet. The computer, open and operating, rested on the afghan that covered her sawn off legs. The sleep mode had been deactivated and the computer screen flipped through random images from Martha's picture files. The iPhone and a cup of coffee sat near Manny's feet on the coffee table. She checked the ring volume of the phone. It was set on high. The ringer on the phone in her pocket was off.

From the kitchen, the aroma of fresh-brewed coffee wafted through the small apartment. She looked up: the hole where the fish-eye lens of her new Nikon camera took in the sweep of the Carriage House from the main door to kitchen to Manny to the bathroom door was obvious, but she had to hope he wouldn't look up. The drill was back in its place in the ground-floor shop. All remnants of dust and particle board had been cleaned up and disposed of. With the click of one button from her hiding place in the coat closet, the camera would start shooting video.

She checked the gauge on the pressure tank, nestled once again into the corner near the main door. It was fully pressurized and holding steady. She had documented the exact location of everything with the camera, and replaced everything exactly as it had been when she had entered shortly after midnight. The hoses were coiled clockwise over the tank and the nail gun was in the exact same position on top of the coiled hoses as it had been for the past several weeks—except the finish nail gun had been replaced with the framing nail gun and its larger sixteen-penny spikes. The safety catch was off.

In the bedroom, Beatrice and Dante lay curled together, like Yin and Yang, on top of the covers. "Stay out of the way, guys," she admonished them. Neither raised a whisker.

Again, she checked the latch on the closet door. The wedge jammed into the throw of the latch and the duct tape were holding fine. The door opened and closed without a whisper. She looked around. She was ready. All she could do was wait.

Sliding into the closet, she settled into the back corner and closed the door behind her. She fluffed the pillows into a nest and threw a blanket over her legs. There was just enough room to stretch them out straight. Trammell's black turtleneck and her own black sweat pants, black socks, and black shoes would keep her from being seen through the slats in the bottom half of the door. Even her coffee mug was black. With a slight turn of the head, she could peer out the one-inch hole she had drilled through the side of the house. Idling away time in the dark, with ibuprofen masking the pain, she would soon be asleep. She couldn't risk being surprised by him. She had to be the one creating the surprise.

She could see down the driveway, its gravel glistening charcoal from the persistent rain, all the way to the road. The green hedgerow bordered one side of the driveway, the main house the other. The back door of the house, the Heidens' Prius and the top of the rented car were visible. Would he wait, or did he have the Carriage House under surveillance? She suspected he would wait. He had to know she was coming home, had to know she was coming for him. He would be cautious, but he would come and he would come to kill the last person who could tie him to Hewitt's forgery ring and the murders of Ralph Hargrove, Povich, and Martoni.

And Lance Trammell.

She realized she didn't even know what Trammell's middle name was. Or if he even had one. There was so much she didn't know. She pulled the neck of his turtleneck up over her nose. Now it smelled more like her than it did him. Would her memories of him fade the same way? Strawberries, the Louvre, and Shakespeare, she reminded herself. Fishing with her father, Paris in the spring, and sunset over the Olympics. So hard to remember what was good in the world.

But she did doze. Road fatigue and injuries and the night spent preparing her trap overcame her vigilance. Her eyes sagged shut. She snapped them back open, then took to pinching herself. Finally, she fell asleep.

She awoke with a start. Her subconscious had picked up something. She closed her eyes and focused. For the longest time, she heard only silence. She glanced out the peephole. Nothing was new in the driveway, except that sometime during her nap, the rain had ceased. The sun had broken through the clouds. Then she noticed the Heidens' second car was gone. Was that what she had heard, the crunching of tires on gravel? Then it came again, a quick and furious scratching. Martha swiveled her head to look behind her. Through the slats she could see one of the cats—it had to be Beatrice—scratching at the closet door. She didn't understand why Martha's lap wasn't available for a nap, why she hadn't been fed yet.

In time, Beatrice stopped scratching, and she disappeared.

Martha resumed her vigil. The Prius pulled in the driveway, and Iris Heiden and the three girls quickly disappeared into the house, lights blinking on. School was out.

Moments later, she saw the wild mane of hair and bushy beard of Harry Callison round the corner of the hedge and immediately come to an abrupt halt. Rebecca bumped into him from behind. So he was playing it straight: father and daughter coming to feed the cats, just like they had been doing for weeks now. He hadn't known she would be here. Good, a small element of surprise tipped her way. Callison turned and said something, pointing behind him and waving with his hand. Rebecca broke into a run, disappearing the way she had come. Callison began to edge down the driveway. He was still in sight when Martha saw him remove a gun from the pocket of his faded Carhartt jacket. Not from his shoulder harness, she noted, but from a pocket. He was screwing a silencer onto the barrel when he disappeared from view.

Martha stood up and pushed the button to begin the video.

She stretched her legs and one arm. Slow and easy, she reminded herself. A coiled spring on the outside, relaxed on the inside. Revel in the paradox. Disarm then disable. An armed man is always more of a threat than a disarmed man. Thank you, Jonesy.

She never heard the key turn, she never heard a step creak or footstep fall. There was just the sudden *poof poof poof* of gunshots fired off through the silencer. She flinched for the briefest instant as Callison's shadow crept past the louvers.

She hit Number 1 on the automatic speed dial of her phone and tossed the phone into her nest of pillows. With the first ring of the iPhone on the coffee table, she came silently out of the door.

The drifting Styrofoam from Manny's missing head and the ringing of the phone distracted Callison enough that he twisted back a second too late. His eyes went wide. With a harrowing scream, she launched herself in a flying kick, her right leg snapping out at the last second to drive the gun from his hand. It skittered across the hardwood floor. Her follow-up jab, delivered with all the force of a killing blow, was thrown off balance by her immobile left arm and glanced off his ear, grazing the back of his head. Still, he staggered and she immediately moved inside his defenses to finish her task.

She snapped a left fist at his face. Only her left arm was strapped securely to her body, and she momentarily faced him with all her defenses down. Callison charged her like a middle linebacker zeroing in on the ball, driving his solid frame squarely into her wounded shoulder.

Again she screamed, but this time from a pain more profound than anything she had ever known in her life.

Those years of practice now saved her. Her body instinctively went into a free fall, letting his momentum and energy be as much his enemy as she was. She hit the floor twisting, and her strong legs flipped Callison over her head, driving him against the sofa and the headless Manny. He bounced off the back of the sofa and started to scramble to his feet, but he only made it to one knee. She used the momentum of the roll to somersault from the floor back to her feet. And her foot lashed out at his face with the short, powerful force of a lethal piston.

He partially deflected the kick with his arm. Still, his head spun sideways. This time her follow-up blow didn't miss, and she drove her right hand into his ear, snapping his head back. He dropped to the floor and tried to roll away. She crushed his knee a with leg strike. A second kick to his jaw sent a tooth and blood flying out. It was Callison's turn to scream.

She towered over him, poised for another blow if he still found the will to move. He didn't, so she did it for him. She grabbed his wild mane of hair and raised his face to the hole in the wall where the camera silently recorded everything.

"How does it feel to be helpless, Callison?" It came out as a whisper. She let his head hit the floor with a bang. "I trusted you. I trusted you, goddamn it. And you set me up, used me, and betrayed me. Used your own daughter to spy on me, you fucking prick. You killed Trammell as surely as if you had pulled the trigger. You were the only person who knew where we were. The only fucking person on the entire planet."

Then her voice dropped low. "How does it feel to know you're going to die?"

She reached inside his jacket, removed a second pistol, and tossed it away. "Feeding kitties appears to be a dangerous job. How long have you and Hewitt been scamming the church?"

A bloody, gap-toothed snarl answered her. His words came out slurred. "Can't prove a fucking thing."

She kicked him in the balls, driving him into the fetal position, where he lay moaning.

"Is Metcalf in on this, too?"

She heard him, but she needed the video recorder to hear him, too. "I'm sorry, Callison. You're mumbling. Is Metcalf in on this, too?"

She brought her foot back to kick him again.

"That prick . . . of a choirboy . . . wouldn't keep a twenty if he . . . found lying on the sidewalk."

In a whisper, she snarled, "Good, so I won't have to kill him, too. How long have you been working with Hewitt?"

His answer was to spit blood and another tooth in her face.

"How long?" For emphasis, she grabbed his chin and wiggled it back and forth. "I've got a lot more bones to break, Harry. How long?"

"Since the Lincoln . . .," he whispered. "Knew it was a fake . . . but couldn't find . . . liked my idea . . . make a little extra . . . This was . . . the big payoff . . . He ran . . . Tried to hide . . . you . . . behind Harbor . . . and that Mormon prick . . . Had to smoke . . . smoke him . . . out. . . . Found the others . . . found you. Old bastard betrayed—"

"He didn't betray you, you asshole." Her voice was harsh, barely audible. Her hand hovered over his face. A sharp stab of the heel of her palm into his nose and he would be dead. They both knew it. "Don't you get it? Hewitt set you up. You and the Reicharts and the rest played right into his hand. For anyone to believe his story, he had to show proof of the Death Angels. And you provided the proof. You made the story so much more believable than a bunch of old documents."

She sat back with a bitter laugh. "Such a fool. The one person I trusted. Was it worth your thirty pieces of silver, Callison? Was it worth the lives of Povich and Martoni and Ralph Hargrove?" She whispered, "And Lance Trammell?"

She rose and strode back to the closet. Looking back, she saw

Callison's hand inching toward his boot. She waited another second before reaching in and turning off the camera. Video time was over. She went to the corner where the nail gun remained undisturbed. When she turned back, she saw he had his hand inside his boot. She marched back at him with the nail gun firing. She was too far away for it to do too much damage, but the nails penetrated his jacket and pricked his skin. It scared him more than hurt him, but it kept his hands busy flailing at his chest instead of reaching for his gun. His jacket looked like a sixteen-penny pin cushion.

She slapped his jaw. "Bad boy, Harry." Harry, Hewitt, Walt, it almost didn't matter. This time all he could do was moan and sag back to the floor.

She pinned his right arm to the floor with her knee and placed the nail gun against the soft part of his wrist. She squeezed the trigger. His body arched and sank back down, all the while twitching like a butterfly with its wings pinned to a board. His right arm didn't move. Patting him down, she found the gun in his boot.

"You did come prepared." She tossed it away.

She straddled him again, pressing the nail gun to his forehead. Her hand shook so much she didn't know if she could hang on to it and finish the job. One more shot, one more. She jammed the nail gun against his eyeball to steady her hand. She aimed up, to drive the nail deep into his brain. One more shot. For Lance, for herself, for a future that now would never happen.

His words came out slurred, but she understood him. "Pull that trigger . . . you'll get needle . . . cop killer."

"I don't think so," she responded. "Self-defense against a corrupt cop implicated in a string of murders? A bad cop who invaded my home and tried to kill me? Sounds pretty straightforward for any jury to decide I was only protecting myself."

"Still . . . can't . . . prove anything."

"Oh, but I can. Look up asshole. That's a camera. I just re-corded your breaking and entering, blowing Manny's poor head to kingdom come, and your little confessional."

She leaned into the nail gun.

"Daddy! I found Beatrice! She's hungry and says you're tak-ing too long to feed her."

Martha almost squeezed the trigger at the shock of Rebecca's voice coming up the stairwell. She heard her steps, saw her enter the doorway, Beatrice in her arms. It took a moment for the scene to register in the young girl's mind. When it did, she dropped the cat and her hands came up to her mouth. She screamed and screamed and screamed.

It took Martha a moment to realize the monster the girl was screaming at wasn't Harry Callison. It was her. The nail gun clat-tered to the floor.

She clutched her good hand to her chest, afraid her heart had burst. She was Walt Boudreau. She was Hewitt Wilcox and Harry Callison and the burnt-faced killer who had shot Tram-mell, all in one.

She struggled to her feet. In a fog, she stumbled to the coffee table, found the iPhone, and dialed 911. Rebecca, paralyzed in the doorway, kept on screaming.

THIRTY-FOUR

The police had not taken kindly to having one of their own nailed to the floor. But Metcalf's return from Utah and the first viewing of the video shot from the hidden camera limited Martha's stay in jail to a single night. Her attorney, Kirk Eckersley, earned his rather substantial fee, practically living that first week at the police station with her. Near the end, he refused to allow her to answer Metcalf's question, "You intended to kill him, didn't you?"

Maybe Eckersley was afraid she would tell the truth, maybe he felt like the detective had overstepped his jurisdiction. So he replied for her. "What she intended, Detective, is irrelevant. All we know for sure is what she did—she subdued a corrupt police officer who entered her home with the very clear intent to kill her. Badgering my client with hypothetical scenarios will not change those facts."

Martha offered nothing in response.

Metcalf stopped calling shortly after that, and the investigation proceeded without further involvement from Martha.

A month passed while Martha's body healed. Her mind was much slower to follow. Whether her heart would ever be whole again, she didn't know.

One weekend, she drove the five hours out to Neah Bay with James MacAuliffe at the invitation of Lance Trammell, Senior. In this remote corner of the country, where ocean and forest differed little from the centuries before, he planned to scatter the ashes of his oldest son. Tall and lean, with gray sprinkled throughout an unruly mop of hair, Trammell Senior wore blue jeans and a turtleneck. Dark eyes set deep in a handsome face weathered by sun and wind made her look away. His handshake was firm but brief.

That Sunday morning, they stood on the bluff overlooking Cape Flattery. Light rain dampened the still morning. MacAuliffe stood at her side. No one had expected John to leave his hermitage in the woods to say farewell to his brother. He didn't disappoint them.

Trammell Senior leaned over the bluff and emptied the urn. For a brief moment, Lance drifted and danced among them. Ashes to ashes, dust to dust, his time upon the stage complete.

She took MacAuliffe's arm. She didn't know if he needed support and comfort at this final goodbye, but she knew she did. Strawberries, the Louvre, and Shakespeare . . . Would she ever find them again?

She and MacAuliffe each placed an arm around Trammell Senior, as he sank to his knees and wept.

The floor of the Carriage House was ruined by the bloody fight with Callison. Her body began to respond to the physical labor of ripping out the old floor, cutting boards, carrying them upstairs, whapping the new tongue-and-groove bamboo floor lengths with a rubber mallet, and nailing them in place. At first, each *thunk thunk thunk* of the nail gun carried the echos of Rebecca's screams. Martha never looked away, never flinched. She faced the young girl and the demon she had become.

In time, with each *thunk* of the nail gun, with each drop of sweat she rubbed into the new wood, Rebecca visited her less often. She sometimes felt the loss, the child's presence there to guide her back to being human.

She resumed her yoga workout on the cold cement floor of the garage. With each session, she found she could hold the meditative trance a little bit longer—two minutes, five, fifteen. She knew a state of forgiveness and peace was in there, but it would take hard work to find it and hold it. With each "*namaste*," she began her quest anew.

When it came time to put the final finish on the new floor, she boarded Beatrice and Dante with the Heiden girls and went to visit her father in Sault Ste. Marie. Before departing, she emailed her resignation letter to Carey, Harwell and Niehaus. She had taken Crystal to lunch to warn her of its impending arrival. Her assistant, young in years, was wise in experience. She had already lined up a new position within the company. Only if the letter actually came in, of course. Of course, Martha said, smiling for the first time in weeks. It was from Crystal that Martha learned that Ben Matthews had fought for and won a settlement from the insurance company for her pro bono clients, Zahit Göksu and his son. The settlement may not have achieved justice, but it would keep the elder Göksu from going bankrupt from the medical expenses of caring for his brain-dead son.

From the airport in Minneapolis, where she would catch a puddle jumper for the hop over Lake Superior, she wrote Matthews a personal note of appreciation. She was grateful for his efforts with the Göksu family, but even more, she valued his role in making her a better attorney. Her only regret was that her needs now took her in a different direction. She had no idea what those needs were, but she was certain they didn't include continuing at CH&N. With no small sense of irony, she sealed and stamped the envelope and her departure from CH&N—just as Hewitt had always wanted her to do.

T he wind blew hard across the ice. Martha burrowed deep into her down jacket and faced the wind with resolve on the spot where Gran had waited for hours, truck lights beaming out across the frozen lake, a beacon by which she might find her way home.

"I still need that light, Gran," Martha whispered, in prayer. "I still need it. Still miss you, I can't tell you how much."

Visiting the cemetery, Martha brushed the snow away from the modest headstones and placed a single red rose on each grave. Gran. Rachel.

When she returned to her father's house, he sat in his easy chair, watching Alex Trebek on *Jeopardy!* The twins had warned her of her father's failing memory, but she didn't see it, as he routinely beat the buzzer with his answers. She pulled up a chair, with no purpose other than to enjoy what time she had with her father.

B ack home in the Carriage House, unwilling to delay the last task any longer, she called MacAuliffe. "I need to do something, and . . . and I guess I don't trust myself. You free?"

She picked him up outside the office of the *Ballard Gazette.* "You've lost some weight," she said, as he slid into the Mini Cooper. He seemed to collapse into the seat, bringing with him the smell of cigarettes.

"Not eating and working eighteen hours a day will do that to you."

"How's the paper?"

"I'm keeping things afloat. Barely. I don't know how Lance did it. I'm going to have to lay someone off pretty soon. We just aren't getting the ad revenues."

"That has to be tough," Martha said. She thought about how the "big story" might have brought new life to the paper, and how it had taken the life of the only man she had loved.

"And I miss him," MacAuliffe said. "A lot actually. We were friends a long time."

Martha squeezed his hand. "I miss him, too, and we'd been friends just a short time."

She found parking and they walked a couple of blocks through Pioneer Square. Store fronts in the historic center of Seattle looked gray and dreary. They ignored a couple of panhandlers.

A queue of men extended down the block from the Union Gospel Mission sign, some with bags and backpacks, some with possessions stuffed into black plastic bags, some young, some old. A few were neat and clean shaven, most were not. Martha and MacAuliffe went to the back of the line. MacAuliffe didn't look too out of place among the homeless of Seattle.

In front of them, a man paced with the nervous energy of someone desperately needing a bathroom. He was middle-aged with a scraggly beard and long, dirty hair streaked with gray. He smelled like a walking dumpster. He carried a rolled-up sleeping bag and a Nordstrom's shopping bag. Two coats covered an addict's emaciated body. He kept muttering to himself as he paced. Finally, he snapped out loud, "This ain't the women's place. This is men's only."

"I know," Martha said. She nodded toward MacAuliffe. "It's his first time. I wanted to make sure he didn't screw it up and go hungry again."

The man reached out his hand and offered a mostly toothless smile. "Welcome, bro. Call me Chet. The good Lord is looking out for you if you made it here. You'll be okay. You'll be okay here."

"Thanks, Chet," MacAuliffe said. "I'm Mac. Appreciate it."

Finally, the line started to move. As they entered the building, Mac whispered to Martha, "You know how to show a guy a good time."

She smiled and said, "They provide overnight accommodations, as well."

"It's nice to see you smile again," MacAuliffe said.

Inside, Martha removed her stocking cap. The buzz cut had grown out a half an inch or so. They worked their way toward the dining room. Almost immediately, Martha recognized Mitch Adair from his photo as one of Santa's elves at the gay Christmas gala. Short and pudgy, wearing round wire-rim glasses and a hair net, Adair plopped mashed potatoes on the plates of the men coming through the meal line. A dirty white apron protected a button-down oxford shirt and khaki slacks.

Martha took a deep breath. Was she ready for this? Did she want to start down the path that would lead her to Hewitt? She scanned the rest of the servers, profoundly relieved that he wasn't among them.

MacAuliffe sensed her hesitation. "You okay?"

She almost took him by the hand and left. Instead, she said, "It's why I needed you to come with me. I promised you a hot dinner. I can't just walk out on you now."

He glanced around the room. "We can leave, Martha. It's okay. Really."

The line shuffled forward, bringing them closer to Adair. The body odor of dozens of homeless men mingled in the hot room with smells of turkey, burnt gravy, Brussels sprouts, and potatoes. Martha hungered for fresh air—and escape. She took MacAuliffe's hand. If he had pulled her out of line and toward the door, she would have followed. Instead, he just held her hand as if it were a butterfly's wing. Unwanted, the memory of the clueless Trammell failing to pick up her hints in the hotel until she started taking off her clothes came flooding back. Men were so clueless. She missed him so.

She squeezed MacAuliffe's hand and let it go. They moved closer to Adair's position in the serving line.

"Welcome back to the Lord's temple, Doc," Chet said to Adair, holding out his plate. When he turned, Martha saw a hand-rolled cigarette tucked behind one dirt-crusted ear. Tobacco or marijuana, she couldn't tell. "Blessed with God's love, I hope? Haven't seen you since the nuptials. Thought you'd abandoned us and ghosted with lover boy. Felicitations in the Lord."

Adair steadied Chet's plate as he scooped on mashed potatoes. "Thank you, Chet. Thank you very much. Yes, I'm feeling blessed. Hugh and I are both feeling blessed."

For a man who looked like a dumpling, Adair's voice came out clear and strong—a voice accustomed to projecting to the back of a classroom.

Hugh? Nuptials? Feeling *blessed*? Had Adair been in on Hewitt's plan? Or could she be wrong and this had nothing to do with Hewitt? The search through Hewitt's bank records and Adair's writings told her she was confirming what she already knew. A simmering anger began to roil in her gut. Blessed? What right did they have to feel blessed? Her feeling blessed had ended with a bullet. And Hewitt might as well have sent the gunman who pulled the trigger. Trammell was dead, her heart had been ripped out . . . and Hewitt was feeling blessed?

"Then, like, spare a bone or two for a friend of the Lord's?" Chet said.

"Chet, you know the rules," Adair said.

"I ain't doin', Doc. Honest as my Baptist brother at a revival. You know I give that up. It's for my new friend Mac here. First timer. Needs some extra love."

"Potatoes are all the extra love I have today."

Chet gave a twitchy nod and stepped forward to the gravy.

"Mashed potatoes?" Adair asked MacAuliffe.

"Yes, please."

"So, first time?"

Hugh, she reminded herself. Hugh, Hewitt. It was time to find out if they were one and the same. Martha wedged in beside MacAuliffe. "Yeah, first time jitters. He's pretty shy. I'm just making sure he gets settled okay." She took a chance. "Chet said you and Hewitt got married. Congratulations."

"Thank you."

"When did this blessed event occur?" MacAuliffe asked. Like Trammell, when given enough clues, he knew what to do. Martha stepped back. "About six weeks ago. It was all rather sudden." An elfin smile broke across his face. "Hugh insisted we elope. One day, he said, 'We're not getting any younger, so what are we waiting for?' We ran away. I can't believe it. I've never done anything so impulsive in my life."

"That sounds wonderful. Where'd you go?"

"A cabin Hugh knew about out at the beach. Near Moclips. It was ideal. Remote, beautiful, nothing works there. No television, no phones, no Internet. We could have been on the moon—well, a wet moon. Rained the entire time."

His face relaxed into an expression that contained all the joy and compassion of a happy man. An innocent man. Martha was certain Adair knew nothing about the fake manuscripts and Hewitt's plot to discredit the church.

"But that was okay," Adair continued, seeming to revel in

finding someone who cared for something more than his mashed potatoes. "We strolled the beach—well, as much as Hugh can stroll—ate good food, talked for hours about history, philosophy—about life. Read books and snuggled by the fire. We even adopted a stray dog. It was perfect. A perfect honeymoon. I've never been so happy."

Martha thought she might get sick right there. Adopted a dog? Snuggled by the fire? Povich. Martoni. Ralph Hargrove. Trammell. Dead, every one of them. Lost their lives while Hewitt strolled the beach with his lover. While she scattered the ashes of her lover to the wind.

"Hey, got your potatoes, so move on." The impatient voice came from the man behind MacAuliffe. "The rest of us are hungry, too. The Doc can lecture another time about his love life."

"I'm sorry, please," MacAuliffe said, stepping out of line and letting the man in to get his mashed potatoes. To Adair, he asked, "How long have you been back?"

"Just a few days." For the first time, Adair really looked at him, his round eyes blinking. "I'm sorry, have we met?"

"No, we haven't. My first time here."

Behind MacAuliffe, Martha stared at the floor, trying to breathe. She had no animosity toward Adair. She suspected he had been used by Hewitt, just like she and Trammell had. She had no doubt that Hewitt cared for Adair—or her, for that matter. But how do you care for someone, love them, and lie to them all at the same time? A paradox Hewitt seemed perfectly comfortable with, had no qualms about.

Well, she had no qualms about ending this little elf's misconceptions, his feeling blessed. She stepped forward.

"Professor Adair, I'm Martha Whitaker, a friend of Hewitt's."

She never heard what he said. What she heard instead was Hewitt laugh. His baritone laugh penetrating the clatter of knives and forks, and of food slopped down on plates, and the shuffling murmur of scores of homeless men. It echoed through her bones. She traced it back to the kitchen, from which a bald man with a clean-shaven face emerged, one hand balancing a tray of cookies, the other hand holding a cane. He was joking with a man carrying a tray of sliced turkey. Then he laughed again, and she was sure.

At the end of the serving line, he set his cookies down and settled onto a stool. Martha jostled men aside, stepped toward him. He had traded the look of the ancient mariner for just plain ancient. His skin was pale and blotchy. His hand trembled as he passed out cookies. A nametag in shaky handwritten letters read "Hugh Adair." He said something to the man waiting for a cookie and smiled the wide smile she remembered so well, a smile of welcome, a knowing smile, a smile of sympathy, of understanding life's hazards, the kind of vulnerabilities that had brought that man to this place. He looked up, startled, and studied her with rheumy gray eyes. "Martha?"

She nodded. "Hewitt." Said his name. Said it to his face. "Hewitt." And all the burden that it carried rose up. The voices of the men around her, the smell of turkey and sweat, of stale urine and fresh cookies evaporated. Do you *know* what you've done? What's been *lost* because of you? Do you know what you *are*? She saw herself grab him by the shoulders, shake him over and over. Heard herself demand answers. Heard herself yelling, I'm barely alive because of you! You bastard, you *bastard*. Why? Why?

But there in the mission, among the homeless and lost, facing the frail figure of Hewitt Wilcox Chappell Adair, *why* didn't much matter anymore. There he was, hiding once again, with the surf washing up against the wreckage of his life; she stood silent.

Why not add Hewitt to a list that started with Walt Boudreau? It would be so easy; she was so tempted.

"Fresh strawberries and . . ." Trammell's voice broke through the pounding in her ears. "Fresh strawberries . . ." The joys of life that she had found in his presence would be forever beyond her reach if she took the next step.

Hewitt rose from the stool, fumbling for his cane, flushed, unsteady. As he came toward her, she saw only her own inner monster. She had taken a half step back from the abyss, and knew she would never recover if she let herself descend into it again. No, she wanted—needed—to stay as far away from revenge as she could.

Justice, however, was another matter. She nodded at MacAuliffe, who stepped out of line to join her.

From the dining room, she heard his plea, "Martha, come back. Please, Martha. I didn't mean for you . . ."

Martha and MacAuliffe walked out of the soup kitchen together. He said he'd get the car and she handed him her keys. Across the road, in the misty yellow ring of a streetlamp stood Detective Eric Metcalf, his long raincoat open and flapping against a tailored suit from the occasional gust of wind. The perfect knot on his silk tie hugged his throat.

"Got your message," he said. "You find him?"

She nodded. As if to settle her doubts and reaffirm her decision, she nodded again. "Yeah, I found Adair. Hewitt, too. He's inside handing out cookies."

With that, she turned and walked away into the rainy night.

ACKNOWLEDGEMENTS

As always, there are so many people involved in bringing a book to fruition that it's hard to know where to begin. If I've overlooked someone, please know it is my short-term memory problems, not a lack of appreciation for your contribution to making *Out of the Cold Dark Sea* a better book.

Profound thank yous are in order to many: To P. S. Duffy for the insights and detailed edits over multiple drafts. Every "Fix!" and "Cliché!" and "I don't understand" made the book tighter, clearer and ultimately better. To Roxanne Dunn, who read every word of every draft and whose criticism helped identify the strengths and weaknesses of the story. God, how I loved to see those triple plus marks! To the Rochester Literary Guild, Dan Dietrich, P. S. Duffy, Debbie Lampi, and Shelley Mahannah, whose support, critical reviews, and unflagging belief that stories make the world a better place nourished and sustained me throughout the many years of bringing this book to print. Dan's frequent phone calls always provided encouragement, insights into the publishing experience, and wise counsel.

I would also like to thank editors William Boggess for identifying some of the fundamental problems of the book and offering detailed suggestions on how to fix them; and Anne Doe-Overstreet whose attention to detail found and fixed all the lingering problems overlooked by everyone else.

Thank you to the dozens of readers—family, friends, acquaintances and complete strangers. Every single one of you made an invaluable contribution to the book.

All errors that remain, whether small or large, are entirely mine, of course.

And finally, to Mary Jo, the love of my life, who has stood beside me through each step of this journey.

ABOUT THE AUTHOR

Jeffrey D. Briggs, a writer and journalist, has been writing about the Seattle waterfront since he moved onto his sailboat thirty years ago. He now lives on land with his wife and dog and can often be found on the shores of Puget Sound, wondering what secrets lie hidden beneath those cold waters. *Out of the Cold Dark Sea*, his debut novel, is the first book of his Seattle Waterfront Mystery series.